Legends of Myr

POHARTAN

Matt Kalesnikoff

Legends of Myr
POHARTAN

How do I choose a dedication?

To my supporters, most notably my family:
Louella, Doug, Nicole, and Kelsie.

To those who read the first drafts.

And to that one person,
who when I told I was writing a book,
literally laughed in my face.

PART I
THE SPARK

CHAPTER 1

A cool, damp, wind blew off Vodana Bay, rushing over the grand city of Tarna and carrying with it the fresh scent of the Northern Sea. The wind swirled around the tall spires of the Water Palace— the centre of strength for the Kingdom of Vodana and the Water Queen—before striking out to the southeast. It rushed over the lush Marden Fields, which were crisscrossed with mighty rivers and some of the richest farmland on the continent of Myr. Fishermen tending their nets and farmers minding their cattle pulled their cloaks tight against the chill before continuing on with their daily labours.

Crossing the border into the Republic of Drevesine, the wind fought its way through the dense forest which covered most of the eastern regions. It passed the walled city of Drevnat, the seat of the Wood Council. Deep within the city, the Council had been locked in its chambers for three days, in a heated debate over recent events throughout Myr and struggling to determine their next course of action. The wind continued south, over the fields and rolling hills where the Drevesine army trained; soldiers sparring while blacksmiths shoed horses and sharpened blades. Joined by a breeze from the East Sea, the wind pushed west over the small farming village of Harten, nestled in the Palter Hills. Across those hills now stretched row upon row of tents, dwarfing the already small town in the centre and choking the surrounding farmland.

The wind continued west along the Hirsen River, eventually crossing over the Lake of Fire in the heart of Pohartan and on to Mount Rhodal: mythical home of the Great Phoenix goddess.

Heated by the fires of the angry, looming mountain the wind passed north over the forge town of Collier, before finally reaching the Black Fortress of Morim.

King Terrin Dramen slammed his chamber window against the now-hot wind. He knew it would have little benefit; the intense heat was unceasing this deep into Pohartan. Usually, he would be happy to have the breeze hot as it may be, for the slight relief the moving air might provide. Not today, however. Today he relished the stifling heat; it was cool compared to his temper and complimented it nicely.

"Tell me about this army on our borders!" Terrin bellowed at the small, scared man quivering before him.

"My... my Lord, it has been growing over the last month, since the unification of Zemiltar." The messenger could not bring himself to meet the King's fiery glare as he gave his report. He had heard what happened to those who delivered this type of news to the King. The messenger was young, surely not yet into his adult years. Wringing his hands nervously, he waited as the King returned to the table.

"And what, exactly, does the unification of the Zemiltar Territories to the north have to do with an army in Drevesine?" roared Terrin, drawing his dagger from its sheath at his belt. The heavy oak table between the two groaned and shook as Terrin slammed his dagger into the map before him, piercing the town of Harten.

"We... that is to say, the scouts believe the High Councilor of Drevesine has struck an alliance with Matrel. Some of the forces appear to be from Zemiltar, they are setting up tents in the hills around the town."

"My Lord, we must strike immediately," the burly Fire General Richmond Arhan growled, pushing himself out of the chair before the fireplace. Terrin did not understand why those fireplaces had been included in the Fortress; they were never lit. Legend said Pohartan was once as cool as Vodana but Terrin had difficulty believing it. "Drevesine could put up enough of a fight against us alone. If we give them time to solidify an army backed by Matrel we may not be able to resist them."

Richmond's imposing figure dominated any room. The man was nearly as wide as he was tall but his body might as well have been made of stone. His intense, deep blue eyes demanded attention and respect, a single look saying he would not tolerate anything less. Most women found him handsome, despite the white around his temples which was starting to show in the blonde hair which cascaded to his shoulders. His knife-like jaw was hidden beneath a close-cut beard, which was also beginning to show white; signs of his experiences, more than his age. In many ways Richmond matched the bear his father had chosen as their house's sigil; beautiful when admired from a distance but undeniably fierce and powerful; not a creature anyone wanted to anger.

King Terrin stepped away from the table and paced back to the window. Below him spread the city of Morim, capital of Pohartan. To an outsider, it was a depressing, menacing sight. Nearly every building was of dark grey or black stone, brought in from the nearby mountains. The window he looked out was one of few in the city, high enough that no enemy could reach it. It was intended to give the King a commanding view should the city be besieged.

Dark grey clouds rolled across the sky, shrouding the city in perpetual twilight. Morim was likely the only place where catching a glimpse of the sun was considered a bad omen.

But for Terrin this landscape, this city, was his home. He could see the beauty and life of the place. In the winding stone streets far below him, he could just see children at play, chasing each other through the crowds. He could hear the sound of singing, blended into the bustle of the market square. For a moment he thought he caught the scent of baking bread over the ever-present smell of sulphur drifting from Mount Rhodal. That one may have been his imagination, or perhaps a distant memory.

He was one of the Fire-born, a true son of Pohartan: one of the "Children of the Phoenix, born from the flaming feathers of the Great Bird herself as she ascended into the heavens." Some believed those stories; the Priests certainly worked to convince the common people of them. Terrin, however, did not. The premise was too bizarre for him. But more importantly, those stories naturally declared the nobles and Priests to be the only true Fire-born and the commoners must strive to be equal to them but knowing they never can be. In his twenty-five years, Terrin had seen many nobles who did not deserve the distinction and some commoners who lived up to the ideals better than most; including Richmond.

It was a tradition for the heir to the throne of Pohartan to serve in the military; it provided vital training but more importantly, it was believed those who were undeserving of the authority and responsibility of the crown would not survive the campaigns against Stalius in the northwest. Terrin had been forced into service earlier than most while his father reigned and he and Richmond fought side-by-side in those campaigns. They served for years on the border, surviving the most heated conflicts seen in the region in three generations. They had the scars to prove their merit and to declare them both to be "Fire-born" as far as Terrin was concerned.

A soft sound behind him drew Terrin's attention back to the room. The messenger was shifting the pack on his shoulder, obviously nervous at Terrin's sudden calm and anxious to be out of the room; intact if possible.

"Anything else to report?" Terrin said softly, forcing the messenger to meet his gaze.

"N...nothing, my Lord."

"Then why are you still here?" Richmond barked.

With a start the messenger began backing out of the room, nervously alternating between bowing and saluting.

As the door closed behind the grovelling messenger and his footsteps could be heard racing down the hall, Terrin turned to his old friend.

"You have to stop bolstering those rumours about how poorly I take bad news."

"Hah! But they suit you, *my Lord*." Richmond always seemed to make the title sound like mockery but was the only person from whom Terrin would accept it. At times it was refreshing to be reminded he was just a man, who happened to have a fancy title. It was also beneficial to have someone around who could be honest with him, instead of the usual nobles who agreed with his every thought in an effort to gain favour. Richmond never hesitated to tell him when he was acting the fool.

"How do our forces stand?" the King asked, returning once again to the window; this time looking to the east, over the fields beyond the city walls. Mount Rhodal dominated the landscape to the southeast, out of view but the ever-present clouds seemed to radiate out from the mountain.

"Four thousand seven hundred forty-two infantry could march from Morim tomorrow, along with two thousand one hundred ninety archers and one thousand two hundred three cavalry," replied the Fire General, his voice taking on the distant, detached tone it always did when talking about specifics.

Richmond was widely considered one of the best Generals in Myr, perhaps one of the best Generals on record, despite his mere thirty-five years. He was able to recite exactly how many men were available, how many horses were trained, even how many swords were in the armoury; he seemed to have an innate sense of facts and figures. Despite this natural ability, he hated them. Richmond had made his name, built his career, on his ability to act in an instant, his ability to turn a force of any size into an elite, effective army. Soldiers shared the story of the Battle of Lortan around their cookpots nightly; relishing in the tale of how Richmond had defeated a force of thousands with just ten men, a Firethrower and a horse.

Terrin had been at that battle. The stories were grossly exaggerated, as the best stories always are. But it was undeniable that Richmond had a knack for unconventional and spontaneous tactics. When Terrin took the throne eight months previous, making Richmond his Fire General was the obvious choice.

"What about Firethrowers?"

"Ten..."

"Ten! You mean to tell me that the army of Pohartan, the *Fire Kingdom*, possesses only ten Firethrowers?"

"Ten which could move tomorrow. Eight are committed to the defence of Morim, seven are under repair, thirteen are under construction and the rest are holding the border with Stalius or scattered throughout the Kingdom."

Terrin paced the length of his small study. "Why do seven need repairs?" he asked, eying Richmond over his shoulder.

"The latest batch of recruits is next to useless," the Fire General shrugged, "One managed to detonate the orb while loading it into the Thrower; incinerating himself, his crew and the three Throwers around him. Another crew managed to launch their orb backwards into the remaining Throwers."

"Pathetic. What was done with the second crew?"

"Hung by their ankles and used for target practice. The others had to know to be more careful." Richmond seemed uncomfortable relating the punishment. A man of contradictions, the Fire General often seemed uneasy with the more brutal and harsh aspects of war. But that did not stop him from getting his job done; another reason Terrin had chosen him to lead the armies of Pohartan.

Terrin ran his long fingers through his short-cut brown hair. Though not as large as Richmond, Terrin was still a powerful man. His time in the military and his training beforehand had sculpted him into an impressive figure in his own right—lean, rather than the Fire General's bulk. He bore the round face of the Dramen family and felt it left him looking younger than he truly was—especially clean-shaven as the King was expected to be. When he took the throne he had certainly been treated as a child by many of the nobles. His fiery temper and immediate displays of control had quickly changed that. Now his Kingdom faced a new threat in the east and he was left nearly undefended with the bulk of his army sitting on the other side of the Kingdom. Yet, if he moved that army his border would be open to the steel armies of Stalius.

He pinched the bridge of his nose with a sigh. "Mobilize the Eastern Battalions, have them assemble near the border. Increase recruiting and training. Find a horse for anyone who can ride and a sword or pike for anyone strong enough to lift it." Terrin opened the door for his friend, ushering him into the hall as the guards outside snapped to attention.

"As the Phoenix rose from the ashes, we will raise an army from the dust if need be, My Lord! The Flame Soldiers of Pohartan will roll over any foe, leaving behind only scorched remnants!" Richmond did love to lay on the dramatics in front of others and Terrin had to fight the urge to laugh. He hoped he was the only one who noticed the hint of mockery in his friend's tone. He was not sure even Richmond was safe if the Priests suspected any insincerity in his faith and adherence to the guidance of the Great Phoenix.

As Richmond strode away, already barking orders to guards further down the hall, Terrin turned to the young guard beside the door. The lad's armour shone in the lamp-lit hall, the black wolf of House Dramen in the centre of the Flame of Pohartan on his chest. In the months to come this young man, honoured by his post among the King's Guard, would likely be forced onto the front lines with the rest.

"Have Donel bring my seal and ink, I have need of them."

*　*　*

Richmond stormed down the hall towards his office in the barracks wing of the Fire Fortress. With an army massing on the border and most of the Kingdom's forces on the other end of the land, he had to make the most of every minute.

The dark stone of the Fortress seemed to consume the light of the lamps which lined the corridor as Richmond passed doorways and connecting halls without a glance. His boots pounded on the red and orange tiles which covered the floor in this wing of the fortress.

Numbers flashed in his mind's eye as he struggled to calculate how he could raise the army he would need. One thousand, three hundred and sixty-four boys of fighting age in Morim, not yet recruited. One thousand nine hundred and eight if we loosen our requirements. Two thousand and thirteen swords and only four hundred and eight lances in the armoury. The forges of Collier can suit and arm one hundred men from nothing in a day if we make some sacrifices in quality. The stables house...

A splash of red cloth in front of him snapped Richmond back to reality just in time to avoid walking over Jermal, High Priest of the Great Phoenix. Jermal's tall but wiry frame was further dwarfed by the broad Fire General. His red robes were adorned with small rubies and gold scrolling along the collar: noticeably absent was the wolf-and-flame emblem of Pohartan and the royal house. The Order refused to wear such "earthly symbols", seeing themselves as separated and superior to such matters. A heavy gold chain hung around his neck, bearing the seal of the High Priest of the Order of the Great Phoenix; a mighty bird, resembling a hawk but supposedly the mythical Phoenix, with its wings outstretched in flight. It looked as though that chain would pull the slim, skeleton-like man to the ground. The High Priest bore a resemblance to a bird himself, with his large eyes and a hooked nose. He even had a tendency to bob his bald head as a bird would.

Richmond stood nose to nose with the aged priest, staring at his piercing, intruding eyes. When face-to-face with Jermal, Richmond always felt as though the man could look into his deepest thoughts, into his very soul. He knew it was not true, or he would not have survived their first meeting but it was a challenge to meet the High Priest's glare.

"Fire General'kar Arhan..."

Richmond cringed at the suffix added to his title. It was an archaic denotation of a commoner and was a deliberate reminder he was not Fire-born. The Order of the Great Phoenix claimed to pity the common people, seeing them as injured young birds who must be mended and cared for but would never be able to fly with the ease and grace of the undamaged Fire-born. High Priest Jermal took that feeling further than others: into disgusted loathing.

Jermal's loathing for Richmond had been amplified when Terrin named him Fire General, a position which had previously been held exclusively by the Fire-born.

"Watch where you walk, dal'kar. The fires of the Great Phoenix wait to consume those who defy Her will." Jermal motioned as if to poke Richmond to emphasize his point but quickly retracted his finger before it could reach the Fire General's chest.

"And how have I defied Her will, High Priest?" Richmond struggled to keep the irritation from his voice.

"To impede the work of Her servants is to defy Her will! The time I waste with ones such as you angers Her, as I am being kept from Her work."

"Did you not preach last week that we are all servants of the Great Phoenix? As you are preventing me from my work, are you not defying Her will as well?" Richmond regretted his brashness the moment he finished speaking. Jermal seemed to have a unique ability to get under his skin and he was often unable to keep himself from being glib with the man.

The High Priest's glare intensified and his voice added a chill to the otherwise blistering heat. "Do not pretend you do the work of the Great Phoenix. You are a pawn of the King; the point of the sword which he thrusts at his enemies. You are a dal'kar weapon and tool, to be used as the Fire-born deem appropriate. Do not forget your place." Jermal's rasp had turned to a growl as he spoke, spittle flying from his lips as he struggled to restrain himself.

In spite of himself, Richmond felt his lips curl into a small smile. It was a dangerous game to play but he could not refuse the pleasure he found in frustrating the old man before him,

"Now move from my path, I must speak with the King on matters beyond your dal'kar understanding. We will, however, speak soon. You may need to be reminded of your role in the Great Phoenix's plan."

Richmond knew he would not enjoy that conversation if it ever happened. He would have to remember to avoid the High Priest for a while. *Well, I am already in trouble...*

"May Her fires light your way, High Priest," Richmond said, clasping Jermal on the shoulder as he passed him. For most, it was merely considered impolite to initiate physical contact with a Priest but Richmond knew the touch of a dal'kar—a commoner, in the popular tongue—was repulsive to Jermal. He would feel Richmond's hand on his shoulder for the rest of the day, always distracted by the "contamination".

The Fire General felt Jermal cringe and reflexively withdraw from the touch. He refused to respond to Richmond's farewell and stalked down the corridor without a glance backwards. Richmond laughed as he saw Jermal repeatedly brush the shoulder of his robe. He would have to apologize to Terrin for setting the High Priest on him in such a foul mood.

He stood for a moment to gaze at the tapestry hanging beside him. It depicted past King Timmon of Pohartan clasping arms with the King of Stalius over a field of death. The scene had taken place over a hundred years ago, the last time Stalius had even been a Kingdom, rather than the personal domain and weapon of the House of Ordreg. Brodon Ordreg had taken power over Stalius in the bloodiest coup in recorded history and his brutal descendants have not loosened their grip on the region and its people since.

What concerned Richmond most about Stalius was the fanaticism of its people. The soldiers of Stalius were the most dedicated and loyal he had ever faced. All the lands knew of the crimes committed by the Ordregs, how could the people be so loyal to such monsters?

Richmond shuddered, turning away from the tapestry and returning to his calculations. *The stables house three thousand horses but half the stalls are empty...*

* * *

The door banged open just as Terrin pressed his seal into the deep red wax. He had expected to have great difficulty with this letter but to his surprise found it easy to write. The words seemed to just pour through him onto the parchment. A letter which could destroy his Kingdom and now he sealed it without a second thought.

Looking up, Terrin watched Jermal stride into the room. Behind him, Donel stood, mouth agape as if in the process of asking the High Priest his business, or asking him to wait. It was likely in the man's best interests that he had not been able to get the words out; Jermal was not one to be stopped.

"Good afternoon Jermal," Terrin greeted the High Priest coolly while pushing the letter under the map spread out before him. Its contents were none of the High Priest's concern and Terrin did not want to spark his curiosity.

Jermal returned the greeting with a stern nod. A delicate and complicated relationship existed between the King of Pohartan and the High Priest of the Order of the Great Phoenix since Terrin's great-grandfather had accepted it as the dominant religion of the Kingdom. To the commoners it was simple; the High Priest guided their spiritual life, while the King governed the rest. The reality was not so simplistic, especially with a High Priest such as Jermal.

Jermal certainly saw himself as superior to the young King: to any King. He saw the Order and the way of the Great Phoenix as above all else; above the petty matters of commerce, politics, war, or anything outside the sphere of the Order. Begrudgingly he allowed himself to be treated as equal to the King but never a hair below. This entitlement allowed him to storm into the King's chamber without warning or even a knock. Facing the weight and potential power of the Order and its followers, Terrin had little choice but to accept it. *Enjoy your power while you hold it Jermal. I will only accept so much and you are on the edge of my patience.* Terrin thought, before wiping clean the anger which had begun to show on his face.

"To what do I owe the pleasure of your company?"

Strangely, Jermal took a moment to absently brush his shoulder before responding. "We have found one."

"One what?"

"A Fire-bearer. You requested I inform you when we found one. I am fulfilling that favour."

It had been an order, not a request or favour but Terrin did not bother making the clarification. "A Fire-bearer? Where? When?"

"In a village called Sastan, deep in the mountains to the south, five months ago."

"Five months ago? I ord... requested you tell me immediately if you came across one and you wait five months?"

The Fire-bearers were an ancient order, predating the Order of the Great Phoenix. Historical records told of individuals who could control fire itself. The most powerful could single-handedly raze a city to ashes. Morim had been built in stone thousands of years before as a defence against the power of those Fire-bearers before the King of the day struck an alliance with them and brought them under the authority of the throne.

There had not been signs of a Fire-bearer in over a hundred years—which had allowed the Order of the Great Phoenix to rise in popularity—but Kings had since searched constantly for a descendant who held their unique powers.

Rumours were heard of similar groups in the other kingdoms. It was said their rivalry led to the division of the continent into the Five Kingdoms, each centred around the element controlled by a specific sect, the Fire-bearers settling themselves in the south around Mount Rhodal. Now, only two of those regions even remained recognized as Kingdoms.

That kind of power in a war against Drevesine... we could burn the Eastern Forest to ash! For a moment he nearly forgot the letter he had written but reality quickly cleared his thoughts. It was extremely rare to find a Fire-bearer with that kind of power, even at their peak. The armies of old had hundreds of them and they provided an advantage but not a deciding one. No, as positive as this news may be, he could not let it stray him from the course on which he had begun; he would still send the letter. He had to.

"What do we know of this Fire-bearer?"

"Brianne, female, eighteen years old by our best guess. Her father is dead—killed along the front with Stalius. She and her mother care for her two younger brothers, names unknown."

"Brianne from Sastan... I will send a unit to collect her and her family and bring them here, to me."

Jermal wet his lips, again wiping at his shoulder. "Do not forget the arrangement, my King; any Fire-bearer found by the Order will spend a year studying with us."

Terrin's glare locked on Jermal, his sudden rage overcoming him. "Do not worry, High Priest, you will get *everything* you are entitled to. I will make certain of it."

The two men stared intensely at each other for a long moment. If either were a Fire-bearer, the other would certainly have been incinerated from that glare. It was Jermal who broke away first, turning to the door. He stormed from the room, the door bouncing on its hinges behind him.

The young guard outside turned to look into the chamber, concerned. Catching the King's glare he quickly jumped back to attention, closing the door.

Terrin looked down at the map, finding Sastan.

"Brianne, Brianne, Brianne... will you be able to survive the storm which is about to consume you?"

CHAPTER 2

Brianne Morette put her hands to her aching lower back, stretching under the blazing mid-day sun. Little grew this far into the mountains, so the small ghabi beans she worked to gather would be vital for her family but the painstaking process of collecting them made her resent their value. Her youngest brother, Ren, still crouched beside her gathering beans into his small pouch. Only six years old, he collected as many weeds and stones as he did beans but he was excited to be out of the village and helping; it also kept him in her sight and out of trouble.

They had left Sastan early in the morning, heading into the mountains to find what food they could to sustain them until the next supply caravan arrived. Sastan had begun as a mere miner's camp but as the nearby mine proved fruitful, wives joined their husbands and their families expanded the camp into a village. There were very few green spaces this far into the mountains and in recent years those closest to Sastan had dried up, forcing the villagers to venture further and further out and return with less and less. Sastan depended on outside supplies being shipped in, in exchange for the iron ore pulled from the mine. It had been longer than usual since the last supplies came in and the people were starting to worry. The village council was even starting to talk about shutting down the mine and abandoning the village.

Brianne loosened the blue scarf which she had wrapped around her head, letting her fiery red-orange hair fall halfway down her back. She futilely tried to wipe the dirt from her hands onto her long grey skirt but the journey through the mountains and kneeling to pick the beans had left her skirt as dirty as her hands.

She took a few steps to the edge of the plateau they had discovered and looked out over the nearby mountains, shielding her green eyes from the blinding sun with her hand. Far below her, a small stream trickled through a narrow valley. Those who knew about such things said that valley had once been a mighty river but Brianne found it difficult to believe. Now it served as the main route to Sastan from the larger centres to the north. To the west on the other side of the valley stretched the sharp peaks of the Olandian Mountains. Somewhere behind her, far on the other side of the mountain upon which she now stood, the dark slopes of Mount Rhodal pierced the sky, shrouded by the ever-present dark clouds which swirled around the mountain.

A hawk streaked across the sky, searching for any rodent brave and foolish enough to forage through this inhospitable terrain. Her eyes followed the hawk north until it disappeared from sight. Letting her gaze fall to the distant valley below, she saw a cloud of dust rising, still a fair distance away.

"Supplies, it has to be!" she mumbled to herself before turning to her brother. The dust cloud seemed larger than that which would be kicked up by the usual supply caravan but Brianne could not think what or who else would be coming down the valley; Sastan was the only village, or anything, within leagues. Likely they had just sent extra wagons to compensate for the long time since the last supplies arrived. If she and her brother hurried, they could get to the village before the caravan arrived.

"Ren! Bring the beans, we have to go back home."

With a small sigh, Ren stood, closing his pouch and putting it over his shoulder. "Bri, can I bring my sword?" he asked, picking up the long stick he had found earlier in the day. He had spent most of their journey that morning fighting his own shadow and monstrous soldiers from Stalius she could not see. He dreamed of one day fighting with the armies in the Northwest and finding their father. It had been two years since the news of his death had reached Sastan and little Ren still had trouble understanding why they told him Father would not be able to come home.

"Yes, fine, bring your sword but we have to hurry!" Brianne conceded, ruffling Ren's light hair before taking his hand and starting back along the trail towards the village. He skipped along beside her as they stepped off the plateau and started their winding path down the side of the mountain. Ren was a constant source of positive energy; he was always laughing and playing, in spite of the work he had to do to help the family and the fact that they had to struggle every day for food. She supposed it was the blissful ignorance of childhood but she hoped he would never lose that enthusiasm for life. Now he began to sing as he always did; a song he made up based on what he saw as they walked. With the ball of energy beside her and the imminent arrival of fresh supplies, Brianne could not help but smile; something she had not done for a long time.

* * *

It was early evening when they returned to the village. Unlit torches had been placed around the village square and the people were running in every direction, preparing. Obviously, someone else had brought back word of the approaching caravan.

Brianne and Ren rushed past the Council Hall in the centre of the village. It was the only building with a second storey and the four small rooms it had to rent were enough for the owner—the head of the Village Council Blithe Tordel—to call it The Miner's Pick Inn. Brianne could not remember visitors ever staying there; most often the rooms were taken by local men who had had too much to drink and were afraid to go home and face their wives.

Blithe stood outside the inn. He held a broom but merely watched the activity around him. Brianne suspected he did that a lot: held a broom to look as if he had just been working or was about to begin but never actually getting to it. His gaze caught Brianne and his frown turned into a grimace before he quickly looked away. Very few in the village had been willing to talk to her, or her family, since the incident a few months ago. She wanted to turn and scream at him. *It wasn't my fault! I didn't do anything!* But she resisted and continued on her way.

A short way down the hill, atop which sat the inn, Brianne passed by the newest building in the village. It housed three Priests of the Order who had arrived half a year ago, claiming to just be passing through. After a month they had ordered the mine closed temporarily so the men could be put to work building this house for them. The villagers naturally smiled and agreed and continued to smile when speaking with the Priests but the move had earned the Priests more disdain from the village than even she received.

The Priests were among the very few who would still look at her, unfortunately. The three now stood beside the house, deep in conversation. It looked as though the village may be getting its wish; the Priests had chests packed and their horses saddled and waiting as if they were about to leave. Cadon caught sight of her and the conversation stopped dead as he gestured to the others. The youngest of the three, he was certainly the most handsome man she had ever seen and she had trouble believing there could be anyone more handsome beyond the village. His black hair hung in waves, framing a perfectly sculpted face. Lara said she thought his nose was too large but Brianne thought it was perfect. He always had the warmest, most inviting smile when he looked at Brianne and she had trouble looking away from his deep brown eyes. Today, however, the two beside him made it easy for her to pull her gaze away.

Grady and Farden were identical brothers, old enough to be her grandfather. Their white hair looked as though it was trying to escape the prison of their scalps, stretching out in all directions. Both gave her matching lecherous grins which made her shiver, their teeth yellow and jagged. Lara said one of them had tried to touch her once but she did not know which of the two and did not have any evidence to turn the Village Council against the Priests. Rumours said it was likely Grady, as Farden seemed more interested in watching young boys. She shivered again and hurried on, pulling Ren with her. *The two brothers could go and leave Cadon here.*

Their home was just beyond the village. Made of stone, as all the buildings were, it consisted of just two small rooms. Brianne and her mother slept in the main room, letting Ren and Jahn sleep in the room at the back of the small house. When Brianne and Ren entered, their mother was standing at one end of the table, cutting some sickly-looking sprouts for a stew.

"Mum, do not bother with those! Haven't you heard? Supplies are on their way!" Brianne exclaimed as Ren rushed to hug his mother's legs.

"And the supplies will last longer if we use these now," her mother replied quietly. Ella Morette had always reminded Brianne of a gentle stream; quiet, calming and peaceful but always moving and able to persevere through any obstacle and continue on its path.

Brianne kissed her mother's head. "Where is Jahn?"

"Outside, as usual, reading that fool book again."

Brianne distantly remembered a time when Jahn had been the same as Ren; full of energy and joy. But now he could not be more different from his younger brother. He had been fourteen when their father died and it had destroyed his world. Now, at sixteen, he should have started working in the mines with the other men but instead spent his days sullenly roaming the village or reading the book their father had given him the last time he visited. Ella kept saying she would put him to work soon but "soon" never seemed to arrive.

"I will go get him, we have to get ready," Brianne said, turning to the door. Before she could reach the handle it opened and Andrew's head appeared. He smiled at Brianne. His blue eyes sparkled, his golden blonde hair falling in waves around his boyish face.

"They are almost here but it is not supplies!" he excitedly proclaimed, before disappearing again. Andrew was of an age with Brianne and until Cadon arrived she had thought him the most handsome man she would ever know. She still expected to marry him, if he would only get around to asking. Andrew, however, still seemed a boy at heart, almost as exuberant as Ren.

Brianne shared a confused look with her mother before following Andrew out the door. Her mother picked up Ren and followed on her heels, calling out for Jahn to come along.

They joined the thin flow of people making their way to the village square. Jahn silently caught up with them as they passed the Priests' home. The three were gone, likely to the square with everyone else.

A small crowd had formed facing the inn, anxiously waiting for whatever was about to happen next. Brianne looked past the inn and was surprised to see a large group of soldiers tending to their horses. They wore only light armour but the Flame of Pohartan on their breasts and banner marked them clearly enough. A smaller group stood opposite; two Priests she did not recognize spoke quickly with Cadon and the brothers, their hands flaring dramatically to accentuate every word, with a handful of guards lingering around them.

Andrew came up beside her, taking her hand in his. "Isn't this exciting?" he turned to her, his face split into a broad smile. She could not help but smile at his enthusiasm.

"What is happening?"

"I don't know, I think…" he was cut off as the door to the inn swung open. The five members of the Village Council stepped out, led by Blithe. Immediately behind them came a large soldier, his helmet held at his side.

The soldier scratched his jaw as he surveyed the crowd before him and waited for one of the newly arrived priests to join him. They spoke quietly, constantly scanning the crowd. Finally taking a step forward, the soldier loudly cleared his throat, demanding silence from the murmuring crowd.

"My name is Captain Brandon Galden, commander of the Fourth Infantry Division of the Third Battalion of the Army of Pohartan. By order of the King, all men aged sixteen to forty able to lift a sword—and those women interested in serving—will accompany me and my men to Morim for immediate training and deployment."

The crowd erupted into immediate protest.

"The village will be left with nothing!"

"We are miners, not soldiers!"

"We have already given more than our share for the King's armies!"

Blithe stepped up beside Captain Galden, his hands in the air, slowly drawing the crowd's attention to him and bringing them under control.

"People, people, be calm! The Captain has assured me this will only be a temporary deployment and our men are unlikely to see combat. Furthermore, the army will more than compensate us for our lost time, with supplies which are on their way to us as we stand here."

The crowd seemed to cool. Some of the men, especially the younger ones, even began to appear excited, likely looking forward to an opportunity for adventure. A chance to break away from the monotony of their quiet mining lives and see a bit of the world beyond was an appealing prospect when it involved little risk. Brianne would never accuse the people of Sastan of being intelligent; most were the type to change their opinion on a whim and agree with whoever happened to speak last.

Brianne looked up at Andrew beside her. For once his expression was unreadable.

The Priest had moved beside Blithe, eyes intent on Brianne.

"Brianne Morette, you and your family will be coming with the Order to Morim." He said it quietly: it was not an announcement for the crowd but Brianne heard it unmistakably. Andrew squeezed her hand and was smiling again; he had heard it as well.

"I did not want to leave you but you will be coming too! Isn't that wonderful?"

Brianne managed a weak smile for Andrew's benefit but her stomach churned with worry. Why does the Order want us to come? Jahn is old enough to fight but why mum and I? And little Ren?

The Captain called the crowd's attention back as Brianne stepped closer to her mother, looking for answers she knew she did not have, or at the very least a little bit of comfort.

"Prepare yourselves and say your goodbyes, we move out in one hour."

The crowd once again began to grumble but the hard tone of the Captain's voice left no room for argument. Slowly the people began to disperse, families huddling together as they went towards their homes to gather the belongings of those who would be leaving. Andrew released her hand and ran to his house, flashing Brianne a smile over his shoulder.

Brianne gave her mother a sad look as they turned towards home. Ren was asking what was happening. Before they could begin walking Cadon approached them, smiling broadly.

"Brianne! I guess we will be travelling companions!" he announced cheerfully as he stood before them.

"What is all this about?" her mother demanded, angrily. It was strange for Brianne to hear the anger in her mother's voice. Usually, Ella was calm in even the most volatile situations and before the "incident", the village's people had often sought her level-headed advice to settle their disputes. To hear the momentary break in her mother's demeanour shook Brianne to her very core.

"Oh, you have nothing to worry about Ella, we simply know how special Brianne here is and believe there will be an important place for your family in Morim. All will be explained on the way there." The beautiful smile never left his face.

Brianne rolled her eyes but it was clear even in Cadon's friendly tone that the issue was not up for discussion. His eyes continually flickered to the soldiers, suggesting they were not merely there for protection and escort.

"Come, Mum, let's go pack our things," Brianne said, beginning to pull her mother away.

"Oh, no need! Your effects are being packed for you. See? Those two soldiers are bringing them up now." He gestured, indicating two guards making their way up the hill towards them. They were indeed carrying what appeared to be the family's packs. "Anything valuable left behind can be sent for when we reach Morim, though everything you could possibly need will be supplied to you." His gaze turned to Brianne's brother. "Jahn, you are of fighting age. Go report to Sergeant Morson, there in the green armband."

Jahn opened his mouth to protest but was silenced by his mother's hand on his shoulder. "Go ahead Jahn, we will be travelling with you, remember?" she whispered softly; her calm demeanour returned. With that and his usual expressionless look, Jahn trotted off to meet the Sergeant.

Brianne, Ren and their mother spent the rest of the hour given by the Captain sitting outside the inn, waiting in silence. Well, near silence; Brianne and Ella knew there must be a lot to say but could not seem to find the words. They were about to give up their home, the only life they had known and be taken to Morim, for reasons they did not understand and which frightened Brianne. Ren, on the other hand, began his usual song; singing about the activity around him.

Time passed too quickly and before they knew it they were about to depart. The men and boys of the village were standing among the soldiers, being organized for marching—it seemed none of the village's women chose to take up the call to arms and for them, it remained optional. Most carried some tool they thought might be useful as a weapon; an axe here, a mining pick there. One or two even bore an old, rusty sword. Andrew was one of the ones with a sword, though his shone brightly. The sword belonged to his father, though Brianne was unsure if it had ever been used. None the less, it made Andrew look noble and heroic. For a moment Brianne forgot about Cadon, her mind wandering to thoughts of Andrew, the brave soldier. At least, her thoughts wandered until Cadon stepped before her, pulling two imposing horses behind him.

"Brianne, this is Fire Dancer, she will be your horse for the journey. Ella, you and Ren will ride Blade's Edge. Do not worry, he is not as fierce as the name suggests; his previous owner had a flair for the dramatic. We are to ride out ahead of the soldiers, so we must get moving." He flashed another smile before turning away to fetch his own horse.

Brianne knew little about horses but these two seemed to be of good stock to her. Fire Dancer was white, with a grey mane, while Blade's Edge was a deep brown, with a streak of white down his nose.

Ella mounted Blade's Edge with ease and Brianne lifted Ren to her before mounting Fire Dancer. She looked around. Everywhere mothers, aged fathers, sisters and children shouted and waved their goodbyes to the departing men. Most were tearful, while others Brianne could see were holding back the tears, desperate to keep them at bay until the men left. One young girl, younger than Ren, broke from her mother's grip and ran towards the line of soldiers, her golden hair flowing behind her. The girl's father, Brianne recognized him as Tel Larson, stepped out of the line and swept his daughter into a tight embrace. Lowering her to the ground again he whispered something in her ear, kissed her on the forehead and she reluctantly returned to her mother. She could see tears forming in his eyes as Tel returned to the line of men.

There were no tear-filled farewells for Brianne and her family. She was certain the village was happy to see them go. Cadon, now mounted on his own horse, gestured them forward. Brianne kicked her heels and without a look back rode out of Sastan.

* * *

They had been on the road for four days. They had camped the first night only an hour or so from Sastan, Brianne and her escorts from the Order noticeably separated from the rest of the group. Within the first full day of marching, they had separated themselves entirely from the mass of soldiers and new recruits heading for Morim. A small group on horseback could move much faster than a large group of new soldiers on foot, attempting to train while they marched. The priests were unwilling to wait for the rabble and before Brianne or her mother even realized it they had left the men behind. There was no chance to say goodbye to Jahn or Andrew and Brianne had once again seen her mother break her calm exterior as she demanded the Priests wait for them to catch up.

The unfamiliar Priest leading the party, Murrell, flatly refused to wait. He insisted every moment possible in Morim was absolutely essential and they must arrive without delay. Though he refused to explain why they were being taken to Morim, or what "important place" awaited Brianne. A guarantee of seeing Jahn again once he arrived in Morim behind them placated Brianne's mother for a short time but it had been an uncomfortably silent journey for several days.

Brianne lay awake in her tent on the fifth night out of Sastan. The priests shared a massive tent in the centre of their camp, while her mother and Ren shared a tent on the opposite side. That arrangement had caused yet another outburst from Ella. She did not see why her daughter should be separated from her. Truthfully, Brianne did not understand either but she had learned very quickly things would be as the Priests dictated: there was no room for discussion. The soldiers slept in a ring around the three tents, simply finding any space of suitable ground and sleeping exposed to the elements.

Silence had fallen over the camp hours ago; even the soldiers were now asleep or silently keeping watch. Yet sleep stubbornly eluded Brianne; she had slept little since leaving Sastan. Her body was exhausted from the days spent on horseback; breaks were few and scattered and the midday meal was eaten while riding. But though her body wanted rest, her mind would not cooperate and be silent. Thoughts about the days to come bombarded her relentlessly. Concerns about what they would find waiting in Morim and what Andrew and Jahn would soon face flashed as she tried to close her eyes and begged sleep to take her. Now she lay listening to the occasional whinny or stomp of one of the horses, the deep snoring of the soldiers nearest her tent and the distant howl of a wolf.

The flap of her tent suddenly pushed inwards and a large, shadowy figure entered. Before she could scream he had his hand on her mouth, silencing her.

"Now we can be together, my dear," a deep voice rasped, breath hot and putrid against her face. The figure pushed his weight down on her, to stop her struggling against him as he slid his free hand down the front of her shift, groping her breast before violently pinching her nipple. Brianne tried to squirm away from his weight and scream through his hand but she was trapped; silenced and powerless against him. Panic overtook her as he moved his free hand to her leg, slowly trailing it along the soft skin of her thigh. He shifted awkwardly, trying to free himself from his robes.

His movements allowed Brianne a brief opportunity to free her hand from where it had been pinned under his bony hip. Brianne's mind was aflame. *That pig Grady!* her mind screamed, remembering Lara's story. For their entire journey every time Brianne looked to the Priests, Grady had already been staring back at her. *He must have just been waiting for his opportunity!* Allowing instinct and panic to take control, she grabbed the hand covering her mouth. Her vision was a sea of red, rage flooding her senses; she felt as if her very blood was beginning to boil. Then, for only an instant, the world was calm around her; her mind was focused and steady, every essence of her being directed at the creature's sweaty hand over her mouth. The smell of burning flesh began to fill her nostrils.

With a primal scream of pain, her attacker leapt back, his hand now engulfed in flames which were rapidly spreading up the sleeve of his robes. Brianne dashed out of the tent into the confused chaos of the camp. The beast's scream had woken the entire camp, who were now rushing to see what had caused it. Close on her heels he sprang out of the tent and fell to the ground, two soldiers racing to put out the flames dancing up his arm.

Torches had been lit and Brianne looked at the shape writhing on the ground. He wore red robes and the hair had been burned off one side of his head. On the other side, however, long black locks hung in singed tangles. The creature turned its head towards her, confirming its identity.

"Cadon!" she screamed in rage and disbelief. His right hand seemed nearly gone and oozing burns stretched up his arm onto the side of his face. Even without the disfiguring burns, Brianne could now see him for what he was: a monster. Lara was right, his nose was too large but more importantly, she could now see the eyes and lips she had once thought of as friendly and welcoming were a lie, viler than any look she had received from Grady or Farden.

The adrenaline of the experience passed and the fear and rage left as suddenly as it had overcome her. Brianne broke down and cried into her mother's shoulder. Now, at least, the world would recognize Cadon for the monster he was.

CHAPTER 3

The sun was high overhead when the messenger reached the front lines between Pohartan and Stalius. The Sixth Battalion of Pohartan stretched out across the horizon as far as the eye could see in both directions. The concentration of troops was the greatest here, along the main road to Scrail, Stalius' capital; further down the line it thinned out slowly, eventually to equally spaced outposts in the more remote regions.

Donel had been dispatched from Morim nearly a month earlier, with a small group of soldiers to accompany him. As ordered by King Terrin, they had ridden hard and fast for the border, nearly running their horses to death in the process.

The King had handed him a sealed letter, with the very strict but very clear instructions that he deliver it to Ordreg and to let no force from God or man stop him. Donel had no thoughts on what the letter may contain but was determined to fulfill his duty.

The small party slowed their horses as they approached the encampment. Before they could reach the mass of tents and men, two soldiers strode from the camp to meet them.

"We are here by order of King Terrin," Donel announced, stopping his horse, "We will speak to your commander. We will be crossing the border and will need fresh horses."

The two soldiers looked at each other and quickly glanced back at the camp before the older of the two stepped forward to speak, a greying beard visible under his helmet. "Very well sir, this way," the man gestured, turning back to the camp. Donel dismounted, throwing his reigns to Captain Mandar, who rode beside him.

"Wait here with the men," Donel ordered.

Captain Mandar simply nodded silently. Donel held no official military authority and no noble blood, nor was he particularly large and intimidating but when set on a task he was as single-minded and stubborn as an ox. Nothing would sway Donel from the path on which he had been set. Likely that was why the King had chosen him for this particular mission. Regardless, the King had made it clear Donel was in charge and the men in his escort knew his orders were law.

Donel followed the old soldier along a winding path through the camp towards the command tent. He had no military experience himself but Donel could not shake the feeling that something was not right in the camp. He had difficulty placing his finger on the issue, until they passed a blacksmith silently sitting beside his mobile forge, watching him intently. *The forge is cold!* the realization struck Donel.

Though he had never been in the field himself, one of his responsibilities in Morim was to oversee the army's supply reports and requests. The amounts of ore and metal required by an army and a reasonable understanding of warfare told him a blacksmith's forge in a force this size should never be cold: there were always horses to be shoed and armour and weapons to shape and mend.

Before he could ask his escort about the blacksmith they reached the camp's command tent. It was a large, tri-peaked structure, with the separate banners of Pohartan and House Arhan flapping from the central pole far above.

As they reached the tent's entrance the soldier moved to announce his arrival but Donel rushed past him and threw open the flaps himself, entering the candle-lit interior.

General Lukas Arhan rose from his seat, while a large, unfamiliar man rose from a seat across the table. Two mugs sat on the table between them, likely—if the stories of the General were to be believed—filled with rather strong ale from the islands north of Vodana.

Lukas Arhan was the father of Richmond Arhan and looked like an aged version of his son. Donel recognized him from Morim when the previous King had named him General of the Sixth Battalion. Despite his age—he was somewhere after his sixtieth year—Lukas was a hard man. Perhaps even larger than his son, he bore the same intensity and radiated power. Though Donel did not recognize the other man, he recognized the armour easily enough. The gauntleted fist pin which held his cloak indicated a soldier of Stalius, while the black stripes down the side of his deep-blue tunic named him one of the elite Tiger Brethren. Donel was not familiar with Stalius' rank symbols but knew the man must be high-ranking to be sitting so casually with General Arhan.

"What is the meaning of this?" Lukas growled, his hand instinctively grasping the sword hilt at his hip.

"Easy General. I am Donel Kademar and under the King's orders, I am travelling to Scrail. I and my men will need fresh horses for the journey and will be leaving before nightfall." Donel handed the General his orders from the King but made no mention of the other letter he carried. His instructions were to hand that letter to Ordreg personally and no one else. That objective was more easily achieved if fewer people knew of the letter's existence.

General Arhan looked over the orders carefully, examining the red seal at the bottom before throwing the parchment onto the table. Donel watched the other man's eyes skim over the words, his stern face cracking into a small smile as he returned to his seat.

"Easy enough, you will have your horses but the rest is in the hands of Colonel Tronbul here," he motioned to the Staliusian officer. "You will be travelling on a diplomatic mission through his territory."

"What is your business in Scrail, boy?" Tronbul asked, now openly reading the orders laid out before him.

"I am to see Hi'ral Ordreg on behalf of King Terrin Dramen. As General Arhan said, it is a diplomatic mission."

Tronbul snorted a laugh, "There has not been a 'diplomatic mission' between our kingdoms in twenty years. The last envoy from Pohartan decorated the walls of Scrail until the elements and ravens wore their bodies down to dust. What makes you think you will fare differently?"

"That envoy had the opportunity to speak with Ordreg first, which is all that matters. I expect at least the same chance." Donel met Tronbul's glare defiantly, ignoring the clear threat.

"Aye, you will have that chance. Hi'ral Ordreg loves to have the court hear the pathetic pleas for mercy from Pohartan." The Colonel turned away briefly but returned his gaze to Donel with a sly grin. "You and you alone will cross the border and travel to Scrail, escorted by myself and a small party of Staliusian soldiers. We say in Stalius that a man needs only his hands to defend himself, while a woman needs a man or a dagger. So, you will be allowed to carry a dagger but no other weapons."

"And you will guarantee my safe passage to Scrail?"

Tronbul's smirk grew and his eyes flashed to Lukas, who nodded ever so slightly. "It is done then. I will gather the men. Do not dally, we ride out immediately." He gulped the last of the ale from his mug and strode from the tent, turning in the direction of the Staliusian camp before the flap closed behind him.

"His terms are his terms, you have little choice but to accept them if you hope to reach Scrail. And I warn you; if I know anything about the man, he will add some more creative and unpleasant, conditions as you go." The General returned to his seat, taking up the remaining mug of ale.

"And just how well do you know him, General? Your camp sits idle while you drink with the enemy? What is happening here?"

With a growl Lukas hurled his mug at Donel, barely missing the younger man's head.

"Do not presume to know my business, boy! You claim to be on a diplomatic mission from the King, yet dare to chastise me for exercising my own diplomacy? Know your place and get out of my sight!"

Donel stormed out of the tent and charged towards Colonel Tronbul's camp. Along the way, he threw his sword in a pile waiting to be sharpened. The weapon had been more for appearances anyway; he did not know how to use it beyond trying to stick the other person with the sharp end before he could stick you.

Crossing the field between the camps he began to hear the growl of tigers. To the right he could see a cleared space within the Staliusian camp where large white shapes dashed back and forth, leaping at each other and rolling to the ground when they crossed paths. Believed by the people of Stalius to hold supernatural powers, tigers were worshiped in the western regions of Myr. To an enemy army they and their trainers – the Tiger Brethren – were a terrifying, nearly unstoppable force.

Donel shivered in spite of himself. Tronbul being of the Tiger Brethren, his tiger would almost certainly be accompanying them to Scrail. Those beasts were violent and unpredictable at the best of times and this journey would be far from the best of times. Donel pulled his gaze from the tigers and returned his thoughts to the path which lay before him.

* * *

The gargantuan doors to the Hall of Swords loomed above Donel. Each two-storey door was adorned with a giant steel tiger, its teeth and claws bared. He was exhausted, barely able to stand. It had been a long journey over the increasingly hilled and rocky terrain of Stalius. Colonel Tronbul had let him sleep only a few hours each night. The remaining time guards on rotation would watch him perform whatever meaningless task Tronbul devised during the day of travel. Some nights he was forced to gather stones and then move them from one pile to another and back, while others he was forced to dig a pit, before refilling it and digging another. When Tronbul lacked inspiration, Donel was left to simply stand in one position for hours.

Scrail was located in the mountains, where the temperature dropped and snow could be found year-round. As they neared the city, Tronbul decided he would take most of Donel's clothes—leaving him little more than his smallclothes and tunic. Compared to the perpetual warmth of Morim, Donel did not know how, or why, anyone could live in these harsh conditions.

They had reached the city less than an hour previous and he had been amazed at the pristine streets. Every city he had visited in the past had beggars leering out of alleyways and trash blowing in the breeze; but not Scrail. Each shop sign shone brightly, polished to perfection and each was aligned perfectly with the next. There were also surprisingly few people to be found. Shop owners stood outside, chatting softly with each other or calmly, almost half-heartedly, trying to entice the few travellers to inspect their wares.

The Fortress of Scrail was located in the centre of the city. It was a massive structure, almost seeming a mountain in its own right, which dominated the city and surrounding valley. Tronbul led the group directly to the fortress and with a few whispered words to a guard, they were escorted directly through to the Hall of Swords, where they would meet Ordreg immediately. The Fortress was as pristine as the streets. Servants hovered everywhere as if simply waiting to tackle anything which dared mar the perfection of their corridors. At one point Donel glanced behind them and servants were already hard at work cleaning the mud and snow brought in by him and his escort.

Everywhere scenes depicting the glory of Stalius, especially House Ordreg, could be seen. Countless portraits of a strong, masculine, imposing young Rodok Ordreg lined the walls, mixed with dramatic portraits of his ancestors, gloriously overseeing the scene of some great Staliusian triumph.

Donel took several deep breaths as the guards reached to open the doors for them. His journey was about to end. He had achieved his objective: he was about to deliver his message to Rodok Ordreg, in the name of his King. The steel tigers seemed to lunge for him as the doors opened, allowing them access. Forgetting the ordeal of the previous days, Donel gathered his remaining strength and with head held high strode into the Hall.

The Hall of Swords was aptly named: every wall was covered from polished floor to high ceiling with interlocked and crisscrossed swords. Different sections of wall were adorned with different styles of sword; some short, some long; some curved, some straight; some as tall as a man, some barely longer than a dagger. Legends, perpetuated by the House of Ordreg, said each sword in the hall had belonged to an enemy of Stalius who had been defeated in battle. Torches dotted the walls, their light reflecting off thousands of polished blades. As if the history of each blade were somehow projected with those flames, the room took on a bright, yet intangibly dangerous light. Above, the high, domed ceiling was also covered with blades, though each was pointed directly downwards. The Hall was intended to intimidate ally and enemy alike and that goal was undeniably achieved. None could enter that hall without feeling the weight and strength of steel—of Stalius—surrounding them.

Donel was not familiar with most of the styles of blade. To his left he did, however, recognize a section of sharply curved Kurali knives: the iconic weapon of Drevesine's secretive Forest Legion. The elite members of the Legion were among the most skilled fighters and assassins on the continent. They had a reputation for being able to hide in shadows while the sun was at its peak and strike their target without notice whether they be in the centre of a crowded city, or isolated in a distant sea. The idea any force from Stalius had defeated enough of them to form a wall with their blades was unfathomable.

The largest collection of blades was displayed directly opposite the main entrance through which Donel strode, where it could not go unnoticed. Almost half the room was adorned with the longblades of Pohartan, recognizable even to Donel. The torches glinted off the Flame of Pohartan on each pummel. Those flames were made from a range of materials from copper to ruby, depending on the wealth of the owner of the blade. The effect of the torches on those swords was thousands of tiny orange and red eyes, glowing, watching the proceedings in the Hall.

Men and women crowded the Hall, they fell silent as Donel and his escort entered. Most appeared to be soldiers, their armour shining under heavy blue and black cloaks. Towards the centre of the Hall, a few who Donel assumed to be nobles could be identified by their finer clothes and lack of armour. To one side, apart from the others, stood half a dozen men in dull grey robes, their hands folded into opposite sleeves. All eyes turned to Donel.

The arriving party's boots echoed on the stone floor of the hall, which was polished to such a sheen Donel could clearly see his own reflection—and the reflection of the thousands of blades dangling above his head. Halfway to the men waiting in the centre of the hall, Colonel Tronbul roughly pulled Donel to a halt. Before them stood two men, while the largest white tiger Donel had yet seen lounged at their feet.

The man to the left appeared not much older than King Terrin—likely not yet reaching his thirtieth year. He wore dull grey robes similar to the men to the side but his bore fine designs stitched in silver up the sleeves and over the collar. Although Donel had never met either of these men, he knew immediately the other must be Rodok Ordreg, though he looked only vaguely like the portraits depicting him which lined the streets of Scrail and corridors of the Fortress. Those images showed a strong, young, virile man. They cast a sense of power, authority and security. Perhaps the man before him had once been the same man as the portraits but no more.

The Rodok Ordreg who stood before him was aged. He stood tall but his eyes looked weary. White hair cascaded down his back, unkempt and tangled. He wore bright armour but it seemed to struggle to contain his girth. No, Donel did not see an unshakable leader of a powerful empire; he saw a man far past his prime, who seemed to be using his golden years to indulge in pleasure and excess.

Donel noticed there was no sign of a throne, or even a seat, for the aged leader and remembered what Tronbul had said of his great leader—just one of many stories the Colonel had shared on their long journey, celebrating the glory of the great Hi'ral Ordreg. Ordreg insisted he was not superior to any common man and as such had long ago decreed since those who meet with him in the Hall of

Swords must stand, he would as well. Donel was unsure what to make of the man before him. He had little time to contemplate it, however, as Ordreg spoke.

"So, you bring a message from Pohartan for me? A plea for mercy, I assume? Has your child King finally taken his head from between the legs of that swine wife of his and seen how hopeless his armies are in the face of the force of Stalius?" His voice was rough but strong. The waiting crowd erupted in laughter.

Donel waited silently for the laughter to subside. It continued far longer than he thought it should—as it went on it sounded less and less authentic but refused to cease. Finally, Ordreg raised his hand to the crowd and the laughter stopped with a nearly tangible suddenness.

Reaching into the pouch hidden under his tunic, Donel pulled out the letter given to him by King Terrin. Cracked and creased from the journey, it still clearly bore the King's unbroken seal in bold crimson wax. He stepped forward to hand the message to Ordreg but was met part way by the man in the grey and silver robes. Donel was instinctively reluctant to release the letter to any but Ordreg personally but decided this must qualify and let go of the parchment. To Donel's satisfaction, the man simply turned and walked the letter the remaining distance to Ordreg. The tiger still laying at Ordreg's feet stretched and yawned.

The Hi'ral cracked the seal and opened the letter. His eyes scanned the words quickly and a cynical smile crept across his wrinkled face.

"Is this some joke? Does your King attempt to mock me?" He passed the letter to the man beside him, who read it quickly. "I would have your thoughts Mikale."

"Terrin Dramen is not known for his sense of humour. The seal is certainly his and the writing does not appear to be a forgery, Hi'ral."

"What of the contents? Can this offer be serious? Does he not understand it will be the death of his Kingdom?" All humour was gone from Ordreg, his face creased in bewilderment.

"Sir, this letter is written by a desperate man: a man who has few options and likes none of them. I read it as a serious, legitimate proposal."

Bewilderment slowly turned to amusement as Ordreg considered the words of his man, Mikale. A low, rolling chuckle began from deep within Ordreg, slowly growing to a full, uncontrollable howl of laughter. The Hi'ral crossed his arms across his extended belly and threw his head back in an unbridled expression of whatever hilarity he saw in the message. Slowly, awkwardly, the crowd began to join in their leader's display, though they were not in on the joke.

Eventually, the overflow of laughter subsided and Ordreg returned his attention to Donel, wiping tears from his eyes as the last chuckles escaped his lips. He glanced down at the tiger at his feet, whose head had risen at the commotion, eyes alert.

"You have not read this letter, have you? You have no idea the weight you have carried here?" Ordreg asked, his smile showing sickeningly yellow, crooked teeth.

"No, I have not. I am but the messenger, fulfilling the orders of my King." Donel replied slowly.

"The man has brought about the end of his Kingdom, the end of his home and does not even recognize it. He is blinded by his duty to those who have placed themselves above him. Do you not find that sickening? This man who calls himself King, calls himself 'Fire-born', this Terrin Dramen, can change your world with the stroke of a quill and the people know nothing of it." It was clear to Donel that Ordreg was no longer addressing him directly. The Hi'ral's gaze had moved over the attentive crowd, his arms waving in dramatic emphasis of his speech. "Stalius will never again see such tyranny, such absolute power. The House of Ordreg serves the people, they do not rule them. People CAN NOT BE RULED! Stalius must remain a strong example to the world of the power of the common people! Soon, all Kingdoms will overthrow the shackles of the oppressive nobility and beg to be part of our glorious community!"

Again, the crowd erupted in thunderous, extended applause. For long minutes Ordreg basked in the ovation, beaming. Finally, he brought silence to the hall once again and returned his attention to Donel.

"You may tell your King I accept his offer. Go, now, I give you leave to return to Morim. Tronbul will escort you back to the border safely." Ordreg waved his dismissal and Donel turned on his heel and began to walk back to the massive steel doors.

He heard a low whistle behind him, followed by an inhuman growl. Something pounded on the stone behind him, approaching with unimaginable speed. Donel attempted to turn but caught only a glimpse of white in the reflection of the floor before he was thrown down, a giant weight crushing him.

At the moment before the teeth closed on his throat Donel's gaze fell once again to the wall of Pohartan swords. Though nothing more than illuminated metal and gemstones, the flame "eyes" of the hilts seemed to stare back at him. Their unblinking stare was one of sadness and defeat and then all went dark to the sickening sounds of tearing flesh and riotous laughter.

* * *

The raven swept out from the towering peak, sailing down-wards on currents of air as it became accustomed to the added weight of the message tube on its leg. As it neared the rooftops below, it beat its wings tremendously, charging back up towards the clouds.

Becoming once again comfortable and confident in the air, it banked sharply to the southeast, passing over the vast grey Fortress of Scrail below. Its brethren loomed on the walls and under eaves, watching intently the commotion at the southern gate. A small group of humans, their silver bodies lit by the setting sun, forced a new feast onto the end of a long wooden spike and slowly raised it into the air.

The raven broke from its course and circled, watching, tempted. The feast was fresh, the juices still moistly dripping from gashes in the flesh. The two soft spheres in the head would be the prize to be consumed but they would first be fought over fiercely. The other ravens began to caw and beat their wings as the humans strode away from the feast. Soon the competition for the prime pieces would begin.

Training outweighed the craving, however, and the raven returned to its course. The message heavy on its leg, it put the setting sun behind itself and struck out towards the human city, shrouded in darkness and heat, to the southeast.

CHAPTER 4

Terrin's mind raced as he pored over the reports laid out in front of him. Technically it was Richmond's job to review these reports but Terrin insisted he remain involved. Too many Kings in Pohartan's past had detached themselves from the daily maintenance of the Kingdom and the result was almost always disastrous. Pohartan had almost crumbled when King Symon Miltur handed control to his council, who were firmly in the pockets of Vodana.

It was not that Terrin did not trust Richmond—in fact, Richmond was the only person Terrin trusted completely—but the King simply could not let go. He could not let such vitally important, though banal, matters and decisions take place without his knowledge and control.

The reports he reviewed now were the most recent and likely last, of the recruiting records. These were from the furthest reaches of the Kingdom, reporting on the number of new recruits brought out from each tiny village. At times the reports were detailed, discussing the relative ability and apparent potential of each group; however, most contained only a village name and a number. The numbers ranged from as low as two, to as high as one thousand; those, of course, being from some of the other larger cities in Pohartan.

Terrin could not help but worry the numbers would ultimately be too few. Another pile of reports before him detailed the growing threat along the border with Drevesine. The initial military camp around Harten had grown considerably. Scouts reported camps throughout the region growing, bearing the flags of Drevesine and its numerous noble houses. Though no camp was close enough to the border to be an obvious declaration of intent by itself, it was undeniable Drevesine was preparing to march.

A knock at the door brought Terrin's head up.

"Enter" he commanded wearily. The past weeks had certainly taken their toll on him. The Fortress—the entire Kingdom—was a chaotic hive of activity. Messengers flew through the corridors on errands for anyone who managed to catch them standing still for more than a moment. Lords met at all hours; either in large, loud, public halls, or quiet, secret chambers. Those "secret" meetings concerned Terrin but only distantly. The lords often involved were minor and fools: proven by their apparent belief they could meet anywhere within his halls without his knowledge.

The clamour of the city outside his window, which he had enjoyed short months ago, was also gone. Now all which could be heard was the clang of armour, the ring of hooves on stone and the barking of orders. Morim had become the centre of a sprawling camp. Nearly fifty thousand souls had answered the call—the order, really—to war and more were arriving daily. But the new arrivals were slowing steadily. The recruits from major population centres had arrived weeks ago and now they waited for only the last, from the most remote and distant villages.

It was an amazing feat and among the largest armies ever assembled in Pohartan. Terrin had Richmond's efficiency to thank. He had demanded an army and the General certainly delivered.

Now he could only hope it was enough.

A young messenger entered the chamber and snapped to attention in front of Terrin. He was a handsome lad and thus far seemed reliable but Terrin could not yet be sure. He was new to Morim, one of the recruits deemed entirely unfit for frontline service. He was undeniably eager, however and enthusiastic to play this minor, yet essential, part for his Kingdom. It would be some time yet before Donel would return with word from Stalius. Until then, this boy would serve well enough.

"What news do you bring, Byron?" The King's fierce eyes locked with the messenger's and the youth involuntarily flinched, casting his gaze downward to the message in his hand, which he extended towards the King.

"A raven has just arrived with this message, my Lord. The markings indicate it is from Scrail."

In a rush, the King snatched the message from Byron's hand, causing the boy to jump backwards half a step.

A raven from Scrail? Donel was to return with word himself. Matters this important are not to be left to birds! Terrin ripped the lid off the small tube, casting it aside as he unrolled the message within and began to read.

You seek a truce? An alliance even? Hah! Your pathetic Kingdom is not deserving of such a recognition! But, in my infinite mercy, we may be able to reach an agreement. My southern army grows weary of supervising that ridiculous rabble of children and invalids you have placed at our border. It has been too long since the blades of Stalius have tasted the blood of Drevesine... Send orders to your General at the border. Have he and his force serve under Staliusian banners for the coming campaign and you will have your temporary peace. Those who survive the war to come will be returned to you.

Ensure your next message is sent with someone able to provide better sport to my tiger.

Hi'ral Rodok Ordreg
High Fist of House Ordreg
Steel Guardian of Stalius

Rage overtook Terrin. He crumpled the message in his fist, casting it aside. Overwhelming anger swept through the King, begging and screaming to be released. His vision blurred with a red haze. His body shook, his teeth bared. Terrin locked eyes with a terrified Byron and his rage found its outlet.

Beyond Terrin's control, he heard a guttural scream escape his lips as his strong right arm caught the shocked, unprepared young man across the jaw. Byron dropped to the ground, his hands jumping to his face. The jaw was certainly broken; Terrin had felt the bones crack against his fist.

Terrin put his weight on his hands on his desk. Trickles of blood flowed onto the reports from the knuckles of his right hand. His mind was clear, the rage was gone but looking at the boy on the floor before him, he had no time to submit to the remorse he felt.

"Be gone," he said. The softness of his voice surprised even him.

Byron rose on unsteady legs and stumbled to the door. The guards outside looked at him quizzically but knew better than to ask questions, or even risk a glance into the room.

As the door closed again, Terrin flexed his hand. It hurt and he had cut his knuckles on the boy's teeth but nothing was broken. He would deny himself any medical care. He deserved more than scratches but it was the penance he could afford to take at the moment.

He turned to the window overlooking the city, his mind returning to the message which now lay crumpled at his feet.

To turn an entire battalion over to the enemy, even if they claim to be an ally? A battalion of over ten thousand men, no less! But what choice did he have? He could neither leave that army standing—not with the size of the force Drevesine was building—nor could he withdraw it without an agreement with Stalius.

What did the banners above the men's heads matter, when they were fighting for the same purpose? The Sixth Battalion was led by Richmond's father, a man who had proven his loyalty to Pohartan time and again: a man who owed his current position to Terrin's family.

As these questions tormented Terrin's mind, horns sounded from below his window.

Looking down, he saw a small party entering through the Fortress gates. The bright red robes clearly indicated several priests of the Order, accompanied by a group of soldiers. At this distance, however, he could not make out the remaining two riders. Or were there two on the second horse?

There was only one answer to who those arrivals were and it likely meant the only good news he had received in months.

Terrin turned to the door and had to struggle not to run through the corridors to the main courtyard. He was determined to reach the new arrivals before Jermal and his vultures had the chance to snatch them away.

* * *

The King threw open the towering double doors of the central courtyard, entering the muted sunlight of the large, open area.

Servants swarmed the new arrivals, who had already dismounted, offering food, water and cool towels to wash away the dirt and dust of travel. Grooms led the horses off to the stables to the east, ready to provide them with the same offerings and care.

The similarity struck Terrin as humorous and he almost let himself laugh, almost. Why should the horses receive any less attention and care than their riders? They too would soon face the horrors of war; face violent and terrifying deaths in the name of Pohartan. And, like the horses, the riders were little more than tools to be used. Oh, they may feign a degree of freedom and choice but they too were merely weapons to be directed by their superiors.

A dozen paces ahead of him Jermal approached the gathered party earnestly, his eyes locked on the young, red-haired woman.

Terrin strode forward with a determined, yet measured pace. He could not appear to be trying to overtake the High Priest but he would certainly close the gap between them as much as possible.

He surveyed the group as he approached. The guards had already dispersed, likely hoping to find a tankard of ale before they were noticed and given a new assignment. Terrin missed the simpler days of being a common soldier. You risked your life constantly but soon became numb to that danger. A soldier's life was a blur of battles, highlighted by the brief rests between, where men who had become closer than brothers laughed and drank around their cook fires. Laughed at stories of conquests—both on the battlefield and in the bedchamber; drank so they would not consider which faces would not be gathered to share such stories at the next opportunity.

Several Priests remained and Jermal was hurriedly speaking with one, whom Terrin assumed outranked the rest. His eyes caught on another Priest in the group. The man's head and arm were heavily bandaged but patches of severely burned flesh were still visible.

Apart from the Priests, looking around anxiously, were three commoners. The young woman with the red hair could only be Brianne, the Fire-bearer. From the look of her, the older woman at her side was surely her mother. Clinging tightly to the mother's leg was a young boy, whose wide eyes looked directly at Terrin.

As Jermal continued to speak with the other Priest, Terrin strode toward the nervous family, brandishing his most comforting smile. He briefly met the gaze of the two women but it was the young boy he addressed first, kneeling down to his level.

"Hello, my name is Terrin. What's yours?" At the mention of his name, the women made quick, unpracticed, curtsies but Terrin dismissed them with a small wave, not looking up.

"I'm Ren!" The sudden energy in the boy was heart-warming. Ren extended his little arm and Terrin grasped his wrist, as soldiers often do.

"Well Ren, welcome to Morim! How was the journey here?"

"Long and boring! All we did was ride horses. I like riding horses but this was too much riding horses. And the food wasn't very good. I like when my mum cooks food but they didn't let my mum cook food. The soldiers cooked and weren't very good at it. Their mums should have taught them better."

"Well Ren," Terrin could not help but laugh softly at the boy's infectious energy, "you will not need to ride horses for a little while and I promise the food here is pretty good. Probably not as good as your mother's but we will try our best."

Terrin rose as he heard Jermal approach behind him. Turning, he greeted the High Priest with a curt nod and glanced at the two Priests beside him: the leader of the new arrivals and the bandaged one.

"What happened to you?" he asked the man with the bandages.

"It seems there was a misunderstanding on the road and an accident," Jermal answered quickly.

"Misunderstanding? Accident? He tried to rape me, there's your bloody misunderstanding!" Brianne had stepped forward, her face red with anger but her mother's hand on her arm prevented her from going further.

Terrin locked eyes with Brianne. He could see the anger in their emerald depths: the fear and loathing she held for this man. He could see the truth of her words in them.

For the second time that day, rage overtook him. His ears caught the ringing of steel as he drew his sword from its scabbard at his hip. His body moved without his conscious control and his sword thrust forward.

Crimson blood erupted over the blade as it punched through the burned man's neck. The man's mouth opened wide but only blood flowed out, gushing and gurgling as he struggled to take his final breaths.

Terrin, back in control, calmly pulled back his blade; the body dropped to the ground. Blood continued to gush from the cut, which had nearly severed the man's head, as the heart gave its final, futile beats. A pool of blood quickly expanded from the corpse; the others stepped away but Terrin let it sweep under his heavy leather boots.

He looked at the people around him. The second Priest looked horrified, as did Brianne's mother, whose face had gone pale. Jermal's face was curled in rage; it was clear he was on the verge of a tirade. Brianne stared at the body and Terrin saw the slightest smile touch her lips. *Oh, there's certainly fire in this girl,* he thought to himself. It was little Ren's face which concerned Terrin but his mother had pressed it into her dress. Terrin could not be certain how quickly she had acted and how much he had seen.

I should not have done that in front of the boy. I should have waited, should have told his mother to cover his eyes, turn him away… He had just taken a life but it did not faze him: he had taken many on the battlefield. What shook him to his core was the thought of what he may have just taken from that boy.

"You, you… you cannot simply kill a member of the Order! Without reason, without trial!" sputtered Jermal, spittle flying from his mouth as his arms waved wildly. "This girl led him on and then attacked him!"

Terrin heard a short, indignant laugh from Brianne. His rage had subsided to a cool, controlled anger. It was nearly tangible within him but he was in control. His wife, Ami, said this anger scared her more than his rage. When he entered a rage, she said, he could not be held responsible for what he did. But this anger… every action was intentional and deliberate.

"Do not presume to tell me what I may do in my Kingdom, in my Fortress." His voice was calm but its strength and intensity sent a chill through the air which seemed to dampen the mid-day heat. Terrin turned to face Jermal and raised his sword to the older man's throat. The point pushed against his skin, just shy of drawing blood. Still warm, the other Priest's blood trickled slowly from the blade down Jermal's neck, pooling on the collar of his robe.

"This… creature tried to touch a young girl against her wishes. You and your Priests attempt to hide this, deny this. You attempt to PROTECT him? By all rights, you should share his fate. Can your Great Phoenix protect you if I move my wrist?"

The two men locked eyes for a moment which seemed unwilling to end. The temptation was almost overwhelming. He had but to flex the muscles of his arm and Jermal would fall lifeless before him. The largest thorn in his side would be removed, permanently.

With a slight sigh, Terrin withdrew his blade, knelt to wipe it clean on the dead Priest's robe and returned it to its scabbard. He could not afford to kill the High Priest. His Kingdom faced war; he could not divide it now to satisfy a personal grudge. The large thorn would become a patch of brambles as the Order rallied, looking for justice.

Jermal, visibly shaken, regained his composure.

"What of your soldiers, King? You think they are innocent? Are you so naïve to think they do not have their pick of the women they encounter, willing or not? You were a soldier once, you know the life. Where are the mass executions of those criminals? Where is your benevolent justice for those women?"

The High Priest was right, of course. Such acts were commonplace among the soldiers; it was an expected part of the job, especially in conquered towns and villages. At worst the officers took part alongside their men, at best they looked the other way. No King had ever attempted to stop the practice: they risked a military revolt. So it continued, known, officially discouraged but ultimately ignored. But Terrin refused to cede the point and though it made him cringe, made the only argument he could.

"The dal'kar cannot be expected to control their basic urges. The Fire-born and your Priests among them, must be held to a higher standard." The words were bitter in his mouth.

Jermal's mouth snapped shut, silencing his retort. He could not argue further without having to concede to a similarity between the Fire-born and the common people. Instead, he changed the subject, redirecting attention back to Brianne and her family.

"As agreed, Brianne is to come with the Order for training. We will take her now."

Jermal stepped towards Brianne but Terrin's extended arm brought him up short.

"You will have your opportunity but not yet. She and her family will spend the night together. Her training will begin in the morning."

Jermal opened his mouth to protest but fell silent as Terrin's hand fell to the hilt of his sword.

With a final glare for those gathered, including little Ren, Jermal turned and stalked from the courtyard, the remaining Priests following in his wake.

Terrin released the remainder of his anger, letting its weight lift off his shoulders. He looked again at each family member. Brianne's mother still looked shocked and pale; her eyes stared into the distance as her hand absently smoothed her son's hair. Ren was softly crying into his mother's dress.

Brianne, however, met his eyes. Her green eyes were piercing, commanding. They refused to release his for a long moment.

"… Welcome to Morim."

It was an idiotic thing for him to say at this point but it was all he could manage. He signalled a servant waiting to the side and the young girl rushed to escort the family to the guest chambers. Terrin turned on his heel and began to walk from the courtyard, the blood from his boots leaving a trail on the stones behind him.

"Thank you." Brianne's voice came from behind him. He hesitated for an instant before continuing, without looking back.

* * *

Terrin pushed the heavy oak door of his chamber closed and leaned against it with a deep sigh, finally letting his body relax. He had spent hours aimlessly stalking the corridors, considering the events of the day and those to come.

Brianne's arrival was one of the final pieces to fall into place. His army was growing and nearly as large as it ever could be but time was running out.

"What news do you bring, my love?" his wife, Amiela, asked from her chair at the other end of the room, placing the large, leather-bound book she had been reading carefully on the table beside her. She sat with her legs curled under her, her delicate chin resting on her hand, her bright blue eyes gazing at him.

He was again struck by her beauty as she smiled sweetly at him. Her golden blonde hair fell in waves past her shoulders to her chest. Her delicate facial features gave her an appearance of perpetual youthful innocence. Today she wore a long, yellow dress to complement her hair, adorned with a pattern of golden gemstones at the neck and ruffles of soft white lace at the cuffs of her sleeves.

"My love? The news?" she asked again, as he stared at her blankly. Terrin brought his attention away from her appearance to her question. Her soft features and gentle voice hid her shrewd and sharp intellect: she was among the most clever and intelligent individuals he knew.

"Ordreg has agreed to the arrangement and Brianne has arrived,' he said quickly. Still leaning against the door, he pulled off his heavy leather boots. The drying blood which covered much of them cracked and flaked to the floor as he tossed them aside.

He was reluctant to share too much detail with Amiela, including Ordreg's terms. Theirs was a marriage of alliance and convenience, not of love. Their union had been arranged in the time of his father's reign to secure her family's wavering support of the Dramen house. Terrin had no doubts that she had since grown to genuinely love him, however, and she was the perfect picture of a caring wife. None the less, it was difficult for him to open himself to her and share his fears and concerns.

"Well, that is wonderful news, on both counts! Now we can begin to move against Drevesine." She rose from her chair and glided across the room to him, wrapping her arms around his waist and rising on her toes to kiss him. He returned the kiss only halfheartedly. Too much ran through his mind to let himself fall into her arms and lips. Instead, he pushed her away gently and strode to the bedchamber. He heard her soft sigh behind him as he closed the door and she returned to her reading.

Terrin dropped his sword-belt against the bedpost and let himself fall onto the bed, not bothering to remove any more of his clothes. A million thoughts fought for control in his mind. It would soon be time to move the armies but how long would it be before Brianne was ready? How useful would she prove? Was his arrangement with Ordreg a mistake? It almost certainly was but what other choice to did he have?

Reports from the front, faces of soldiers new and old, Brianne and her family, military tactics: all flashed through his mind's eye, refusing to let him focus on any one long enough to find an answer or form a decision. He found his eyes growing heavy, the long day—the long weeks—weighing down on him. As he finally felt himself drift into slumber, two faces remained. Two faces, which had begun the day filled with excitement and ended it filled with terror. Two faces which had changed that day and may never return to their previous state, because of him. Two faces he would be long in forgetting: Byron and Ren.

CHAPTER 5

Brianne glared back at Jermal. She hated this man, with a passion. He and the other Priests, had been trying to "train" her for several days now, with no results. She was not surprised by their failure. What could they possibly know of the power which they claimed lay deep inside her, or how she could control it?

The Priests spent much of their time studying ancient texts on the people they called Fire-bearers, scraping for any clue as to how they accessed and harnessed their power. Most thought it came through relaxation and focus and merely encouraged her to clear her mind and simply will the candle which they set before her to light. But if it were as simple as a thought, Jermal would be reduced to a pile of ash by now.

He alone took a different approach. The High Priest believed her power could be reached through stress and intense emotion. Given the events of the trip to Morim, she could not blame him for this belief but she also hated him for it. Jermal was becoming ever more creative and cruel, in his attempts to ignite her rage and thus her power. His first and continuing, strategy was to keep her separated from her mother and brother.

They had come to collect her early that first morning in Morim. The King had done his best to ensure their comfort, as he had promised. They had been treated to the largest feast she had ever seen. A large variety of meats and vegetables, bread and cheeses and any type of wine she could imagine had been laid out for them. An entire roasted hog sat on a silver tray next to a large stuffed chicken. There was a massive slab of seared beef, surrounded by plump spiced potatoes. She recognized little else on the table: the variety of everything astonished her. Most had probably gone to waste.

Ren had rushed to the food almost immediately, his little fingers grabbing at each dish, eager to try everything. Though he was quiet, evidently the horror he had just witnessed in the courtyard was replaced already in his mind by a love of food. Brianne envied him for that; it seemed nothing could bring Ren down for more than a short time.

Brianne and her mother, however, could not so quickly forget and struggled to summon an appetite. She had seen blood before and grotesque injuries. In Sastan accidents were common, whether they be mining or hunting. When Brianne was a young girl those injuries were often brought to her mother to care for, until Carly Ferrer moved to the village, anyway.

But Cadon's death was very different. The rage she saw in the King's eyes as he drew his sword, the raw power which pushed it through Cadon's neck, the sickening sound of the slash and the thud of his lifeless body on the ground... and the blood. She had not known the body held so much of it and the smell had been almost overwhelming.

No, the two women were not very interested in the meal. Each nibbled on some bread and cheese, avoiding the range of meats. Ella drank several servings of wine but Brianne limited herself to chilled water. How they managed to keep anything cool in the oppressive heat of the famed Fire Fortress was a mystery to her.

After the meal, they had been escorted to their quarters for the night. Like the meal, they were the most lavish she had ever seen. The outer chamber was lined with exquisite furniture, the walls bore bright tapestries depicting scenes of sunshine and green meadows—a stark contrast to the war and death-themed décor of the rest of the Fortress.

Beyond was a single, massive bedchamber. Three full-sized beds sat waiting, covered in luxurious pillows and linens. They looked to be three fluffy, pure-white clouds, save for the Flame of Pohartan embroidered on each piece.

In spite of each having their own bed, the three weary travellers washed and all crawled into the middle bed. Even with the three of them occupying it, there was still room to spare.

Ren had been the first to fall asleep: a day of excitement and the largest meal he had ever eaten taking their toll on him quickly. Ella followed soon after; she could not fight the effects of the wine. But Brianne did not sleep so easily and she lay awake for long hours listening to the gentle breathing of her mother and brother.

It was not just Cadon which plagued her thoughts: he had deserved the fate he suffered. But she could not pull her thoughts from the King. She could not know his true motivations, perhaps he was merely a cruel and violent man, as so many whispered in hushed tones. But she could not help feeling he had acted in her defence. And his eyes as she met his gaze after Cadon's body fell… They were not the cold eyes of a feral animal: she saw compassion in them, even sorrow.

Eventually, Brianne had drifted to sleep but it felt as if only moments passed before the Priests arrived to claim her, for there were no windows in the room by which she could judge the time. They stormed in without warning. They were insistent and demanding, though not aggressive and had Brianne rushing out the door before she fully understood what was happening and without a proper opportunity to say goodbye.

Now, three days later, she was convinced that had been Jermal's intention and it fueled her hatred of him.

He stood in front of her now, staring, as he often did. It irritated her, as she was left to simply stare back silently, waiting for his next attempt to get a reaction from her.

He had tried every angle he could conceive and it frightened her how much he seemed to know about her. He told her terrible stories of what Jahn was likely to face serving in the military; numerous gruesome ways he may meet his end. He told the same stories of Andrew and when they failed to get the reaction he desired, he changed his tactics, telling stories of the women Andrew would be with, that he would forget her quickly and completely as he raped across the countryside along with his fellow soldiers. Jermal suggested that her father had died a coward and a traitor. He even began to tell stories of what would happen to her, or her mother— or even Ren—should they ever be captured by enemy soldiers.

The man had a sickening talent for descriptive detail but no matter the reaction he received from Brianne, there was no fire.

Brianne could tell he was growing impatient with words and wanted to try more extreme measures. He had struck her in the face once. It had come as such a surprise; she had not had time to react. She knew that was just the tip of what this man was willing to do, wanted to do but for now, the other Priests protected her, if indirectly.

She had seen the disapproval in their eyes when Jermal struck her. He may be the highest ranking among them but she could sense he was reluctant to risk losing their favour. So as long as there was another Priest present and thus far there was always at least one other at all times, she should be free from the true reaches of his cruelty. For now, two other Priests sat at the far end of the room in front of towering bookshelves. Each was engrossed in a thick volume.

"What do you hate most, Brianne?" Jermal finally asked, his eyes unblinking. His voice pained her ears, his putrid breath assaulting her nostrils.

"You," she replied simply. She refused to waste her time and energy on the deference and pleasantries she had seen too much of in Morim already. Why should any man be placed above another? Brianne would greet any new acquaintance, regardless of what title they gave themselves, with courtesy and respect. Let it fall to them to prove themselves unworthy of such regard. Jermal had immediately proven himself unworthy and Brianne refused to offer him any special considerations, which—to her great amusement— seemed to infuriate him endlessly.

His face tensed at her response, though surely he had to have been expecting it and she saw his eyes flash to the other priests.

"Leave us," he said over his shoulder.

The two Priests at the back of the room looked from each other to Jermal and back but did not move.

"I said leave us!" Jermal bellowed, his wiry frame shaking with anger.

Both Priests appeared shaken and quickly rose from their seats, rushing from the room. As the door swung closed behind them Jermal's gaze returned to meet Brianne's, his eyes burning more than she had ever seen them.

"I have had enough of your games, you insolent bitch. For some reason, the Great Phoenix has deemed you worthy of this incredible power and we are going to find a way to get to it, so we can put it to work for Her. We are finished with those other Priests and their pathetic ideas about relaxation. Idiocy! The amount of time we have wasted already... Fire is not calm, fire is not peaceful. Fire is chaos, activity, rage, destruction. That is how we will reach it." Jermal's arms flailed dramatically as he spoke, his face contorting as he enthusiastically formed each word.

"Sounds enjoyable," Brianne said calmly, taunting him.

"Enjoyable... yes, yes it will be. But not for you." A cynical smirk came over the High Priest's face.

Suddenly he drew his arm back and struck her across the face with the back of his hand. She was stunned by the force of the blow, amazed the frail-looking man before her could manage that speed and power. An instant later his fist found her stomach, knocking the wind from her lungs.

As she struggled, bent over, to regain her breath Jermal continued to rain blows on her, striking her shoulders and back, her sides and arms; anywhere he could make contact. He seemed to have the energy of a much younger man. She managed a look at his face; his eyes were ablaze and a sickening smile of pure pleasure spread across his lips.

The blows were slowing very slightly, their force lessening: Jermal could not deny his age and maintain this vigour for very long. Past the surprise of the vicious attack, Brianne prepared herself to fight back. She was not going to be subdued so easily and let this man do as he pleased to her. Turning slightly, she accepted his blows to her hunched back and with every ounce of her strength rammed her elbow into the High Priest's groin.

Jermal's attack stopped immediately, his face gone pale and his hands reflexively clutching his manhood. Silently, unable to even utter a moan, he fell to his knees.

Brianne stood over him. Her body hurt from his strikes but she held herself tall. Looking down at the High Priest she raised her arm to strike him, to return the beating he had just given her. But then she felt something begin to rise deep inside her. She closed her eyes, trying to focus on the feeling. It was a feeling of warmth but not just warmth… intense heat, somewhere within her.

The feeling began to grow and spread over her body. She arched her head back as it overcame her. It felt as though her body was aflame but her mind was clear, clearer than it ever had been. Brianne embraced the feeling. Somehow it seemed natural, normal: she had never felt this sensation before, yet her instincts took control.

Focusing on the heat which engulfed her body, Brianne began to shift it, control it. She gloried in the power which coursed through her, drawing more and more. With less than a thought, she was directing it, driving it from around her body into the upraised palm of her right hand. With a flash which illuminated the room, a ball of flame appeared above her hand. It should have burned her flesh but she felt nothing.

Turning her hand, she cast the flame away from herself, over the High Priest's head and into the shelves of books at the back of the room. The dry, ancient papers erupted instantly.

Jermal, eyes wide, rapidly crawled to the door, still unable to stand. She let him leave. With the power which ran through her, she could have reduced him to ash with a thought but she resisted. Control was hers now and he had to know it. There was nothing more he could do to her, nothing she had to fear from him.

So Brianne stood, spreading her arms to the power and the heat. The flames jumped from the shelves to the table and continued to spread but they did not concern her: she would not be harmed by them. Let them burn. The furniture in the room would be ash in moments and the heavy oak door was beginning to smoke but the stone of the Fortress would not allow the flames to spread any further and they would soon die out.

A smile spread over Brianne's face and she began to laugh gently.

*   *   *

Terrin paced along the front of the formation of soldiers standing at attention awaiting their marching orders. Richmond walked beside him, studying the soldiers, ensuring each was prepared.

This group was the most skilled in the now-vast Pohartan army. They were all career military men who had experience either against Stalius or in skirmishes with the numerous tribes of Zemiltar to the north who often attempted to raid over the border.

The battle-hardened faces of the soldiers, each with their fair share of scars, stood in stark contrast to the freshly polished armour they wore. Their breastplates were a deep shade of orange, with the flame of Pohartan bright in the centre. Their sleeves were a bright crimson, some officers wearing a matching cloak. Many bore orange plumes rising from their polished, pointed helms. The front ranks held long pikes, each with orange and crimson ribbons streaming from below their sharpened steel tips.

This was the elite First Battalion, the Fire Wall as they called themselves. The name was derived from their appearance: everything was intended to give the image of a wall of fire rolling towards the enemy. These men would be the front and centre of any major battle, which gave them great importance but also great risk. Each man in the Fire Wall had been hand-chosen by the Fire General.

Terrin clasped his hands behind his back as he walked, if only to keep them still.

He was nervous but how could he not be? He was standing before one of the largest armies ever assembled and it fell to him to order their march. It would be the first and last campaign for the vast majority of them.

Though confident in Pohartan's victory, Terrin had no illusions it would be an easy one. Many would die in the months to come: it was merely a matter of trying to ensure the last man standing on the field was one of yours.

He felt better inspecting these men than he had some of the other, newer, units. These men were all proven veterans: they knew what they were facing because they had faced it before and survived. They had killed and seen their friends cut down. Their stoic faces fit the circumstances perfectly.

Most of the army was comprised of fresh, young recruits. They were still expecting a monumental adventure, about which they would tell their grandchildren. Some expected to come out of battle as heroes and legends, somehow thinking they would single-handedly decide the war. Some even expected to come out as wealthy men. Terrin was perplexed as to how they expected that to happen: soldiering was not a route to riches.

Whether expecting notoriety, stories, or wealth, what each of those young men forgot was they must survive first: dead men tell no tales, nor enjoy riches. Terrin knew better the true expectations a soldier could have from war: mud and blood. They would march in mud, they would camp in mud, they would battle in mud, kill in mud and in most cases die a bloodied mess in the mud. The men he now observed knew this bleak reality.

The younger soldiers had actually been smiling when he inspected their groups. It angered Terrin and his glare quickly suppressed those smiles. One soldier had stood out to him, however. Perhaps it had been the lack of a smile, or perhaps the piercing emerald eyes which did not shy away from his gaze as the rest did. Whichever it was, it had caused Terrin to pause and still, he dwelled on the experience, though now he understood why.

"The boys around you are smiling like court fools but you have the look of a veteran. How old are you boy?" he had stopped to ask.

"Sixteen, my Lord."

"And what, at sixteen, do you know of war which those around you do not seem to?"

"War… is death, my Lord."

"Death? Not glory or honour? Not fame and riches? Or whatever else these boys seek to gain?"

"The only glory or honour in war is found if it can be won without drawing blood, my Lord."

"A wise sentiment from such a young man. Unfortunately, it seems Drevesine has taken that option from us. What is your name, soldier?"

"Private Jahn Morette, my Lord."

Terrin understood then why the boy's eyes had caught him so: they were the same piercing emerald as his sister's; for Terrin had no doubt this boy standing before him was Brianne's brother.

He had merely nodded and walked away then, forcing his mind to return to the inspections. The process was a charade anyway; Terrin knew the soldiers would be as prepared as they could be. Unfortunately, for most that merely meant they had been trained to put their armour on properly, salute and stand in an orderly formation. There was simply no time for more. They would have some opportunity for training on the march but for most, it would be luck, not skill or training, which saw them through the first battle.

No, the inspection had little meaning for him. The true purpose was simply for him to be seen. For the younger men, it was exciting to see their King so close and for the veterans… they needed to see not him but his confidence. They needed to see that their leader would be marching with them towards victory with his back straight and chin up, not uncertain or afraid.

So he paced before them, hands clasped behind his back, head high, doing his best to keep his face firm.

Now he approached the small group of mounted men who would march with him at the head of the army.

Three Generals sat atop their towering warhorses, one for each of the waiting battalions. Two Battalions were already assembled at the border, awaiting the new recruits which would join them from this group. Each General had their bannerman behind him, the pendants of their battalions and flags of the Generals' Houses waving lazily in the soft breeze high above their heads. Two more bannermen sat waiting, each with a large flag of Pohartan waiting to be unfurled. Each also held the reins of a horse, waiting for the King and Fire General. The man holding the reins to Terrin's horse also bore the flag of House Dramen. Richmond refused to have the flag of House Arhan flown, insisting he served only Pohartan and the King and leaving the flag for his father to fly. Terrin appreciated the gesture.

Terrin nodded to the waiting Generals as he mounted his horse, each hitting a gauntleted fist to their chest in salute. He strode forward and turned his horse, Mi'drak, to face them, taking in as much of the waiting army as he could. He paused for a long moment before speaking. This was the last moment of peace Pohartan would have for a long time, Terrin wanted to stretch it as long as he could, squeeze every bit of tranquillity out of it. He hoped the others were doing the same. But he could not hide in the moment, he could not ignore his responsibility and so he finally spoke.

"Pohartan has enjoyed a long period of relative peace. We have been able to live our lives without the shadow of war. Our industries have flourished, our families have grown.

"But now, Zemiltar and Drevesine have become jealous. Their armies stand poised at our border, preparing to strike. They want our land, they want our people. They will take the food from the mouths of your children, they will kill without mercy.

"You have been called from all corners of the Kingdom because none would be safe from this menace and so all must face this threat. It falls to us to defend our families, our neighbours, our Kingdom. We will not have peace until the forces which stand against us have fallen to our blades!

"You, the army of Pohartan, the strongest army this King-dom has ever mustered, will be the heroes of which legends speak! Your names will live on for eternity as the saviours of Pohartan!

"You will face death in the months to come but many among you know that in war, death is a mercy. Death is Mercy and war… War is Death." The last words came out as a shout and somehow raised a cheer from the assembled masses. Though his words could not have travelled far, the cheer rippled through the ranks, rising to a roar as it was taken up by thousands.

Terrin lifted his crowned helm from the pommel of his saddle and placed it on his head. Raising his hand in the air he turned to the east. He thrust his uplifted hand forward and kicked Mi'drak ahead. With the signal, thousands of men and horses be-hind him took their first step towards war in unison.

Richmond trotted up beside Terrin. A short distance behind were their two bannermen, the twin flags of Pohartan flowing above them. Next came the remaining three Generals and their men, followed by the first ranks of the First Battalion.

"Well, how was that?" Terrin asked, turning to his friend. The bannermen were not far behind but with the racket of the army behind them—trumpets and drums had started, to celebrate their departure—they were well out of earshot.

"Perhaps you should leave the rest of the speeches to me," Richmond laughed in response.

"That bad?"

"Stealing the food from their children? Really? I was a little surprised you did not tell them the enemy would rape their mothers too."

"Actually, I almost did," Terrin admitted, "But it seemed to work at least."

"True but let's be honest: motivation is easy this far from the battlefield. Let these boys see some of their friends die, then see if you can get them excited enough to cheer their way onto the field again." Richmond's jovial mood turned solemn quickly.

"Fair enough. I suppose I will leave that one to you."

The two rode in silence for a short while before Richmond responded.

"I do not think I will go with 'war is death'… Not sure where you thought up that one."

"Well, it is true, is it not?"

The Fire General simply nodded and grinned grimly. The silence returned as they rode out of the valley north of Morim.

It would take hours for the army to make its way from the vast valley behind the King and Fire General. Each battalion consisted of thousands of soldiers, divided into various divisions and companies of cavalry, infantry and archers. Between each battalion squadrons of Firethrowers crawled forward, their heavy machinery being pulled by teams of horses. Somewhere in the mass was High Priest Jermal and his small contingent, including Brianne.

Behind the last battalion came a second army, nearly as large and arguably as important as the first. They were the hordes which followed and sustained any fighting force. The supply wagons and their drivers, the blacksmiths and craftsmen needed to maintain the armour and weapons. Cooks and nurses, farriers and merchants and of course whores ready to take what little money the soldiers may have as the long campaign became increasingly lonely and the soldiers became more eager to seek relief in their womanly comforts.

As the first ranks were making their slow progress out of the valley, the constant cloud cover parted for a brief moment, allowing the sun to shine through and illuminate the valley and soldiers below.

CHAPTER 6

The march to war was a long and arduous one. They broke camp at dawn each day but travelled at a snail's pace, barely covering any land before setting up camp again at dusk. They could move no faster than the Firethrowers, which were a labour to transport over the rocky and hilly terrain of eastern Pohartan.

Richmond knew Stalius was preparing their army to march and should be somewhere behind them. He hoped they would reach them before the border: the first battles would be much more difficult without that extra power. Stalius did not have the burden of heavy artillery to slow them down and thus should be making better time but it was still a significantly longer distance for them to travel.

But he could not allow himself to simply rely on Stalius' arrival, rely on their extra numbers to sway the battle for them. He had to plan as though they would be alone against Drevesine and the forces from Zemiltar. The problem he faced now was the difficulty getting accurate reports from the scouts. Most did not return once they were sent out and those who did usually had not gotten close enough to gain very useful information. Pohartan soldiers were no match for the stealth and efficiency of Drevesine's Forest Legion in even the relatively light forests around the border.

He wished he knew of what the Brianne girl was capable. He wished she herself knew. Though she had made quite the spectacle in Morim days before the army left, she had since been unable to do much more than light a candle, or hold a small flame above her hand for a few moments before it sputtered and died. Though amazing feats in themselves, such abilities held little military value to him. He could do far more damage with a Firethrower, or even a flaming arrow shot by a trained archer.

Richmond studied the maps before him endlessly as he thought. Knowledge of the terrain was the only real asset he had in planning. He knew roughly where the enemy was and had to assume they were at least a couple thousand men stronger than Pohartan's force. That advantage would be exponentially exaggerated if his force was dragged into the forests, where they would be destroyed by the Forest Legion. The alternative, however, was to allow himself to be bottlenecked onto the roads and fields between hills.

He had the option to set the Firethrowers on the forests, burning them to ash. However, that was a dangerous strategy in the extreme. A sudden shift in the wind could send a wildfire sweeping over his own army. However he analyzed the situation, Drevesine had the advantage. It would take all his talents—which he felt were always exaggerated by Terrin—and a fair bit of luck to find a way to crush the enemy.

For a moment he found himself wishing his father were with him. He would be soon enough, as he marched from the Western border. Lukas Arhan had taught Richmond everything he knew, essentially raising him on the battlefield after Richmond's mother died not long after he was born. Though he hated to admit it, much of his success as a soldier and General was grounded in an effort to impress the older Arhan. Lukas had always been a cold and distant man, reluctant to express any feelings of warmth towards Richmond—if he had them at all. Military strategy was the only commonality they shared, apart from their appearance and it had led to a very strained relationship between them. However, despite their difficult personal relationship, Richmond could certainly use his father's knowledge and experience now, as war loomed closer.

The five Generals he did have available to him crowded around the table in the small tent. They stood silent, waiting for him to speak. That angered him as well; he needed ideas, suggestions:

not silent, waiting eyes. The army marching from Morim had finally connected with the friendly forces awaiting them.

"Well, what the hell are we going to do?" he asked, looking up at the five pairs of eyes staring at him, his tone clearly expressing his weary frustration.

"Die." It was General Marcus Lamner, commander of the Second Battalion, who responded first. Richmond rolled his eyes in annoyance. Lamner was a strong General—he would not hold the position if he were not—but he had a dark, pessimistic sense of humour, which was extremely trying at times. Richmond knew the man well enough to recognize his attempts at humour, though he had never seen him crack a smile.

"Maybe contribute something useful, Marcus," Richmond barked, "What do you think Simone?"

Simone Atlee, General of the Fifth Battalion, was the first woman in the history of Pohartan to hold such a rank. Historically women were not allowed in the military but Simone had fought hard to enter the ranks. Even after she had been allowed to enlist, it had been a long time before a commanding officer gave her the opportunity to fight. However, once allowed on the battlefield, she had proven unstoppable, quickly surpassing and outshining her male counterparts. Her success had inspired Terrin's father to loosen the restrictions on women in service, allowing them to enlist if they so chose but excluding them from active recruitment.

She was also the youngest and most recently promoted General. When the King ordered an army raised, General Todd Carter resigned. He was old and ailing. He insisted he be allowed to spend his remaining years with his grandchildren and not on a battlefield hundreds of leagues from home.

So Richmond was forced to find a replacement and eventually settled on Atlee—much to the chagrin of the other Generals, who struggled to take her seriously. But Richmond needed someone with proven determination and drive, someone who would not squirm and buckle when the odds were stacked against them. He could think of none more qualified than Simone.

"We should charge at them, take them head-on." Dendrik Saer, General of the First Battalion answered, causing Simone, who was about to respond, to snap her mouth shut with an audible click.

Dendrik was a mountain of a man, a head taller than any of the others in the tent—even Richmond—and proportionately broad. His military record was one of awe and legend, virtually unmatched by any General living or dead. His position as General of the Fire Wall was hard-earned and well deserved. However, he had a tendency to prefer brutal, head-on assaults. More often than not, they were successful for him, even against larger opponents. Fortunately, Dendrik also had no qualm following orders which instructed him otherwise. He understood clearly the hierarchy of rank and his place in it—high as it may be.

Richmond watched Conrad Bartel's expected grimace in unison with Simone's stifled response. Conrad was the polar opposite of Dendrik in every way. Physically diminutive, he always favoured stealth and surprise in attacks. Enemies became especially cautious and paranoid when they knew they faced Conrad Bartel, as he seemed to have a supernatural ability to position soldiers where they were least expected to be.

"You do not like Dendrik's suggestion, Conrad? What would you have us do?" Richmond pressed.

"Charging up the middle would be a slaughter. Yes, we may come out on top but the cost would be huge. At the very least allow me to take the Third around and position ourselves behind the enemy."

"And how do you propose to get behind the enemy? Their camp is massive and with that blasted Forest Legion up every tree, you would have to go leagues around; either into Zemiltar or nearly to the coast. We do not have the time to waste waiting for you to get into position." Dendrik stabbed at the map before him with his fingers as he spoke.

"What if we burn the forests? Clear the way with the Firethrowers?" Nedly Furell, of the Fourth, suggested.

"Too unpredictable. We would first need the wind to be in our favour, which is pure chance and hope it does not change. Even if the wind works for us, we would need to wait for the fires to burn themselves out. We simply do not have time. We are going to be essentially marching straight into battle," Simone finally spoke. Richmond smiled slightly to himself. It was pleasing to see he had made a good choice by selecting the woman: she understood the situation as he did.

"Simone is right but so is Conrad," Richmond sighed. "A hard charge up the middle would be extremely costly to us, with no guarantee of victory, especially with the dense forest in the way. The Forest Legion would pick us off as we tried to drag the Firethrowers through that, or even up the roads."

The discussion dragged on late into the night, as it had every night of the march: the same ideas being suggested and dismissed, the maps being studied and marked for any reasonable route to the enemy.

*   *   *

The small fire burned brightly in the circle of seated men. The flames reflected off their armour and danced over one soldier's blade as he sharpened it. There was no true need to sharpen the blade: it had been sharpened in Morim and had not yet tasted flesh but Jahn found the rhythmic *whoosh* of the whetstone sliding against the steel soothing.

Kervil stirred the cookpot hanging over the fire idly. The stew smelled surprisingly pleasant, especially for a soldier's meal. Kervil's family owned an inn in a town Jahn had never heard of in western Pohartan. Now he struggled to recall its name… *Tonhurst, was it?* It did not really matter.

Jahn eyed the men with whom he shared a fire. It was a lie to call them "men". Tumas was the oldest among them and he was only a season or two older than Jahn. Amad insisted he was of an age with the rest but Jahn remained skeptical. His bulky armour made his already minuscule frame seem almost laughable and Jahn was convinced he could not have experienced more than fourteen summers.

But "men" they insisted on being called and so Jahn tried to view them as such, including himself. They were enlisted in the military, preparing to die for their Kingdom. What other rite of passage must they take to be considered men if they were not now? Even if most did not yet need to shave.

"Jahn, put the sword away and pay attention, man!" Petren chided, backhanding Jahn's knee to bring him out of his apparent daze.

With a grimace, he dropped the whetstone back into his pack and slid his sword back into the leather scabbard propped beside him. The sound of the sword sliding into its home was oddly satisfying itself.

"What was the question?" he asked, seeing the eyes of the five others on him, waiting.

"What is your girl's name? Back home in Sastan. The one waiting for you when this is all over," Kervil repeated, giving the pot another stir.

"I do not have one," Jahn replied, matter-of-factly.

"Atta boy, Jahn!" Amad proclaimed, "The rest of you are fools, trying to cling to one girl from back home. We are going to come back heroes and have our choice of any woman we want!"

"Oh? And I am certain you are used to having your choice of women, aren't you Little Pup?" Tumas quipped, tussling Amad's hair. The action and nickname earned him a harsh glare from Amad.

"Bloody right I am! Back home I could barely keep them away. I would have my pick when I wanted to steal kisses behind Master Harmon's blacksmith shop but sometimes I would have to hide out in the woods just to get some time to myself." Amad's arms flailed to accentuate his story, his bravado ruined by his voice cracking as he spoke. "I tell you boys, I would have five girls at a time if I wanted."

"Your fingers do not count as 'girls', Amad," Tumas said quickly, launching the others into an outburst of laughter and shattering Amad's confident smirk. Even Jahn had to let himself smile, a little.

Though not significantly older than any of them, Tumas was quickly filling the role of older brother to them all. He would crack a joke at your expense at every opportunity but there was a sincerity and maturity to him. Jahn and the others in his little squad, had felt an instant connection to Tumas; they knew they would be able to count on him in a pinch.

Amad, face red with embarrassment and frustration, opened his mouth in retort but Kervil cut him short.

"Settle down gentlemen, the food is ready," He began to dish out the stew and pass servings around the small circle.

Jahn was starving. It had been a long time since breakfast and a hard day of marching. The small amount of dried meat they had been rationed around midday was enough to keep them moving but not to satisfy anyone's hunger.

Kervil passed him a bowl of the steaming stew and Jahn dug in greedily. It tasted as good as it smelled. The meat and vegetables were issued by the army but Kervil carried a small pouch of spices in his pack. Jahn hoped those spices did not run out anytime soon.

You should not be here, Jahn thought while he ate, looking at smiling Kervil. You should be back at your family's inn, cooking there.

Jahn looked at each of his comrades in turn, finding himself thinking the same about each.

Hulking Tumas, the blacksmith's apprentice, belongs at a forge.

Fennel—slender and a hand taller than the rest of them—is a merchant's son, not prepared for the physical work of soldiering.

Squat Petren—the quiet son of a farmer—should be tending his fields in the north.

And Amad... Amad was always unclear on what he had been doing before being pulled into this mess. Jahn suspected it was because he had been playing, as a child should: too young to begin apprenticing.

Then Jahn came to himself and returned to his introverted daze as he ate and the others talked and laughed around him, throwing elbows as they mocked and teased one another.

What would he be doing if he was not here? What was he doing before the military came to Sastan and his family was dragged away? He did not have an answer for himself. Perhaps he would have finally been pulled to the mines, or perhaps he would still be spending his days alone with his thoughts, flipping through his father's book.

I suppose I might as well be here, he solemnly thought. As good of a place for me as any.

A short distance away he watched Sergeant Morson approaching through the camp.

"All right ladies, pack it up, douse those fires! We have an early march and I would not want you princesses complaining about being tired!"

A collective groan rippled through the small groups, each around their own fires but people began to move. Armour clanged and boys grumbled. There was a loud sizzle and putrid stench as one of the groups apparently chose to douse their fire by relieving themselves on it. Sergeant Morson stormed over to them, clapping each on the side of the head and shouting obscenities.

In the other direction, Jahn saw Andrew stand among his squad. He appeared to be giving instructions to the boys—men—around him. Perhaps he had become the "Tumas" of his own group.

Jahn had not had the opportunity to speak with Andrew—or anyone else from Sastan—in weeks. The army had done its best to separate the boys from the same village or town; apparently so if a squad was lost, it would not devastate an entire village.

Shrugging slightly and letting the brief moment of homesickness pass, Jahn rinsed his bowl with his waterskin and dropped it into his pack, pulling out his bedroll. They would sleep where they were, under the stars. The night would be warm and though they were entering more lush regions, rain was unlikely.

*   *   *

Brianne watched the flame of the candle flicker and dance before her, casting fleeting shadows across the walls of her small tent. She had lit it herself some time ago: the candle had burned halfway down since. It was the most she had been able to achieve since that night in Morim. She could *feel* the movements of the flame. She could sense each tongue as it whipped out from the centre. Somehow she knew where the flame would flicker next, in the instant before it moved there. She had seen little of Jermal since that night. He was never far from her, however. They had set her tent in the middle of the Priests' camp. That camp travelled with the main army, yet remained distinctly separate.

Slowly, quietly, Brianne steadied her breathing, focusing on the feeling of the candle. Left, back, left, right, back, back, flare, fizzle, spark… she knew what was coming next. As she charted the dance she reached out with her mind, preparing. As the flame made a sudden leap to the right she was ready and *grabbed* it, *pulling* it away from the wick. The flame floated in the air, held by her mind and Brianne smiled.

She had been practicing these small things for weeks. That night in Morim had awakened the power in her and shown her how to control it. While the Priests were watching, she feigned incompetence, sweating and panting trying to create the smallest spark. While in the privacy of her tent, however, she was improving rapidly. It appeared both Jermal and the other Priests had been correct about her power. As Jermal believed, it had been ignited by intense emotions such as anger and fear, as had happened in the camp leaving Sastan and in the Fortress in Morim. But now that she had experienced it, felt it within her, it was hers to control and she was learning to access it through calm focus.

She swirled the flame in the air before her, it leaving a streak of light behind itself for an instant, drawing its path. Extending her hand, she let the little ball of flame twirl between her fingers and over her palm. From one end of the tent to the other she flicked the flame, careful not to let it touch the walls: she was not nearly ready to control the fire that would cause. She laughed a laugh of pure joy and pleasure. This was not the power and control which she had felt in Morim but it still felt wonderful: she felt complete. And it had been achieved by herself, at peace, without Jermal's brutal attack and the ensuing rage.

The tent flap burst in with a sudden flourish, pulling Brianne's focus from the candle before her and the flame blinked out. The tent remained well-lit by additional candles, spread around the perimeter to hide the shadows cast by the flames she was trying to manipulate.

Jermal stalked into the tent, his perpetual scowl directed at Brianne.

"Come, the King demands your presence," he demanded brusquely before storming out again.

Brianne hastily blew out the remaining candles and composed herself before following the High Priest into the muggy evening air. She followed Jermal as he led the way towards Terrin's command tent, which was situated in the middle of the First Battalion's sprawling encampment.

She scanned the faces of the men around the small fires they passed. She did not know in which battalion Jahn or Andrew had been placed and was constantly hoping to catch a glimpse of one of them. She had not seen either since Sastan. Now, in the masses of men which comprised the army, she knew her chances of simply stumbling across them were slim, yet she continued to look.

However, the men they passed now seemed to share a common trait, suggesting to her the two she sought were not in the First Battalion: they were all older. Not "old", though one or two had hints of grey in their hair, but "older". Not one face she saw showed the tenderness of youth. It was difficult to guess ages with the added grimness of experienced soldiers but Brianne thought the youngest here had at least five years — five hard years — on her.

No, there were no fresh recruits here. There was no riotous laughter rising from these circles of men, no energetic fistfights in the lanes between tents and fires. These men were more sombre, sobered by both age and experience in battle. Though a deep chuckle did rise occasionally—they were not statues, after all—most sat in hushed conversation or complacent silence.

Jermal was keeping a set distance between them. Brianne sped up slightly to close the distance, a question forming on her lips. The question faded as he noticed her approach and increased his own speed to maintain the distance between them. Brianne smiled to herself, increasing her speed again slightly. To her pleasure, Jermal moved more swiftly, not allowing her to close the gap. With glee she continued to push him, forcing the older man to a near-jog.

Petty, petty man! She laughed to herself as she watched the High Priest struggle between maintaining his composure and dignity by not running, yet keep her at a comfortable distance. Surely he hoped it appeared he was merely in a hurry and it was she who must struggle to keep pace.

A stray cat skittered across the path between her and Jermal. There were hundreds of them in the camps, prowling, hunting for scraps from the soldiers or the vermin which also seemed to follow the army.

There were dogs too. Some had been owned by the soldiers before they were recruited, some had merely been found and adopted by the squads. Men happily passed the mutts scraps of their rations and the dogs placidly lay at the feet of their generous masters.

How long before they eat those beloved pets? Brianne was startled by the darkness of the sudden thought but allowed it to play itself out. Father told us the reality of war. Campaigns stretch and rations become scarce, men become hungry and desperate... how long before these men stop seeing those animals as companions and instead throw them in the cookpots? Weeks? Months? How long would this war plague the land, for that matter? Years?

She watched the cat stalking through the night. A mangy dog lounging by one of the groups of soldiers offered it a half-hearted growl as it passed and received an equally apathetic hiss in return.

Looking at Jermal's back she could not help but wonder how long it would be before someone turned on him. He was not the beloved childhood companion, nor was he the mangy but lovable new friend. No, Jermal was a wild-eyed mongrel in a dark alley, baring its teeth and laying back its ears at anything which drew too near. Surely the dogs would at least outlast the man.

Terrin's command tent soon loomed before them. It was a two-peaked structure, with the flag of Pohartan flapping listlessly above each peak. Two guards flanked the entrance, their auburn armour shining dimly in the waning evening light.

Watching their rapid approach, one of the guards poked his head into the tent. When he re-emerged he nodded to his partner and the two held back the flaps for the approaching pair. Jermal charged into the brightly lit tent without sparing a glance for the soldiers. Brianne was fairly certain he would have charged straight through even if they had not opened the way. Brianne offered the soldiers a small smile as she followed the High Priest.

The tent was spacious by most standards but sparsely furnished and decorated. To one side lay a collapsible cot, its sheets were strewn about haphazardly. A tall washbasin sat next to it and two closed chests sat next to that.

The ground was covered in mismatched rugs, some bearing fanciful depictions of the Flame of Pohartan, though most were merely solid, earthy colours. Several camp stools sat unused on the opposite side of the tent, accompanied by pieces of armour and miscellaneous weapons—presumably belonging to Terrin.

The centre of the tent was dominated by several folding tables, placed together to form one large surface. The table tops were bare, save for a folded piece of red fabric but to the sides of the tables were bins overflowing with rolled and folded papers: maps, certainly. Scattered around the tent were tall candle stands, providing ample lighting for Terrin's meetings, which she knew often stretched late into the night.

Four men stood at three sides of the table. Brianne recognized the two on the sides as Generals but she did not know their names, nor which Battalions they led. At the far side of the table, directly opposite the entrance, stood Fire General Arhan and Terrin.

Richmond looked grim and imposing, as he always did. He wore a simple tunic, exposing his bulging arms in the warm evening air. His hands were clasped behind his back, feet spread wide in a firm stance. The candlelight which illuminated the tent interior glinted off a large double-sided axe resting at his hip. His face was stoic, his weighty gaze focused on Brianne.

Beside him, Terrin looked almost timid. He was dressed simply by a soldier's standards, let alone a King's. He wore a crimson shirt of undoubtedly fine material but it was unadorned. The neck hung unlaced and the sleeves were pushed up to the elbows, revealing his sculpted forearms. He stood comfortably, thumbs hooked onto the belt which held the sword at his hip. Even that sword was simpler than she would have thought a King to carry. She had not noticed it in Morim, in the courtyard as he pushed the blade through Cadon's neck. She took the time to notice the simplicity of the weapon now, however. It bore the Flame of Pohartan on the rounded, polished pommel but that was the only decoration. The grip was black leather, worn with age and use. If she looked carefully, she could see the indentations where Terrin's fingers lay as he wielded the weapon. The grip connected to a simple, slightly curved, metal crossbar, which itself rested at the mouth of an equally undecorated black leather scabbard.

She knew very little of swords—or any weapon—but it was evident even to her that this one was not merely a noble man's decorative accessory she had seen during her brief time in Morim, as nobles came hoping to see the novel fire-wielding girl. This was a practical tool, designed to fulfill its purpose effectively and nothing more.

A visible wave of distaste crossed Terrin's face as he looked at Jermal but his expression softened when he turned to Brianne, even allowing a warm smile. His eyes, however, made her rethink her description of him as "timid" in comparison to Richmond. They were by no means cold or unfriendly towards her, they were merely… intense. It seemed she could see into his depths through those eyes. Though a simple brown, the colour seemed to swirl, drawing her in.

"Welcome, Brianne, thank you for coming so quickly," Terrin said softly, a genuine ring of pleasure in his voice.

Jermal's face grew darker, likely at the obvious lack of acknowledgement from the King. His breathing was laboured as he recovered slowly from the brisk walk here.

"I believe you have met Fire General Arhan?"

"Yes, we met briefly one day in Morim. Good to see you again, Fire General," she replied politely.

It had been a very brief meeting. The Fire General had poked his head into one of her "training sessions". He had been very cheerful and friendly—a welcome change from Jermal's cold distaste—and she had immediately liked the burly man. However, when he saw she could not, as of yet, use her abilities to any measurable degree, he had soon left.

Now he offered her a friendly nod and smile, which seemed genuine as well. She had already spent too much time with Jermal and the Priests that a hint of genuine emotion was such a welcome change. Jermal quite openly despised her, while the other Priests could seem pleasant enough but it never had any depth. To them, she was a puzzle: an experiment to be studied and feared. It was refreshing to interact with people who seemed at least capable of true warmth and emotion.

"Excellent. These are Generals Saer and Lamner, of the First and Second Battalions, respectively," Terrin continued. "I am going to cut straight to the chase Brianne. In three days we will be at the front lines, our army will reach that of Drevesine and Zemiltar. Drevesine has requested a meeting when we arrive. We hope this meeting will be a chance to talk some sense into them and avoid this war. I would like you to be there, with the four of us here."

"Why..." she started to ask, flustered but she was abruptly cut short by Jermal.

"Outrageous! How long have you known about this meeting? I must be present!" He spurted through clenched teeth.

"No, Jermal," Terrin said simply, calmly. Though his voice held firm, his eyes belied the anger he felt, yet carefully controlled.

Jermal was visibly taken aback by the simplicity and directness of the King's response.

"No? No! I am the High Priest of the Order of the Great Phoenix! I demand to be at a meeting of such potential importance to the Kingdom, instead of this dal'kar trollop!" he raged on, gesturing to Brianne.

She arched an eyebrow at him but let the exchange between him and the King continue uninterrupted.

"I said no, Jermal. This is a matter for the crown and military, there is no need for a representative of the Order to be present. The agreement is five individuals and I have chosen my five." Terrin's voice held its calm edge but his knuckles had gone white clutching his sword belt. His eyes were aflame and his body very nearly seemed to be quivering with the anger he barely held in rein. The unwavering finality of his decision was clear to everyone in the tent, including Jermal.

The High Priest's rampaging anger abruptly switched to a cold rage which sent chills through Brianne.

"So be it," was all he said but the words cut the tense air in the tent, hard and sharp as steel. He straightened his back, turned and walked purposely from the tent.

"I apologize for him." Terrin's eyes returned to her. His hands and body had relaxed the moment Jermal left. His eyes had lost their fire but retained their intensity.

"Thank you but I have become accustomed to him over these past weeks."

"True enough I suppose," Terrin chuckled slightly. "I apologize for that as well. Your training is one thing I have not been able to wrestle from him, yet. I do not envy anyone who must spend that much time in his company."

"It has not been too bad as of late. He keeps his distance since that night in Morim." She smiled to herself, remembering the sight of the High Priest crawling to the door, clutching his groin.

"Why me?" She remembered her original question.

"Because they will not expect you to be there. They will expect me to bring Generals and they will likely actually expect to see Jermal. But you… they do not know you, or of what you are capable. Your very presence will throw them off, distract them, make them easier to speak with."

"We would like to see what you can do, as well. How far has your ability come?" Fire General Arhan added.

"Not far, I'm afraid."

"Show us."

With effort Brianne cleared her mind, focusing on one of the candles scattered around the room. It was easier to work with an existing flame than create one from nothing, though she had been improving at that.

She pulled the flame from the candle, leaving a thin wisp of smoke rising from the wick. The flame formed into a smooth sphere and drifted towards her, passing between the heads of Richmond and Terrin. The two men jumped, having not seen her collect the flame from behind them.

She held the sphere of rolling flame over the table, pushing her will into it and forcing it to grow. It reached the size of a head before her effort and concentration were stretched to their maximum. She let it shrink down to the size of her fist and held it there momentarily while she thought.

With a playful smile, she cast it towards Terrin, stopping it inches from his chest. To her surprise, he did not so much as flinch, though the other men had dropped their hands to their weapons, panicked. He raised a hand to them, motioning them to remain calm. His eyes flicked to the ball before him but then returned to her, holding steady, studying her.

She had the ball circle the King several times, then shift and dance around each of the other men. Terrin held firm, while each of the others flinched away, twisting their heads to follow the flame.

Finally, beginning to sweat from the exertion, she sent the ball of flame back to the candle from which she had taken it, allowing it to settle and shrink onto the wick.

Without a flame dancing around them, the men were able to smile at each other, apparently pleased with the demonstration.

"We should put her with the archers. That kind of control would be invaluable..." General Saer began before he was cut off by General Lamner.

"All we would need to do is get her close to their leadership. An attractive woman would get close more easily than any soldier or assassin and they would never see it coming."

"Gentlemen, there is time for strategy later," Terrin interjected, raising his hand to silence them. "Brianne, that was perfect. I would like you to practice a small demonstration for the meeting. Something simple, casual even."

"I think I can manage that."

"Excellent, thank you. That will be all for now, you may go back to your tent to rest and practice."

"Thank you, my Lord, Generals." She did her best curtsy, still fairly unfamiliar with the movement and turned to leave. As she stepped towards the entrance she heard Fire General Arhan clear his throat.

"Oh, of course!" Terrin said suddenly, "Brianne!" She turned, "This is for you. I would like you to wear it to the meeting. I had it made for you, so it should fit. I will send a seamstress to you tomorrow if any adjustments need to be made." He slid the folded cloth across the table towards her.

She took the bundle in her hands, pleasantly surprised at the softness of the fabric on her fingers.

"Thank you, my Lord," she said again as she turned and left the tent.

She had no trouble finding her way back through the encampment without Jermal's guidance.

Night had fallen more fully in the short time she was in the King's tent. The soldiers were letting the fires die down slowly. While some still sat in quiet conversation, many were preparing to sleep, if not already snoring.

Brianne rushed through the camp towards her tent, her thoughts firmly on the dress folded in her hands and what it signified.

As she approached her tent she looked off to the crowd of tents to the left. At that moment, in the torchlight, she saw Jermal step from his tent and thrust his hands into the sky. Difficult to distinguish in the darkness, she thought she saw a raven take flight and strike out westward.

Thinking nothing of it—he was likely just sending a message to his disciples in Morim—she entered the warm glow of her own tent.

CHAPTER 7

A powerful gust of wind ripped across the shallow valley, rustling the canvas of the small pavilion erected in the centre. The blazing sun was nearing its mid-day peak, causing the assembled riders to shield their eyes from the brightness. They were far enough from Mount Rhodal for the skies to clear and it was still taking those accustomed to the ever-present overcast to acclimate to the persistent light.

Terrin sat atop Mi'drak at the edge of the valley, gazing at the pavilion. To his right rode Richmond, his face stern. He wore his full armour and had weapons strapped to every available space. He was an imposing sight to behold, intended to intimidate and unnerve those they were about to meet.

To his left rode Brianne atop Fire Dancer. She looked resplendent in the crimson dress he had had made for her: Terrin found his gaze wandering down the plunging neckline. From his vantage point atop the tall Mi'drak, his view was pristine; the soft indent at the base of her neck forming an arrow, guiding his eyes to the mounds of her bosom, gently rising and falling with her breath. With a start he caught her eyes shift to him and he quickly forced his gaze back to the path ahead. He needed to remain focused on the coming meeting but struggled not to fixate on the young woman beside him. Hopefully, she would prove as distracting to the envoy from Drevesine with whom he was about to meet.

He forced his mind back to the matter which brought them here, to this valley between the massed armies. Drevesine had requested a meeting: Terrin knew little more than that about their intentions. Both armies were poised to fight; Drevesine had consolidated their forces and fortified Harten and the surrounding hills and Terrin's force sat on the cusp, within striking distance.

Terrin could not help but hope this meeting would prevent the coming bloodshed. If he could only convince Drevesine and Zemiltar to back down, then he could return his armies to the border with Stalius, their agreement rendered null and void. Thousands of men and boys who marched with him could simply return home: return to the mothers, wives and lives they had been forced to leave behind. To achieve that, he would need to focus on keeping a short leash on his temper.

Across the field, he could see the banners of the Drevesine group, also waiting. He could make out five riders, as had been agreed. With a relieved sigh he signalled behind himself for the small contingent of soldiers he had brought to remain where they were, hidden among the trees at the edge of the valley.

Readying himself, he raised his own banner high in the air, waving it in a small circle. As the Drevesine banners waved, returning the signal, both parties strode towards the centre pavilion.

* * *

Terrin dismounted Mi'drak a few paces from the pavilion, signalling his companions to follow his example. Below the canvased covering of the pavilion waited a long table, the other party dismounting a short distance on the other side. That party consisted entirely of individuals from Drevesine, to Terrin's disappointment and frustration. While the King had entered the valley full of hope and optimism, the composition of the party he was meeting quickly darkened his mood.

He could recognize only two of the five individuals as they slowly approached the centre table. Leading the group was Jase Ekman, a member of the Wood Council, beside him walked a fellow councillor, Eve Kome. Both had attended Terrin's coronation on behalf of their Republic.

It was not difficult for Terrin to put a stern expression on his face as they reached the meeting point, as he was annoyed at the faces he saw and, more significantly, those he did not. "Where is HardOak?" he demanded. That the High Councilor had not deemed this meeting worthy of his time and sent his underlings in his stead was insulting.

"The High Councilor had other pressing matters to attend to, I am afraid," Jase responded as he and his companions aligned themselves across the far side of the table. "We are fully empowered to find peace through this discussion, however."

Terrin simply glared at them for a moment as the tinglings of frustration began to blossom into anger in the back of his mind.

"Allow me to make introductions," Jase began after a moment of uncomfortable silence. "To my left are Eve Kome and Lorence Yarlad, Councilors of the Wood Council representing the southern reaches of Drevesine. To my right is General Todd Navillus, leader of the army of Drevesine and Daimian Nightcloak, of the Forest Legion."

Intrigued by the final man, Terrin eyed him. There were many legends about Nightcloak and his Forest Legion. Many described the Legion as more of a cult than a military unit, with Nightcloak firmly at their head. The man certainly had the bearing and apparent confidence of a secure leader as he stared back at the King, unblinking. The tone of Jase's voice as he introduced the man implied a level of disconnect between the two.

"Where are the representatives from Zemiltar?" Terrin demanded, not bothering to introduce his own companions.

"Zemiltar?" Jase began, his voice uncertain. "The Zemiltarans with us are..."

"So you admit to your alliance?" Terrin cut him off; his temper had surfaced. The feeling was all too familiar to him. An instant before, he had been calm. Irritated but calm. Then the anger rose like water filling a leaky boat but lightning fast. His rational mind told him it did not belong in this situation but there was no holding back the flood and that quiet voice of reason was swept away.

"What alliance? They are mere..." Jase stammered, taking half a step back at the suddenness of Terrin's change in composure.

"Do not try to deny it!" Terrin shouted, slamming his fist on the table. "Foselak marched an army here and you came to join it. What is it, have we grown too prosperous? Do you foolishly believe my rule to be fragile and think you see an opportunity!?" He felt the spittle fly from his lips as he raged, his vision was blurred with anger. There was no stopping the tirade now.

Absently he noticed the eyes of those opposite him widen and shift to his left, where Brianne stood. On the periphery of his vision, he caught sight of small balls of flame circling around her. He smiled inwardly, pleased she was playing her part; putting them on edge, her power accentuating his statements. The internal smile did not reach his lips, however, as he raged on.

"King Dramen, we assure you..." Jase attempted to say before he was again cut short.

"Enough!" Terrin bellowed back. "I am not interested in hearing more of your lies! We came to this meeting in good faith, in an effort to prevent war. You come spouting bullshit! It is obvious this meeting is a mockery! Why else would HardOak not attend? Why else would you not bring a leader from Zemiltar and try to deny them?"

He continued, as the Drevesine delegation stood mouth agape, clearly surprised to have their pretense exposed so easily. "We came here to seek peace, to find a way to avoid this war. You come... why? To lull us into a false sense of security? To make empty promises so you can stab us in the back?"

"Well, Pohartan is not so foolish! We will not fall for your ploy! You have taken on more than you ever could have expected this day. The Flame Wall of the Pohartan army will roll over Drevesine, leaving only ash and scorched earth in its path of destruction!" Terrin felt as if a weight was being lifted off his shoulders as the words poured out. He was barely in control, a mere passenger being dragged along the raging rapids. But those rapids could not extend forever. Ever so slowly the voice of reason which had previously been swept away began to surface again.

He stood in the uncomfortable silence as he pulled his raging temper back into control, his mind clearing slowly.

"King Dramen..." Jase began again. While the Councilors stood stunned, appearing as children who had just received a stern dressing-down from an angry parent, the expressions of Nightcloak and General Navillus had grown progressively darker as Terrin spoke.

"Save your meaningless words. We will see you on the field." Terrin cut him off one last time with a growl. Spinning on his heel, he stalked back towards the horses, his party falling in behind. The Drevesine contingent was left speechless.

Often after his temper had been released Terrin was left to struggle with confusing feelings of guilt and shame. He did not enjoy who he became during those times but had found few reliable means by which to keep that anger at bay: its power overtook him so swiftly, so completely. Those feelings began to pry at him now but he ignored them. The arrogance of Jase's attempted lies was still fueling a deeper, more controllable anger.

As they approached the horses Terrin saw Brianne turn towards the pavilion. The balls of flame which had been swirling around her suddenly shot back. Terrin turned to watch Jase and his companions jump back as the flames struck the table before them and the canvas above, catching and spreading unnaturally quickly. The group from Drevesine fled from the flames as Terrin smiled, taking the image as an indication of how the coming war would go.

* * *

Brianne smiled as she watched the pavilion burn and the men retreat through the smoke. As she mounted Fire Dancer she caught Terrin smiling at her. It was a bizarre smile, as the anger was still evident on his face but it was an approving smile.

She could not help feeling pleasure at that smile as well and the thought of Terrin's approval of what she had just done. She was not completely sure why she had decided to set fire to the pavilion; it had merely felt correct.

Fire Dancer began to trot alongside Terrin's horse as they made for the edge of the valley. *King! Not Terrin! I must remember to call him King, even in my own mind.* She was unsure what to think of the young King but it did not truly matter what she thought. He was the King and saw her as a weapon, a tool. Sure she had seen him looking at her several times since they started out that morning but certainly, that was the dress doing its job. It was the finest she had ever seen, let alone owned but even it was intended as a weapon and tool of distraction.

As they rode, Brianne heard a sharp call rise up from the valley behind them. She did not recognize it, nor did she know what it signified but Terrin—King Terrin—and Fire General Arhan seemed to understand. They exchanged a quick look and kicked their horses into a gallop. King Terrin drew his sword, while Fire General Arhan pulled the shortbow from his saddle and nocked an arrow. General Lamner and General Saer followed suit, readying their own weapons and galloping behind the King and Fire General.

Brianne hastily followed, afraid. With difficulty she formed another ball of fire, holding it beside her. It took a lot from her to hold that ball, maintain that focus, while atop the galloping Fire Dancer but panic forced her.

A moment of fear swept over Brianne as they entered the forest. She was not used to riding through this dense of forest, or at this speed. But Fire Dancer was well trained and well named, leaping over fallen branches and shrubs and between trees like a flickering flame.

The smell of death hit her. It was not as strong as when King Terrin had killed Cadon, as it was mixed with the fresh scents of the forest but there was *more* of it.

They flew past the bodies of fallen Pohartan soldiers, their weapons still resting on their hips, untouched. A few had arrows jutting from their bodies, looks of pain and shock on those faces which were not buried in the dirt and greenery of the forest floor. Most, however, had their throats slit wide. They lay on their backs or propped against trees as they had fallen, dead eyes staring unblinkingly at the canopy of leaves above.

Richmond loosed an arrow and a figure fell from a tree off to the right. Its green and brown cloak flapped and fluttered as it fell, blending into the surroundings and making it difficult to follow its path to the forest floor.

Brianne had not thought to look up but did so now. She saw nothing but leaves and branches.

Richmond loosed another arrow but nothing fell. Trusting him, Brianne cast her little ball of flame where he had aimed his arrow. With a scream, another figure fell to the ground, this time in flames. The scream was stifled by a loud thud as the body hit the hard-packed ground. The heads of the men riding before her swivelled left and right scanning the trees, searching for targets.

She felt the air beside her split as an arrow flew by her ear. She watched as it buried itself in the neck of General Lamner ahead of her. His body went rigid for a moment, his head lolling to the side, before going limp. He fell forward over the neck of his horse, which continued to gallop with the others, carrying the dead weight of its former master.

A mass dropped from the branches above her, landing behind her on Fire Dancer's back. The horse neighed loudly and Brianne screamed as one arm wrapped around her waist and she saw a glint of steel rising beside her.

Strands of her flowing hair were cut by an arrow launched towards her. She winced, squeezing her eyes shut as she heard the sickening *thunk* of the arrow striking her attacker.

The arm at her waist went limp and then fell away as the body slid from the haunches of the galloping horse. Brianne opened her eyes again to see King Terrin turning away, nocking another arrow in his own bow. He must have followed Fire General Arhan's example and forgone his sword.

Brianne's heart raced, her breath was heavy, fear and panic sweeping over her. She could not hope to hold a flame any longer and gave up the effort and letting the power rush from her, instead clinging low to Fire Dancer as she raced through the forest.

The trees began to thin out, the shrubbery on the forest floor growing less dense. The other riders began to slow, weapons still in hand but lowered now.

"Fucking Forest Legion! They were watching our men the entire time! Just waiting to slaughter them!" She heard King Terrin shouting and swearing to Fire General Arhan, their panting horses slowing to a trot. They exited the last trees of the forest and continued onto the road which would take them back to their army's camp.

General Saer brought his horse beside that of General Lamner, checking its burden. King Terrin looked back at the aged General, catching his eye. General Saer solemnly shook his head, adjusting the body on the horse and patting his fallen comrade's back before moving his horse away a short distance.

"The Second Battalion will need new leadership," King Terrin was saying to Fire General Arhan as Brianne brought her horse up beside the men.

"Slim pickings in the Second but maybe I can pull someone from the Fourth, or even the First. I will find someone," Fire General Arhan responded, his eyes already in a far-off place as he worked through the options in his head.

"Can you believe their insolence? Their audacity!? Acting the victim, denying their own actions… That Jase is a deranged fool, the whole blasted Wood Council are! Not even bringing a representative from Zemiltar to this blasted meeting! As if we do not know they are there…. Oh no my friend, I tell you, they want this war. There was never a hope of stopping it!"

"Without a doubt, Terrin. They must have been trying to placate us before attacking. I see no other purpose for this charade of a meeting," the Fire General replied.

It was Fire General Arhan who first noticed Brianne's arrival.

"Burning that pavilion was beautiful, well done." He nodded approvingly in her direction.

"Yes, excellent work. Let us hope you caught one or two of them," King Terrin added, turning to Brianne.

"Thank you, my Lords," she said simply.

"They almost had you in the woods there. Are you all right?" She thought she caught a hint of concern in Terrin's—*King* Terrin's—voice.

"Yes, I am all right. That was an amazing shot, thank you."

He shrugged. "We cannot afford to lose you," he responded, returning his gaze to the road ahead.

They continued the rest of the way to camp in silence. Brianne's own thoughts danced around as quickly as her still-racing heartbeat. She relived the terrifying, yet exhilarating, events of the day. In a flash, memory and realization struck her. *I killed a man, in that tree...* It had happened so quickly, in such chaos. It had been driven by instinct. She had seen Fire General Arhan loose and had sent her flame following the arrow.

That scream....

The breaking of branches as the smouldering body fell...

The sickening thud and crunch which silenced the scream...

I am a weapon...

CHAPTER 8

The rain fell softly on Terrin's head, a steady *pat pat pat*. He let it fall upon him, allowing it to trickle through his hair and down his face and neck. His clothes were already sodden and he felt each step squish in his boots as he passed the sentry lines heading north.

Rain was scarce in Morim. On the rare occasion it fell from the ever-present clouds most would flee inside. Terrin never understood that. Did they suddenly fear to get wet? Not Terrin. As a boy, he and his friends—few as they had been—would race outside at the sound of the first drop hitting the hard stones of the street.

They had laughed and cheered as the rain fell harder, at times dancing among the droplets with their arms outstretched; at times simply lying flat and letting the rain douse them.

Anyone else caught in the rain would look at him as if he were mad, while they themselves covered their heads and ran about their unavoidable errands. He would not care, however. He often found himself out in the rain even after his friends had gotten over the novelty and returned home. At those times he would walk as he did now: alone with his meandering thoughts until his mother, or more often a servant, found him, or the rain stopped.

As an adult, rain always now brought him back to those innocent, care-free days. Though as rare as rain was in Morim, it was far more rare for him to have the time or opportunity to enjoy it as he once had. He had that opportunity now.

It was early morning, the day after the meeting with Drevesine: the day the war would truly begin. He and the Generals had spoken late into the night as the rain drummed on the canvas above them. The rain would actually work in their favour and had allowed them to put the final elements of their battle plan together. Terrin was experienced enough to know plans rarely lasted far beyond the first step of the soldiers but it was still vital to have at least some form of guiding framework for the Generals to follow.

Terrin had attempted to sleep once his Generals left to their own tents but it had been fleeting at best. The soothing sound of the rain was no match for the events of the days past and those to follow rampaging through his psyche.

Eventually, he had given up on getting any meaningful rest and wandered into the rain, unable to resist the call any longer.

Richmond would certainly berate him for leaving the camp, particularly alone. It was a great risk, to be sure: though sparsely treed, members of the Forest Legion were potentially scattered throughout the woods around the Pohartan camp and would love the opportunity to kill the King. But Terrin let his feet carry him where they pleased and did not stop as he found himself leaving the camp and entering the still-dark forest.

The war he was about to wage fought for control of his mind but he resisted those thoughts, letting the rain wash them into the mud, to be left behind in his footprints. Terrin opened his mind, allowing any other thoughts which chose to enter have free rein as he walked.

The image which seemed to dominate his thoughts was that of his mother: the ringlets of her dark hair framing her face; her warm eyes; and her bright, loving smile.

Samara Dramen had been a quiet, reserved woman. When she spoke, she spoke softly and without aggression. But when she spoke, people listened. Terrin's father could carry on bellowing in an attempt to bring a council meeting to order and be ignored but the soft sound of Queen Samara clearing her throat could cut through any rabble and bring any raucous crowd to rapt attention. She had been respected for her intelligence and insight but more than that she had been loved: loved for her warmth and her compassion as she showed the citizens of Pohartan genuine caring and they adored her. The people loved her, Terrin's father loved her but of course, Terrin loved her most of all.

He remembered her silken voice as she sang him to sleep each night. He remembered her gentle, genuine laugh: a pure expression of joy which brightened any room. He remembered the sparkle in her eye as she listened attentively to his childhood tales of adventure. What he remembered most was her face as she looked at him. The small, patient yet genuine smile she seemed to have for him alone and the pure love he could see in her eyes.

Now, standing in the rain he could almost smell her favourite floral perfume and he could feel her lips on his forehead, just above his right eye where she had kissed him goodnight, every night after finishing her song.

Mixed with the rain, the tears which began to roll down his face were hidden to the non-existent observers. His feet had taken him to the top of a large hill, giving him a perfect vantage over the forest and the rising sun, just beginning to peak over the horizon and start its journey across the sky, apathetic to the events which would take place in its light.

Terrin let the tears fall and let the thoughts continue. He knew what was coming next: the thoughts he had avoided for fifteen years now, forced away whenever they tried to emerge. Now he let the memories play themselves out.

He had been ten years old when his mother died. She had been trying to bring a brother into the world for him and both mother and infant had been lost. He always thought of it as "for him". Though knowing better as an adult, Terrin still carried guilt for his mother's death on his shoulders. He had begged for a brother; pleaded with his mother, pleaded with the gods to bring him one. Not understanding the process, his child's mind saw his mother's pregnancy as an answer to his prayers; a gift for him.

Then, one rare sunny morning in Morim, his father had burst from their chambers, screaming for the midwife.

Terrin had been confused, scared, as servants rushed about in chaos. He had wanted to go into the bedchamber, where he could hear his mother screaming in pain and his father shouting frantic and irrelevant orders but Mistress Ralos—his mother's handmaid and a surrogate aunt to Terrin—held him firm.

And so he had stayed, for what seemed an eternity, staring at his parents' chamber door, shaking with fear and confusion.

Finally, the screaming stopped and another eternity passed before his father opened the door. Terrin had never seen his father so dishevelled, had never seen his eyes so vacant and lost. The King shared a brief, meaning-filled look with Mistress Ralos before speaking.

"Terrin, come here son. Your mother wishes to see you," he said, his voice hollow.

Young Terrin raced into the chamber. To one side the midwife and several servants huddled over a small, unmoving form but Terrin was focused on the bed where his mother lay.

Her hair was slicked to her head with sweat and her usually sparkling eyes seemed dull. Somehow she managed that special smile as he raced to her side. Though he could not put words to it, he understood what was happening and burst into tears.

"I'm sorry mother! I'm sorry! I do not need a brother! I'm sorry!" he sputtered between sobs.

His mother brushed her fingers through his hair, gently pulling his head close to hers and kissing his forehead, just above his right eye.

"Shhh, my sweet boy, shhh…" she said weakly. Then she began to sing the song she sang to him each night. Terrin sang along, through his sobs. With each line, his mother's voice grew weaker, more distant. He was left to finish the song by himself as his father pulled him away.

That was the first time Terrin could remember feeling the blinding rage. He had lashed out at anyone near him for days, refusing to leave his own chambers, even for his mother's funeral services.

Now he felt no rage. He felt little of anything. The burden of the crown and the looming war were a distant awareness. He was not King Terrin at that moment, he was not nobility: he was a ten-year-old boy, losing his mother.

Terrin began to sing. His voice was barely audible and his lips barely moved but in his mind, his mother's voice rang loud over the treetops.

* * *

Richmond watched as the men hitched the last of the Firethrowers to their horse teams, preparing for the battle. The other Firethrowers were already on the march, trailing behind the front ranks of the First Battalion as they moved along the road which approached Harten from the south.

They were to be the main thrust of the attack, as they insisted on being, closely followed by the Second. The Firethrowers were charged with keeping the sides of the road clear of enemy soldiers as the Pohartan soldiers marched towards the valley.

The sun was just beginning to rise and push back the rain clouds. The dissipating rain had been a stroke of fortune for them: now the Firethrowers could shoot into the sodden forest to keep any Forest Legion soldiers away from the advancing army, with minimal risk of the fires spreading wild and turning on the Pohartan soldiers.

It would still not be an easy march or battle. Though the Firethrowers may keep the road clear for the march towards Harten, everything would change once they entered the valley surrounding the small town. The valley would be a dense sea of soldiers, waiting for them and as the battle began there they would be too close for the Firethrowers to be used effectively.

The Fifth Battalion would have the worst of it. They were assembling to the north and were charged with striking through the forest. To her credit, Simone had not flinched at the assignment; though they all knew it meant a large portion of her men were forfeit. They were to punch hard through the forest, ideally to strike at the flanks of the soldiers which would be engaging the First and Second Battalions in the Harten valley. The true purpose of the

Fifth, however, was to draw the Forest Legion to them. They were to be fodder, plain and simple. The cost to the Fifth would be large but Richmond hoped it would be enough to ease the way for the First and Second but more importantly the Third, who was now breaking camp and beginning to trickle to their position in the southeast.

Richmond mounted his horse, Ursa, surprisingly swiftly for such a bulky man so heavily armoured, as the last Firethrower and horse team were paired. He kicked his heels and guided Ursa along the ranks of soldiers slowly marching up the road, towards the dense forest. He acknowledged the salutes of the men he passed with a nod as he trotted ahead. Their faces were stoic. They knew toward what they marched and had steeled themselves to the likelihoods it entailed, as seasoned soldiers do. He raced past line after line of men, their armour blending into a wall of crimson and amber as he picked up speed, heading for his place beside General Saer near the front ranks.

Neither of the men was the type to lead from the back, to try and remain in a safe location and guide the battle. Such a philosophy had its merits but simply did not suit these men: they preferred to be in the thick of things. Richmond had begun his career as a basic infantryman and was used to the chaos and danger of the battlefield. Thinking back, the commanders he had respected most were those who fought beside him; including, for a period, Dendrik Saer.

One of the Division Commanders was saluting and walking away as Richmond reached Dendrik, who sat atop his horse. The road was wide enough to allow the men to march in lines of ten. Five such lines marched in front of Dendrik now, forming their iconic Fire Wall at the head of the battalion. Behind that wall, with the General, laboured four Firethrowers and their crews.

Dendrik saluted as Richmond brought his horse alongside the older man.

"Everyone's on the move," Richmond informed.

"Where's Dramen?" Dendrik asked, acknowledging Richmond's statement with a simple nod.

"Fair question. The sentries said he wandered out of camp shortly before dawn. I assume he will be here shortly. He knows the plan." Richmond hoped his tone was calm, hiding the concern he felt.

To Richmond's relief, Terrin, mounted on Mi'drak, trotted up beside the men as if summoned by the mention of his name.

"Good morning, gentlemen," he said.

"Where did you go this morning?" Richmond asked. "You look weary."

"Just needed to clear my head."

Richmond shrugged, accepting the answer. He had experienced years of similar behaviour and explanations from his friend and King.

"Well, let's get on with it then," the Fire General said as the three trotted towards battle at the head of an army.

* * *

Brianne gently patted Fire Dancer's neck as they strode forward between the smoking trees. She knew the small action was more to calm her nerves than those of the gelding: Fire Dancer was war-trained and calm, while Brianne had never felt so anxious.

Being here was her own doing, so she had no one else to blame. In fact, she had asked to be at the front, with the King and Fire General. *What was I thinking?* She asked herself, shaking her head.

Instead, she rode among the Second; a compromise between her and the King. King Terrin felt she was not ready to stand in a full-fledged battle and had tried to persuade her to stay back with the Fourth, who sat in reserve. For reasons she no longer remembered—perhaps she was just full of adrenaline from the meeting with Drevesine—she insisted she take part. She largely regretted that conviction in this moment.

She forced herself to take a deep breath, made difficult by the cloud of smoke over the roadway and regain her determination. King Terrin and General Arhan were somewhere ahead among the constant booms of the Firethrowers, perhaps already engaging the enemy in the valley. Somewhere to the southeast both Jahn and Andrew—she had managed to coax information about their assignment from the new General of the Second—marched through the forest to battle. How could she simply stay behind while everyone else fought? So once again she swallowed her fear.

Nolan Warsch rode beside her, chatting pleasantly but inanely. The new General of the Second Battalion irritated her, though she did not have a fair reason to feel that way. He was very friendly and charming and certainly handsome. Brianne appreciated his flowing chestnut hair, his rigid jaw and his bright smile. She had seen some of the women of the camp swoon over him as the army prepared to march earlier that morning but for her, it was more of an acknowledgement of his beauty than actual attraction. Something about the man simply irked her.

He was asking her about Sastan as the men ahead came to a stop. A soldier on horseback came galloping from the front, coming to a sudden stop in front of General Warsch.

"Sir, the First have engaged the enemy. They were able to push a short way into the valley but have stalled."

The General's tone took on a serious edge as he turned to the business of war.

"Any orders from Dramen or Arhan? Surely they do not expect us to simply stand behind them and wait."

"No orders, sir. The King and Fire General are right in the thick of the battle," the soldier replied, shaking his head.

"Bloody fools and their heroics. How can you lead soldiers while you are busy trying to protect your own neck?" the General muttered half under his breath. The soldier looked around conspicuously, trying to pretend he did not hear Warsch call his superiors—including the King, no less—"fools".

"All right, thank you." Warsch called behind him, "Balon! Forward!" Major Balon trotted to the General's side.

"Get yourself to the front and push the men forward. We are bottlenecked on this road and need to help the First push further into the valley."

"Yes, sir!" Balon saluted, jogging ahead.

"I wish we could get off this road and around through the forest. Those Firethrowers may have kept the Forest Legion at bay but they have also blocked us in," Warsch continued, still mostly to himself.

Brianne glanced over the forest rising on either side of the road. Smoke billowed through the branches from patches of flame scattered among the trees. The sodden shrubbery and muddy ground seemed to keep the flames from raging wildly but it would be nearly impossible to maneuver any meaningful number of men through.

Not far to her right, a small bush was completely engulfed in flame and Brianne reached for it with her will. With some effort she *collected* the flame from the branches, leaving smoking tendrils rising from the charred remains as the flame rose into a single, roiling ball above the bush.

Testing, she split the ball in half. One portion she cast deeper into the forest, where it struck a new shrub and began to consume it, returning to natural flame.

The remaining portion continued to churn mid-air, tongues of flame fluttering over its form. Concentrating, Brianne began to *squeeze* the fire. She wanted to get rid of the flame entirely—something she had not yet thought to try. The ball of flame shrunk into itself slowly but did not wither and die. Instead, it grew more intense as the flame was forced into a smaller and smaller space. Soon she had an orb no larger than her fist but of such intensity it was nearly palpable.

Brianne released her conscious self. She stopped thinking about what she wanted to achieve and just let her instincts make it happen. It was not an easy state to reach but she had learned to trust her subconscious to know what to do.

Beginning slowly but gaining force and speed at an alarming rate, the intensity of the flame shot towards her, drawing out of the ball she had formed. It was not the flame itself moving towards her but its energy; its essence. She could see it racing for her, though she was certain it was invisible to those around.

The force of it almost knocked her from Fire Dancer but she held firm. A nearly overwhelming wave of heat rushed over Brianne, threatening to consume her. But as quickly as it began, it was over. The heat disappeared, as had the ball of flame.

Warsch stared into the trees, where the ball of flame had been. He had only seen it form and then shrink and disappear.

Brianne panted, out of breath from the residual effects of the heat and exertion and looked at General Warsch.

"I think I can take some men through."

*   *   *

Jahn adjusted his breastplate as he wove through the dense trees. The strap was digging irritably into his shoulder and he could not seem to get it to sit properly.

Petren marched along to his right, with Fennel a few paces to the left. Soldiers wove between the trees in all directions. The entire Third Battalion was traipsing through the forest, heading north to Harten.

They had been listening to the boom of the Firethrowers for most of the day—it had to be near mid-day by now—but a short while ago they also heard the horns announcing the charge somewhere in the distance, indicating the First had reached the valley.

"Hey, Jahn!" a small voice called from behind him, where Amad was struggling to pull his armoured legs through a dense thicket of shrubs.

"What?" Jahn hollered back without looking.

"How many do you think you will kill? I am going for at least ten!"

"Bullshit, Little Pup!" Tumas shouted, "At the first sign of the enemy you will be hiding under a bush, your trousers wet with piss!"

Some of the men in earshot chuckled.

"Shut up Tumas, or I will be pissing in your mouth! Well Jahn, how many?"

"As many as try to kill me, I suppose," Jahn replied solemnly, "At least, I hope I get those ones."

Amad released a quick laugh, which died off as he caught Jahn's meaning.

"Well… you're depressing…" he heard Amad mumble.

It was true, Jahn supposed, he was depressing. The others were constantly cracking jokes or boasting about what great heroes they would be. Jahn tried to joke along, tried to smile with the rest but he could not; especially as the battle drew closer.

The others noticed his sullen attitude and it had built a wall around him. He was part of the squad in practice: he ate with them, trained with them, slept next to them and would soon fight with and for them but he was not truly part of the camaraderie.

He adjusted his shoulder strap again, this time thinking perhaps he had managed to get it to settle into the proper position.

Jahn continued to scan the branches overhead, as they had been instructed to do but continued to see nothing. Several times he had passed the body of a member of the Forest Legion lying on the ground, with an arrow or two jutting from its torso and usually with at least two Pohartan soldiers lying dead nearby. Amad had raced to the first couple Legion bodies, looking to loot one of their Kurali knives but they had already been claimed by other soldiers.

His squad was deep enough in the centre of the crawling battalion he did not believe the Forest Legion posed a particular threat to them. Most were likely drawn to the First and Second on the road, or the Fifth, who had started marching through the forest to the west hours ago. Those who remained in the area either chose to stay concealed or revealed themselves and caused as much damage as they could before they fell—long before Jahn's group reached them.

Jahn's eyes continued to pan but his mind began to drift off once again.

Perhaps an hour passed. One more fallen Legionnaire was passed, this one surrounded by four downed Pohartans. Suddenly, Jahn realized the trees were gone: they had entered the valley of Harten. Ahead a writhing mass of soldiers swelled in front of a backdrop of flame and smoke. The smell of smoke and blood and the clash of swords were heavy in the air.

Amad pushed past him, sprinting with his sword waving wildly in the air, screaming at the top of his lungs. The others were running too, into the mass which was just beginning to notice them as the first soldiers crashed into their flanks.

Jahn took a long, deep breath and drew his own sword. Then his feet were moving with the others: his sword held firm at his side and his jaw clenched shut.

PART II
THE FLAME

CHAPTER 9

The sound of Jahn's breath pounded heavily in his head, in rhythm with his racing footsteps. His shoulder strap continued to dig into his flesh but the annoyance was vague and distant.

Ahead, his comrades crashed bloodily into the side of the enemy, who were primarily entangled with soldiers of the First and Second. Some were turning to the new threat but most just as a sword slashed between their armour. The majority had no inclination they were now being pressed by a third battalion as they engaged in one-on-one clashes for their lives.

Jahn saw little Amad as he approached the mass, sword ready. The petite young soldier was darting madly through the chaos. Where most engaged a single enemy soldier, Amad never stopped moving. His sword flashed from side to side, making small jabs at every Drevesine soldier he passed. A slash to an arm or leg or a jab to the side and Amad had moved on like a wisp of smoke. But it was enough; each victim was distracted or debilitated enough for another Pohartan soldier to seize the advantage and land a lethal blow.

Nearing the mass, Jahn chose his target. A soldier in Drevesine green at the edge of the crowd was just turning to face the new onslaught, directly in front of the charging Jahn.

A guttural roar escaped Jahn's lips as his momentum brought him into his adversary. He swung his sword hard towards the soldier's neck but met only steel and air as his sword was deflected by that of his enemy.

Jahn struggled to pull his feet under him and turn to continue the attack. He faced the other soldier, who stood with his sword ready. They locked eyes in the chaos which surrounded them as men crashed into each other on all sides.

The soldier's face seemed a contradiction: his teeth were barred, fierce. His eyes, however, were frantic, full of terror. Sweat dripped down his face from under his helm: he looked no older than Jahn himself and Jahn wondered if this were the other soldier's first battle as well.

There was no time to explore these thoughts, however, as the soldier swung towards Jahn. It was a basic swing; coming down from the right but Jahn barely got his blade into position to counter it. He struggled to recall the drills he had been run through a thousand times since being enlisted.

Their encounter felt much like one of those drills. Each played their part, alternating between attacking and defending, working their way through the basic and practiced forms. But Jahn was already beginning to slow, struggling to hold his footing. More and more he fell to defensive stances, missing his opportunities for a counter-strike. His adversary was certainly an equal swordsman in skill—better would have capitalized on Jahn's moments of hesitation and left him in a bloodied heap—but held the advantage in strength and stamina.

The young Drevesine soldier recognized this as well and the realization gave him an extra burst of motivation, as he pushed Jahn back. Each strike came closer before Jahn could weakly deflect it.

Then Jahn fell. His heel caught on something behind him and he was on the ground.

In front of him, the soldier raised his sword to deliver the decisive strike. While Jahn weakly held his sword aloft, hoping for the strength and luck to deflect a few more blows before the boy's sword met his flesh.

A cackling streak of silver and crimson dashed behind the soldier, who let out a shriek, falling to one knee, his hands dropping to the back of his upper leg.

Jahn saw the advantage and without thought drove his sword into the boy's side, as he had been trained, between the plates of his armour.

His hand dropped from the hilt of his sword, buried deep in the Drevesine soldier and Jahn fell back, exhausted. The lifeless body fell on top of him and there he stayed.

*   *   *

Brianne raced between trees, two dozen Pohartan soldiers keeping up surprisingly well in their bulky armour.

The fires which ran along the road had not spread more than a quarter of a league out. It had taken much of Brianne's strength to carve a way through, with these men huddled around her, sweating from the intense heat as they trod through the inferno.

Beginning to fear they were lost in a sea of flame, Brianne may have been the most relieved when they broke from the fire into untouched forest.

Once safely away from the flames, they had stopped a moment to catch their breath—as best they could in the smoke-filled air. To Brianne's surprise, the men then looked to her to lead them on. And so, despite her best judgement, she did. Brianne was no woodsman and it was virtually impossible to pinpoint the sun through the trees and smoke but she made her best guess at the proper direction and began to walk, soldiers in tow.

It was not long before they started seeing the bodies.

They were scattered at first: solitary Pohartan soldiers, felled by a brutally slit throat. As they continued, picking up speed, dozens could be seen: more and more frequently felled by arrows.

As the number of Pohartan casualties grew, so too did the number of green-cloaked forms of the Forest Legion. But it was not an equal matching: there had to be at least ten Pohartan dead for each Drevesine.

So now they ran: the men with their bows in hand and necks craned upward. Brianne appeared unarmed but was prepared to hurl a ball of flame at the slightest whisper of movement above.

Ahead, the sounds of shouts and movement began to cut through the trees. Brianne focused her energy, forming two small balls of flame in the palms of her hands.

She raced past the first green-clad figures before she even saw them, nearly crashing into one of them. One of the soldiers running with her did collide with it, however, and the two went down together with a heavy thud.

Brianne strained her eyes and began to distinguish the scattered human shapes from the foliage into which they blended. With ferocity she cast her balls of flame at those closest, watching their cloaks burst into flame. She heard the steady twang of arrows being loosed around her, along with the distinct sound of steel sliding free from scabbards.

And so they descended into pandemonium. Brianne's forehead beaded with sweat as she hurled fire in every direction. Around her, the Pohartan men clashed and died but so too did the Legionnaires, caught by surprise as they had been.

Ahead, Brianne could see flashes of silver and amber dancing among the trees and continued the charge in that direction. They met the other force and for a moment were greeted with raised blades and gritted teeth before recognition set in. Among the mass, Brianne locked eyes with General Atlee, her helmet gone and hair dishevelled

"East!" Simone shouted over the chaos. Her men were clustered together, facing outwards with shields raised high, hoping to deflect arrows. Brianne could not judge how many remained but it was far fewer than should have been there.

East the mass moved, Brianne's force integrating itself into the larger group. Men continued to fall but they pushed on, determined.

"We have to get out of this bloody forest!" Simone screamed, firing an arrow into the trees. She followed the shout with a stream of curses in a language which Brianne had never before heard, as she continued to nock and loose arrows.

Brianne continued to hurl balls of fire over the heads of the Pohartan soldiers, as they trotted through the dense forest. Many hit home but some missed their mark, flashing into the branches and colliding with distant trees.

It seemed an eternity: soldiers racing through the woods, fighting for their lives. The new soldiers provided a surge of renewed vigour in the besieged soldiers, giving them that drive to push. Brianne was beginning to fear they were not going to make it through, as Pohartan soldiers continued to fall.

Finally, they emerged from the treeline, into the valley of Harten.

Chaos reigned ahead. Men clashed with guttural screams as steel met steel. Figures were nearly impossible to distinguish in the writhing mass, smoke rising above.

Brianne looked at Simone beside her but the General was looking off to her left. Brianne followed her gaze and saw what she saw. Cresting over a low hill was a swarm of fresh Drevesine soldiers; their armour yet unsullied by the mud and blood of the battle towards which they charged.

Without missing a step, Simone turned their force, charging to meet the new arrivals before they hit the side of the unsuspecting Pohartan soldiers in the fray. Exhausted, feeling unable to move her legs or form a clear thought, Brianne did not hesitate to follow, her own soldiers close behind.

* * *

Richmond dared take a moment to wipe the sweat from his eyes. He could feel the heave of each of Terrin's breaths as they stood back-to-back. Their heads swivelled as they moved as one. The battle wore on in all directions around them, as they worked their way through the chaos. As the battle began, they had been leading the soldiers deeper into the valley and the mass of the enemy army but now all sense of direction was lost and irrelevant.

Richmond felt Terrin shift and step away as the King moved to meet another opponent. He did not look but listened to the sound of Terrin's sword meet the enemy's. There were two quick clashes of steel against steel, followed by the distinct sound of metal tearing through fabric and sinking into flesh. Terrin was back, breathing heavily.

Richmond's own blade was slick with blood, which was also splashed across his armour. Early in the battle—an eternity ago—he had taken a shallow cut to his left arm. The wound existed distantly in the back of his mind, buried deep by a flood of adrenaline but it was there. His left arm was growing weaker, forcing him to abandon his favoured double-handed axe. It would certainly need treatment if he survived the battle but would not be what brought him down.

Off to his left—west, by his best guess—balls of fire arced across the sky; their roar and crash lost in the din of battle.

A green-clad soldier emerged from the mass before Richmond, his sword raised and face contorted in pure, unbridled bloodlust. Rather than take the defensive, the Fire General lunged at the man. His sword plunged downward through the man's right eye, exploding out the base of his skull. Richmond smoothly pushed the enemy's falling blade away with his gauntleted free hand, pulling back his sword and letting the body fall in a heap.

"How many was that?" Terrin asked over his shoulder.

"You have to be kidding! I lost track ages ago!"

"That does not mean much; you have trouble counting your fingers."

Richmond could not help but release a burst of laughter. Even in this mess, Terrin had not lost his wit and quick tongue.

Two enemy soldiers broke off from the mass and charged for Terrin and Richmond, who pivoted to meet their blades. Richmond was the first to strike, surging forward while bringing his sword down in a high arc over the assailant's left shoulder. The enemy soldier took a half-step back and brought his blade up, guiding Richmond's harmlessly to the side. Richmond used his forward momentum to charge his shoulder into the other man's chest, pushing him back several paces.

As Richmond danced back and forth with his opponent, Terrin stared at his own foe. The soldier was bouncing on the balls of his feet, passing his sword from hand to hand, as if coaxing Terrin to strike first. The King rose to the bait and charged forward, sword first. The enemy sidestepped smoothly, grabbing at Terrin's shoulder and pulling an unsteady Terrin past him.

Terrin regained his footing quickly, spinning and bringing his sword up in time to deflect a strike at his exposed back. Cursing himself for making such a novice mistake, he refocused, bringing his sword up in a traditional duelling stance.

"Well look at this," the Drevesine soldier began, "I get to be the man who kills the Mad King of Pohartan." He was smiling gleefully, spinning his sword in a flourish as he took a slow step closer to Terrin.

A blonde head rose over the enemy's shoulder as his legs were taken out from under him. Richmond roared as his sword came up in a spray of blood after passing through the man's knees. The Fire General spun as the enemy soldier fell, carrying through the momentum of his swing to bring his sword down across the soldier's face, splitting his head in two.

"I had that one under control," Terrin said, looking at his panting friend.

"Of course you did," Richmond replied, wrenching his sword free from the wreckage it had created.

A horn blared somewhere in the near distance, three short bursts. Richmond and Terrin looked around; few Drevesine soldiers remained standing in the immediate vicinity and those that did turned on their heels and ran. The Pohartan soldiers raised their weapons in a cheer, letting their fleeing enemies pass.

One green-clad soldier had a Pohartan soldier down on the ground before him as the retreat signal sounded and took the opportunity to push his pike through the man's chest before turning and attempting to retreat with the others. Unlike his counterparts, he was met by a wall of steel, as Pohartan soldiers who had witnessed his last act descended on him from all sides like a swarm of wasps. A barely recognizable bloodied heap was all that remained as they dispersed and joined their cheering comrades.

Richmond and Terrin shared a look and a slight nod, clasping forearms.

"I had that last one," Terrin said simply, igniting a blast of laughter from Richmond.

CHAPTER 10

Brianne stumbled. Her mind and body were in a state of exhaustion the likes of which she had never experienced, nor thought possible. She drifted through the aftermath of the battle as if it were a dream; a nightmare, more accurately. Bodies covered the landscape, twisted and contorted into grotesque angles. Limbs lay stiffening in unnatural positions if they remained attached at all. Faces were frozen in rage or terror. Underfoot, the once-solid ground had been churned to mud. Pockets in the ground were filled with fresh blood; a million tiny, crimson lakes nestled between the mountainous corpses.

She trod through the human wreckage, searching. She barely knew for what she was searching, in truth. Someone she could help, she supposed. Intermixed among the dead were the nearly-dead, their moans and pleas filling the morose air. Incoherent wails were interrupted by cries for various women's names but above all else, the universal cry for "Mother".

Her efforts seemed futile—those her meagre skills could help were also combing through the bodies, wearing make-shift slings and bandages. Those still on the ground were far beyond her abilities.

Nearby, a Pohartan soldier crouched beside the moaning body of a fallen Drevesine soldier. With a smooth motion, the Pohartan pushed his ready dagger into the throat of the fallen soldier, his moans turning to a weak gurgle before falling silent a moment later. Without rising, the soldier turned on his heels to another wailing comrade, this one in matching crimson and amber. This time the soldier hesitated a moment, looking at the body. Brianne was near enough to see the tattered remains of a thigh, severed muscles dangling where the rest of a leg should lie in the mud. The kneeling soldier made his judgement and plunged his dagger again into the warm flesh of the man's neck before rising and moving on.

Brianne doubled over, emptying the contents of her stomach onto the ground, trying desperately not to hit the bodies near her. She stood there a moment, hands on her knees, as she caught her breath and strove to regain her composure, struggling not to retch again. Slowly she straightened and continued through the carnage, gingerly stepping over and around the scattered bodies and limbs.

A hand clasped her ankle and she gasped. Brianne looked down at the gauntleted hand, her eyes following the arm to the shoulder. Above the shoulder rested a helmeted head. Blood covered the portion of the face she could see. One pained eye looked up at her. She gasped again as she looked at the rest of the man's head; the entire left side of his helmet was deeply smashed in, creating a divot where half his skull should be.

As she was held captive by that single eye—the other was buried somewhere in the cavern of his skull—the light left it and the hand at her ankle fell limp.

Her thinly held control was lost and she emptied the remaining contents of her stomach beside the fallen soldier. She did not bother to look for which side he had fought: it did not matter anymore.

Helplessly, she passed moaning bodies beyond her ability. Somewhere there were soldiers and nurses better trained than she, rushing to save those they could but they were far too few.

A body ahead caught her attention, though she could not tell what about it stood out to her. It was heaped with the rest; silver armour obscured by blood and mud. Yet it seemed to call to her and so she slowly, cautiously, drew closer.

The soldier's helmet had been lost and a deep gash split the back of his skull. Tufts of golden hair lay among the blood-soaked remainder of the young soldier's head. Flecks of grey dotted the gore and Brianne could only assume they were pieces of brain matter. Again she doubled over, heaving. There was nothing left in her to bring up but there she stood; throat burning and body convulsing, the taste of bile overwhelmed by the odour of blood.

There was nothing she would be able to do for this soldier; he was leagues beyond the help of any save his Creator, yet she could not turn away, nor prevent her feet from drawing her closer.

She crouched over the body now, fingers reluctantly reaching out, tentatively touching a miraculously un-sullied lock of softly curling hair. Panic and realization swept over her. There was a reason she had been so drawn to this body: she knew this soldier.

Without regard for the blood and gore, Brianne worked her hands under the soldier's heavy armoured shoulder, attempting to turn the body. At first, nothing moved and Brianne pressed harder. With a deep *thuck,* the mud released its captive, allowing her to shift the body, revealing his face.

Andrew's blue eyes met hers, cutting through the blood which coated his soft features. Death had stolen their lustre, leaving them dull and cold. His jaw hung askew, exposing his bloodied teeth and bloated tongue; a far cry from the joy-filled smile to which she was accustomed.

Brianne's mind screamed in agony and rage but the sound did not have the opportunity to escape her lips as she fell sideways, her body numb and darkness settling in.

* * *

All was quiet as Jahn pushed the Drevesine soldier away from him. "Quiet" was a relative term: the wails of the dying were as crickets on a crisp Sastan morning compared to the roar of the battle.

Jahn did not believe he had lost consciousness, though he remembered little of the battle which had rumbled over him after he fell. It was as though he were simply removed from the physical sensations, passively watching the figures move above him through vacant eyes.

His legs sluggishly resisted his attempts to move them now, angrily numb from the hours—had it been hours?—lying still under the weight of an armoured body. Jahn forced them to obey his will and stood, wavering slightly.

A sword lay discarded nearby and Jahn claimed it as his own: it was identical to any other sword used by the military. Distantly he remembered forcing his original sword into the abdomen of another young man but lacked the drive to retrieve it. Wiping his new acquisition on a nearby body, the action did little to clean the blade, he slid the sword into the scabbard at his hip and began to walk on shaky legs.

A young woman rushed to his side, bandage at the ready in her blood-stained hands. She wore a heavy black dress with the Flame of Pohartan embroidered on the left breast. Her hair was tied back by a broad strip of red cloth, several stray brown strands stuck to the sweat of her forehead.

Jahn waved her off absently. She hesitated only a moment before turning to the nearest moan, continuing her gruesome work.

Though he walked through a sea of death, Jahn remained focused ahead. There he could see soldiers, alive and upright, milling about purposefully and knew that was where he needed to be.

The town of Harten lay before him in the distance, seemingly largely untouched by the battle. As he drew closer, the bodies began to thin out and the extra space became occupied by the remnants of what had been a portion of the Drevesine camp.

The town itself was deserted of civilians, instead occupied by soldiers and their accompanying entourage of tradesmen and servants. Most rushed about at a determined pace, obviously carrying out specific tasks. Many, however, simply stared and wandered listlessly. Jahn supposed he belonged to the second group and likely appeared no more coherent.

After walking over the field of death, it was a shock to see so many still alive. It was more of a shock to see those who were not only alive but composed. Ahead a tall soldier was shouting orders to those around him, sending them running in different directions in a scene of controlled chaos.

Jahn's head rolled to the side, glancing down a narrow alley. There, a group of soldiers had already managed to loot a cask of ale and were drinking in wanton celebration; before the order orchestrated by the tall officer could set in, no doubt.

Further down the alley a pair of pale legs stuck in the air, straddling the half-exposed torso of another soldier. Jahn acknowledged the likelihood the woman was an unlucky resident who had failed to flee, rather than one of the willing whores who followed the army but did not dwell on the thought, choosing to continue on his way.

The officer was waving his arms, shouting at a sheepish looking group of soldiers, a small pile of mismatched valuables sitting at their feet.

"There will be time to collect this shit later, boys! I told you to make sure those buildings were clear of soldiers, not trinkets! Now get your useless asses into that inn to the right and make sure there are no stragglers," he barked.

The soldiers snapped a salute and trotted off to their duties without a further word. The officer gazed down at the small pile and crouched to pick up a necklace, which he quickly pushed into a pouch at his waist as he stood, turning to Jahn.

"Welcome back to the land of the living. You look like shit, son. Battalion and division?"

"Third Battalion, Fourth Infantry, sir."

"Third, eh? We were sure glad to see you lads come running out of the woods." The officer clapped Jahn on the shoulder, "Captain Galden is out that way" he gestured back behind Jahn, "and you lads are on cleanup detail. Enjoy." Jahn saluted weakly and turned on his heel, walking back in the direction he had come.

He passed the alley again. Now he turned to see the men had abandoned their cask, undoubtedly having emptied it and had joined the man and woman further down the alley. He veered to the right, away from the group and in the direction the officer had pointed.

Through the town he wove, passing more soldiers on errands or hiding from officers. He happened to look up to see a pair of eyes disappear from an upper window, whether civilian or enemy they would be flushed out before too long.

The town of Harten was much larger than Sastan, with many streets intersecting and dark alleys stretching between cramped two and even three storey buildings. Harten was of course dwarfed by Morim but Jahn had seen little of the capital. They had been camped outside the high stone walls and the training regimen did not allow free time to enter the city. Jahn had only seen the tower of the Fire Fortress, looming over the walls, along with the peaks of a few other roofs scattered across the city.

Out of the town, at the edge of the battlefield, he saw a group of Pohartan soldiers moving about several large mounds and made his way toward them. As he approached he began to pick out bits of red and silver in one heap, while another appeared dark, with a few pale patches. Jahn missed a step when he realized what the piles were: one was pieces of armour, while the other was the bodies from which that armour had been stripped.

Amad met him as he approached. The boy's face was caked in grime, beads of sweat cutting meandering lines through the filth. But his eyes were bright and wild.

"Good to see you made it, Little Pup." Jahn managed the weakest of smiles; little more than a twitch at the corners of his mouth.

"Bloody right I made it! That was fucking amazing, wasn't it?" Amad was practically jittery with excitement. "How many of those bastards did you take down? I lost track of mine but it was a bloody lot!"

"I... did not keep track," Jahn mumbled, reluctant to lie, yet unwilling to confess the truth.

"Those fuckers took down Kervil. I saw it. Piece of shit took him from behind; sword through the neck. So I returned the favour. Gutted that bastard like a pig."

Jahn nodded, taking in this information. "What about the others?"

"Haven't seen Petren yet. Otherwise, we seem to be in one piece. We were a little worried about you but here you are!"

"Here I am. So, clean-up?"

"That's right. Pick a body, strip anything useful from it and throw it in the piles. Sergeant says we will be relieved soon enough to either make camp or go after those bastards but might as well do what we can in the meantime. Some bullshit about 'teaching us the cost'," Amad scoffed, bending to another body.

Jahn shrugged and went to work. The cost of battle was readily apparent to him; first it had claimed his father, though that had been distant and intangible. But now he had lived through one, he had had the very tangible experience of a blade in his hands, desperately fighting to stay alive. And he had taken another boy's life with that blade.

"Amad, what about the Drevesine bodies?" he asked, standing over the corpse of a grizzled soldier in green armour. What could be seen of the man's face was aged and scarred, spotted with grey stubble. Most likely he was a veteran but his experience had not been enough to save him.

"Take anything valuable or useful. Weapons and armour can be reused or melted down. Leave the body to rot, they deserve no better," Amad shouted. He was struggling to pull the helmet from a body. Jahn watched him strain for a moment, twisting and prying before an audible crack resonated and Amad fell backwards, helmet in his hands, head still inside.

Amad let out a sickening chuckle, to which Jahn struggled to attach an emotion. Ignoring the context, he almost would have said "amusement". Jahn shook his head and bent back down to his gruesome work, waiting until he was given different instructions.

* * *

Terrin shielded his eyes from the sun as he watched the Pohartan flag slowly rise over The Wooden Warrior—the grandiose name given to the inn at the centre of Harten. The Flame of Pohartan came to life, illuminated by the sun as the flag snapped and fluttered in the breeze. He had claimed the inn as his headquarters going forward, as he and the Generals debated their next move.

They would have to discuss how vigorously to pursue the enemy. The battle had been won but it was by no means decisive; the enemy army was still large enough to prove a significant threat and could not be left to regroup and recover from today's defeat. Drevesine also undoubtedly had more men in reserve and available to be recruited. Terrin, on the other hand, had the most men he would be able to muster until Stalius arrived and was now marching on enemy soil.

The question before him was whether to pursue the Drevesine army in full force and try to push a decisive and quick end or hold back and await the reinforcement from Stalius.

Richmond stood beside him, bare-chested, his armour already stashed within the inn and a bandage tied tightly around his arm.

"Well, that is quite the sight," The General said with a low whistle, gazing up at the flag. "When was the last time the Flame flew over Drevesine?"

"Around the same time we were allies with Stalius. I sense a trend."

"Peace in the West and expansion eastward? I am in favour of such a trend."

"Let us not forget how it turned out last time, my friend. There is a reason this town, not to mention much of the Great Wood, is no longer part of Pohartan," Terrin replied grumpily, scratching the light stubble he had allowed to grow along his jaw over recent days.

"You, my Lord, are one hell of a downer," laughed Richmond, clapping Terrin on the shoulder with a massive hand.

"I do my best. On that subject, do we have a casualty count?"

"Not yet. Soon, I am sure but it does not look too bad, aside from the Fifth. Simone took a hell of a beating in those woods. They had a smaller force down here than we expected. Might have been a fair fight if we had just thrown in the First and Second. With the Fifth coming from one direction and the Third from another, it did not take long for them to break." Richmond looked particularly pleased with how the battle had played out.

"They will soon be back in greater numbers if we do not pursue them quickly."

"The decision is yours to make, Terrin but I do recommend discussing it with the other Generals."

"Well that is why I am standing here waiting, is it not?" The words came out much more sharply than he expected and Terrin quickly suppressed the flash of anger which accompanied them. "Any sign of her yet?" he asked, calming his tone and changing the subject.

"Not yet." Richmond did not need to ask whom Terrin meant by "her". "Reports say she came out of the forest with Simone, hurling fire in all directions. The two of them, and the remainder of the Fifth, intercepted a company of Drevesine before they could blindside us. Probably saved hundreds, if not thousands, of lives."

"But she has not been seen since?" Terrin asked, trying to hold back the slight catch in his voice. He was merely asking about the status of a very valuable weapon…

"No, sir."

"What the blazes was she doing with Simone anyway? She was supposed to be with Warsch!"

"Well, there comes Nolan, why don't you ask him?" Richmond pointed over Terrin's shoulder at the approaching General.

"Ho! My King, General! Lovely day for a victory, is it not?" General Warsch strode up to the waiting men, his armour shining brightly. He looked untouched by the battle, his attire unsullied beyond a bit of mud on his boots.

"Nolan. How stands the Second?" Terrin asked directly, ignoring General Warsch's jovial mood.

"Five hundred lost, give or take: dead, nearly dead, or unaccounted for. Another several hundred with injuries from which they should recover," Nolan recited absently, his eyes wandering over the area.

"'Give or take'? 'Several hundred'? If you're going to be a General in my army, Warsch, you damn well better wrap your head around some specific numbers. Vague estimates are damn useless to me," Richmond fumed.

Visibly shaken by the verbal lashing, Nolan's mood took a noticeable decline. "Yes, sir! I will get the exact numbers for you as soon as possible, sir!"

"General Warsch, where is the Morette girl? She was to remain with you, behind your battalion," Terrin asked, his intense gaze holding the General's eyes.

"That one's crazy. Dull and quite the looker but she has a death wish. We were stalled on the road, so she took a group of men into the trees to try and get around. Cleared a path right through the flames! It was incredible, to be honest. Just disappeared into the smoke."

"She was to stay with you, Nolan. You were supposed to be keeping an eye on her, keeping her safe! Not giving her a squad and letting her traipse off into a fucking burning forest!" Terrin growled, grabbing the General by the collar of his cloak.

"Easy, Terrin," Richmond soothed.

"My apologies, my King! But... well, have you met young Miss Morette?" Nolan stammered, "I would fear more for the burning forest than for her. I tried to talk her out if it but she had her mind set and there was no turning it! I gave her my best men! And she seemed to have things under control!"

"She does seem to be a strong-willed young woman, Terrin. I do not imagine I would have any more luck than Warsch here of turning her from the course she chooses. Remember the difficulty even convincing her to stay as far back as the Second? Besides, we know she made it out of the forest; an open battle should be easy compared to trees full of the Forest Legion," Richmond said calmly, drawing Terrin's hand back from Nolan's throat.

At that moment, General Atlee rounded a corner a short distance from the inn, helping along a limp, listless Brianne; the young woman's arm draped over the General's shoulder and her feet barely shuffling along.

Terrin ran to the two women, taking Brianne's other arm around his shoulders and wrapping his own arm around her waist, taking her weight from Simone.

"What is wrong? Is she hurt?" he asked rapidly.

"No, sir. Well, not physically," Simone replied "One of the men from the Second saw her walking among the bodies after the battle. Those lads have been watching and following her like puppies since they came barreling through the trees and pulled us out of there." She gestured over her shoulder, to where a knot of Pohartan soldiers was following behind.

"I ordered them to return to General Warsch here but they are damn determined not to let this one out of their sight. Their interest in her seems... honourable, at least. Regardless, one of you will need to deal with them."

Richmond walked to the group of men, shouting at them as he approached. "Men, what the hell do you think..."

Terrin blocked out Richmond's tirade as Brianne shifted and let out a small moan at his side. It was pleasant to have her warm body pressed against his, as she leaned on him for support.

"Anyway, sir," Simone continued, "Corporal Bradford there says he saw her bend to move a body, then faint. He scooped her up and ran her over to me. As I say, she seems unhurt. She is likely just over exhausted and overwhelmed; it's a nasty mess out there."

"All right, thank you, Atlee." Terrin nodded to the General. "Atlee, Warsch, head inside, we have a lot to discuss as soon as the others arrive."

Both Generals saluted and turned towards the inn. Nolan rushed to the double doors first and made an elaborate flourish as he held one open for Simone. His broad smile was met with a cold scowl from the female General, as she opened and passed through the second door.

"Richmond!" Terrin's shout interrupted the Fire General's harangue. "Have one of those men run for a medic for Brianne, then get yourself inside."

Before Richmond could turn to relay the order, a pair of the soldiers were off at a sprint to follow it. The others walked to the front of the inn and took up posts by the door. They saluted Terrin solemnly.

"What are they doing?" Terrin asked Richmond as he approached.

"They are an odd group, I will have to explain later. For now, there's no harm in them taking up guard duty, I suppose." Richmond shrugged.

Terrin shook his head, absently. He shifted Brianne's weight slightly and walked into the inn, followed by Richmond. Nolan stood behind the wide oak bar, a fine thin glass of some lightly coloured liquor before him on its well-worn surface. Simone sat on a stool in front of the bar, silently tolerating Nolan's onslaught of charm and compliments and she drank deeply from a heavy stein.

Richmond grabbed a large bottle from behind the bar and continued towards the large private rooms in the back, signalling the others to follow.

Terrin turned to the right, striding past empty tables and their mismatched chairs. The room was neat and orderly: it had been evacuated calmly long before the battle, not in a chaotic rush as his soldiers broke through the forest. There was a small stage set before the large fireplace against the wall, which would normally be occupied by some travelling musician, trying to earn a room for the night. Now, the room was silent of the normal music, laughter and the solid din of conversation.

Only his heavy footsteps and the soft shuffling of Brianne's feet could be heard as he made his way up the stairs at the far end of the room, to the guest rooms of the upper floors.

CHAPTER 11

Terrin turned to the left at the top of the stairs, pushing open the first door he came to. It opened into a small, simple guest room. A single bed nestled in the far corner, below a small window. Against the wall adjacent to the door sat a table with a washbasin and water pitcher and two sturdy oak chairs.

The King guided a barely conscious Brianne to the bed, where he gently laid her down, lifting her feet onto the thin blanket. The room was hot and the air stale; Terrin rose and stepped to the window, opening it a crack. The smell of battle—smoke, blood and excrement—was heavy in the air but the soft breeze created some welcome movement to the stifling air in the room.

Brianne shifted slightly, releasing a soft moan and Terrin looked down at her gentle face. Her eyes were fluttering as if fighting with themselves over whether or not to open and wake her.

Footsteps sounded on the stairwell. Instinctively, Terrin's hand went to the sword on his hip as he spun to face the door.

"My Lord?" a voice called out and Terrin relaxed. He stepped towards the door, opening it to reveal a young Pohartan Private looking lost at the top of the stairs.

"Here, Private."

"My Lord!" the soldier snapped a sharp salute, "General Furell sent me to inform you the Fourth is entering the valley and setting up camp, with the supply train in tow, sir!" The boy snapped another precise salute, holding the position.

"Thank you, son." Terrin was briefly amused at himself for calling this soldier—apparently not significantly younger than himself—"son". "There should be a medic headed this direction. Wait for them out front and send them to this room, then return to Furell and have him come to the inn."

With a quick "Yes, sir!" the soldier was back down the stairs.

Terrin returned to the room, closing the door behind him. He dragged one of the heavy chairs across the floor to a spot near Brianne's bed. Removing his sword belt and leaning the weapon against the wall at the head of the bed, he sat.

He felt lost as to what to do, how he might be able to help her. If she was not breathing he could share his breath with her but she was. If she was bleeding he could stop the blood but she was not. He impotently reached out and gently shook her shoulder. She shifted slightly, releasing another small moan but nothing more. Terrin folded his hands in his lap, helpless.

There he sat, watching her, waiting for competent help to arrive. She wore the dress he had given her, its silk draped over her curves, shifting as her chest rose and fell. Parts were singed and frayed, while blood, though not her own, marked the sleeves and hem.

The pillow below her head appeared thin and a quick poke confirmed its poor quality. Terrin rose from his chair, looking around the room, seeing only the table, washbasin and second chair. With some reluctance, he left the bedside and crossed the room to the door. He quietly opened it, peaking cautiously into the hall, listening for any approaching footsteps. Distantly he heard a roar of laughter from Richmond below him but nothing else.

Silently he scolded himself for behaving as he had as a child, skulking through the Fortress, seeing how long he could stay out before being spotted by a guard or servant.

Confidently, he strode across the hall to the opposite room. It was the mirror image of the room in which Brianne lay; he snatched the slim pillow off the bed, tucked it under his arm and returned to the hall.

The next room was slightly larger, though more cramped: there was a second bed but not proportionately more room for it.

Terrin swiftly grabbed the flimsy pillow from each bed and turned back to the door.

He hesitated a moment, his ears primed. *What was that?* he thought, recognizing a sound so soft it seemed more a memory of a sound previously heard. He was standing between the two beds, his legs in a wide stance brushing the thin cover on each. He stood there several moments, unmoving, unbreathing and heard it again: the faintest shuffle.

With remarkable speed he dropped the pillows he held, bending and reaching under the bed to his left. Without looking he grasped the first thing his hands touched and pulled.

From under the bed came a young boy—he could not have been more than eight years old—screaming and squirming. Terrin pulled him upright, holding the boy in front of himself by the shoulders, several inches off the ground.

The boy's eyes were wild with terror, his body quivering and legs flailing wildly. His cries were largely unintelligible, though the word "please" persisted throughout.

"Silence!" Terrin bellowed, giving the boy a quick, hard shake. The boy went still and silent for a moment and then began to cry, tears bursting from his eyes and streaming down his face.

Terrin stood transfixed as he ran through his options. Finally he lowered the boy to the ground, grabbing him by one arm and pushing him towards the door.

In the hall, Terrin pointed his captive towards the far end of the corridor, where a second staircase led to the inn's back entrance.

"Go!" he commanded, giving the boy a hard shove. He took several shaky steps forward, looking back over his shoulder at the towering Terrin. Finally, safely out of arms' reach, he broke into a run, disappearing down the stairs like a jackrabbit into its warren.

Terrin combed his fingers through his hair, watching the empty corridor for a short while. He heard the slam of the door at the bottom of the stairs as the boy escaped into the alley behind the inn.

Behind him, footsteps could again be heard on the main staircase and he turned to see two women crest the stairs; the medics he had sent for, dressed in the dark Pohartan garb. He held up a finger to halt them, darting back into the double room to retrieve the pillows he had collected.

"Here," he said simply upon returning to the hall and leading them into the room where Brianne lay.

The two women did not waste time with formalities and rushed past him to the bedside, hovering over the young woman. They descended on her, placing their hands on her head and patting down her body looking for wounds. Terrin squeezed in beside the bed, gently lifting Brianne's head and sliding the additional pillows under it.

"Well?" he asked.

"Her body is not severely injured, only a few minor scrapes and scratches, but her mind seems to be having difficulty. We see it often in young soldiers: they are not able to comprehend the nastiness of battle and their mind shuts down while it works to reconcile what they have experienced."

Terrin was familiar with the symptoms: he had seen them strike many soldiers. Usually, however, they ended up curled in a ball somewhere, muttering to themselves. Some never seemed to recover, not fully.

The older woman seemed to understand the concern written across his face and her tone softened sympathetically. "I am certain she will recover, my Lord. Likely exhaustion and dehydration are playing the largest part. We will care for her and wait here for her to wake."

The other woman picked up the pitcher from the side table and finding it empty, lifted it in a signal to her partner and left the room.

With another look at Brianne, Terrin sighed.

"Thank you," he said simply, with a nod and left the room.

Terrin paused as he passed the bar at the back of the common room. He crouched down, sifting through the bottles hidden below the counter. He had been in enough Inns in his soldiering days—with or without the innkeeper being present—to know where to look for what he wanted. Most of the liquor was on display on the lowest shelves; within easy reach for the innkeeper to grab frequently. Higher calibre labels, less often requested, were kept on the higher shelves, primarily so those with a little extra coin could make a show of requesting it be brought down. Rarely were those higher bottles of any significantly better quality than the ones below them: they merely had a recognizable name and reputation.

But any connoisseur—or veteran soldier—knew to look below the bar. These were the bottles which were not worth wasting on the average traveller, just looking to drown out their evening. There was no need to display them, as anyone who could afford to drink them knew to ask for them by name.

He pushed aside a light coloured Vodanan wine and a dark draught from the Otrenia region of Drevesine and spotted what he had hoped to find: Kalmak, an amber whisky from a region of Stalius of the same name. Though there were finer whiskies to be found in palaces and castles, this label would not be out of place there and was top-rate for a town inn. Terrin had grown a deep fondness for it during the campaigns along the border with Stalius.

Standing, he grabbed a glass from the bar and then a second, anticipating Richmond's interest. He turned down the short hallway beside the bar and strode into the large private room at the end.

Richmond was seated at the head of a large oak table, reclined with his stockinged feet up on its polished surface. He was tipping back the bottle in his hand but set it aside as his eyes caught that which Terrin was holding, a smile creeping across his face.

Dendrik Saer sat to Richmond's left and grabbed the abandoned bottle, taking a long swig. Across from him sat Conrad Bartel, with Nedly Furell beside him.

At the other end of the table sat Simone, reclined as Richmond was, silently tolerating an onslaught of banter from Nolan, who was perched on the table beside her feet, fine glass in hand.

The clamour of conversation stopped as Terrin entered the room, save for Nolan, who, having his back to the door, took an extra moment to realize the King had entered and silence had fallen.

"I visited the Northern territories once, you know. Lovely place! There was a quaint little bakery in one of the towns, where I ate the most delectable sweet roll... but I am certain you are familiar with them, having grown up there."

"Warsch. You are wasting your time," Terrin interrupted, causing the General to jump. "The only reason she would let you show her your cock is so she can cut it off."

The Generals in the room burst out into laughter, the loudest guffaw coming from Simone herself, who sprayed a mouthful of ale over the table before her.

"Sorry, my Lord. Merely engaging the lady in some light conversation," Nolan stammered as he pulled out a chair for himself, face red.

"It is not a conversation if you are the only one yammering, Warsch," Simone jabbed.

"And I am fairly certain you are more of a lady than she, anyway," Nedly mocked, reaching over to give Nolan's glass a strong flick of his finger. The fragile glass shattered in Nolan's hand, causing another eruption of laughter from the room.

"Gentlemen," Terrin cut through the laughter as he poured two glasses. "Who was responsible for clearing the town of civilians? Specifically the inn?" He slid a glass across the table to Richmond, who caught it and rose in his seat, removing his feet from the table.

"That would be Captain Lotera, of Warsch's Second," Richmond stated, eliciting a nod from Nolan.

"Lotera? A good man. Shame," Terrin mumbled largely to himself. "Well, gentlemen, well done," he said, changing the subject and raising his glass to a quick cheer. "What next?"

"We follow and crush those bastards," Dendrik answered quickly, a nearly gleeful grin creeping over his face.

"I agree with Dendrik. They are on the run, now is our best opportunity to roll over them." Nolan nodded towards the senior general.

Richmond took a slow sip from his glass, looking deeply into the amber liquid. "We cannot strike them in full force. We routed them here but we also took a big hit. The majority of our soldiers are green as that grass outside. We are not ready for another full assault."

"They have the advantage of the land and the forest; we cannot set fires the entire way. And we do not know how many more men there may be out there. Where are the Zemiltarans? We need the support of Stalius before we take them on," Simone added, absently swirling her draught. Richmond nodded approvingly.

"They are running wounded, with their tails between their legs! And you want to give them the opportunity to regroup, recover and get reinforced by Foselak's barbarians? How is that a reasonable plan?" The passion behind Nedly's voice turned his face red.

Terrin pulled out a chair beside General Saer and took a seat, taking a deep swig of the whisky in his hand. He locked eyes with General Bartel across the table. "What do you think, Conrad?"

General Bartel took a long moment to answer, releasing a deep sigh. "You know my tactics. I ultimately side with Simone and Richmond. There are too many unknowns for a full assault. But, waiting for them to recover would also be a mistake. Do we have any word on Stalius' arrival?"

"A month at best. Two, realistically." Terrin answered, "The latest report puts them charging across Zemiltar. They are not likely to face much resistance but it is impossible to know for certain.

"So my generals are divided and are telling me it would be a mistake to either attack them or not attack them."

"That seems to be about the state of matters, my Lord." Richmond nodded, with a rueful smirk.

Silence fell over the room, save for the sounds of beverages being swallowed and cups banging back down on the table. Nolan began to whistle a low tune until a sharp glare from Dendrik cut him short.

"Richmond." Terrin broke the silence, the edge of an idea forming in his mind. "Remember Dristyrl? During the Jorhuin campaign?"

The Fire General sat a moment, his eyes wandering to a far off place in his memories.

"I remember a desperate run to that little shithole town, Stalius' damn tigers nipping at our heels the entire way."

General Saer sat up, "Aye, it was a cold winter. Every damn night those white beasts would glide out of the snow, fucking ghosts they were. We did not dare stop to make camp for near a fortnight." His puzzled look softened, as he began to grasp the King's thought.

Richmond understood as well. "You want to be the tigers this time. Keep the main force in pursuit but a safe distance behind and send small groups to harass them along the way." He began to nod slowly, though remained restrained. "We ended up winning that battle, Terrin. We, the pursued. And they had fucking tigers."

"Barely. We barely made it behind the walls of Dristyrl after taking massive casualties." Terrin's voice grew stronger, more resolute, as he spoke. "The only reason we were able to hold the town until reinforcements arrived was you, Richmond. Drevesine will not have the benefit of you." Dendrik offered a nod at this, without a hint of bitterness—despite having been the superior officer during that particular campaign.

"These sound like bullshit barbarian Zemiltar tactics to me," Nedly spoke, not being swept into the King's fervour. "Hiding in shadows, striking and then running away. Cowardice, really. The Fourth is rested and at full force. Let us take the lead and we can decimate these running dogs before the week is out."

Conrad clapped his hands together, practically salivating at the plans being discussed. "No my friend. Not cowardice... cunning! We will be the night, be the darkness. Every moment they will be looking over their shoulders but as they look over the left, we will be on their right, striking and disappearing in a wisp of smoke, barely seen from the corner of the eye. This, my friend, is how wars were meant to be fought."

The discussion continued for several hours, as the sun set outside the inn and the remainder of the army continued its efforts to clean up the battlefield and prepare an easily broken down camp, awaiting word from their superiors.

Points were brought against Terrin's proposition, many of them fair and valid; however, the King had set his mind almost immediately as the plan began to form in his mind and would not be dissuaded. As always, the only one with a hope of convincing him otherwise was Richmond, who seemed firmly in his corner.

Eventually, the King called an end to the meeting, a plan set in place. The Generals parted ways to relay orders to their subordinates. They would march in the morning, in pursuit of the Drevesine army: though the Fourth may be ready to move, there was little debate the remaining battalions needed at least a night to return to even minimal effectiveness.

Terrin leaned on the bar in the common room as the Generals took their leave. Richmond had taken a room on the third floor and made for the stairs, stretching his broad arms and releasing a loud yawn. He offered a weak salute as he ascended and was gone from view.

Nolan was the first to reach the door and swiftly held it open for Simone immediately behind him. As she passed through, he attempted to follow but was pushed aside by Dendrik, close on Simone's heels. Terrin let himself smile at the dejected expression on Nolan's face as he found himself holding the door for the remaining Generals.

As the door swung closed behind them Terrin stifled his own yawn and made his way to the staircase. He too had claimed a room on the third floor—not the largest suite, as may be expected of him—but it was not yet his destination.

*   *   *

As Terrin entered the room Brianne was seated at the edge of the bed, one leg curled underneath her. Across her lap lay Terrin's sword, unsheathed She was dressed in the Pohartan livery of the medics, her boots and fine red dress discarded in a crumpled heap at the foot of the bed.

She looked up as he entered, a lock of hair falling across her brow and a smile skittering over her lips.

"Good evening, my Lord," she said with a slight nod. Terrin thought he heard the same good-natured mockery in her tone which he was accustomed to hearing from Richmond. The Fire General had earned that tone through a long friendship and trying times but it felt just as natural and welcome coming from Brianne.

"Good evening, Brianne. The medics should not have left you alone!" he felt furious.

"They said the same," Brianne laughed. "It was difficult to convince them to leave. But once they were convinced I was awake and well enough, they were able to agree others needed far more help than I."

"So you are well then?" Terrin remained standing at the door. He was unsure how to proceed, having expected to find an unconscious Brianne still attended by the pair of medics.

"Yes, reasonably so." He could see the exhaustion in her eyes but they retained the brightness he had observed when she first arrived in Morim. "I am afraid that lovely dress is not, however. Singed beyond repair in a number of places." There was a genuine tone of sadness in her voice.

"I will have another made for you," Terrin said, shuffling his feet.

"I appreciate that but the same would only happen again and there is no sense in having to stitch a new dress for every battle. I will need something different, something stronger. Perhaps leather? May I meet with your armourer?" Brianne lifted the sword from her lap, bouncing it on her palms as she looked at Terrin, an eyebrow slightly cocked.

"Of course, I will send him to you at dawn. Whatever you need will be his top priority. ...You intend to continue fighting then?"

"I have never seen such horrors as I saw out in that field. I was not prepared for that, could have never prepared for that..." her voice took a far-off tone, fading away for a moment before regaining its strength. "But here we are. The enemy is still out there and they are still a threat to those I love. How could I stop fighting, as others continue?"

"We could certainly use your... skills," Terrin replied, stepping further into the room.

"And a sword, I would like a sword. And someone to teach me to use it." Brianne weakly swung the King's sword in a sloppy arc before her.

"What need do you have for a sword, when you have your fire?"

"What if I do not have my fire? You do not know how it works and nor do I, really. What if one day it decides to leave me? Would you walk into battle with only a single weapon, my Lord?" Arm shaking slightly from the unfamiliar weight, Brianne lifted the sword to point at Terrin.

"Fair enough, we will find you a sword." Terrin lightly pushed the point of the blade back down and Brianne returned the sword to her lap. "Now, leave matters of war for the morning, for tonight you must rest. You can be at ease here: the inn is secure, I will be checking it again myself before returning to my rooms."

Brianne smiled and as Terrin reached for the hilt of his sword she grasped his wrist. Craning her neck, she brought her lips to his. Terrin inhaled sharply in surprise but did not immediately pull away. Her lips were soft against his, inviting. For a fleeting moment, her tongue darted between his parted lips, dancing with his. Then the moment was over and Brianne pulled away, still smiling.

"I would rest now. Goodnight, my Lord." She lay down on the bed, turning her back to him. He thought he saw her cheeks redden in the moment before she buried it in the pillows.

Speechless, Terrin fetched his scabbard from its rest against the wall and slid his sword home. He then turned without a word and left the room, closing the heavy door behind him.

He stood a moment in the hall, blinking, as he struggled to process what had happened. Unable to make sense of it, he shook the thoughts from his head, turning instead to the task of ensuring the inn was truly clear. *Who had been in charge of securing it?* He thought. *Ah yes, Lotera. Pity that, he was a good officer.*

CHAPTER 12

Jahn stood over his pack, looking to his squadmates still packing their own belongings. They had only received the orders to prepare to march minutes before but Jahn had little to ready. Thumbs hooked behind his sword belt, he released a long sigh. His fellow soldiers were in good spirits; a change encouraged by a generous extra ration of liquor the night before to the soldiers who had experienced their first battle. His own spirits were improving as well. Perhaps this soldiering business was actually a good match for him: he felt comfortable in the structure, the routine.

Where Kervil should have been stood a new soldier: Uteer. His squad had been nearly decimated in the battle and thus the remaining soldiers had been spread out to fill holes elsewhere. He was a fine addition to the group, blending in smoothly. Already he was taking part in the jokes at Amad's expense and chatting casually with the others.

"You should have seen Trey, from my last squad. Took five of those others to take him down! And three did not walk away from it," Uteer exclaimed, barely a hint of sadness remaining in his voice at the mention of his lost friend.

"We have Tumas for that," Amad said, beaming. Tumas was momentarily taken aback by the compliment. "... Or at least, Tumas likes to take on five men at once!" Amad finished, moving his hand back and forth in front of his mouth and pushing his cheek out with his tongue.

The other men of the squad laughed loudly. Tumas, however, grabbed his water canteen and hurled it towards Amad. The younger soldier leaped back quickly enough to only catch the canteen on his shoulder, rather than his face and the others laughed harder.

Jahn found himself smiling and laughing along with the others. Perhaps not as hard as they but he was part of it, which broadened his smile a small amount.

Petren—who had rejoined the squad shortly after Jahn had— stooped to pick up the thrown canteen, tossing it back to Tumas, who was now smiling himself.

The motion of a figure over Petren's shoulder caught Jahn's attention and his smile dropped for a moment. Leaving his pack where it lay and leaving his squad confused, he wordlessly pushed past them and pursued in a jog.

Flying past tents he took a sharp right and his smile returned. There in front of him, weaving through the camp, was his sister. He had not seen her since the army and the Priests had parted ways on the road from Sastan to Morim and they had not spoken since the day they were collected from their home.

Jahn's jog turned into a sprint. "Brianne!" he shouted as he approached. The nearby soldiers turned for a moment, returning to their business when it became obvious the shout was not for them.

Brianne stopped and turned as well, a bright smile crossing her face as Jahn approached. Before he could say any more she threw her arms around him in a powerful hug. Jahn surprised himself by gleefully returning the embrace, even lifting his sister off her feet for a moment.

"Oh Jahn, it is so good to see you in one piece!" Brianne said as they parted, only to pull him back for a second brief embrace.

"Look at you! You are quite the man and it has only been a few months!" She held him at arm's length, taking a good look at him. "Actually... you look a lot like Father in that armour." Her voice softened at that but the smile deepened.

"What in the blazes are you doing here with the army, Brianne!" Jahn asked, confused.

Brianne's smile became mischievous as she took a step back. Jahn gasped as a small ball of flame appeared between them. Brianne lifted her hand and the fire danced about with the gentle motions of her wrist. Finally, his sister raised the palm of her hand and the flame hovered above it as it shrank and disappeared.

"There is so much to tell you, dear brother," Brianne laughed at Jahn's perplexed expression.

But Jahn's mind was already processing. "That fire, back home, years ago… That was you, wasn't it?"

Brianne sighed. "Yes, it was. I certainly did not mean for it to happen, I did not even understand *how* it happened at the time… but now I understand that it was me."

Memories returned to Jahn, momentarily wiping the smile from his face. Memories of the flames leaping into the night sky, the shouts of the townsmen as buckets of water were brought from the well beside the inn. The wail of Miss Hitair, burying her face in their mother's blouse, refusing to look at the inferno and the silhouette of Brianne emerging from it.

"But, you do not intend to be in battle, do you? Even with that neat trick, this is no place for you! It is far too dangerous!" Jahn pleaded.

"I have already been in battle, Jahn. I will not let you and the others I care for, go off and fight while I could be helping but instead do nothing." Brianne's fists went to her hips, a stance Jahn found almost comically reminiscent of their mother. "It seems I can handle myself quite well on the battlefield, little brother."

Jahn knew his sister and the tone her voice had taken: there would be no dissuading her. "Very well," he said, resigned. "Promise me you will at least be careful. Well, as careful as one can be. Make sure you always have a real soldier to watch your back." Brianne rolled her eyes but pulled Jahn in for another hug.

"Have you seen any of the others from home? Andrew?" Jahn asked and was taken aback by the sudden darkness which passed over Brianne's face.

"I am sorry, Jahn, Andrew… was killed in the battle."

Jahn's heart dropped. It was expected others would die in battle, he had already experienced it but the news hit him hard none the less. Despite not seeing him frequently since leaving Andrew had been one of the few remaining positive links to home, to the calm, simple life they had left behind.

"Son of a bitch," Jahn muttered. And then he put Andrew out of his mind—a skill he was not excited to be acquiring but seemed necessary regardless.

Brianne looked at the sun and sighed. "Jahn, I must go."

"Yes, yes of course. Do not let your little brother hold up your important business," Jahn chided.

Brianne laughed, giving him a gentle punch on the arm before pulling him in for a final, long embrace.

"I love you, brother," she whispered as she held him close, kissing the side of his head.

"I love you too, Brianne," Jahn replied, giving his sister an extra squeeze before pulling away. "Be safe."

"And you. I will find you again, as soon as we have the opportunity! We must talk more!" Brianne took a few steps backwards before turning, returning on the path she had been walking.

"Goodbye, Brianne!" Jahn called from behind her, receiving a wave and smile from his departing sister.

* * *

The camp was being broken down as Brianne strode through. Soldiers were streaming about as ants in a controlled, orchestrated chaos. They were to begin marching promptly, in pursuit of the Drevesine army. The mood was positive; almost jovial. Friends lost the day before had been honoured and toasted that night and the seasoned soldiers were already focused on the battles ahead, morale boosted and confidence high from a resounding victory.

Weaving through the crumbling tents, she left the main camp and entered the support camp. Stopping a woman rushing past, Brianne got directions to the tent and craftsman she sought.

"Master Kinade?" she asked, approaching the back of a man directing a younger man in the packing of his implements onto a large cart. The man turned, his scowl turning into a smile as he eyed the young woman before him.

"Yes, that is me," he said pleasantly. Master Kinade was a broad man, with arms as thick as his legs, which appeared as tree trunks sprouting below his heavy leather apron. He was a head taller than Brianne, his once-brown hair now mostly grey, with only whispers of its former hue. He would be a very intimidating man, if not for his broad smile. His eyes practically glistened with happiness.

"I am Brianne..." she began, Master Kinade interrupting her almost immediately.

"Yes, yes of course you are! The King sent me word to come see you. I promise I was about to! Young Ihan here, you see, he is a good lad—shows some real promise—but he still needs a lot of supervision I'm afraid, or I would have been to see you already. My cart here is my mobile workstation, I could not have it improperly sorted, you see." The young apprentice, Ihan, looked up at the pair briefly. He caught Brianne's eye and blushed, quickly returning to his work.

"Rest easy, Master Kinade, I was not impatient and am happy to come to you." The man's smile broadened, which Brianne had not thought possible. She felt herself smiling back in response.

"Well, lovely. How can I help you? The King's message was... unclear as to what you needed."

"Armour, Master Kinade. I need armour."

"Ah, yes. That is what the King's message said, you see. So few women in the military these days. I can count the armour I have crafted for women on one hand. The most recent has been General Atlee. Will it be armour like hers, then? It is not a significant adjustment from the men's armour, you see. Just a little more room in the chest, a little less in the shoulders…"

Brianne politely raised her hand to stop his verbal onslaught.

"I am looking for something a little different. I do not need the bulk. I need something more… fitted. Something that does not weigh me down, that moves with me." Brianne rubbed her hands down her body, attempting to indicate the fit she was looking for. She caught a blushing Ihan looking over again and cast a wink in his direction, sending him scurrying back to his work.

Master Kinade's eyes sparkled.

"Yes, yes, I see. Well, we can certainly get that made for you! I will, um, need to take some measurements. Or I can call one of the seamstresses to come take them!" He began to turn, casting his eyes about for someone to help him.

"That will be all right, Master Kinade, you can take the measurements. Or maybe Ihan needs the practice?" A loud clamour rose from the opposite side of the cart, where Ihan had stumbled, dropping the tools he had been carrying. Master Kinade let out a burst of rolling, joyous laughter, which caused heads to turn in their direction.

"I do not believe he would be able to read the measurements, at the moment. I will take them." He grabbed a ribbon from the cart beside him and led Brianne to his tent.

Brianne stripped to her smallclothes and was pleased to see she had read him correctly; Master Kinade remained strictly professional as he worked his way around her, making the necessary measurements. He spoke endlessly, barely seeming to take a breath: about his family, his experience working leather, his excitement at the opportunity to make something different from the standard armour and saddles he was usually commisioned. A thousand questions she did not have the opportunity to ask were answered for her. He did not even bat an eye as he adjusted her breasts, simply noting down the needed measurements.

Once he finished and she dressed, the two sat in conversation for a while, discussing the less practical aspects of style and design for the pieces. Master Kinade showed a remarkable talent as he drew detailed sketches, erasing and redrawing small details until they reached an agreement.

When Brianne left the tent Ihan was leaning against the packed cart, chatting with a young woman. The girl was batting her lashes and twirling her hair about her finger, giggling as Ihan gently touched her arm. Brianne rolled her eyes but smiled at the young couple.

"Sianne! Get out of here and back to Mistress Pait! Ihan, this cart better damn well be packed perfectly!" The smile had left Master Kinade's face but Brianne could still see the joy in his eyes—he was putting on a show and enjoying it.

The two young romantics—realistically not much younger than Brianne, though she felt she had aged years in the past days—did not recognize the burly man's charade, however, and jumped. Sianne squealed, turning on her heels and rushing off through the camp. Ihan turned to his mentor, quickly launching into an explanation of where Master Kinade's equipment was all packed.

Brianne waved farewell to Master Kinade, receiving a broad smile in return—with, of course, his back turned to Ihan. She turned away and rushed back through the camp to her meagre belongings, needing to determine where she would be placed in the coming march.

*   *   *

Terrin raised his free hand to silence the assembled soldiers, the other clutching his sword at his side. Richmond, Brianne and the Generals occupied the front row, with a variety of officers arranged behind them. Opposite the inn sat a small raised platform, on which Terrin now stood. All around soldiers shuffled their feet, falling to silence in anticipation of the coming spectacle.

The sun was still working towards its peak. The camp had been broken down and the soldiers were ready to march; however,

Terrin had one matter to resolve before they could pursue the Drevesine army.

Captain Lotera kneeled beside the King, hands bound behind his back. He stared forward, barely blinking: his gaze looking off to a distant place which no others could perceive. The Captain was a man of middle age, grey just beginning to brush the temples of his hair. Though his armour was dishevelled, he held his back straight and head high.

"Captain Lotera," Terrin began, squelching the last murmurs of conversations from the crowd "was charged with ensuring the town was clear of enemies. It was his responsibility to see each and every building emptied. Every nook was to be searched for lurking assassins. The Captain failed in this responsibility. I, personally, found a potential assassin lurking in the very inn in which your King, Fire General and Lady Morette had taken rooms."

"Captain James Lotera," Terrin turned to the soldier "You are charged with endangering the life of the King through gross incompetence. I have judged you guilty and shall enact the appropriate punishment. Have you any final words?"

Lotera cleared his throat, his gaze returning to the present and those gathered before him. "I have failed my King and Kingdom. I have brought shame to my name and accept my end."

Terrin hefted his sword and set his stance. "While this blade brings justice, with it comes forgiveness. Go now to the next life, free of the burdens of your failures in this. May you rise again in Her glory."

The Captain leaned forward, willingly resting his head on the stump which had been brought to the platform. Without hesitation, Terrin brought his sword down over the man's neck. The motion was quick to the eye but slow for the King, who felt every sensation of the action. First the flex of his muscles, pushing the blade through the air. He felt the moment the steel first bit flesh, that first instant of resistance. Then the blade met bone, slowing imperceptibly at the denser material; however, the power of Terrin's swing overwhelmed the strength of the man's spine and the blade continued through. Next, it passed through the flesh and arteries of the front of the man's neck, as a knife passing through breakfast jelly. Finally, it met the dense wood of the stump. At that moment Terrin felt his muscles relax, releasing the force of the swing, bringing it to its conclusion.

"… you rise again in Her glory," the crowd was repeating the customary invocation, the King's fatal swing taking only a brief moment. Captain Lotera's head dropped from the stump and rolled off the edge of the stage, coming to a rest between the feet of Richmond and Brianne. Brianne glanced down at the head, her hand shooting to her mouth as her body heaved. However, she recovered her composure quickly and Terrin saw her steel herself.

The crowd stood sombre and quiet, a gentle cough briefly breaking the silence. Lotera had been a good officer. He was well respected by his subordinates and well-liked by his superiors. Terrin had not enjoyed the need to enforce the law in such a way but he could not let such a breach of security pass. A relaxed attitude to responsibility would spread through the ranks like a weed given an opportunity to take root. He had seen it before, when officers became lax in their duties, their soldiers gladly followed their example. It began with simply letting their equipment dull or wear and ended with an unreliable soldier not where they needed to be at a crucial moment of battle.

"To your positions, we march immediately. Dismissed!" Terrin shouted. The eerie, unique sound of hundreds of soldiers saluting in unison struck the town, followed by the shuffling of thousands of feet, clink of armour and the rise of hushed conversation.

Terrin stepped off the dais to Richmond and Brianne. He looked down at the severed head lying in the gravel at his feet. Lotera's eyes were wide, staring into his own. The head rolled to the side as Terrin nudged it with his foot, turning the empty eyes away from him. Pulling a cloth from behind his belt he wiped his sword clean before sliding it into its scabbard, dropping the cloth to further hide the glare of the Captain's head.

"Brianne, have you had the opportunity to speak with Master Kinade?" Terrin asked.

"Yes, my Lord. He is working on something for me."

"Excellent. I will ensure it remains his top priority." Terrin turned to Richmond. "Have Lotera's body placed with the others."

Richmond nodded. "What of his family?"

The King glared, silently.

"Yes, of course. Just thought I would check."

"See to the Captain quickly and meet me at the front." Terrin offered a quick salute to Richmond and a nod to Brianne, before turning to follow the mass of soldiers.

Brianne watched the King depart for a moment. When she turned to the Fire General he was holding the Captain's head by the hair and signalling two nearby soldiers to assist him with the body.

"What was that about the man's family?" Brianne asked, keeping step with the Fire General—opposite the side where the head dangled from Richmond's hand.

"He does not want them killed."

Brianne stopped for a moment, puzzled.

"Well, I would hope not. Why was that an option? Why did you have to check with him?"

"Endangering the King has always been treated akin to treason," Richmond replied as if it was a satisfactory explanation. As the soldiers picked up the body Richmond pointed them out of the town, towards the battlefield. Raising his free hand, he stopped them before they completed their first step. Reaching down, he tore the brass three-tongued flame clasp which fastened the man's cloak.

"To his family," he said to one of the soldiers, handing him the clasp—Lotera's designation of rank. The boy nodded and the two soldiers began dragging the body away.

Richmond turned to Brianne as if remembering she was there and they had been speaking. He raised his eyebrow at her puzzled expression, recalling her question.

"Ah, yes." The Fire General smiled. "The punishment for treason has historically been death, not just of the accused but of his or her immediate family. Terrin, however, has avoided enacting the second part of the punishment."

Brianne was shocked. "Did Captain Lotera know?"

"The traditional sentence? Of course he did. All soldiers do."

"No. Did he know Terrin would not pursue it?"

Richmond pursed his lips, looking off as he thought. "Probably not. Terrin has only had to act on three cases of treason during his reign. Those were all shortly after taking the throne and were high members of the court. They were handled quickly and relatively quietly, so I doubt the change is well known." He shrugged, turning and following the soldiers.

Brianne stood a moment, trying to process what had happened in the previous few minutes. In the distance, trumpets sounded. Not knowing what they were meant to indicate, she cast a final glance over the splotch of blood drying on the dais before turning the direction which the King had taken.

CHAPTER 13

Terrin thrust his arm forward, signalling those with and behind him to begin marching. The mass of men at his back lurched forward in unison, the distinct sound of clanging armour and stomping feet filling the air. There was no pomp and pageantry as there had been when the army departed from Morim. They were in the midst of war now, focused. Drums could be heard in the distance behind him — a guide to get the newer soldiers marching in step. The First Battalion immediately behind the King, however, needed no such aid.

Richmond rode to his right, while Brianne sat resplendent on her horse to his left. She wore a simple Pohartan dress — the style of the palatial livery, though made from a finer fabric. He gazed at her as she stared over the landscape while they passed from the valley around the small town and into the narrow strip of gently rolling farmland which surrounded it. In the near distance, they could see the tall oak trees of the Great Wood scraping the sky.

There had been some little debate over where Brianne would ride for the march — Terrin had learned quickly that arguing was of little use. As they approached the Wood they would be moving deeper into the ranks of the First Battalion, so she would be as safe with them as she would be anywhere else practical.

Though a casual trot for the horses they rode, they pushed the marching soldiers to a quickened pace; their foes had a reasonable head start on them. Though the Drevesine army would too need to pause and regroup: they could not simply sprint back to the capital of Drevnat with their tails between their legs.

"Brianne, I see they found you a blade," Terrin observed, nodding to the shortsword bouncing at Brianne's hip.

"Fire General Arhan did, my Lord. It seems to be a quality blade, though I have not yet learned to use it." Brianne lifted the blade a few inches out of the scabbard before letting it drop back home with a soft *click*.

"We will have someone work with you whenever we make camp. At least make sure you do not jab yourself on accident," promised Richmond. "Maybe Atlee, or someone from this little company of yours," he smirked.

Terrin turned to look behind him, where a line of ten men rode behind the other Generals and their bannermen but before the front ranks of the First. They were men from Warsch's Second, formally: the same who had followed Brianne into the burning forest and had barely left her side since. They were led by Sergeant Bradford, whose promotion had been recommended by Atlee after the battle. Terrin, Richmond and Warsch had spent some time debating them; they claimed to be devoted to the protection of Brianne but Terrin had not spoken to them directly and was not sure if that devotion was akin to that of a soldier to a skilled commander, or a follower to a deity. He could not, however, find valid arguments against Brianne having extra protection and so had allowed them to form their own unit and ride ahead of the column with her.

"They have given themselves a name, did you hear, Terrin?" Richmond beamed, apparently excited to see Terrin's reaction.

Terrin rolled his eyes. "Great and what have they decided to call themselves?"

"The Phoenix Guard."

"Well shove an ember up my ass... At least it is not another fucking fire-themed name." Terrin's face paled at his curse as he turned to Brianne to apologize but she was caught up in a fit of laughter.

A Pohartan rider was waiting alongside the road a short distance ahead and Richmond kicked Ursa forward to meet him.

"A scout," Terrin said, turning to Brianne. "There must be something of interest ahead."

Terrin saw the scout gesture to a farmhouse just visible through the trees ahead and to the east and Richmond nodded to the scout before returning to Terrin.

"There are too many footsteps leading into that house up there and there are several horses out behind. Nice horses. Military-grade horses."

Terrin nodded. "Take care of it."

Richmond returned the nod and rode back to General Saer. Together they pulled a selection of soldiers from the First and directed them to the farmhouse. As they left at quick jog Richmond reined his horse back beside Terrin.

"Any word on Jermal?" Terrin asked idly, as they watched the soldiers approach and surround the house.

"Nothing new," Richmond replied.

Several of the soldiers could be seen raising flaming arrows, firing onto the roof of the moderately sized homestead.

Terrin saw the slightly puzzled look on Brianne's face.

"Jermal left camp before the battle. He and his Priests packed their belongings and were gone. The sentries said they headed west." Terrin shrugged. "I am not overly concerned, really. Good riddance, that man was a thorn in my side. The march will be easier without having to appease him."

"Besides," Terrin continued, "I may be able to call this desertion and maybe, just maybe, be able to turn that into a legitimate justification for killing him next time I see him."

The farmhouse was some distance from the road but they could see figures in green and silver armour flood out of the burning building. The Pohartan soldiers were waiting and met them with first a hail of arrows, then barred blades. The clash that ensued was quick and decisive. A smaller group of people could just be seen attempting to flee out the side of the building but were spotted by the soldiers and were felled by a volley of arrows. Finally, the soldiers dragged burning timbers to the barn and other buildings of the yard, setting them ablaze before trotting back to the column.

* * *

The army marched on through the increasingly dense forest. They remained on the main throughway in pursuit of their prey, where the road was wide enough for the army to march and the forest had been cleared for thirty paces on each side.

With enough space for the massive column to march together, the Forest Legion had shown little activity: the few times they attempted to strike the side of the column retaliation was swift and decisive. It was assumed the Drevesine forces were among the trees, tracking their progress but confrontations were infrequent.

Jahn, buried in the middle of the column, had little concern for the Legion. He was focused simply on continuing forward. He marched on with his head held high: he felt good, better than he could remember feeling for a long time. Wispy clouds cut the heat of the afternoon sun, leaving the air tepid on Jahn's skin, though his heavy armour and equipment left him sweating.

He was surrounded by his squad, as he always was; men he was beginning to see as friends. Jahn also could barely remember the last person who he would classify as a friend. There had been other boys he had played and laughed with in Sastan but they had stopped talking to him after Brianne's incident. He could still clearly see their mothers' frantic eyes and harsh muffled tones as they pulled their sons away. He had stopped being bothered by the forced isolation not long after, when news of his father's death reached them.

But for months now he had been forced to spend every moment with these men and he could not deny they were slowly breaking down the walls he had spent years building. To his surprise, he felt glad to let them.

Amad stumbled suddenly beside him, causing Jahn to frantically reach for his sword before realizing there was no threat.

"What the hell was that, Amad? Steal a couple extra rations of rum?" Petren asked, giving Amad a firm punch in the shoulder.

"Nah, my huge cock slipped out and unrolled and I tripped over it," Amad quipped back.

"Been pulling on it too much? Stretch it out?" Jahn shot back, receiving an approving nod from a laughing Petren over Amad's head.

"Shut up, 'Professor'," Amad bit back.

"'Professor'? What the hell is that, Little Pup?" Tumas, marching behind Amad, asked, giving the younger soldier a light shove.

"Jahn's nickname! He's always reading that book of his, like the professors in the Universities of Vodan or Drevesine!"

"What the hell do you know of Universities, Little Pup?"

"Better question, what the hell do you know of books, Amad?" Fennel added from beside Tumas.

"My brother went off to study at one! He wanted to become a magistrate. He told me all about them: about their Professors, always walking around with a pile of books in their arms and their heads in the clouds," replied Amad, confidently.

"Well that is a stupid name for Jahn," Fennel frowned.

"He *does* always have that book out," Tumas considered. "What is it, anyway? Your diary?" There was a faint hint of mockery in his tone but the question was genuine.

Jahn sighed. The book his father had given him sat in his pack. He had carried it with him when he left his house for the last time and had managed to keep it close since. On quiet nights around the fire, or even while in the autonomous trance of long marches, Jahn would pull it out and read the well-worn pages. He knew the words already: he had read it so many times. The pages containing his favourite passages were little more than scraps, held loosely in place. The first page bore an inscription written to him by his father.

He had turned that page so often it had come loose months ago and he had to use resin to bind it to the inside of the cover to preserve it.

"It is just a book my father gave me," Jahn said simply.

"Well, what makes it so special? What book is it?" Tumas pressed.

"It is Hermulen's Treatise on War and Warfare. My father gave it to me the last time I saw him before he... before he died." Jahn's voice trailed off and there were a few beats of silence from his friends, at the suddenly solemn mood.

"Who's Hernimul? And what the hell is a treaty?" Amad finally asked.

Petren gave Amad a rough shove, "It is HER-MU-LEN and shut the fuck up."

There were a few more moments of silence before Uteer spoke up from beside Jahn. "I am sorry for your loss Jahn. My father is gone as well." Uteer had a slight accent, common among the Northern provinces, along the Zemiltar border.

"What happened to him?" Jahn asked.

"I wish there was some grand story. That he died heroically in battle perhaps. Or rescuing an innocent child from a fire... but he was a simple man. He was a farmer. One quiet morning we were in the barn and he was teaching me how to shoe a horse. We had this big roan mare, Lulu. Well, Pa was crouched behind big ol` Lulu while she ate from a bale. A rat popped out of the hay right under her nose and gave her a good spook. She gave a swift kick and it must have caught Pa just right in the head because he dropped to the floor and did not get back up." Uteer's voice shuddered slightly at the last few words and Jahn dared not look at him as they continued forward a few more paces.

"My father was a soldier," Jahn began. "He was a great man. Big as a giant and strong as one, too. But he had the kindest heart. Everyone in the village loved and respected him. When I was young, he would always tell me grand stories of his adventures. He was the greatest soldier on the Stalius front! He told me all his comrades looked up to him and he told me of the battles he was in and how he led the charge to win each." Jahn's voice grew stronger as he relished the opportunity to share the tale of the great man he knew as his father.

"He told me about fighting the tigers. Some people did not believe Stalius' armies actually had tigers but my father told me about them. One night his squad was camped out near the border and out of the darkness leapt three of the great beasts! The size of oxen but all claws and teeth. My father's squad-mates were too afraid to move but not him. With a spear in one hand and a sword in the other, he brought the first two down quickly. But the spear broke and the sword was jammed so far into one of the beasts he could not pry it free. So the last one he faced bare-handed. He told me he got onto its back and twisted its neck until it snapped. He saved his whole squad that day." Jahn was walking straight-backed by the end of the story, his chin held high in the air, as he was filled with pride for his father's heroics.

Petren looked back to Tumas and the two shared a solemn, skeptical look before Tumas clapped Jahn on the shoulder. "That is wonderful, Jahn. You should be proud to have such a great father."

"I am," proclaimed Jahn, his back becoming even straighter, his head raised even higher.

"If he was so great, how did he die?" Amad asked, receiving another hard shove from Petren, who got a dark glare in return.

"I do not know, exactly," Jahn admitted reluctantly. "When word came, there were no details. We were simply told he fell in battle."

"Well, I am certain he did not go down easily, Jahn. From the sounds of it, he must have taken down half the enemy army first!" Tumas gave Jahn another reassuring pat on the shoulder.

"Oh, I have no doubt!" replied Jahn, wistfully.

The army marched on. Jahn's squad walked in silence for quite a while, as conversations droned on among the soldiers around them. Finally, the prolonged silence was broken as Amad once again stumbled, tripping over a large stone poking up in the roadway. The action broke the quiet tension and the squad returned quickly to their usual banter; finding any opportunity to mock their friends, tossing escalating insults back and forth and laughing together at their own cleverness. Jahn smiled and laughed along, tossing his own verbal barbs as they came to him and losing his breath laughing at himself when one of his friends shot back a particularly sharp quip.

*　*　*

The lone soldier struggled through the drifts of dense snow. His armour was heavy and the cold caused it to resist his every movement. He pressed on, feeling the presence of his pursuers, though he could not see them through the wildly blowing snow. The chilling wind cut at his face, his beard wet with sweat, frozen into an icicle on his face. He cast his red-plumed helmet into the snow, exposing his head to the cold. He did not care; anything he could toss which would gain him some speed.

The sound of the howling wind filled his world until it was joined by another, deeper sound. A shape cut through the blizzard before him, seen more than felt. Another dashed by his side, this one just a hair away. They were everywhere around him.

Exhausted and alone, the soldier stopped. His legs refused to continue on, as if they were trapped in the thigh-high snow. He desperately reached for his sword. Clasping the hilt, he pulled but the blade would not let free. Was it frozen in place? He did not know. He reached for the long knife at his other hip but it was not there. Had he tossed it aside as well? Why would he have done that?

He heard the sound in the wind again. It was a deep growl. Or was it several deep growls? He could not tell. But he knew it meant his end and he knew it was growing louder, closer. In desperation and panic he reached for his sword again but where it had sat moments before was now just frigid air.

Looking up, a shape slowly approached him through the flurry, its eyes ablaze, cutting through the mist. A pair of eyes opened to either side of the first beast: there were now three bearing down on him. Desperately he tried again to flee but the snow was now to his waist and he could do little more than twist his torso.

With a snarl two of the beasts leapt forward, revealing their steel teeth. One bit deep into his right shoulder, while the other latched onto his left arm. He howled in pain, a sound which rose above the blowing wind and the growls and gnashing teeth of the beasts. With a toss of its head, one beast tore his arm from his body, shaking it as a dog shakes a captured squirrel.

The first beast slowly stepped forward, locking eyes with the soldier. The blizzard lifted as it came into view, revealing itself. The great Tiger skulked forward, white and black fur covering its immense muscled form. It seemed to grow as it approached, initially meeting the man at eye level but towering over him as it reached him, its hot breath striking the man as it licked its sword-like teeth.

Desperately, the man flung his head from side to side, unable to move more than that. He locked eyes with a figure he had not seen before, far to his left. With terror in his eyes, he screamed, "PLEASE, HELP ME!"

The girl stood silent, watching. She wanted to help, she wanted to reach out. She knew there should be something she could do to help the man, she had it within her to save him. But instead, she did nothing and watched as the mammoth tiger snapped its jaws shut over the man's face, splitting his skull in half.

Brianne shot awake with a scream.

The tent flap blew inward as a soldier jumped in, pike lowered. Torches outside provided a meagre glimmer of light and the soldier's eyes darted around the inside of the tent before he relaxed.

"Are you all right, my Lady?" Corporal Canbur asked frantically. He was second-in-command of the Phoenix Guard. At least one of the group, often two, stood guard outside her tent at all times.

"Yes, Corporal, I am fine. My apologies. Merely a bad dream." Brianne was still catching her breath from the nightmare as the Corporal returned to his post outside her tent.

She had dreamed of her father frequently since the battle. They were always unpleasant dreams. The previous night it had been he who she found on the battlefield, instead of Andrew. Walking that field continued to haunt her. She could remember every detail, every moment, in vivid realism. But she made a conscious effort to put those thoughts from her mind in the presence of others, instead putting on a strong face. It was not until she was alone in her tent for the night that she let the tears come.

Brianne lay back in her cot, forcing her eyes to close again. Immediately the image of her father being ripped apart by the giant tigers flashed before her and her eyes shot open. Her father had shown her sketches of the beasts on his last visit home and she had seen them depicted in tapestries at the Fire Fortress in Morim but her subconscious morphed them into massive, unstoppable, blade-toothed beasts to haunt her dreams.

Sitting up, Brianne hung her head between her knees for a few moments, willing away the dark thoughts. They departed but did not go far; simply resting at the edge of her consciousness, ready to pounce the moment she let them.

With a sigh, she stood and dressed. She did not know what time it was but knew sleep would not return to her quickly. Leaving the tent she met the Corporal and his counterpart, Private Veritan. Both were young men, not much older than she. They snapped to attention and saluted quickly. Giving the soldiers a nod, Brianne began to step away from the tent. The men fell into step behind her and she stopped.

"Gentlemen. I need to take a walk and get some air but I will not be leaving the camp. I will be perfectly safe. You may wait here." The soldiers did not look entirely pleased but stepped back to their positions outside her tent. It felt extremely strange to Brianne to be giving orders and absolutely bizarre that these men seemed to obey them.

She started to weave her way through the camp, with no particular destination in mind. The hour was late and the camp was quiet. A few piles of embers sat glowing, with mounds of sleeping soldiers around them. The sound of hundreds of soldiers snoring filled the air. For a moment she considered trying to find Jahn but picking him out of the sea of sleeping soldiers would be impossible. As she walked, she formed a small ball of flame before her, letting it float in front of her at her waist, illuminating the path.

They had found a clearing centred around a large hill to make their camp as they pursued the Drevesine army and she found herself making her way to that hill. Some men had attempted to make their camp on its slopes, lying with their feet facing downhill to avoid rolling down in the night. She picked her way around these men—some of whose efforts had failed and they appeared to have rolled into their fellow soldiers, still sleeping soundly. The crest of the hill was free of soldiers, the slopes too steep to be practical.

At the very top of the hill was a large boulder, atop which a shadowed figure sat, silhouetted in the bright moonlight. Brianne slowed but continued her approach. She had thought to climb the boulder herself and supposed the company of this insomniac soldier would not necessarily be unwelcome.

As she approached, she allowed the ball of the flame to rise, increasing its size slightly. The figure turned at the approaching sound and light and Brianne was able to see it was not a mere restless soldier: it was King Terrin.

She stopped short. "Forgive me, my Lord. I did not mean to disturb you." Brianne began to turn away.

"No disturbance, Brianne. Would you like to join me?" The King stood on the rock, crouching down and offering Brianne his hand to help her climb up. Brianne ignored the hand and deftly climbed on top of the boulder. She saw Terrin smile slightly before returning to his perch. She sat on a flat section of the boulder near his side, dangling her feet over the edge. The ball of fire she had been holding winked out of existence as she released her focus on it, returning the two to the relative darkness of the moonlight.

There was an extended moment of silence between them before Terrin broke it. "Nice night," he said awkwardly.

"It is," Brianne agreed, "Though I do wish I were sleeping through it."

"I find it difficult to sleep through most nights, lately," sighed the King, "and often come out to stare up at the sky while the camp sleeps."

"What keeps you awake?"

"Responsibility, I suppose," Terrin replied. "This army is my responsibility and beyond that the Kingdom is. If we fail, what will happen to the people who relied on me to keep them safe?"

The King gestured out in front of them. "Not far that way is the Drevesine army, undoubtedly with their scheming, cowardly Zemiltar allies. They are camped around a small village called Prinol. It is too small to house them and does not have walls, so they cannot fortify it and will have to move on. We have finally caught up with them and can begin our strategy of slowly breaking them down as we chase them—unless, of course, they stop and try to make a stand. In roughly two weeks time we will push them to a fork in the road. One branch would lead them to the capital, Drevnat. We cannot let them take that road. A siege would be long and challenging and we want this over quickly. The other path turns toward Zemiltar and that is where we want them. If we can push them out of this forest and into the plains, we can crush them between us and Stalius' army."

"Stalius' army!?" Brianne responded in shock.

"Yes." Terrin ran his fingers through his hair. "The Generals know, of course, though the rest of the army does not, that I have made an alliance with Stalius."

Brianne's mouth worked but no sound came out as her mind rolled over the implications. They had been stuck in a perpetual war with Stalius her entire life. Her father had died fighting that war. An alliance now, a few short years after his death, felt odd. What had been the point of him dying, if the war could end so easily.

"So, Stalius is our ally now?" she asked, unable to keep a tinge of frustration from her voice.

The King laughed. "I am afraid not. Sure, they are supporting this campaign but the moment it ends nothing will have changed between us. I hope to maintain a truce long enough for both sides to return to our homes but we may very well have to fight them as soon as Drevesine and Zemiltar are defeated. A large portion of the force marching with them, however, is our own Sixth Battalion, so we will have the numbers advantage should they choose to make trouble." Terrin continued, his voice going to a barely audible mumble, "Perhaps it would actually be a good opportunity to strike a devastating blow against them..." There was an extended silence, as Terrin appeared lost in thought.

The King shook his head as if returning to himself. "I apologize. What is keeping you awake at this hour?"

"Tonight, a nightmare about my father." Brianne let out a brief shiver, rubbing her arms against a cool breeze which blew over them.

"Where is your father? He was not with you and your family when you arrived in Morim." Terrin looked as though he wanted to put an arm around her, to help protect her from the cold, even lifting his arm a few inches before letting it fall back to rest on the stone.

"Dead." There was a hint of forlorn sadness in her voice. "He was a soldier, on the border with Stalius. We received a letter telling us he died in battle."

Terrin put his hand on Brianne's shoulder for a brief moment of indecision. He chose to pat her shoulder, as one man would console another, before retracting it and speaking. "I am sorry for your loss. There have been some challenging times on that border. Soldiering is a tough life for the soldiers but I imagine it is also very difficult for their families as well."

Brianne shrugged, her gaze somewhere distant. "It was. We loved him and missed him, of course, but every time he came home he seemed less and less himself." She brought her knees up to her chest, wrapping her arms around her legs. "He became increasingly distant and quick to temper. That is, when he was home at all instead of out drinking at the inn."

"My mother and I did our best to hide it from my brothers. We knew the signs to look for and whenever his mood began to shift

I would take Jahn and Ren into the yard, or find some errand for the three of us until he settled down or left to drink."

"Many men struggle to deal with the realities of the battlefield. Some drown themselves in the bottle, some shut down entirely. One way or another, battle changes a person." Terrin turned silently to face Brianne. "But I suppose you have experienced that yourself now."

"I still see it when I close my eyes. I can hear the screams, smell the burning flesh and blood… I try my best throughout the day to put my mind elsewhere but alone at night, I struggle to keep the thoughts away." Brianne rested her chin on her knees, letting a moment pass before continuing. "But I feel stronger for it, too. As I was leading those soldiers through the forests and onto the battlefield, it felt… good. I felt a confidence and strength I have never experienced before."

Terrin chuckled softly, nodding knowingly. "It is a brutal paradox. You never feel more alive than when you are on the brink of death. Every fibre of your body is active and alert, as you focus on keeping that which would harm you at bay. I wish I could say battles become easier over time but they do not. There is a certain level of shock which comes with the first but even clear of the shock the brutality does not lessen. If anything, you have a clearer head with which to process the true nature of war. You have to make conscious decisions in your movements to bring death, rather than letting panicked instinct control you."

"We were… I was worried about you when they brought you out of the field to the inn in Harten," Terrin continued, "but, well, you seemed to have improved."

Brianne was glad to have the darkness hide her cheeks reddening at the memory of the inn in Harten. "I am sorry for my behaviour that evening… I was not myself. I do not remember being pulled from the battlefield or being brought to the inn. My mind was away from my body, caught in a loop of terrors. I saw those soldiers die over and over. I watched their skulls crushed by great war hammers. I saw their bodies engulfed in flames from my own hands…" Brianne shuddered at the haunting memories.

"But when I awoke, I felt such a strong sense of… myself. I had entered that valley and come back out the other side. I felt invincible. Maybe it was still adrenaline from the battle but I was almost out of my mind, as if I was watching myself from above. It was wildly inappropriate of me. Since that day I have been having wild swings between the two extremes: feeling terrified and alone and feeling stronger and more confident than I have ever felt before."

"There is nothing to apologize for," he said, shifting himself closer to Brianne. "I was taken aback, certainly but not displeased."

Brianne leaned against the King, resting her head on his shoulder. They sat together in silence that way for some time, until the first rays of the morning sun began to rise over the horizon.

CHAPTER 14

Brianne's breathing was heavy, sweat dripped from the end of her nose. Her muscles screamed in protest as she raised the sword in her hands, barely deflecting the other blade striking towards her. With a grunt she threw her shoulder into her attacker, knocking them back. As quickly as she could she spun, bringing her blade towards the neck of her off-balance opponent.

"Good, very good," Simone commended, as the dulled blade stopped several inches from her throat. "But remember, usually your opponent will be larger than I, sturdier. If you had not been able to throw me off balance, such a close attack could have been disastrous for you. Half of winning the fight is being able to read your opponent: identify their strengths and weaknesses. Let's go again."

Brianne was standing bent with her hands on her knees, fighting for breath, trying to suppress the urge to empty her stomach. She did not believe she would be able to move, let alone duel. Yet when Simone moved against her, she found her body moving almost automatically through the motions the experienced soldier had been teaching her.

With a quick step back she raised her blade to meet Simone's. Grunting and straining she met the woman's blows, pushing them aside as they came towards her. Brianne knew Simone was not coming at her with her full strength and skill: they were still in the early stages of her training, trying to have her gain some competence in the most basic tactics. As Simone prepared another flurry of attacks, Brianne saw her opportunity—the opportunity Simone was most likely intentionally creating for her. With a yell Brianne sidestepped Simone's swing, leaving her leg extended. Using the other woman's momentum against her, Brianne brought the pommel of her sword down on Simone's back, pushing her forward while kicking her legs out from under her.

The General went down with a hard thud but came up with a broad smile. The soldiers loitering around watching the pair let out a loud cheer.

"Excellent. While your opponents may often be larger than you, that size can be their weakness if you can use their momentum against them. A rolling boulder is dangerous but it also cannot stop itself."

The edges of Brianne's vision were starting to blur and she managed a weak "Uh-huh" before vomiting on the ground between her feet.

Simone laughed. "That is a sure sign we have done enough for today." She waved to one of the nearby soldiers, who threw her a canteen. She pulled the lid from the canteen and took a long swig before handing it to Brianne. "Take a drink and a rest, you are doing very well."

Brianne took the canteen and filled her mouth, swishing the cool water around before spitting it out to clear the vomit. Then she drank greedily, not caring as she spilled water over her chin and down the front of her tunic. She was dressed as Simone was, in a soldier's tunic and breeches. She pulled free the laces at her neck, fanning herself with the fabric. From the corner of her eye, she saw a pair of soldiers pointing and leering and silenced them with a stare.

Her time spent sitting with Terrin had calmed her from the nightmare which had so shaken her the night before. At some point, their hands had found each other and were reluctant to let go as the sky turned from black to orange, yet they did separate as the two parted with basic, sheepish pleasantries. Brianne had returned to her tent and fallen into her cot, drifting off to sleep almost immediately, smiling to herself.

Not more than an hour could have passed before Simone woke her, anxious to resume the training sessions they had shared nearly every day of the march.

"We are not moving today," Simone said now, "It looks like Drevesine is resting in Prinol for now and the King decided we could use the rest as well: we have been pushed nearly to our limits to catch up with them. It will be good to give the men a break and the supply wagons a chance to catch up. But do you know what that means for us, my dear?" She gave Brianne a wide smile.

"An afternoon training session?" Brianne guessed.

"Afternoon!?" Simone scoffed. "Try a second morning session! I can smell breakfast cooking. Get yourself something to eat and then I want to see you back here in two hours."

Brianne groaned but did not argue. Though her body screamed at her, she enjoyed the training sessions with the female General. It felt good to have a sword in her hands: a far cry from the life of gardening she could have expected at home. To feel the adrenaline of matching her skills against another, of fighting for her life—if only in a mock battle with an opponent skillfully pushing her just to the edge of her blossoming abilities. She passed the training sword to a soldier leaning against a barrel nearby and offered Simone a salute. "Yes, Ma'am", she said with a smile.

Simone returned the salute with a smile and returned to a fighting stance, signalling the young man who had caught the training sword to approach her.

Watching the two spar for a few minutes, Brianne was awed by their grace and speed. Blade met wooden blade faster than her eyes could follow as the two danced around each other. She could only imagine how sluggish and inept she must look by comparison.

Finally, Brianne turned away from the spectacle and started back to her tent. She may be clumsy and ungraceful now but she knew she was slowly improving. Her ever-present Phoenix Guard escort this morning was the leader of the group, Sergeant Bradford. He had not been as easily swayed by her insistence on the safety of the camp as her guards from the previous night.

"Sergeant," —though a friendly fellow, he insisted it was improper for her to call him by his name—"shall we find some breakfast?" she asked, turning and walking backwards a few steps to address the man.

"Sounds like an excellent idea to me, my Lady."

Brianne walked on through the camp, weaving her way back to her own tent. As her route neared the King's command tent, she crossed paths with Richmond.

"Hello, Brianne! How are you?" the Fire General asked with genuine warmth and cheer in his voice.

"I am well, Richmond." The two had become close over the weeks of travel, often sharing long, pleasant conversations while on the march. He insisted she call him by his name rather than his rank, pointing out she did not fit in the traditional military hierarchy.

"Excellent, excellent. Looking forward to the day of rest, I am sure. Have you been told we will remain camped?" He stopped as he reached her, hooking his thumbs behind his belt in a relaxed pose.

Brianne pushed a stray strand of hair from her face, tucking it behind her ear. "I do not believe Simone will allow me to have much rest. She has another training session planned for me before noon. But it will be nice to stay out of the saddle for the day. I am not used to riding such distances."

Richmond nodded knowingly. "If Atlee is pushing you too hard, I can have a word with her. We would not have you worn out."

"Oh no, no. I am happy for the training. Tired and sore, yes but more than willing to press on. I have a long way to go."

"I have spoken with Atlee about your progress and seen you train myself: you are doing exceptionally well, from what I can see. You have a great talent with the sword." Richmond's smile added weight to his compliment and Brianne could feel her cheeks colour.

"Well thank you. I still feel more likely to cut myself than my foe but hope I am improving."

"Go get yourself something to eat," Richmond gestured away, turning towards the command tent. "I am sure you will need the strength and energy for Simone."

"I will, thank you. Enjoy your day, Richmond." Brianne continued on her way to her own tent, now not far. She was nestled within the ranks of the First, not a great distance from Terrin and Richmond's central command area. Her tent was in its own isolated little clearing within the camp, accompanied by a smaller tent for Sergeant Bradford and a cookfire and bedrolls for the remainder of the Phoenix Guard.

The soldiers of the Guard stood as she entered the small area and she nodded to them with a smile. Bradford saluted as he turned away, joining his men. They all returned to their seats, offering the Sergeant a bowl filled from the cookpot hanging over the fire.

Brianne entered her tent to find her own breakfast waiting for her. She pulled the light linen from the tray revealing an assortment of fruits, a thick heel of bread and a large wedge of cheese. She felt guilty for the relative splendour of the meal in comparison to whatever stew the soldiers were able to pull together.

Biting her lip she concluded the debate in her head. Picking up the tray she left her tent and carried it to the seated ring of men. Stifling any debate, she passed the tray around the circle while filling her own bowl from the pot.

The group sat in uncomfortable silence as they began sharing the meal. The food they had prepared for themselves was little worse than some of the stews she and her mother had prepared for their family in the days waiting for the next supply wagon to arrive at Sastan, so she was not put off by the soldiers' rations. Her tray reached her again nearly full but she saw that a couple of pieces of fruit were missing and a small chunk had been torn from the bread. She tore her own portion from the bread and broke off a piece of the cheese before passing the tray on again. This time around the soldiers were more willing to take their share from the tray.

Slowly over the course of the meal the soldiers loosened up, with concise responses to Brianne's questions evolving into stories and jokes. By the end of the meal, they were all freely talking and laughing together.

* * *

Richmond nodded to the soldiers standing guard as he pushed into the command tent. Terrin was standing at the far side of the central table, staring down at the map laid out before him. General Conrad Bartel stood beside the King, while General Nolan Warsch stood opposite, his back facing the entering Fire General.

"Richmond, welcome," Terrin said, not looking up from the map. General Warsch turned to greet Richmond, clasping his forearm firmly for a moment.

The map laid across the table detailed the area south of Drevnat in which they found themselves. Markers stood on the map, indicating the locations of the Drevesine army as well as their own.

"Where the hell is the Forest Legion, Richmond?" Terrin straightened his back, crossing his arms over his chest and resting his chin on his fist in consternation. The King seemed to be in a foul mood.

"I do not know," replied Richmond, simply. "We have had no sign of them for several days now. Our scouts have been able to reach and observe the enemy in Prinol without their harassment." Richmond walked to the side of the tent, where a folding camp table stood bearing a pitcher and several goblets. He poured himself a drink from the pitcher—simple water, to his disappointment—and returned to the table beside Nolan.

"What of the Drevesine regular sentries?" asked Terrin.

"They maintain a constant patrol," Conrad spoke up. "But they are sloppy, complacent. They stomp loudly through the brush in pairs, chatting idly. They work on a regimented schedule, patrolling their sections in predictable patterns." He gestured to the map as he spoke. "It is my opinion they have become lazy, having constantly relied on the Legion to be the true defence against surprise attacks."

"Well that is good, is it not?" Nolan asked. "Why are we not more excited about not having to deal with the Legion and instead being left with incompetent guards?"

Terrin bent back over the table, studying the markers. There was one representing the Forest Legion but it had been moved aside. "Because, Nolan, I get suspicious when things work out in our favour like this." The King picked up the Legion marker, bouncing it on his palm. "Why would the Forest Legion, arguably their greatest asset, abandon the army while they sit in this village?"

"There has often been tension between the Legion and the Council," Richmond offered. "Maybe Nightcloak does not want to lose more of his men in this conflict."

"Perhaps." Terrin sighed, dropping the marker back on the table. "I suppose sometimes luck needs to turn in our favour, eh? Or, perhaps, they are just laying low."

Richmond nodded. "It would be a strong strategy: disappear, let us feel safe from them. We start sending men into the forests again, feeling secure and they spring their trap. It would only work once but could be a painful blow if we sacrifice too many men."

"So, what do we do?" asked Nolan.

Terrin and Richmond shared a long look. They had been working closely together for years and could tell a lot about each other from a look, speaking volumes in subtle facial movements. After a moment they nodded to each other.

"We continue as planned," Terrin explained. "We have a great opportunity here, with them halted in Prinol. We do not risk a full assault; our forces are not yet ready, we do not know the lay of the land, nor do we have time to move into a more advantageous position. Instead, we will begin our strategy of harassment."

Picking up where the King left off, Richmond continued. "With their weak sentry lines, we should be able to strike at them in the night. We will form two small raiding parties. One will circle to the east, the other to the west. They will sweep over the sentries in their areas as quietly as possible, then move on the camp."

Nolan looked at the map, mulling over the plan in his head. "How big of raiding parties? We cannot hope to overwhelm them."

"Our goal is not to overwhelm them, Nolan," corrected General Bartel. "Our goal is to give them a quick jab in the side, then disappear as quickly as we came in. We reduce their numbers slightly but more importantly we keep them on edge. They are not sure what happened, how many of us there were and most importantly: what might happen next."

"And what if the Forest Legion is lying in wait?" Nolan questioned, scratching his jawline.

Terrin sighed again, running his fingers through his hair. "Then we lose the men we send, another reason to keep the raiding parties small." The notion of willingly sending men to slaughter pained him. Open battles were one matter but if the Forest Legion were still in the area, slaughter is exactly what it would be. They could not send a large enough group to effectively fight the Legion but also remain stealthy enough to slip into the camp and raise havoc. "At least we will know one way or the other."

"I assume you will want some of my Second for this operation?"

"Yes, you will select a group to strike from the east; Conrad, select a group from your Third to hit from the west at the same time." Terrin moved two of the markers from the pile representing their army to flank the Drevesine position on the map.

"The good news," Richmond started, "if you can call it such, is now that the scouts have been able to get closer they have seen Zemiltar flags in the village."

"I fucking knew it, those snakes!" The King's outburst was a combination of outrage and vindication. He brought his fist down hard on the table, causing the markers to jump and scatter. Richmond's water goblet tumbled from the table, spilling over his boots. "I knew those bastards were lying! They held back the Zemiltarans at Harten but here they are, together."

Both Conrad and Nolan took a step back as the King raged.

"They dared lie to me! To my face! We will destroy them!" Terrin grabbed the central marker representing Drevesine from the table—a tall green piece with carved leaves at its top—and snapped it in half in his hands. He threw the pieces to his side, before resting his hands on the table.

Taking a few deep breaths, the King steadied himself. "This *is* good news, thank you, Richmond. I look forward to being able to crush the lot of them after we push them back out of this forsaken forest." His voice had returned to its normal cadence, the flash of anger passed. "We make our first strike tonight."

*   *   *

Jahn crouched behind the trunk of a large oak tree, trying to suppress his heavy breaths. The sound of his heart beating wildly in his chest pounded in his ears and he felt certain those around him could hear it through the darkness; that the sound would alert the guards ahead. He slowly drew his sword from its sheath, limiting the sound and keeping the blade low so it would not glint in the light from the soldiers' torches.

Collecting his breath, Jahn slid to the next tree to his right. He was working his way around the two soldiers, preparing to come up behind one of them, while Amad moved in the other direction behind the other. As he reached the next tree, he looked back to see Tumas take his place at the last.

Sergeant Morson had come to them late in the afternoon of that day, informing them they had been chosen for this operation along with several other squads, whose members were crouched in a rough line among the trees. They had been told to strip most of their armour: its sheen and clatter could give them away too easily. The next few hours had been spent in the forest south of their camp, rehearsing their movements. Every time one of the officers who stood as surrogates for the sentry soldiers they would be facing heard them approach, they were forced to return to their starting positions and try again. As darkness fell, they had barely achieved a single success of sneaking up on the officers. So now they crept through the forest in the black of night, thrown into the real scenario, each knowing their role but few feeling confident.

Jahn slipped to the next tree; two more and he would be in an appropriate position. This tree brought him dangerously close to his target and he could feel his hand shaking. He felt uncomfortably vulnerable without his armour. They were each dressed in simple black trousers and tunics, with even the Flame of Pohartan embroidery removed.

He could hear the soldiers talking, their menial chatter hopefully covering the sound of his footfalls as he moved to the next tree. Further ahead he could see the torches on the edge of the Drevesine camp. It felt too close: a yell from one of the sentries would likely alert the camp. From his vantage, Jahn could see a bell in the hand of his target soldier. It would take only one firm clang of the bell to alert the soldiers. He would have to move quickly to ensure the soldier did not have the opportunity to ring it.

One last tree and he was in position, ready to rush up behind the soldier's left shoulder. He looked through the darkness and thought—hoped—he saw Amad slide into his position a short distance away. Now out of the soldiers' line of sight, he let his blade hit the torchlight for an instant, flashing his signal back to Tumas, letting him know he was in position.

The next few moments passed agonizingly slowly. He crouched silently, waiting for the signal to strike. There was no alternative now. The signal would come and if he did not move, or even if he moved too slowly, the operation would fail as the camp was alerted. Time seemed to slow, each heartbeat stretched as he waited.

The loud crack of a branch breaking caused the soldiers' heads to snap forward and Jahn rushed in. Three strides brought him to the soldier. Jahn brought his left arm firmly around the soldier's torso, pinning his left arm—the arm holding the bell—to his body. Simultaneously he brought the sword in his right arm up in front of the man, slicing through his throat. The soldier dropped to the ground with a gurgling, choking final breath. The bell fell to the ground with a dull toll.

Everyone froze. To his side, Jahn saw Amad standing over the body of the other soldier, eliminated in a similar manner. Their heads turned to the camp, anticipating.

Nothing moved.

Jahn picked up the torch the other soldier had been holding and ground it into the dirt, extinguishing it. In the darkness, he could just see his fellow soldiers quietly moving forward. He turned and joined them in a crouch, moving towards the edge of the camp.

Off to their left, a bell tolled a single note and the skulking soldiers froze again. Among the torches lighting the border of the camp Jahn could see a Drevesine soldier moving. He stood at the edge of the torchlight, squinting into the darkness. After a few moments, he turned back into the camp and Jahn exhaled — in his imagination he could feel the collective exhale of his compatriots as they began to move again.

They had no way to signal the soldiers who should be approaching the far side of the camp, so there was no way to coordinate the attack. Their instructions were to launch the assault as soon as they were in position. They were in position now, crouched at the edge of the camp's torchlight, blades drawn.

A low whistle started off to Jahn's left: Sergeant Morson signalling them to attack. The men of the line copied the whistle, ensuring it passed down the line. Jahn imitated the three-note tune, then sprang forward.

Jahn was closest to the torch and pulled it from its stand as he moved past in a trot. The men were still silent, wanting their first strikes to land before the enemy knew what was happening. The wandering Drevesine soldier was in front of him. He had just started to turn when Tumas rushed past Jahn and jumped on the man. The two went down with a clash, as Tumas' blade sank into the man's torso.

To the side, two members of their squad — Uteer and Petren, Jahn thought — descended on a group of soldiers sleeping around the smoking remains of a doused cookfire. They moved among the men quickly and efficiently, plunging their blades into each sleeping soldier's throat. The last man was just starting to rouse when the blade found him.

Running past the first rows of sleeping soldiers, Jahn had his target in his sights. There was a large tent not too deep into the camp. He had no idea what would be in the tent but if the Drevesine army was organized as the Pohartan army was, it would likely be the tent of the commanding officers of this section: Captains if he was lucky but Sergeants at least.

Jahn slashed the guy rope of the nearest corner, giving the supporting post a firm kick. As the tent began to fold in on itself, Jahn threw the torch into the canvas. The material caught quickly and Jahn heard the frantic shouting and rustling of the men inside, struggling to understand what was happening and escape.

The camp was rousing now. Alarm horns sounded in the distance, from the other side of the camp and were echoed nearby. Jahn saw one soldier raise a horn to his lips and ran him through with his blade, cutting the note short. It was time to leave.

Turning to escape the camp, Jahn was joined by Petren. Together they swept over a group of soldiers in the process of rising and reaching for their weapons. The two moved quickly and ruthlessly, slashing at the weary soldiers with lethal efficiency, leaving behind them a trail of bloodied corpses as they left the camp. They were joined by their fellow soldiers as they trotted into the trees. Behind them enemy soldiers, individually and in small groups, were beginning to compose themselves, some attempting to pursue the attackers.

Ahead, Jahn saw a dozen points of light bouncing among the trees. As he and his allies raced passed, the Pohartan archers raised their flaming arrows, firing a volley into the pursuing soldiers and chaotic camp. Two volleys of unlit arrows followed the first, forcing the Drevesine soldiers to dive for cover and abandon their pursuit. The archers then turned, joining their fleeing allies.

Jahn raced through the trees as fast as he dared, dodging around dark trees and barely avoiding tripping over buried roots on the forest floor. He felt strong. He felt confident. He felt *good*. Embracing this previously unexperienced rush of adrenaline washing over him, he let out a loud *whoop* as he ran; a call that was taken up by the other soldiers and echoed through the darkness.

CHAPTER 15

A dozen balls of flame darted around the tent in a frenzied dance. Brianne felt a bead of sweat roll down her forehead, blinking it away as it hit her left eye. The sweat was not from the heat of the flames but from the effort to keep them moving in the complex pattern she had devised.

When not training with Simone, Brianne used much of her free time practicing with the flames, even while in the saddle on the march. She wished for the opportunity to practice with larger flames, to see how large she could create and how large she could suppress. Her Phoenix Guard had gotten used to their cookfire acting unexpectedly, as she lifted it from the logs or doused it before relighting it for them. It had proven impossible to find an opportunity to work with much of a larger flame, as she was constantly surrounded by flammable materials. Instead, she had devised a series of smaller exercises for herself, which she worked through and practiced until she mastered them before finding a way to make them more difficult. She could feel the power inside her at all times now, just a thought away from rushing through her body.

Working with the flames brought her peace. It forced her mind to focus, not allowing it to wander to the memories of the battle. The flames were a powerful, unrelenting force: near unstoppable, especially when pushed by her will. The more she worked with the power, the more she felt those same qualities of strength and perseverance in herself.

There were numerous scorched sections of her tent canvas from her practicing. Times when she had lost track of a flame or sent it flying a direction she did not intend. The confines of the tent added an element of difficulty, as she struggled to keep the flames moving without hitting anything. Now, however, she felt in control as the balls of flame moved and danced. With so many pieces at play, she felt she was at the edge of her ability: which meant it would soon be time to increase the difficulty.

A knock on the post at the entrance to Brianne's tent drew a sliver of her attention away from the flames for a moment and two of the balls crashed together in a small explosion. The other balls shrank out of existence as Brianne deliberately withdrew her power from them. She released her hold on the power which dwelt inside her and it dimmed from her consciousness but did not disappear. It remained present in the back of her mind, as if it were a figure looming just at the periphery of her vision. But it was a welcome figure, a reassuring figure.

"What is it?" she asked, splashing her face with water from the pitcher set on a table beside her cot.

"A Master Kinade to see you, my Lady." Private Veritan poked his head into the tent. "With his apprentice and a package."

Brianne smiled. "Thank you, Private. I will be out in a moment." The young soldier nodded and pulled his head back out of the tent. Brianne could hear him relay her imminent emergence to the waiting men, only barely muffled by the canvas of the tent.

She took a deep drink of the water, then wiped her face with a shirt she had discarded on her cot before stepping into the afternoon sun outside the tent.

Master Kinade stood waiting with his hands clasped behind his back, a wide smile on his face. "Good 'fternoon, my Lady!" He dipped his head respectfully.

"Good afternoon, Master Kinade," Brianne replied pleasantly, his positive mood immediately infectious. "It is good to see you again."

"Aye, you as well! It has been a hard march, to be sure. We have been trailing behind the army with the rest of the followers and I surely thought we would never stop for a proper rest! Push the horses all day, with barely enough of a stop at night to get a proper bite to eat before sleepin' under the wagon and moving on again first thing in the morning." Master Kinade looked at the soldiers standing outside her tent. "Though I suppose I shouldn't be complaining. I wasn't doing the marching, like these lads here. Too old for that by far. I was riding in the wagon most of the trip, working on my leathers."

"Is that what brought you here to me, Master Kinade?" Brianne asked, eyeing the large bundle being held by the young man behind Master Kinade, whom she recognized as his apprentice Ihan.

"Yes, yes, of course!" Master Kinade replied, clapping his hands together happily. "I finished these pieces a couple days ago and I must beg your forgiveness for not getting them to you sooner. We could barely keep up with the army until you made this here camp and actually stopped for a night." He turned and took the package from the younger man, pulling back the wrappings as he turned back to Brianne.

Brianne took the package, cradling it in her arm. It was heavier than she expected. Looking in, she saw folds of soft black and crimson leathers. The intoxicating aroma of the fresh leather wafted over her, bringing a wide smile to her face as she breathed it in deeply.

"Everything is there, my Lady. Everything we discussed and a couple extra touches I thought you might appreciate." Master Kinade gestured to the younger man with his thumb. "I had Ihan here do some of the work, it was good practice for him, you see, doing some of that fine detail work. But I promise you he did a swell job. I inspected each piece and had him try again if it was not up to my standards."

"I am certain they are of the highest quality. Thank you, Master Kinade." Brianne offered her hand to shake those of Master Kinade and his apprentice. "If you will excuse me, I am eager to take a closer look."

"Yes, yes, of course, my Lady. Should you need any adjustments, please send for me. I do not know how long the King intends to keep us here but I really do my best work while not bouncing in a wagon."

Brianne nodded, thanking the men again before turning to her tent. She felt giddy as a young girl who had just been given a present. As the tent flap fell closed behind her she embraced her power. She did not summon any flames but the mere act of holding the power brought her that heightened sense of confidence and strength. She wanted to feel powerful as she tried on her new armour.

* * *

The sun was just setting as Jahn and his squad left their camp and entered the surrounding woods, heading towards the Drevesine camp. The enemy had surprised them by not leaving the village that day, which provided them with another easy opportunity for a quick night attack. Their strategy would have to be different this time, however, as the scouts would undoubtedly be more alert.

After their successful attack the previous night, Sergeant Morson's Company—which included Jahn's squad—had been selected to run another operation. It had been Jahn who suggested they strike in the twilight hours, rather than waiting until the dead of night. Hopefully, the enemy would believe they were in the lull of the perceived safety of daylight, anticipating a later attack.

Sergeant Morson walked beside him now. Again they had left the majority of their armour behind, sacrificing the protection in favour of quieter and faster movement. Most of the soldiers were dressed in simple brown tunics and breeches, with hoods pulled over their heads. Some, including Jahn and Sergeant Morson, wore the green cloaks of the Forest Legion, pilfered from those few the army was able to bring down along the march. The cloak Jahn wore bore an ominous arrow hole through the breast.

The Legion had not bothered them on their last raid, nor had they seen any sign of them in days. Nevertheless, they remained a constant threat in Jahn's mind. He scanned the trees constantly, searching as best he could for the hidden assassins.

The soldiers walked through the trees in silence for a long while, approaching the camp. They had run through their plans over and over throughout the day, breaking down the details as best they could. There was nothing more to discuss at this point: they were left to simply execute the plan and hope it went as expected.

Closer to the enemy camp they came to a stop at a signal from Sergeant Morson. The soldiers spread out and crouched behind trees and shrubs, finding whatever cover they could and settling in. They were still a distance from the expected enemy scouts but took every precaution as they waited for the sun to finish setting.

Jahn crouched behind a large oak tree, anxiously rubbing his hands together and absently toying with the hole in his cloak. After he had recommended the time of the attack, the commanding officers had invited his input in developing their strategy. Some of his suggestions had been accepted and incorporated into the plan, earning him an important role in its execution. But it was a role that put him at the greatest risk and he struggled to keep his nerves calm.

Approximately an hour passed and the soldiers were doused in the last hints of the setting sun. In their own camp—and hopefully, the enemy's—most of the soldiers would be sleeping, as the rest tossed in their bedrolls or watched the dying embers of their cookfires.

At another signal from Sergeant Morson, Jahn rose and began to walk forward. He was joined by the Sergeant and Tumas, along with two other soldiers from other squads who he had formally met that day. The five of them were clad in the green cloaks and walked confidently through the trees. The remaining soldiers followed behind, moving among the trees as clandestinely as they could manage.

Through the trees, Jahn caught his first glimpses of the Drevesine soldiers standing guard. There were three of them, hovering about a torch propped in a stand dug into the ground. They stood less casually than the guards of the previous night, their hands on the hilts of their swords or staves of their pikes, while their eyes scanned the darkness ahead of them.

Despite their improvements, they were still woefully unprepared to be guarding. Huddled around the torches as they were, their eyes did not have the proper opportunity to adjust to the darkness falling over them. They would be largely blind to anything outside the ring of light in which they stood. This worked to the benefit of Jahn and the men walking with him, who would be reaching the edge of that light in a few more paces.

"Hey! Who's there!?" one of the guards finally shouted, as the Pohartan men drew closer. Jahn and his similarly dressed comrades made no effort to hide beyond the natural camouflage of their cloaks as they continued forward. One of the guards half-raised a horn to his lips, as the others raised their weapons, nervously shifting their weight from foot to foot.

Sergeant Morson stepped forward, just into the ring of light. The Drevesine soldiers calmed visibly. The one with the horn, who had originally spotted them, spoke up. "Well, where the fuck have you bastards been!? We sure could have used you last night." He lowered the horn to his side, while one of the other guards sheathed his sword. The third guard lowered his weapon but did not withdraw it. His look remained frantic and skeptical.

The Sergeant took another measured step forward as the rest of the cloaked figures entered the light. He offered a dismissive wave of his hand. "Our movements are not your concern. We are where we intend to be."

"Fuck you," the Drevesine soldier spat. "Last night those jacks slipped right into our camp, from all fucking sides. Murdered a goodly chunk of our boys before running off. General Navillus is right pissed at you boys."

"I have come to speak with the General. If you will let us pass." Sergeant Morson spoke gruffly. The soldier stepped aside, inviting them to pass with an exaggerated wave of his arm.

The option of attempting to assassinate General Navillus had been discussed. With their cloaks, they may be able to reach him if all the Drevesine soldiers were as easy to convince as these were. Ultimately, the thought had been dismissed. The commanding officers would not be so easily fooled and the Pohartans did not know the details of the relationship between the army and the Legion; a group of Legionnaires attempting to reach the General could very well raise immediate alarm.

Jahn walked forward with the others, involuntarily holding his breath as time seemed to slow. He approached the soldier who still had his blade drawn, attempting to pass him as casually as possible. Jahn's own blade was drawn and clutched close to his side, hidden by the cloak. The two locked eyes as they passed. The other man's gaze dug into Jahn, who could not determine if the look was one of suspicion or mere disdain.

As Jahn's foot fell on the other side of the man, he heard the distinctive *twang* of bowstrings. With a whirl that sent the hem of his cloak fluttering, Jahn spun, plunging his bared blade into the back of the Drevesine soldier, pushing him to the ground. The arrow jutting from his neck pushed through the other side before the shaft snapped against the ground.

Sergeant Morson and the Pohartan soldier to his other side were similarly guiding the bodies of the other Drevesine soldiers down. Jahn pulled his sword from the man, its crimson-soaked blade catching the torchlight. He nodded to the Sergeant and turned towards the camp as the other Pohartan soldiers emerged from the darkness.

Jahn turned in the direction of the camp. The tents and sleeping men were still some distance off, their torches and dying fires just barely visible through the trees. Between the Pohartans and the Drevesine camp stood a portion of the army's horse lines. Row upon row of horses whinnied in the near darkness, accented by the occasional stamping hoof. Amidst the rows lights from hooded lanterns bobbed — patrolling soldiers, grooms, or farriers minding the horses.

The Pohartans moved quietly among the horses, striving not to startle the beasts. They were well-trained war horses, used to men passing around them: they responded with little more than a toss of their heads.

Jahn cut the first line he reached, patting the nearest horse to keep it calm. They wanted to cut as many lines as possible before the horses or nearby men reacted.

Turning, Jahn crashed into someone who had been walking along the horse line in the dark. In the moment he had to react, Jahn looked over the other young man. He was no older than Jahn and was dressed in simple clothes, bearing the leaf sigil of Drevesine. As the young man blinked at the unexpected figure in his path, events suddenly unfolded all at once, moments crashing together.

"Pardon me, si..." the boy's words were cut off as Jahn covered his mouth with one hand, pushing his sword through his chest with the other. The boy's body dropped to the ground and in the near distance the light of a lantern turned toward Jahn.

The *twang* of a bow sounded and the lantern bearer fell, his lantern clattering to the ground loudly.

"Bradson?" a voice asked, as another figure approached the fallen body. That figure was overtaken by a Pohartan soldier and the two grappled to the ground. Raised voices began to sound around Jahn, as the Drevesine forces became aware of the enemy in their midst. A sharp whistle sounded nearby; a signal from Sergeant Morson that it was time to take their leave.

Jahn rushed to a Drevesine soldier who had drawn his sword. The two clashed amidst the rising chaos and clamour. Jahn was fueled by determined adrenaline, while the soldier he faced was still uncertain of what was happening around him. Their blades beat against each other in a brief exchange before Jahn seized the advantage. Ducking to the right as his opponent thrust, Jahn slashed at the man's exposed side, his blade biting deeply. Stunned by the injury, the man fell to one knee, dropping his blade. Moving the momentum of his swing into a turn, Jahn brought his blade down again, striking the man's neck, dropping him to the ground in a lifeless heap.

Horses were now darting around him in a panic. Many of those whose lines had been cut had lit torches tied to their tails and were frantically running to escape the flames chasing them. Other horses had dead rodents, caught by the Pohartans earlier that day, tied under their noses. Those horses bucked and reared, adding to the pandemonium as they tried to get away from the creatures.

Through the darkness Jahn saw a smaller Pohartan figure—Amad—running along the front of a line of horses still tied in place. Panic was rising among those horses, for as Amad ran by them he had his blade barred, striking at the horses' legs as he moved, wounding as many as he could.

The calamity had reached the camp, as some of the horses raced through the tents, trailing flaming torches. While some soldiers attempted to catch and calm the beasts, more turned their attention to the cause of the chaos, taking up their weapons and racing into the fray,

Jahn turned and began to run towards the forest, dodging between charging and raging horses. Ahead he saw the back of a Drevesine soldier, sword in hand, standing over a still body clad in brown. The soldier's head was darting around, searching for the next threat. His gaze found Jahn but moments too late, as Jahn's sword was already slicing through the air to strike the man's head.

Freeing his blade from the man's skull, Jahn kept running. As he entered the trees, arrows began to fall around him, striking trees with a heavy *thunk*, or *swish*ing into the underbrush.

He was joined in his race through the forest by more figures. As more and more came together they slowed. Reaching a small patch of trees they stopped, leaning on the trunks and panting. Jahn felt he would never catch his breath. As the soldiers looked at each other and began to clasp hands in celebration the sounds of pursuit rose behind them. Reluctantly, Jahn pushed his legs to continue carrying him away. As the trees raced past and the shouts behind them fell away, the fleeing soldiers laughed and whooped, running into the night.

CHAPTER 16

Terrin stood at the edge of the clearing, holding the reins of Mi'drak and looking over the village of Prinol. The Drevesine army had stayed in the village three nights, breaking camp and leaving as the morning sun rose. Now the village was left apparently deserted. The fields around it had been flattened by the camped army, abandoned scraps blowing about in the midday breeze.

The Pohartan Army had prepared to march the moment scouts reported the movement of their enemies and were now leaving camp, taking to the road in pursuit. The King had selected the troops he needed to join him in a forward force and investigate what was left behind. A small group of mounted Pohartan soldiers trotted towards the King, having completed their preliminary sweep of the village.

Richmond, leading the group, reined in his horse as he neared Terrin. Dismounting, he patted Ursa's neck before closing the distance to the King on foot. "Not much to see," began the Fire General. "No obvious signs of soldiers. We did not sweep every building, so we cannot be certain. Looks like they cleaned the place out."

"How about civilians?" Terrin asked.

"Must have left when the army did," Richmond shrugged. "Knew we would be coming up behind them. I sure as hell would not want to stick around for an enemy army to march in."

Terrin nodded. Raising his hand, he gestured towards the village. Loud creaks of heavy machinery moving rose behind him and the Firethrowers were readied.

Turning back, the King looked to the waiting Captain. "Flatten it."

The Captain nodded. "Loose!" she shouted.

Each of the dozen Firethrowers aligned in the field kicked back as the firing mechanisms were released. A deep *whoosh* filled the air as the orbs flew through the sky.

The soldiers cheered as the orbs struck their targets, exploding on impact. Fire spread quickly from where the projectiles hit, rapidly engulfing buildings.

"Reload!"

Soldiers grunted as they turned heavy cranks, bringing the arms of the Firethrowers back into position. At each machine, two soldiers gingerly lifted one of the heavy orbs from the cart carrying them, transferring it to the bucket of the Thrower. As they stepped back, the soldier standing at the release lever nodded to the Captain. It was a precise, practiced routine; each member of the crew fulfilling their role in careful sequence. Almost in unison, moments after being told to reload, the Throwers were again ready.

"Loose!" the Captain shouted again. Levers were being released as she finished the word and another dozen orbs streaked through the sky. They disappeared into the village, the earth shaking as they struck their targets and exploded.

"Excellent work, Captain," Terrin nodded to the woman. "Have your crews prepare the Throwers for movement. I will leave these soldiers here to stand guard should the enemy appear. The army will be coming through shortly and you can return to your position among them as they pass."

"Understood, my Lord." The Captain saluted before turning, shouting orders to her soldiers.

Terrin gestured for Richmond to join him as he mounted Mi'drak and turned away from the rising inferno of Prinol and started down the road to reunite with the approaching army. His

immediate retinue of bannermen and a small contingent of the assembled soldiers fell into step behind him. Richmond caught up
with the group quickly, coming up beside the King.

"How went the raid last night?" Terrin asked the Fire General.

"Well enough. The enemy is getting smarter, more alert. We
lost eleven men. Captain Galden relayed his Sergeants' reports that
they killed 'probably a hundred', so still a win for us." Richmond
adjusted the axe on his hip. "We are certainly preventing them from
sleeping soundly. Our men report that they spied many of the soldiers sitting awake around their campfires, swords ready in their
laps."

"I certainly would not want to be among the unlucky ones
stationed around the periphery of their camp at this point." Terrin
could not help but laugh softly to himself. "I still do not understand
how Morson got a Firethrower close enough to their camp, in the
middle of the night, through these trees."

Richmond laughed along. "I imagine they are left trying to
figure that one out as well. Most of the men we lost went down covering that machine's retreat."

They heard the clamour of the approaching army before it
came into view: the pounding of thousands of feet marching in
unison, the clang and clatter of armour shifting. Above it all rose the
sound of a thousand voices singing. The soldiers were in good spirits after their respite—a respite for those not involved in the night
raids, anyway: a majority of the army—and their voices rang out
over the trees.

Terrin reined in Mi'drak, waiting for the army to reach his
party. The song took him back to his days of being a soldier. There
had always been an extra level of responsibility on his shoulders,
being the heir to the throne but those days he had felt the freest. His
father held the throne and with it the weight of the Kingdom; they
had been but a distant concern for Terrin, a worry for his future self.

Instead, Terrin had been free to travel the countryside with the army, treated no differently than any other soldier.

His early years of service had been the hardest. He had been stationed among the Sixth Battalion, along the border with Stalius: The battalion was at the time commanded by General Saer. There had been a skirmish with the enemy nearly every week, as Stalius attempted — and occasionally succeeded — to break the lines and the Pohartans had to throw them back. Occasionally their momentum would carry them over the border into enemy territory, where they, in turn, would strike at the border cities until the enemy was able to regroup and push them back.

For seven years he endured this constant action, his identity as a soldier, man and future King forged by it. Each morning waking, prepared and expecting to face a battle that day or the next. Despite its challenges, Terrin thrived in the environment. He relished the feeling of power he experienced in the heat of battle. For years he had struggled to control his fiery temper and the battlefield gave him an outlet through which to unleash his fury. It offered him a balance, allowing him to remain calm and relaxed during the fleeting times of relative peace. Often he would turn down opportunities for a respite off the front lines, whether through the normal rotation of his Company, or summons to court from his father. He knew where he belonged and it was not lounging in some town or enduring monotonous Council meetings.

When Philup Thurwer — then General of the First Battalion — passed away, General Saer was promoted to the position at the head of the Fire Wall. He took with him some of his brightest, including Richmond and Terrin. In his absence, his Colonel, Lukas Arhan, was promoted to General and took charge of the Sixth.

As part of the First, Terrin's days were markedly quieter, battles and skirmishes less frequent. The battalion served along the northern border shared with Zemiltar. It was a time of official peace between the Kingdom of Pohartan and the disjointed tribes which occupied the centre of the continent, loosely forming the region of Zemiltar. As such, the soldiers served primarily as a local militia:

policing the communities and offering arbitration in disputes. Only rarely would they have to hunt down a raiding party from one of the tribes of Zemiltar.

It was in those years that Terrin developed a reputation for his temper. Without the constant release of battle, the rage he often felt building inside him found different, oft unfortunate and unfair, outlets.

When his father passed a few years later and he was forced to return to Morim and take the crown, he felt he was being shackled. Gone were his days of freedom; charging through fields with a company of soldiers behind him, throwing himself into the enemy; his days of laughing and drinking with common soldiers, celebrating a victory or commemorating a defeat. Instead, he was stuck wandering the confined halls of the Fire Fortress. Those council meetings he had long avoided suddenly filled his days, as he suffered through the banal nattering of Lords and Ladies concerned with the minutia of running a Kingdom. Many of those nobles became the targets of the King's now-famous anger, as he became increasingly frustrated with the mundanity and confines of royalty.

Terrin's expression must have become distant, as he realized Richmond was staring at him quizzically.

"What is on your mind, Terrin?" Richmond asked quietly, his voice meant to carry only to his friend.

The King took a deep, heavy breath before answering. The air was a curious mix, as smoke from the burning village blended with the residual stench of the army which had been camped there—horses and feces, primarily—and the fresh scent of the forest and open air. Terrin smiled. "That it is good to be back, my friend. It is good to be myself once again."

* * *

Jahn was jostled awake by the bump and sway of the wagon rolling over the uneven roadway. As his Company had been among those involved in the overnight raids, they had been granted the privilege of riding in wagons for this portion of the march. They were meant to be catching up on lost sleep but the constant knocking of the wagon made more than a few minutes of rest at a time nearly impossible.

Instead of attempting to return to sleep, for the moment Jahn looked at the faces sharing the wagon with him. Some of the faces he had been used to seeing were notably absent, replaced by others, strange and unfamiliar.

After the raid of the horse lines, Jahn had learned the fallen soldier whom he had avenged had been Petren. The following night, as his squad frantically fought the enraged enemy back from the fleeing Thrower, both Uteer and Fennel had been killed. Jahn could still see them both as they fell: Uteer, taken by an arrow in the back as they ran; then Fennel calling out behind them, falling to a sword at the moment Jahn turned and looked to him, eyes staring into terrified eyes.

That left three of them — Tumas, Amad and himself — left alive from their original squad. Of course there had been some reorganization and two new soldiers had been added to their ranks to fill some of the gaps. Jahn suspected it would not take long for those new soldiers to blend into their group, becoming as close with them as the others had been. But for now, merely the day after the loss, the soldiers were mostly quiet as the wagon creaked along the road.

Gazing about, Jahn met the eyes of one of the new soldiers, Megen. She was sitting with her back up against the side of the wagon opposite him, legs stretched out beside his. Like him, she was from a mining village in the southwest of Pohartan. When the military came to her village, she had been the only woman to volunteer. Megen smiled slightly and nodded to Jahn, who responded in kind. There was little to speak of, as they yearned for rest among their fitfully sleeping companions.

Next to Megen, on the opposite side of Jahn's outstretched legs, lay one of those soldiers currently sleeping and the other new face in the squad: Omerin. Omerin was a large, muscular man, a few years older than the rest of the squad and had served in the military prior to the outbreak of this new campaign. He lay with his arms crossed over his chest, his bald head bouncing with the movements of the wagon.

Jahn was startled by a tap on his shoulder. Turning, he found Sergeant Morson towering over him atop his horse, trotting alongside the wagon.

"Good morning, sunshine," the Sergeant nodded down to Jahn.

Awkwardly struggling to upright himself, Jahn inadvertently jostled his sleeping companions awake. Eventually he got himself up into a kneeling position and offered the Sergeant a quick salute, "Good morning, Sir!" His fellow soldiers, now awake and aware of the ranking soldier in their midst, also quickly turned themselves in the wagon bed to face him, saluting.

Morson matched their salutes with one of his own, then returned his focus to Jahn. "You have impressed the powers that be, young man." He reached into a pouch bouncing on his hip and pulled out a metallic disc, the size of a large coin. "They appreciate your strategic contributions. And I have seen you face the enemy these past nights. You remain focused and controlled, you act quickly and decisively. Though..." his tone changed, "you still need some practice with that blade: you are quick but sloppy. A foe with his wits about him would not have too much trouble with you."

"Yes sir, thank you. I will practice my sword work at the first opportunity." Jahn was not used to receiving praise and did not know how to properly accept it, choosing to ignore it. Criticism, however, he had a lifetime of experience accepting—or at least hearing.

"See that you do, Corporal." Sergeant Morson flipped the disc to Jahn.

Catching it, Jahn looked down at his hand. In his palm sat disc of polished steel, two parallel lines slashed across the front, raised over the Flame of Pohartan. The back of the disc bore two curved and bent pins, which pricked his palm from the catch, drawing tiny droplets of blood which Jahn ignored. It was the symbol of the rank of Corporal.

"Stick that on your tunic and these folks with you become your problem," the Sergeant gestured to the rest of the wagon. "As Corporal you remain under my command but become responsible for the rest of your squad. So, all the responsibility, none of the power. Does that not sound like a delightful position to be in?" Morson spurred his horse forward, away from the wagon. "Get some sleep, soldiers," he called back.

Jahn sat back down against the side of the wagon, turning the badge over in his hands.

"Congratulations, Jahn!" Tumas offered from Jahn's left side, with a genuine smile.

Amad, on Jahn's other side, offered a salute with one hand while performing an obscene gesture with the other but both were accompanied by a pleased smile equal to Tumas'.

Across the wagon bed, Megen was casting him an appraising look and offered a quiet "Congratulations" when their eyes met. Omerin was the only one not to offer some form of approval to Jahn. Instead, he glared at the younger soldier for a moment, scratching his heavily bearded chin. With an audible huff, he turned his head away, returning to his sleeping posture and attempting to drift off.

Perhaps he will not blend into the group so smoothly, Jahn thought to himself as the wagon rumbled into the valley in which the village of Prinol had once stood. Plumes of smoke were rising from the remains of many of its buildings. The last stalwart structures along the edge of the village were slowly succumbing to the blaze, their charred remnants finally crashing to the ground, exhaling clouds of ash and dust.

*   *   *

Brianne rode into the valley atop Fire Dancer. Simone rode beside her, with the Phoenix Guard and Simone's Colonels behind them. Ahead, a dense line of soldiers snaked its way through the valley, skirting the smouldering ruins of Prinol. Brianne turned to look back, peering over the shining helmets of the ranks of soldiers behind them. The tail of the marching army was lost along the bends of the road.

"… my sister never supported this choice," Simone was saying beside her. The two had been discussing their families before Brianne became distracted by the change of scenery.

"What about the rest of your family?" Brianne asked, returning to the conversation. She and Simone had spent a lot of time together over the march and were quickly becoming close friends.

"My mother was the one who most supported me joining the military. She was so proud, so confident I would succeed. My father offered his support but reluctantly. He wanted me to stay home where it was safe, marry a good man and just focus on running my home. However, once he saw that I was determined to follow this path, he helped me enlist. He knew I was not meant for that life." Simone smiled at the memory but the smile fell away as she continued. "My sister stopped speaking with me that same day. Though I am not home often, the times I am she seems to find an excuse to stay away. I have not even met her two youngest children."

Brianne nodded, knowingly. "That is unfortunate. I understand the feeling you are speaking of, of not being meant for that traditional life, though I had not been able to articulate it before I left Sastan. As a young girl, I envisioned myself marrying Andrew. I imagined he would build us a new house in the village; he would work in the mines, as the men did and I would tend the house and children, as the women did." Brianne shrugged, "I did not feel some great passion for that future: it was just an expectation. My friends would speak about the same plans, their eyes sparkling at the idea and we would laugh about our future children falling in love."

"That has all changed now, however," Brianne went on. "I do not imagine I will be returning to Sastan. I know Andrew will not be." Her voice trailed off as horrific images of Andrew's crushed face flashed before her eyes.

Simone let a moment of silence pass between them. Brianne had told her of finding Andrew's body among the devastation outside Harten.

"Where is your family now? Your mother and Ren. Have you heard anything about them?" Simone asked finally.

"I do not know. But, I suppose I have not asked." The realization upset Brianne. She had certainly not forgotten her mother and youngest brother but why had she not enquired about them? Were they being treated well in Morim still? Had they been sent back to Sastan? A wave of homesickness came over her as she realized Ren's birthday had passed since she and Jahn left Morim with the army, he is seven years old now.

"I hope they are well. Perhaps they have been allowed to return home: my mother would like that, though it would likely feel empty without Jahn and me there."

"Hopefully this campaign will not last too long and you will get a chance to see them again," Simone offered in a cheerful tone. "I sent word to my parents that I have been promoted to General but I would have loved to be able to see their faces when they received the news."

Brianne became distracted again as they neared the remnants of the village. Smoke drifted up from the husks of buildings, charred stone walls were leaning precariously over the streets. The talk of family and home cast a veil over her image of the village: she could see the streets arranged as those of Sastan. She could see Master Kleen's blacksmith shop in the ruins and The Miner's Pick Inn smouldering in the middle of the village. The similarities to her home were striking and haunting, though Brianne supposed most villages of similar sizes shared common features.

"I am going to go take a look at the village," Brianne said suddenly, turning Fire Dancer away from the column and urging her to a trot towards the wreckage. Behind she heard horses follow her—the Phoenix Guard, always at the ready.

"I am not sure this is wise, my Lady," Sergeant Bradford stated warily, pulling his horse up beside Brianne. "What are you looking for?"

"Nothing, really," Brianne mused. "I just feel the need to take a look around. This village reminds me of my own." She looked at the man riding beside her, the concern on his face. "I am certain it is empty, Sergeant."

The man sighed but made no effort to dissuade her, instead drawing his sword. The sound was echoed by the soldiers riding behind them drawing their own blades.

Smoke hung heavily in the air as they passed the skeletal remains of the first buildings. Little was left of the structures but Brianne supposed they had been private dwellings. *Were we in Sastan, this would have been Lara and her family's home, with Kenton Welvar and his family living next door.* They crossed a narrow street and passed among what would have been another row of homes.

They stopped in the wider street which followed. Ahead of them, the street opened into a small clearing, surrounded by buildings. The village's main hall sat across the clearing, the charred remains of the second storey roof leaning precariously inward. As they watched, the frame gave in to its fate and collapsed with a loud groan and crash, kicking up a cloud of ash. As far as Brianne could tell, it was the last building to surrender.

Though many of the people of Sastan had shunned her and her family in recent years, it had still been her home. She still had years of positive memories to compete with those negative, lonelier times. Years of running through the village green in front of The Miner's Pick, playing with the other children. The Autumn and Spring festivals, where she and Jahn would sit with their parents, not understanding the conversations of the adults around them but listening in rapt attention.

Andrew had stolen her first kiss under the tree down the street, behind plump Marc Owen's bakery. She had slapped him, shocked at his sudden rash action but had been unable to keep the smile from her lips or the colour from her cheeks as he ran away, laughing merrily at his victory. In Prinol such a tree sat near the centre of the village, though in the opposite direction of that in Sastan. How many young lovers had shared such experiences under its branches, now charred and twisted?

"I could have lived in this village. These could have been my family and friends' homes and livelihoods," Brianne spoke, mostly to herself.

"I came from a reasonably wealthy family, my Lady," began Sergeant Bradford. "Not the level of nobility but certainly never wanting for food nor shelter. I am embarrassed to admit, it took me a long time to realize the lucky position I was in. As a younger man, I would glare and sneer at beggars if they approached."

"That is… an odd confession, Sergeant," responded Brianne. She could not see the connection between the village, her wandering thoughts and his sudden statement.

Sergeant Bradford continued, seeing the confusion on her face. "My point is what my grandfather would say to me. He could see my arrogance at my privilege. He had spent his early years in squalor, unlike me. Over his life he had built a modest estate for his family, from which I benefitted. He never forgot from where he came, nor those who had not been as fortunate as he and wanted me to gain perspective. He would continually tell me, usually accompanied by a slap to the back of my head, 'There but by the grace of the gods, go you'."

Brianne nodded as the Sergeant continued. "War is a nasty business, for everyone it touches. It is easy to forget its effects when you are on the side that is winning and the battles are not taking place near your homes. Whenever I am feeling prideful I look to my slain enemy, or a destroyed village such as this and remind myself of my grandfather's admonition. At times, I can still feel his slap."

Brianne smiled softly up at the taller man, who himself was smiling slightly at the memories of his grandfather. "Your grandfather was a wise man. And it seems he has instilled this trait in you as well. Thank you for sharing his words."

Sergeant Bradford bowed his head in reply. "We do as we must for our Kingdom, to protect our families but we must never forget the experiences of our enemies. They keep us grounded."

CHAPTER 17

"We have to burn it!" General Furell insisted, pounding his fist on the table to emphasize his point. "If they make it to Drevnat, we would be drawn into a long siege and then what have we achieved?" Some of the Generals gathered around the table in the King's tent nodded in agreement. They had been debating their strategy for some time and tempers were starting to rise.

Simone was one of the hold-outs to the plan of burning the forest. "Perhaps we have already won. They threatened us at our door and we pushed them back. We can keep them running the rest of the way home and our point is made: our strength is known. Let them reach that safety; they will not threaten us again anytime soon."

Terrin ran his fingers through his hair, suppressing his frustration. They had discussed the plan ad nauseam weeks ago and he had thought they were all agreed. Now that they were days—hours, really—from needing to act, the Generals were making their final suggestions of alternatives. The Drevesine and Zemiltar horde were on the brink of the fork, where one path would lead them to the safety of the capital; the other, the open fields of Zemiltar.

"Gods be damned, Simone. Would you be so easily cowed?" Nedly Furell accused. "If you were in their position, would you merely hide under the bedsheets, while the enemy presented their back to you and walked away?"

"I am afraid I agree with Ned. We have to keep them out from behind those walls," Dendrik Saer offered. "Perhaps it is a matter of your inexperience, or your womanly ideals, Simone but it would be foolish to leave a force this size at large."

Simone lost herself for a moment, tired of being belittled and disregarded by the other Generals. "Listen, you old bastard. I will shove my 'womanly ideals' up your ass so far, you will pass them with your morning shits for the next week. I stand at this table by merit and my opinions will be respected as if there were a cock attached to them. The fact I would avoid bloodshed if possible does not make me weak."

For several extended heartbeats, there was tense silence in the room. Simone and Dendrik stared daggers at each other from across the table, as the other Generals stood transfixed.

A loud guffaw from Richmond broke the tension. "Well, welcome to the table, Simone! It is about bloody time."

The anger left Dendrik as water leaving an upturned pitcher, though his face remained stoic and stern: his default state. "Duly noted, General Atlee. However, I still disagree with your strategy."

"I am sorry, Simone but I must admit I have been swayed." Nolan had been Simone's last ally in the debate and Terrin could see her disappointment as he abandoned her. "We have the advantage with Stalius coming in, it is best for us to destroy this enemy completely. Our optimum chance to do that is to push them out of the forest."

Simone sighed, disappointed but accepting she was outnumbered. "Very well. However, we are still talking about burning the Great Wood. Aside from the ecological implications, the logistics still elude me. How do you propose we achieve this? We cannot possibly expect to drag the Firethrowers through the forest, fast enough to get around and ahead of the enemy."

"The young Morette girl, obviously," Dendrik responded.

"Is she capable of handling a fire of that size? Not to mention the danger of such a mission. Do we want to throw her into such a vulnerable position?" Simone seemed skeptical.

"It is not like you, Simone, to speak of needing to protect a woman from danger," Terrin noted. "I am confident she has the ability—she is our best option, regardless—and she is a soldier in this war as much as the rest of us, we might as well use her."

"How is her blade work coming?" asked Nolan. "Not that I would expect her to need it, with her abilities and that Phoenix Guard of hers."

"Exceptionally well, actually." Simone smiled at the progress her friend had made. "She learns quickly and moves gracefully as, well, a dancing flame. I mentioned this to her. She claims embracing her power helps her focus, yet refuses to acknowledge she has made such great progress."

"So we are finally in agreement then," Terrin said, looking among his companions. Each nodded in turn, Simone's approval coming reluctantly. "Richmond and Conrad, please stay so we can break down the details. Simone, would you please send for Brianne to join us? The rest of you, return to your men. Make sure they are resting, so we can continue marching the moment the sun begins to rise.

"No need to send for me, I am here," Brianne said, causing heads to turn to her as she entered the tent. Terrin had made it clear to his guards that she had the freedom to come and go as she pleased, including to such meetings as these.

The dismissed Generals nodded and saluted as they took their leave, Simone clapping Brianne on the shoulder in greeting as she made her way from the tent. Brianne stepped to the table opposite Terrin and Richmond, offering a greeting nod to Conrad. "Evening, gentlemen."

Terrin stood transfixed by Brianne, standing across the table. She was clad in close-fitting black and deep crimson leathers, armoured similarly to the archers, though with finer, customized pieces. Thickened plated leather bracers protected her lower arms and up over her shoulders. Her shirt reached her neck, though she had left the lacing loose. A padded and plated corset encircled her torso, accentuating her natural shape. Belted at her waist was the sword she had been given, held in an ornate scabbard. The belt's buckle was modelled after the Flame of Pohartan and glinted in the torchlight of the tent. Terrin was most surprised to see her wearing fitted trousers accented by boots which reached nearly to her knees, rather than a skirt.

Her hair was tied back with a thin leather strip and draped forward over her shoulder. The strands of hair hanging over her chest obscured the intricate pattern of flames etched into the leather over her heart.

"We have a plan, I presume?" she asked, meeting Terrin's gaze.

The King had difficulty finding his words, as her emerald eyes glittered in the flickering torchlight.

"The beginnings of one, Lady Brianne," Richmond, seeing his friend at a loss, answered for Terrin. Terrin was grateful for the assistance, as it gave him the opportunity to gather himself.

The King cleared his throat. "Yes. We need to make sure the Drevesine army does not take the road to Drevnat. We believe you will be able to assist with that."

"How so?" asked Brianne. As she did so she leaned forward over the map laid out on the table, examining the area it represented. Terrin found himself distracted again as her posture provided him with a slight glimpse down between the open laces of her shirt. A sharp kick from Richmond snapped his attention back and Terrin looked over to find his long-time friend smirking at him. Terrin admonished himself for becoming so easily and thoroughly distracted: now was not the time for such thoughts.

Brianne looked up at him, awaiting his response and he struggled to keep his embarrassment at his wandering thoughts from showing on his face. He relayed the elements of the plan they had determined thus far and together the four of them worked together to finalize the remaining details.

With the final pieces in place, the group parted ways for the evening. Brianne was the last to leave and as Terrin watched her walk to the entrance of the tent, he once again could not keep his eyes and mind from wandering. He knew she caught his downward gaze as she turned to look back at him on her way from the tent. As he began to attempt to stammer out an apology or explanation, she merely offered him a mischievous smile and disappeared from the tent, the flap falling closed behind her.

*   *   *

Brianne rested her back against a large tree, a short distance from the side of the wide road which slashed through the dense forest. They had spent a long day of hard riding and her legs were screaming at her. They had ridden along the road as far as they could until their scouts caught first sight of the rear scouts of the enemy army. Then they had cut into the trees, carving a large arc through the forest in an attempt to avoid and overtake the marching Drevesine army.

The charge had been tense, as they desperately sought to win a race their foe did not know they were involved in. They had to take the shortest route they could, without alerting the enemy to the presence of several dozen soldiers charging through the forest. There was the constant threat of running headlong into a group of soldiers, or worse, a contingent of the Forest Legion.

Somehow they had made it, with Richmond and a Sergeant Morson navigating them to the road leading to Drevnat, about a league north of the fork. The Phoenix Guard was scattered among the trees nearby, speaking in quiet pockets while constantly scanning the surrounding area.

Richmond and the Sergeant were standing at the side of the road nearby, relaxed with their feet spread and arms crossed. Brianne was not paying attention to what they were talking about but every few moments they would laugh together.

Sergeant Morson turned away from the Fire General and approached Brianne, who rose, somewhat reluctantly, to greet him.

"Lady Morette, we did not have the opportunity to formally meet, I am Sergeant Morson." He extended his hand to her, palm up, expecting to receive hers gently, perhaps to kiss her knuckles in a gentlemanly way. Instead, she grabbed his hand with her own and offered a firm handshake.

"It is a pleasure to meet you, Sergeant," She said firmly, meeting his gaze with her head held high.

"Hmm, you must have strong lineage, my Lady. You are an impressive figure yourself and your brother is performing strongly in my Company."

Brianne's face lit up at the mention of her brother. "Oh, you know Jahn! It is good to hear he is doing well. You will keep him out of too much danger, won't you?"

"As best I can, given the circumstances, my Lady." The Sergeant's voice was shaky, his tone unconvincing. Brianne did not, however, have the opportunity to question him.

"Brianne, Morson. Rider approaching," Richmond called from the road, gesturing south.

Brianne's gaze followed the Fire General's signal as she and Sergeant Morson picked their way to the road. The scattered soldiers cut their conversations short, joining the movement. Brianne spotted the rider approaching at a gallop. He wore a crimson tunic sporting the Flame of Pohartan—a scout Richmond had sent forward.

"Sir, the enemy vanguard approaches. The main force has reached the fork." The soldier reined his horse in as he offered his report, punctuating it with a sharp salute to the Fire General.

"Thank you, get yourself behind us." Richmond turned, addressing the surrounding soldiers in a shout, "Everyone back!"

He turned to Brianne. "Are you ready?"

"As much as I can be," she nodded. Richmond and Sergeant Morson backed up the road a dozen paces, leaving Brianne standing alone. She turned to face the south. A bend in the road limited her view but she imagined she could hear the hooves of the approaching enemy.

Taking a deep breath, she opened herself to her power, as she had done thousands of times to this point. In a rush, the energy and warmth filled her. Her senses heightened; the weariness of travel left her. Focusing, she formed a massive roiling ball of flame before her. The inferno swirled in a circle as tall as she, just off the surface of the road. She poured her will into the flames, increasing their intensity.

With a wave of her arm—an ultimately unnecessary gesture but the movement gave her the sensation of better control—she cast the ball of flame into the trees to her left. She held the fire there for a few moments, ensuring the fresh green trees caught. As she pulled her will from the ball, leaving the flames to leap from tree to tree of their own will, she formed a second sphere in the road. She repeated the process, casting the flames to the other side of the road.

Now each side of the wide road was a roaring inferno. She could hear the soldiers behind her, shifting nervously. Ahead, however, the road remained clear. The sound of pounding hooves rose through the crackling flames, as a line of green-clad soldiers galloped around the bend in the road.

"What the bloody..." Brianne heard the start of a shouted string of curses from the oncoming soldiers as she embraced the flames again. Pulling energy from the existing flames and fueling them with her own, she built a wall of flame towards herself, across the road.

Her entire world became flame as she was surrounded. She could distantly hear herself screaming among the inferno, swirling no more than an arm's length from her. It was a scream of power, of strength: never before had she felt the invigoration of this much energy and she thrived in it. This was the opportunity to test the limits of her abilities which she had so long sought.

Reaching out, she embraced the wall of flame with her will and began to push. Slowly the flames rolled forward down the road. Through the wall she heard the shouts of men and cries of horses, desperately turning and fleeing as they were approached by the towering inferno, flames leaping as tall as the treetops.

As the flames moved past Brianne she reluctantly drew back her will. The blaze reduced in its supernatural intensity but remained raging over the road and through the trees before her. Turning, Brianne saw the Pohartan soldiers pushed back an extra thirty paces. Once she was free from the flames and walking towards them, Sergeant Bradford and the Phoenix Guard raced to her side, swords drawn. Richmond and Sergeant Morson followed at a more reasonable pace, as the remaining soldiers held back from the charred trees and roadway.

Sergeant Bradford looked over her frantically. He seemed surprised to see her unharmed, as he himself was already covered in sweat from the flames still so close. "I must admit you had us worried but there was little we could do. I have never felt so lost."

Brianne patted his arm comfortingly. "I appreciate your concern, Sergeant but you need not fear for my safety among the flames. You can keep your focus on protecting me from arrows and blades."

"Well… fuck," Richmond seemed at a loss for words as he reached Brianne. "Dendrik is going to be rather upset that his First no longer has the most impressive Fire Wall."

"We should move, General." Brianne was starting to feel the effects of using so much power, her knees growing wobbly and arms weighing heavily. "This fire is its own beast now. I am holding it back at the moment but the wind is coming this direction and it wants to roll over us."

Richmond's eyes went wide. "Yes, yes of course." Turning, he signalled everyone to a trot. "Move yourselves! Bring out the horses!"

In a few moments, they were mounted and making their way through the trees once again, moving quickly to leave the flames behind. Brianne held her focus as long as she could, ensuring the flames would not overtake them. As she felt certain they were clear of danger, she reluctantly released her hold on the power.

A wave of nausea overcame her and she had to resist the urge to lean over her saddle and empty her stomach. She was glad to be atop Fire Dancer, for she doubted she would have the strength to stand.

"I do not imagine they will be trying to march an army through there now," Richmond said beside her, as Ursa dodged around a tree. "General Saer should have the First charging up the road behind them, so they do not have the opportunity to sit and think about what to do. They cannot take their entire army through the forest, so they will have to follow the other road."

Richmond fell silent as he slowed his horse, the other soldiers slowing theirs as well. Brianne watched him draw his massive axe from his belt and followed his gaze. A short way ahead, in a small clearing, a band of men stood waiting for them. Casually they were waiting for the riders to approach, hoods thrown back, hands at their sides, palms forward to demonstrate they were not holding weapons. They were dressed in cloaks whose colour seemed to shift between different hues of browns and greens.

"Good afternoon, Fire General Arhan." The man in the centre of the group took a step forward. "I am Daimian Nightcloak, First Blade of the Forest Legion." Nightcloak offered a bow, with a flourish of his cloak.

"I know who you are, Nightcloak. What are you doing here?" Richmond's tone was heavy with suspicion and unease.

"Well, to be fair, I am in my forest, in my country. I think the more reasonable question would be what are you doing here?" He did not wait for a response, gesturing to the smoke rising behind them. "Though I do not need an answer to that, it is fairly obvious."

"Are we going to have a problem here, Nightcloak? We have not seen your men for some time." Richmond did not take his eyes from the man standing in front of him.

"Oh, but we have seen yours. We have been watching closely."

"What do you want?" The Fire General's suspicion was turning to anger.

Instead of answering the General, Nightcloak turned his attention to Brianne. "You must be Brianne. Who else could you be, of course? I remember you clearly from our meeting, though did not know your name at the time and not many people these days have your abilities. We were not sure who you were at the time but you left quite the impression."

Brianne steeled herself, suppressing her weariness. Embracing her power once again, she brought forth a fist-sized ball of flame, allowing it to float at her side. She said nothing in response to the man. As soon as she allowed the power to overtake her she felt a strange aura over the area, seemingly radiating from Nightcloak and his men.

"That is quite the impressive trick." Nightcloak kept his voice firm but Brianne noticed him take a half-step to the side, away from her. She glared at him, pushing him another half-step away.

"You slaughtered our men after that meeting." Richmond was flexing his hand over the handle of his axe. Ursa seemed to sense the tension of the moment, shaking its head with a snort. "What say we even the numbers, here and now?"

"Easy now, General." Nightcloak lifted his hands in a placating gesture. "I would suggest we were provoked. After all, we were nearly incinerated after your King stormed off in a huff. We are in a war, my good sir, we both know the cost. You have struck down plenty of our fine young men as well."

Through gritted teeth, Richmond demanded again, "What do you want?"

"There have been some… changes in the country of Drevesine as of late. I have had some disagreements with those in charge. Why do you think we have not destroyed your little raiding parties as they blundered their way through the forests in the dark?" Showing no concern for the General's hard tone, Nightcloak paced with his hands clasped behind his back as he spoke. "No, I have little interest in expending my efforts to defend HardOak's forces. I am not your enemy at this moment, Fire General."

Richmond did not seem swayed, a stern expression locked on his face. Nightcloak continued. "'The enemy of my enemy is my friend', as it were. At the moment, I am more concerned with Har-dOak than I am with you and your raging King." Brianne had gotten to know Richmond well enough to catch the slight change in his expression as he became more curious about what the other man had to say.

"One last time, Nightcloak, what do you want?" Richmond's axe lowered slightly from its raised, tense, ready position.

"Peace, between our forces, for now. You have been picking away at their army but so have we. They are in a near frenzy. I would like to continue this, without worry that our forces will clash if they cross paths. Perhaps," he raised his hand as if an idea had just struck him, "we could even coordinate our efforts."

"'For now', you say? It is not wise to suggest peace, with such a promise of future violence." Though his tone remained firm, Brianne could virtually see the wheels turning within Richmond's head. He was quickly running through the implications and strategic possibilities of such an arrangement.

"The future will depend on your Mad King and his visions for this region once this war ends. At this moment, I want both your armies out of my forest and it appears," he gestured again to the smoke which was rapidly covering the sky, "you do as well. So, here we are, hands outstretched." He stopped his pacing in front of Richmond's horse, extending his open hand to the Fire General.

For a moment Richmond remained still and silent. Finally he returned his axe to the loop at his belt and dismounted, approaching Nightcloak cautiously.

"I make no firm guarantees. However, we will part this clearing in peace. I will share your words with the King." Richmond extended his hand towards Nightcloak, stopping short of clasping the other man's, forcing Nightcloak to cover the remaining distance. He did so and the two stood a moment, hands clasped, staring firmly at each other, each taking measure of the other man.

As the men released their hands Nightcloak turned and began to walk from the clearing, pulling his hood over his head. As he moved he released a low, quick whistle.

The soldiers raised their weapons in a quick moment of panic as two dozen figures dropped from the trees around them. Each was clad in the same colour shifting cloaks. However, they did not attack. Instead, they simply nodded to the soldiers and turned, walking off into the trees.

Brianne released the breath she had not realized she had held at the moment the men dropped from the trees. She looked back to the clearing where Nightcloak had been walking. To her surprise, there was no sign of him or the men he had been with. As she turned again to look among the Pohartan soldiers, she realized she could not see any of the green-clad figures. They should have not yet been able to walk far enough to be out of sight but there was no sign of them.

Richmond remounted Ursa, looking to Brianne. As their eyes met he merely shrugged. "We better get back to the King."

CHAPTER 18

The days which followed passed in a cycle of routines. The armies moved in measured distances, hopping from clearing to clearing or town to town when they could be found: soldiers sleeping on the road and among the trees when no other option was available as night fell and exhaustion overtook them. As the Drevesine army left each village behind, the residents would also flee, left to simply pray to their Gods that their village would be spared by the pursuing Pohartan horde. Some were, while others burned, with the villagers left to wonder at the whims of the King which had led to their misfortune.

As each night fell, the Drevesine soldiers fought sleep, wild-eyed. At any moment they knew they could be swarmed by the enemy. Some nights, figures nearly impossible to see would slip among their ranks, silently slitting throats as the crickets chirped. Other nights, masses of demon-like men appeared at the edges of the camp, spouting fire and destruction. The army's command was learning quickly but as they adapted to each new method of terror the enemy returned with a new creative tactic, circumventing the newly devised defences.

Among the soldiers, despair and fear were fertilizing the seeds of desertion. Promises of freedom from the onslaught once the army escaped the forests and emerged into the plains of Zemiltar kept most soldiers in rank and file but a slow trickle had begun, as disillusioned and desperate soldiers found opportunities to slip away from the main force and try their luck alone in the trees. The fate of those soldiers found missing from the ranks was never known to those who remained. Some may have reached safety but most would be found lifeless in the underbrush had time been spent to attempt to retrieve them.

After weeks of marching and terror, the flora began to thin. Over the course of a day, the soldiers moved from the dense trees of the Great Wood to the welcoming open plains of Zemiltar. The Drevesine army and the allies accompanying it were met by a waiting friendly force of mounted men, waving a dozen banners bearing different sigils of the regional tribes. From the mass a bare-chested, muscled and tattooed man rode forward, flanked by banners depicting a strange winged beast and met the Generals of Drevesine. He warned of another force of armoured men approaching from the West.

The two forces present melded together, mounted men in tanned leathers marching along with green and silver clad foot soldiers. Together they turned to the Northwest, marching away from the dangers of the trees and the enemies approaching from two sides.

*   *   *

The screech of a hawk streaking across the sky was cut short as an arrow plunged into its body, causing it to spiral down to the ground. Terrin watched as the soldier who had fired the arrow sprinted out into the plain to retrieve his kill and salvage the arrow if he could. It was known to the army that Matrel Foselak and other tribal leaders of Zemiltar, used the birds as scouts and so the King had offered a reward for every bird brought down.

Rumours claimed some of the tribesmen of Zemiltar had the ability to communicate with the creatures, able to receive more meaningful reports than an indication of direction. Though Terrin struggled to believe such nonsense, there was no harm in being cautious: after all, a year previous he had believed the stories of individuals wielding fire as a weapon were equally farcical.

Terrin took a deep breath as he looked over the open plains, the Great Wood behind him. His nostrils filled mostly with smoke, as the fire they had started weeks past was still burning in areas far behind them and the wind had shifted to carry the smoke in their direction. Still, there was a different undercurrent to the smell: the grasses and wildflowers of the fields offering a different perfume than the trees of the forest. The King enjoyed the change after so long.

He looked back, watching the small party walk away, disappearing into the trees. Nightcloak and his men had proven invaluable in the past weeks, assisting their soldiers in slipping through the forest and running their own attacks on the Drevesine army. Terrin had high hopes for the future of Drevesine and Pohartan as allies, assuming the other man's bold plans came to fruition as this war came to a close. But the war was not over yet, Terrin reminded himself, turning back to the plain before him.

Brianne rode to his left, this day dressed in a skirt split for riding as part of her new, fierce, appearance. To his right, Richmond rode, weighed down by his plethora of weapons. He had rarely donned so many arms on the march but they would be meeting the contingent from Stalius at long last and they wanted to be prepared.

Terrin himself wore his full armour, emblazoned with the Flame of Pohartan and the Wolf sigil of House Dramen on his chest. The banners which flapped in the wind over their heads, carried by men riding behind them, bore the same images. He had let himself grow a beard on the march, abandoning the foolish custom of clean-shaven royalty, feeling it gave him a more mature, serious, appearance. On his head, he wore the Crown of Pohartan—something he had rarely done in the past but a piece he always carried close with him. Its ruby-dotted gold peaks curved about his head, designed to resemble a wreath of flames.

As expected, a group of soldiers rode towards them, their silver armour shining in the sunlight. Above their heads flapped sapphire and black banners, depicting the clenched gauntlet of Stalius. Among the blue and black flapped a single indigo banner. As they drew closer, Terrin recognized it as the bear of House Arhan. The riders continued forward and Terrin recognized under that banner the figure of General Lukas Arhan, riding alongside a man in Staliusian armour at the head of the group. The group itself appeared composed of a mix of Staliusian and Pohartan soldiers.

"I never thought I would see this," Richmond mused beside him. "Stalius and Pohartan, riding together."

Terrin tightened his grip on his reins. "I would not get used to it. Though I suppose you never know. Perhaps this war with Drevesine will herald in a new era." The skepticism in his voice bordered on sarcasm as he spurred Mi'drak forward. The rest of the party — the bannermen, Brianne's Phoenix Guard and a contingent of men from the First — sprang forward with him. They closed the distance quickly, reining in their horses a few feet from the other party.

Richmond's father was the first to speak, offering a sharp salute, "Greetings your Highness!" He offered a nod of acknowledgement to his son, before casting an appraising look over Brianne, his eyes visibly scanning her body up and down.

"May I present Colonel Henrik Trombul, commanding officer of the Southern Brigade of the People's Steel Army of Stalius." Terrin appraised the man beside General Arhan. He was younger than Lukas but not so young as Richmond. His dark hair was cropped short, greying at the temples. He sat on his horse with his back board-straight, his prominent chin held high so his steely blue eyes could stare down at the King, despite being at a similar height. He offered only a cold nod at his introduction.

"We were told we would be meeting with Ordreg himself," Terrin spoke firmly to General Arhan, offering the foreign Colonel little more than a glance.

"And you will, my Lord. It appears the Hi'ral was not well enough for the ride. We are camped around a town not far from here, where he awaits your arrival." Lukas gestured behind him over the plains. "It is only a couple hours ride, I assure you."

Terrin and Richmond shared a concerned expression, both recognizing the danger of riding into a town controlled by such a tenuous ally. It was unclear how many of the forces there would be Pohartan and how many of his own soldiers Ordreg would have brought. Terrin looked to Brianne in an effort to gauge her understanding of the situation; however, her gaze was locked in a glare directed at Lukas, who was eyeing her hungrily without any effort to hide it as he awaited the King's response.

It was Richmond who spoke up, "Very well then, lead the way."

The elder Arhan pulled his eyes from Brianne and met the gaze of the Fire General. "Yes, sir." He saluted his son, the ranking officer. Lukas and Colonel Trombul turned their horses together, bringing their party in tow. As their horses moved to an easy trot, Terrin and his retinue fell in behind them.

"We are not going to walk into a town full of Staliusian soldiers, are we?" Brianne asked.

"Of course not," answered the King.

* * *

They could see the edge of the Staliusian camp in the near distance as they reined in their horses. The party in front of them continued on for a short distance before their halt was noticed and a loud whistle brought them to a stop as well.

Lukas Arhan brought his horse around his group of soldiers and he came to meet the King's party at a canter. "Is there a problem, my Lord?"

Brianne did not like the man. His blatant lecherous staring was all the reason she should need but that was not the only aspect which put her on edge. She could not quite identify what put her hackles up about the man, perhaps it was merely the circumstances of meeting him as he marched alongside the enemy she had been raised to hate. She attempted to convince herself that was the case. Where when she had met Richmond, she had felt immediate warmth and compassion radiate from him, his father was the opposite.

"We will not be entering the town. Have Ordreg come to us here. He made it this far from Scrail, I am sure he can come the extra distance." The King was glaring at the General in front of him. Perhaps, Brianne thought, her feelings towards the man were simply the echo of the King's. She looked past Terrin to Richmond, whose own expression was unreadable but certainly lacked the warmth one would expect between father and son.

"Very well." Lukas turned and galloped back to his party. Brianne noticed the lack of a salute or title directed towards the King.

"What do you think, Richmond?" Terrin asked.

Richmond sighed heavily, taking a moment to reply. "Of Ordreg, or of my father?"

"I would take your thoughts on either."

"Ordreg loves to control any situation. While it is possible his health has deteriorated, you are right: if he made it to this town, he likely could have met us as we exited the Great Wood. I doubt he would be so bold as to attack us in this town with our own forces matching his and the rest of our army so close. He wanted to meet on his terms, make us come to him. He will be annoyed he has to come to us."

Terrin smiled and nodded. "That suits me just fine. What of your father?"

"Same as last I saw him, I suppose. A little fatter, a little older but arrogant as ever."

"I do not like him," Brianne interjected. "I am sorry, Richmond but something about him makes me uneasy."

"That is fine, Brianne," Richmond replied with a bit of a laugh. "Likability has never been one of his traits. And I saw how he was looking at you. You are justified in your assessment of him."

The three fell silent as they watched the other party return to a trot towards the town, leaving them alone on the plain. They were stopped on top of a low hill, giving Brianne a view of the town in the distance, an island in a small sea of soldiers. From what she could see, it was unlike any town she had seen before. The buildings looked to be little more than fortified tents and they were organized in a circular pattern out from the centre like the spokes of a wheel, rather than the grid of streets she was used to.

"What is the name of this town?" Brianne asked.

"I assume you have not been to Zemiltar?" Terrin asked. When she nodded confirmation, he continued. "Well, it is not really a 'town', as we would consider it. This is the home of a particular tribe of the region. Which tribe, I do not know, as I cannot see the banners from here. You see, you will not find this place listed on any map. Notice there are no roads leading to or from it?" Brianne nodded again. "The people of Zemiltar are nomadic. At any time they can pack their tents up and be gone in a blink."

The three continued their conversation as they waited, with Terrin and Richmond explaining to Brianne the social and political structures of Zemiltar. It was fascinating to her, as she had never been far from Sastan, let alone out of Pohartan. Drevesine at least had similar customs and heritage to the people of Pohartan: Zemiltar, on the other hand, felt almost like she was walking into a different world.

Their conversation was eventually cut short as Richmond noticed movement coming from the edge of the camp and pointed it out to the King. "There. Looks like a carriage coming out."

Brianne's gaze followed his pointed finger and she too saw the shape he was referring too. As it drew closer, she could identify it as a bulky black carriage, pulled by a pair of large gray horses. Brianne's breath stuck in her throat, however, as she caught sight of the figures moving alongside the carriage.

The carriage was accompanied by a number of mounted soldiers, which was no surprise but between the soldiers prowled massive white shapes. She had seen those shapes before; in drawings her father showed her, in tapestries in the Fire Fortress of Morim and most recently in her dreams: they could only be the legendary white tigers of Stalius. They crossed the distance from the camp quickly and Brianne was awe-struck by the creatures.

She watched as they darted around the horses and carriage, at times disappearing beneath to pop out the other side. They moved with such grace, dancing nimbly among their companions, stopping and turning on a pin. There were two of the beasts accompanying the party and as they approached they leaped and pawed at each other, rolling in the grass for a moment before rising again and darting to catch up. Brianne was amazed at the calmness of the horses which accompanied the tigers, as Fire Dancer was beginning to shift nervously as they approached.

As the approaching party reached the Pohartan group, the tigers calmed from their play to stare down the unfamiliar people. Brianne could see their muscles tense and flex under their taught, black-striped skin. Emitting a low growl, they began to pace back and forth in front of the waiting soldiers as the carriage was brought around in an arc, to come to a stop with its side door before the King. Though not quite the size she had dreamed, they were far larger than she had realistically expected, their backs nearly reaching the knees of the mounted soldiers.

Colonel Tronbul was first among the Staliusian soldiers. He reined his horse in front of the carriage, opposite Brianne. With a sharp word in a language she did not recognize, one of the massive tigers quit its pacing, moving to stand beside the mounted Colonel. Its low growl stopped but its eyes did not leave the opposite party, its tail gently swishing against the long grass.

Lukas Arhan reined in his horse at the other end of the carriage, facing his son. Brianne scanned the accompanying soldiers, noticing that the General was the only one among them to be wearing the armour and colours of Pohartan. The rest bore the deep blues and greys of Stalius.

The driver of the carriage leapt down from his bench and approached the side of the vehicle. Reaching underneath, he pulled out an extension of the steps down from the door, anchoring it to the ground and creating a raised platform. Circling around to the other side of the platform, he reached up and pulled open the door of the carriage.

Brianne watched as an aged man slowly emerged from the carriage, a younger man in decorated grey robes followed behind him. The older man stood tall after stooping through the door of the carriage but his few steps onto the platform were shaky. His white hair lay dishevelled down past his shoulders, looking as if he had just risen from bed. He wore heavy black robes, draped over his protruding belly. Brianne's eyes were drawn to his yellowed, jagged teeth as he opened his mouth to speak. He too spoke a word foreign to her and the second tiger moved to stand beside the platform. Rodok Ordreg did not need to bend to scratch the beast's head.

"Well, so this is the boy-King of Pohartan at last," Ordreg began, he turned to look at Richmond. "You must be the son of the good General Arhan here. I have had many opportunities to speak with him on the road. I hope you will prove to be as qualified a soldier as he."

He turned to look at Brianne, licking his dried, cracked lips in an unsettling manner. "And this little thing here… I have heard much about you, young lady. Not, however, of your appearance. No wonder the King keeps you around. I bet you keep his cock hard and head empty." The man laughed at his own vulgarity. The Staliusian men laughed with him. Even Lukas let a wide smile cut across his face. "If you want a real ride, you are welcome to come back to our camp with me." Brianne felt her body tense in a cringe at his wink.

"I think I would rather die," she responded before she could think better of it. It was the Pohartans' turn to laugh, as Terrin and Richmond chuckled as Ordreg's grin became a scowl.

"Shall we get to our business, Ordreg?" Terrin asked, preventing the situation from escalating.

"You dragged me out here, so we damn well better," Ordreg barked back.

"The Drevesine army and their Zemiltar allies are camped north of here," Terrin gestured into the distance. "We hold the entrance to the Great Wood. Their next opportunity to make it home is over the Eirne river. It will take them some time to build the bridges or barges they will need to get their force across."

The younger man behind Ordreg stepped forward, quietly whispering something into the man's ear. Ordreg nodded. "I suppose you would like to strike them before they cross that river."

"Yes. With them stalled, this is our opportunity to crush them. We will attack at dawn, in two days time. We will approach them from the southeast. You will then appear to the southwest. They will be overwhelmed, surrounded and trapped between us and the river."

"Two days, you say?" Ordreg looked to Colonel Tronbul. A wordless moment passed between them and the Colonel nodded. "We will be where we are needed," confirmed Ordreg.

Ordreg's smile returned. "Now, my dear young King. Months ago you wrote me a letter. Promises were made in exchange for our assistance in your little war. Otherwise, why would we care? Let the rabble squabble among themselves, I would say and then I can clean up the remnants."

"I remember well the promises I made to you," Terrin cut him off. "Once the battle is won, you will have what is owed to you."

Ordreg raised his chin, glaring down at the King. "Oh, I will, boy. Whether it is given freely, as agreed, or taken by force, I will have it." Suddenly Ordreg spun on the platform, nearly knocking his companion off as he stormed back into the carriage. The young man scanned the three Pohartans mounted before him, locking eyes with Brianne for a moment before following his leader.

Quickly the carriage driver packed the platform away and leapt back into his seat. With a flick of the reins, the horses began to move and the carriage lurched forward. In moments the carriage was bouncing across the plains, returning to the Staliusian camp, the accompanying soldiers following behind. Colonel Tronbul offered a final glare at the Pohartans before racing after, the two tigers following easily at his side.

Only Lukas remained. "Richmond," he said, "I would speak with you for a moment."

"Certainly, father," replied Richmond. The two led their horses off a short distance to achieve some privacy.

"Dare I ask what you promised him?" Brianne gave Terrin an accusatory glare from the corner of her eye, not turning to face him completely.

"What does any leader want from another? I promised him territory. Quite a bit, actually."

Brianne's eyes widened and she turned to look at the King. The mix of surprise and anger on her face must have been obvious, as he raised his hands defensively. "I have no intention of giving it to him, of course," he soothed. Her expression softened only slightly. "I needed his assistance and did what I needed to—promised what I needed to—to obtain it. When this battle ends and the Drevesine horde is destroyed, Ordreg and his men will be next."

Terrin actually smiled. "The man was a fool to accompany his men. It would have been one thing for us to simply destroy his forces but with him here we have a prime opportunity to take him." There was light in his eyes as he spoke quietly of his plans. "Not only will we be able to eliminate this Drevesine threat but we can finally end the generations of war with Stalius."

"Do you not worry about breaking your word?" Brianne asked.

The King spat. "There is no concern for honour when dealing with Ordreg. The man will smile and welcome you into his halls, as he orders men to slaughter your family in your absence. The people of Pohartan will have no concern for me misleading our greatest enemy in an effort to defeat him."

Brianne nodded to herself. Her father had tried to instill in her a sense of honour as she was growing up and she strove to live up to those ideals. But then again, what Terrin said rang true. What was the significance of a broken promise compared to the scale of the war which had continued between the Kingdoms for so long? The war which had taken her father and so many others. *Father hardly lived up to the ideals he preached anyway*, she thought.

Richmond came trotting back to the group, as his father galloped off toward the Staliusian camp without another word to the King.

"What did he have to say?" Terrin asked.

"Little of substance," replied Richmond. "He asked about my life since we last spoke: my time as your Fire General. We have not seen each other since the promotion ceremony."

The three watched silently as General Arhan galloped across the field, reuniting with Ordreg's party just as it disappeared into the camp.

"Odd," Terrin said simply. Richmond shrugged as they turned their horses, kicking them to a canter in the direction of their camp.

CHAPTER 19

Brianne was pulling the straps of her bracer tight when the knock came at her tent post. "Lady Brianne, you have a visitor," announced Sergeant Bradford, accompanying the knock. It was just after dawn of the day after the meeting with Ordreg and the day before they would attack Drevesine. Brianne had intended to make it a day of training with Simone if the woman was available but had not yet had her breakfast.

As she emerged from her tent she was surprised to see her visitor was not her friend, come to collect her for a morning training session. She would never have been able to predict this particular visitor.

Before her, flanked by two of the Phoenix Guards, stood a young man wearing simple brown garb. He looked as though he could be a camp follower; perhaps a farrier or groom. But he stood with his back straight and head held high, nodding slightly in greeting as Brianne looked him over. It took a moment for recognition to set in and Brianne struggled to hide her surprise when she realized this man was the young man who had emerged from the carriage behind Ordreg the previous day.

She must have failed to hide her shock, as he addressed her with a gentle smile. "Hello, my Lady. My name is Mikale. I have an urgent matter about which I must speak to you."

Her suspicion high, she embraced her power. The feel of it running through her gave her strength and heightened confidence. "And why do you wish to speak with me, in particular?"

"I feel you will be most qualified to assist me, my Lady. The others have a reputation for being unreceptive to unexpected visitors. My information, however, is of the utmost importance. Might we speak privately for a moment?" Brianne noticed his evasion of including his own title or affiliations in his introduction, or mentioning specifically the "others"—presumably Terrin or Richmond—he could have spoken to. His plain garb bore no insignia to mark his allegiance or rank.

Sergeant Bradford stood stiffly beside her, his hand on the hilt of his sword. The soldiers who flanked the visitor mirrored his pose. All seemed uneasy, uncertain of this strange man requesting an audience with the woman they were sworn to protect. Brianne spent a long moment staring the man in the eye, attempting to gauge his character. She had no illusions of some divine skill she bore for discerning a man's intentions but years of simply being a woman had given her plenty of opportunities to practice. He held her gaze firmly but not angrily, nor lustfully. His expression read to her as one of determination but with a layer of pleading.

"My tent will have to suffice for privacy," she said finally. Sergeant Bradford opened his mouth in protest but a hand on his arm and a pointed look from Brianne cut him off. He huffed in aggravation but made no further protest.

"Yes, that will work. Thank you, my Lady," Mikale said, ducking past her quickly into the tent.

"I will be all right, Sergeant," Brianne said to Sergeant Bradford, attempting to placate his lingering worried expression. She gave him another reassuring pat on his arm before following Mikale into the tent.

Mikale was standing in the centre of the tent as she entered. He looked up, speaking a word quietly to himself. Brianne felt a wave of power wash over her, akin to the feeling she had experienced when Nightcloak and his men disappeared into the trees.

"What was that?" she demanded.

"We will be free to speak plainly now, my Lady. No noise will pass from this tent." His reply was calm and casual, with no hint of malice.

"How? Did you cast some kind of spell?" Brianne was more curious than concerned.

A look of confusion crossed the man's face for a moment, before realization seemed to hit him. "Of course, I suppose you have had little proper training. The people of Pohartan have little experience with the Vein." He smiled at her, much as a teacher would smile upon a favoured pupil. "The power you tap into to wield your flames. In Stalius we call it the Vein—like a vein of ore in the mountains, or the veins which carry our blood through our bodies. When you are open to the Vein, letting its power flow through you, you will be able to sense others who are likewise connected. I have used my own connection to the Vein to seal this tent from eavesdroppers."

Brianne was fascinated and wanted to ask for more information. No one had been able to provide her much useful knowledge about her power: where it came from, or how she could best control it. The Priests had been merely throwing out wild theories from ancient books. Jermal, despite his vileness, had managed to open the gate for her but every stride forward she had made since was that of a blind man stumbling alone through a maze.

"There are others with powers, like mine?" Brianne asked, both excited and skeptical.

"None exactly like you, to my knowledge," replied Mikale. "There have not been any able to wield fire as you do for a great while. But other abilities in other areas have remained alive, even thrived. There is a wide world out there beyond the borders of Pohartan, my Lady."

Brianne stepped past Mikale and took a seat on her cot, mind racing. Since the incident in Sastan had made her family outcasts, she had felt so alone. The idea that she was not, that there were others at all like her, others able to tap into this power, shook her.

"I would love the opportunity to teach you more about the Vein, my Lady," Mikale started hesitantly. "I am First Sage of the Cereb'Ani. Our order is dedicated to the study of the Vein and the powers which flow through it. But now is not the time." His tone became more frantic as he wrung his hands anxiously.

"Why have you come to see me? And why could you not go to the King or Fire General?" asked Brianne.

"I have urgent news to relay to your leaders but I feared to meet with them in person. As I hinted earlier, they have a bit of a brutal reputation in regards to messengers…"

Brianne cut him off. "I can assure you, the King is a different man from what lies I am sure your leader has told you. But we are here now, so please, share your news."

Mikale exhaled heavily as he began. "Ordreg is planning to betray you. We believe the moment the battle ends, he will turn his soldiers against yours."

Brianne could not help but laugh slightly. It seemed Terrin had a similar plan, so would likely not be surprised at this news. Though she felt comfortable with this Mikale, she was not so foolish as to reveal the King's plans to him. "Why would you tell us this? Why would you betray your Hi'ral?" she asked instead.

"Rodok Ordreg is a vile man." Genuine anger entered Mikale's voice as he spoke. "The Cereb'Ani have been working for some time to bring him down. But he puts on a strong performance for his people: his hold on power is absolute. He controls any information which reaches the people, ensuring it not only does not disparage him but that it paints him a hero. He is seen as like a God to the common man in Stalius. Any who get a glimpse of the truth and dare speak it are dealt with brutally. Deep in the mountains are numerous labour camps, to which the families of dissenters disappear. The guilty themselves are the lucky ones, as they are merely swiftly and silently murdered.

"We see an opportunity with this war," he continued. "We have not had the proper chance to remove the Hi'ral; have not found strong enough allies. We are a peaceful order, you see: sworn to do no violence ourselves. Our vows have been tested under

Ordreg but they are what define us. But if your King can defeat Ordreg, we can begin to heal Stalius."

"So what do you require of us?" Brianne stood, facing Mikale. She was of a similar height to the man and was able to meet his eyes levelly.

"I simply had to make sure your King knew of the coming treachery and assure him that he will have the assistance of the Cereb'Ani when the deed is done. We can rebuild a new Stalius, as an ally to Pohartan." Mikale smiled.

"How does plotting your leader's death fit with your pacifist vows?" There was more of an edge to her voice than she intended.

Mikale's smile faded. "As I said, my Lady: our vows have been tested. We have been pushed to our limits. While we have vowed to do no harm, we cannot blind ourselves to the harm Ordreg and his line have done to Stalius for generations. Much debate has occurred among the Cereb'Ani but desperation has led us to make peace with this solution: for the good of the Republic, Ordreg must be removed."

"I understand," Brianne offered her hand to the man, "I meant no offence."

Mikale took her hand in his, his smile returning. "Will you pass along our message, my Lady? Ensure your King does not fall into the tiger's jaws?"

"Yes, of course." Brianne nodded, returning the man's smile.

"Most excellent, thank you. And should we both see peace after this war, I extend an invitation to you to come to the Cereb'Ani Temple in Scrail. We would delight at the opportunity to learn more about your particular connection to the Vein." Mikale's smile widened. Another wave of power washed over Brianne; she assumed Mikale had dropped his protection against outside listeners.

"That would be wonderful," Brianne said, leading him from her tent. Sergeant Bradford and the other members of the Phoenix Guard were hovering about the entrance, a clear look of relief crossing their faces as she emerged unharmed.

Mikale bowed deeply, "Farewell, my Lady. Thank you for your time. May the Gods see you through the coming days."

Brianne returned his bow with a nod. "Peace be with you, sir."

The man from Stalius turned on his heel, offering a polite nod to the surrounding soldiers. Calmly he strode from the little clearing around Brianne's tent.

"Escort him out of the camp," Sergeant Bradford commanded to one of the other soldiers, a Private Leitier, who sped after the man.

"Is all well, my Lady?" the Sergeant asked, turning to Brianne.

"Yes, Sergeant. But I must go speak with the King." She began walking in the direction of Terrin's tent without waiting for a response. Sergeant Bradford fell into step behind her, signalling to the others to be at ease.

* * *

A soft breeze shook the canvas of the tent around Terrin. He enjoyed the sound, found it soothing. The remnants of his breakfast sat on a tray atop a small folding table beside the cot on which he lay. He relaxed with his hands behind his head, staring up at the ceiling canvas of the tent. The afternoon would bring long meetings with Richmond and the Generals. Scouts would be returning with final reports of the terrain and the enemy's position and the last details of their battle strategy would be put into place.

But until then, Terrin had a rare opportunity for a moment of peace. Thoughts of the coming battle raged in the back of his mind but he fought to suppress them, letting himself simply breathe.

A brief knock was all the warning he received to Brianne walking into his tent. His rapid move to stand was slowed as he realized there was no imminent threat or report from the expected scouts. Instead, he rose slowly, finding himself smiling at the woman who approached him. Her body swayed as she moved, the leathers of her new armour hugging the curves of her waist and hips.

"Good morning Brianne," he said warmly.

"Good morning," she returned his greeting with a smile. "I had a visitor this morning, from Stalius."

Terrin's joyful mood dropped suddenly. "Who? When? What did they want? Why did they come to you?" The questions fired from his mouth, a dozen more remaining unasked in his mind.

"His name was Mikale Talode. He called himself the First Sage of the Cereb'Ani."

"Yes, we know of him." Terrin scratched his chin. "He was with Ordreg yesterday. What in the world did he come to you for?"

Brianne shrugged, "He brought a message for you. Apparently he was too afraid to speak with you directly. He did not want anyone to know who he was, so perhaps he also did not think he could get an audience with you."

"Not a crazy notion, I suppose," Terrin replied, considering. "Many people wish to speak to the King at any time. My guards would likely turn him away long before he reached this tent, particularly if he was not forthcoming about who he was. What was his message?"

Brianne leaned against the table in the centre of the tent, crossing her arms over her chest. "He says Ordreg plans to betray you. That once Drevesine is defeated, he will turn his men on yours."

Terrin smirked. "Of course he will, I would expect no less. This is not some great revelation. Why would this Mikale risk himself, both at our hands and those of Ordreg, to bring this message?"

"He claims to be an ally to us," responded Brianne. "He asserts that his Order works against Ordreg. They wish to see him removed but lack the will or ability to get their hands dirty in the act. He claims the Cereb'Ani will be able to lead Stalius to a peaceful alliance with Pohartan after Ordreg falls."

Terrin paced the few steps across the tent in front of Brianne. "That is good news, of course." He continued to pace as he thought aloud. "I will share this news with Richmond and the others but I do not see how it changes anything for tomorrow. We will work with Stalius to bring down Drevesine and Zemiltar—your new friend made it sound as though that was still part of Ordreg's plan?" Brianne nodded. "Then we will turn our forces on Ordreg. This only confirms that is the correct course of action. With our six battalions—including the men under Lukas—Ordreg does not have a hope of overwhelming us. Unless, of course, we fall to Drevesine but then this is all moot.

"Thank you for bringing me this information, Brianne." His smile returned as he looked at her; her bright red-orange hair framing her face, her captivating emerald eyes shining with life.

"Of course," she said, rising from the table. She slowly walked towards the entrance of the tent, her hand moving to the flap. She looked back at Terrin, seeming almost reluctant to leave.

"Brianne..." Terrin started. He did not have a conclusion for the thought but did not want her to leave.

"Yes?" she replied, stepping away from the tent entrance, closing the distance between them.

He took her hand in his, staring impotently, mouth agape. He knew what he wanted: he wanted to take her in his arms, kiss her and throw her down on his cot. As the sun rose tomorrow morning, they would be riding into battle. She would be an integral part of that battle and as confidently as he spoke about defeating Drevesine, Zemiltar and Stalius, there was every possibility either of them would fall and not see another day.

He had been spellbound by her from the moment he first saw her in Morim, he admitted to himself. Though he was married to Amiela and respected her deeply, there was little love there, little physical passion. When he first met Brianne he had merely known her as beautiful. Over their months together he had learned there was so much more to her. She was fierce and infinitely clever. While she cared for her family, she was wildly independent.

These were the thoughts racing through his mind as she reached her hand up to grasp his head and pull it down to hers, pressing her lips to his. His body tensed in surprise for a brief moment but quickly relaxed, allowing him to lean into the kiss. He wrapped his arms around her waist as her tongue parted his lips, dancing in his mouth with his own.

Brianne slid her hand up his chest, pulling at the laces of his shirt. She stepped back and smiled at him, breaking the passion for a moment as she pulled at the straps of her bracers, throwing them to the ground as they came free. Terrin stepped forward to kiss her again, his hands blindly fumbling over her body to release the remaining straps of her armour.

They parted again, each pulling their own shirts over their heads, throwing them to the ground. Terrin bit his lip as he looked at Brianne's exposed body for a long moment, taking it in: her soft, pale skin, the gentle curves of her alert breasts.

Brianne pushed him backwards, causing him to fall onto the cot behind him. She laughed softly as she knelt over him, straddling his legs. She pulled his head towards her chest and he needed no encouragement to begin kissing her breasts. Her delighted laughter transformed into gentle moans.

The wind continued to flap and flutter the canvas of the tent as the two lovers carried on, abandoning their stresses from days past and fears of the days to come. To them, the outside world faded away, all that remained was the bliss and comfort of their bodies moving together. Outside the tent, as the sounds from the interior rose, guards nodded to each other, laughing knowingly.

* * *

The sun blazed down on the assembled soldiers, sparring in a cleared section of plain separated from the main camp. Grunts and shouts filled the air, accented by the clang of steel. Lines of soldiers stood facing each other, crashing together in a brief bout then parting ways again. Battle was coming and the commanders insisted the soldiers spend their day in a final effort to improve their skills.

Jahn wiped sweat from his brow, panting. Despite the heat, they had been forbidden from removing any of their heavy armour. The combination of exertion and heat from the sun was starting to blur Jahn's vision.

Omerin, his sparring partner, stood across from him. He too looked worn down from the effort, bent forward, resting his hands on his knees. The man was a fierce opponent; strong, experienced and willing to put his full effort into even a training session. Jahn had chosen Omerin to be his partner specifically for these qualities. Heeding Sergeant Morson's warnings about his own sword work, he recognized he needed to be pushed hard to improve. In the past weeks, he had received many bruises and a few scars from the other soldier but every day he fought on, his feet moving slightly faster, his blade blocking strikes slightly more frequently and reliably.

"Take a break. Get yourselves some water," Jahn called to the soldiers of his squad, seeing the same exhaustion in the faces around him. It would not do to have them completely worn out for the following day's battle. A quiet cheer rose from the soldiers as they stepped out of their places in line, making their way to the water barrels.

As he reached one of the barrels, Jahn dropped his helmet to the ground. Tempted to dunk his entire head in the water, he resisted the urge and instead splashed his face with cupped hands. The water was warm from sitting exposed to the sun but refreshing regardless. He lifted the large ladle hooked to the barrel's edge, drinking deeply.   As he looked up from the barrel, clearing his eyes of the water he had splashed over himself, he found Megen standing opposite him.

"Corporal," she nodded, extending her hand to take the ladle from him. He handed it to her and she drank greedily, spilling much of the water over her face and down her chin. Her dark hair was dishevelled from being crumpled under her helmet, with strands struck at odd angles across her forehead.

"How goes the training, Megen?" Jahn asked as he took the ladle back from her, retrieving for himself another, more civilized, scoop of water.

"Well, considering the conditions. Tumas is a strong opponent: we keep each other on our toes..." she trailed off. Her eyes darted around them. The other members of the squad were divided among other barrels in the grouping, speaking quietly among themselves. Megen lowered her voice, leaning in closer to Jahn. "I cannot help but wonder, however, why we bother."

"What do you mean?" Jahn asked, lowering his voice to match hers.

"I mean why are we even here? Why have we charged out into this damned field?"

"We follow the King," Jahn stated, confident it was a sufficient response.

Megen's voice dropped even quieter, such that Jahn had to lean closer to hear. "Have you not heard him called the Mad King? My last squad was always grumbling about him. The whole Company was, really. I am surprised you have not been, as you have been most forced into danger and lost so many already.

"Think about it, Jahn. Sure, maybe Drevesine had an army in Harten but they weren't doing anything, were they? The King just called up this army and charged in. Did he even try to speak to them first?" She looked around again. The other soldiers were engrossed in their own conversations, paying the two of them no attention. "And those villages he burned on the way here. What purpose did that serve, other than wild brutality?"

Jahn was flummoxed. The son of a soldier, he had been raised on the assumption that one should be loyal to their Kingdom and King. The way Megen spoke now was bordering on treason. His skin crawled with discomfort.

"Drevesine was threatening us, all of us," he offered. "Why did you join the military, if not to defend Pohartan?"

"Oh, I joined to defend Pohartan and my family." Megen's brown eyes were wide as she looked into Jahn's. "But is that what we are doing? We are destroying innocent villages in Drevesine and now chasing a foreign army across foreign territory. You tell me, how is that protecting my sisters? I am telling you..." she took a deep breath, taking a final glance about to ensure no one was paying them any mind. "... this King Terrin is mad. His rage is going to lead us into disaster."

Jahn was left alone, mind reeling, as Megen walked away. Since the King had taken the throne, Jahn had heard murmurings about him. Usually they were the babblings of men who had had too much drink and forgotten themselves, so he had ignored them. Jahn had only seen the King once, the day they left Morim. Such a brief experience gave him little opportunity to take measure of the man. Though Jahn knew Brianne was somewhere in the camp, working closely with the King.

Megen's words ran in cycles through his mind as he considered them. Were Mother and Ren any safer for the army being in the fields of Zemiltar? He had not questioned the purpose of burning the villages they passed through but uncertainty was beginning to creep into the furthest reaches of his mind. What if he had lived in one of those towns? How would he see the King and army then?

Afternoon faded into evening before the training soldiers finally broke ranks for their meal. Jahn had earned more bruises from Omerin than he should have, as his mind continued to become distracted with complex thoughts. Megen had so easily and thoroughly planted seeds of doubt deep into his mind. Throughout the evening she continued to cast him meaningful looks over the cookfire as the others laughed and joked together, distracting themselves from thoughts of the morning, sure to come too quickly.

CHAPTER 20

"Fuck," Richmond muttered under his breath. "Fuck!" he said again, shouting the curse for all to hear. Reports of this development had come in the last hours of the night but seeing it laid out before him was a different matter.

Behind him, the soldiers of the First Battalion stood in rank and file, their amber armour shining as the sun crept above the horizon. To either side of the standing soldiers, ranks of cavalrymen waited, their horses whinnying and stomping in anticipation. The entire Pohartan army was stretched out across the plain, standing in formation, awaiting the order to charge.

The scene which they faced, however, was not what had been expected even the day before. As expected, ranks of soldiers in green stood facing them, weapons at the ready. Basic defences—a wall of pikes anchored into the ground—had been prepared. Alongside the green-clad soldiers, hundreds of men in tanned leathers sat on horseback, whooping and hollering as the Pohartan soldiers came into view. But behind those first defensive ranks of soldiers was a flurry of activity.

The wide, glistening river was littered with large, flat barges. Above each flapped white triangular banners, a blue droplet of water visible on each: the banner of Vodana. Quickly running into place to support the waiting Drevesine soldiers were ranks of white and blue armoured soldiers. As they leapt from the barges, Drevesine soldiers would climb on to be ferried across the rushing waters.

"How in the hell did they get Vodana involved in this!?" Terrin, mounted beside Richmond, demanded of no one in particular.

"I do not know but they are getting them over the river."

"Well, we have to get down there and crush them before they can get enough across!" Terrin shouted. As he did so, he kicked Mi'drak forward. Horns were sounded in a rush, ordering the charge. Richmond spurred his own horse after Terrin, hearing the pounding of the soldier's feet behind him.

A yell of rage and determination rose from the army as they charged across the plain. It was supplemented by the pounding of hooves as the cavalry raced in from the sides of the formation, joining Terrin and Richmond in their rush to the enemy.

Ahead, the standing Drevesine soldiers braced themselves behind their pikes, waiting for the impact. Before the Pohartan mass could reach them, the Zemiltar horsemen charged out from behind the defences, meeting the enemy in the field and the battle was begun.

The men from Zemiltar moved like spirits among the comparatively sluggish Pohartan cavalrymen. It was said they had learned to ride before they learned to walk and they moved with their horses as if their minds were connected. Arrows flew from shortbows wielded by the shouting riders, as others brought down armoured riders with long hooked pikes. The downed soldiers were left to frantically swing blades at targets as they flew past, or be trampled in the melee.

Richmond felt a jolt of pain in his chest as an arrow ricocheted off his armour plating. Despite their superior training and experience in mounted combat, the Zemiltarans were used to facing off against other tribes, armoured as they were in leathers and fabrics. Only a direct hit from their bows would pierce the thick Pohartan armour.

Richmond raised his own bow, firing into the chaos. He lacked the speed and skill of the enemy but his targets were more vulnerable. He brought down two riders before the battle became so dense and chaotic that he could not safely take aim.

He returned his bow and instead took up his great axe, barely dodging the hook of a pike swung at him by a passing Zemiltaran. Quickly he turned Ursa, kicking him into a gallop after the man.

The enemy, too focused on finding new targets, did not see Richmond racing up behind him. With a grunt, Richmond swung his axe as he came alongside the man. Carried by the momentum of his swing and his racing horse, the axe ripped through the air in a low arc. It caught the man in the centre of his back, nearly cleaving him in half in a burst of blood as it dragged him from his horse to fall limply to the ground.

Richmond guided Ursa with his knees as they raced through the chaos to the next target. A screaming man swung a large pike in Richmond's direction. Richmond caught it in his free hand. With great effort and strain, he managed to remain in the saddle, while the man at the other end of the pike was forced from his by the unexpected resistance. As he fell, he released the weapon. Tumbling on the ground, he was crushed beneath the hooves of a Pohartan soldier's horse, who had been running behind him.

Richmond hefted his new weapon, dropping his axe back to his belt. As he rode past another enemy rider he caught the man about the neck, dragging him from his horse. The Fire General raced on through the pandemonium, not checking the fate of the fallen man.

It was difficult to make sense of the chaos but Richmond thought they were winning. The Zemiltarans had the speed and skill but the Pohartan soldiers were better protected and seemed to have the advantage of numbers.

Thunderous explosions shook the ground and Richmond looked up. The Firethrowers had been moved into position and were firing on the enemy force. However, instead of the orbs crashing into the soldiers on the ground, they were exploding mid-flight. Flaming debris rained down from the explosions, most falling harmlessly over empty ground.

"Fuck!" Richmond swore again, sparing a moment to look up at the spectacle. The Firethrowers were their most useful tool to diminish the enemy's numbers before the foot soldiers struck and he had no idea why the orbs were not striking their targets.

A second volley of orbs soared through the air. Again, most exploded impotently mid-flight but one or two managed to complete their flights, crashing devastatingly into the encamped Drevesine army. Richmond let out a short roar of approval before a rider rushed towards him, forcing his attention back to his immediate surroundings.

Instinct drove him as the rider closed the distance in a flash, a scythe-like blade bared and swinging. Richmond anchored the pike against his side and charged as if wielding a lance in a tournament. The longer pike gave him the advantage of reach as it dug itself into the enemy's chest. The force tore the weapon away from Richmond, as it drove the other rider off his horse.

There was no time to celebrate the victory, however, as an arrow abruptly cut the air in front of him. While it missed striking him, it hit Ursa in the neck with a sickening thud, burying itself deep in the animal's flesh. The horse screamed as it tripped over itself, crashing to the ground and throwing Richmond from the saddle. Coming out of the fall in a roll, Richmond sprang to his feet, bringing his axe to his hands once again.

Men and horses raced about him. Frantically he swung at man and beast alike while dodging and rolling from the weapons swinging down at him.

To his surprise, a rush of soldiers on foot surrounded him. The First Battalion had entered the fray. Richmond met eyes with General Saer, the ageing General armed and armoured among his men. They only nodded briefly before each turning to face the oncoming enemy.

The Zemiltar numbers were dwindling. While many Pohartan soldiers lay lifeless in the muddied field, so too lay the bodies of the leather-clad men. Most of those who had not yet fallen had at least been unhorsed and were now fighting in close hand-to-hand combat with the Pohartan soldiers.

Richmond spotted Terrin in the melee, his crowned helmet easily recognized. He was facing off, sword-in-hand, against two Zemiltar fighters, who had exchanged their long pikes for spears.

"To the King!" Richmond shouted, thrusting his axe in the direction of Terrin. The men around him took up the shout, following the Fire General in a rush, sweeping over any bewildered men in their path.

The man Richmond rushed did not have adequate opportunity to respond as the large Fire General leapt over the body of a felled horse, bringing his axe down on the man's head. The heavy weapon sliced through the man, separating his head and right shoulder and arm from the rest of his body.

Seizing the opportunity, Terrin turned his full attention to the other attacker. In a swift movement, he batted away a thrust of the spear with his bracer as he brought his sword up, forcing it through the man's chest.

"Thank you," Terrin said simply, grasping his friend's forearm for a moment. The fresh Pohartan soldiers had formed a pocket around the King and Fire General, as they dispatched the remaining unhorsed Zemiltaran cavalrymen.

"Of course," Richmond replied with a nod. Each had aided the other in battle countless times, there was little to be said about such matters.

"Thoughts on the Firethrowers?" Richmond asked. He was grateful for the moment of peace, knowing it would be fleeting. Fighting still raged around them. As if cued by his question, another volley of orbs crossed the sky, with similar results to the last: the majority seemed to strike an invisible barrier far above them, with only one hitting its mark this time.

"Has to be those damn witches from Vodana," Terrin spat, accentuating his frustration. Pohartan and Vodana did not have a relationship of note: either positive or negative. There was little contact or communication between them, so Richmond knew little of their culture. He had, however, heard stories of a society of witches, protected by their Queen.

"Now is our opportunity to charge," shouted General Saer, running to meet the two men. "The Zemiltarans are running back to the Drevesine lines. Those cowards did not leave their formation to assist their so-called allies, letting us crush them."

Richmond nodded. Looking around, the final few enemies trapped within the ranks of the amber-clad soldiers were being dispatched. Most of the Pohartan men were standing weapons drawn, awaiting the next order.

"Charge the lines!" Terrin shouted. A horn blared nearby to carry the order and the men turned to rush the lines of Drevesine. At the same time, another warning shout rose from among the crowd: "Archers!"

As Richmond and Terrin ran within the mass of Pohartan soldiers, a wave of arrows fell around them. The unlucky were struck down, their companions forced to jump and weave around them as they fell. Those fast enough raised shields over their heads and the clink of arrows striking them echoed like rain on a metal roof.

"Close the distance!" Richmond shouted but the men did not need the encouragement. They raced towards the enemy with a unified roar as another rain of arrows fell around them.

Then they were to the spikes. They had been dug into the ground, angled out. Intended to catch horses and break a cavalry charge, the Pohartan soldiers were largely able to dodge around them, though it slowed their progress enough to allow another volley of arrows. Some men were unfortunate, as they charged blindly under their raised shields, to find themselves suddenly impaled. Most, however, were able to weave around the defences, to find themselves crashing into the front line of waiting soldiers.

The Drevesine soldiers stood shoulder-to-shoulder, shields raised and spears and blades jutting through the gaps. It was not enough to stop the tidal wave of Pohartan soldiers.

Richmond swung his axe as he crashed his body against the shield in front of him, severing the head of the spear he had dodged around. The man behind the shield went down with a thud, as his companions were similarly pushed back by the onslaught.

Standing on the fallen shield—pinning the man under it—Richmond swung his axe into the mass of men before him, deftly blocking blows aimed at him. The soldier following behind Richmond through the created hole quickly thrust his sword through the opening in the helmet of the man pinned under the shield as the Fire General moved on.

Chaos reigned again, as Pohartan and Drevesine clashed. Richmond's vision was a blur as he moved from target to target. Each move was the result of years of training fueled by adrenaline as he blocked and countered weapons aimed in his direction. There was no opportunity for planning or consideration: a glint of steel from the corner of his eye and he brought up his axe to catch the falling blade, punching the soldier holding the hilt in the face with his gauntleted fist, causing him to drop to the ground.

The field had been churned to mud and the smell of blood filled Richmond's nostrils. Again, as he had so often before, he found himself back-to-back with Terrin, as they circled through the mass together briefly before individual targets drew them apart.

Too far away to react, Richmond was forced to watch General Saer fall. He was a skilled soldier but his age had been catching up to him. His movements were too slow for this form of combat, with multiple assailants coming from any direction. The General was caught blade-to-blade with a Drevesine soldier when a second soldier approached him from behind. The new attacker, who General Saer never knew was there, seized the opportunity to strike at the General's neck. Saer's blade fell from a limp hand as his body toppled to the ground.

Bodies cluttered the ground rapidly, their amber or green armour becoming nearly indistinguishable under the blood, viscera and mud which covered them.

Sweat dripped into Richmond's eyes as he stepped over an unidentifiable body. He blinked it away and roared as he charged further into the chaos: a deep, bestial sound which seemed to carry over the cries of other men and the clash of steel against steel.

* * *

Brianne could feel ripples of power in the air over the battle-field. She watched as orbs from the Firethrowers flew through the sky and felt a surge of power as they seemingly struck an invisible barrier and exploded.

Charging through the tall grasses beside Simone, Brianne was embracing her power, pulling in as much as she could. The flow was tantalizing, as if calling for her to pull more. As a wave of arrows launched into the air from the ranks of soldiers in front of them, she focused some of her energy. A streak of flame lit the sky, catching the falling arrows. Brianne felt another surge of power from somewhere among the enemy and her flames were hit by a wave of unseen force. She struggled to maintain the flames but was overwhelmed and they winked out. They had, however, achieved their purpose of incinerating the incoming projectiles.

Someone in the enemy camp was wielding a great amount of power—likely multiple people, based on the sheer strength of the power radiating from the army.

They raced towards the front lines. Simone's Fifth Battalion formed the eastern-most wing of the attacking army, tasked with charging along the line of the river, not allowing the enemy to squeeze out from the crushing force of the rest of the army.

However, they had been dismayed with the rest to see the new banners about the camp as they approached that morning. The soldiers in white armour they raced toward now stood out against the greens and yellows of the plain. Simone had relayed the reports of Vodana's arrival to Brianne as they had marched and the fates had apparently determined it would be them holding the far side of the enemy line, trying to hold back the Pohartan attack as their allies escaped across the river.

Brianne and Simone dodged nimbly through the wall of angled pikes. Focusing her energy, Brianne formed a wedge of flames, casting it before her into the enemy lines as a hoe digging a line in the ground for planting.

Men leapt to the side trying to avoid the flames but many were caught in their path. The flames caught their tunics and heated their plates of armour unnaturally quickly, causing them to run panicked into their comrades in a vain attempt to reach the river.

As soon as Brianne felt resistance strike and begin to suppress her flames, she released her focus from them, cursing. As she hit the charred ground where the front lines of the enemy had stood moments ago she drew her sword.

Still she hurled balls of flame in all directions. At almost the same instant she had a clear line of sight on a white-armoured figure, a small ball of flame streaked towards them. Some of those balls winked out of existence before striking their target. The more balls she threw, the more winked out and more quickly.

Frustrated, Brianne focused on using her sword. She retained hold of her power, as its flow through her sped her reactions and reflexes.

Never before had she used the weapon outside of her sparring matches with Simone and other soldiers of the Fifth. A small part of her rebelled against the notion: striking an enemy with a blade was not the same as using her power, it was more intimate, more personal. She suppressed this tiny protest, as it held no place in the sea of violence in which she found herself.

Breathing deeply, she approached an enemy soldier, prepared to strike. Before she had the opportunity, however, Sergeant Bradford raced past her, bearing down on the man and pushing him to the ground. A short scuffle ensued but it was the Sergeant who rose.

Brianne turned quickly to the next nearest enemy but again a member of the Phoenix Guard reached them before she could. They were forming a ring around her, protecting her.

Feeling both frustrated and thankful, Brianne sighed. Again she turned to her powers, hurling balls of flame over the shoulders of her defenders, into the masses of men surrounding them. As quickly as she began throwing flames, they were again being suppressed: someone was actively working against her.

Brianne changed her strategy. Rather than hurling the balls of flame from herself into the enemy, she merely manifested them around her target. It was a more difficult task for her but seemed to be more effective for a short while, as her invisible opponent was slower to counter them.

A new thought struck Brianne. As she continued her attacks—already more failing than succeeding—she focused on the power which came to match hers. Straining with the mental effort, she felt for it as it engulfed and extinguished her flames. With the next strike, she thought she could get a sense of the direction from which the power came.

"This way!" Brianne shouted and the ring of soldiers with her at its centre carved a path through the enemy.

They moved slowly, as the battle was thick around them. Inevitably, the circle began to shrink, as soldiers in the Guard fell and the others closed in the gaps left in their absence. Private Veritan was the first she saw fall, as a Vodani soldier stuck a spear in a gap in his armour as he raised his sword to strike. Brianne wanted to pause, wanted to mourn. The demands of battle would not allow it, however, and instead, she thrust a ball of flame into the face of the enemy soldier.

As they progressed Brianne blindly created bursts of flame in front of them, among the press of Vodani soldiers. As before, more were suppressed than succeeded but with each attempt Brianne studied the patterns of the power working against her, refining her direction.

The ring of soldiers opened briefly as Simone stumbled through. Her helmet was gone, her hair clinging to a bloodied gash on her forehead. But she was standing, still, alert.

"Simone!" Brianne screamed. "Are you all right?"

Simone took a moment to catch her breath. "It is only a scratch." She waved away Brianne's worried look. "Where are we going?"

"Someone is fighting my flames and presumably the Fire-throwers," Brianne gestured ahead. As she did, Corporal Canbur fell, shrinking the circle another degree. Now there was barely room for the two women to walk among them. "I intend to find them."

Simone nodded. Having had a brief moment to catch her breath, she pushed into the circle beside Sergeant Bradford. She shouted orders for those who could hear them to join the push. Few did, as most were occupied in heated individual duels.

And on they pushed through the field. It felt as if hours passed with Brianne conjuring pockets of flame, locked in a contest of wills with an unseen opponent. Their group progressed on, as all around them white armour clashed with amber.

Eventually, Brianne was forced to use her own sword, the small reluctant voice quieted by the carnage and desperation. Her first victim had broken through to her by cutting down Private Leitier. He had not had time to gain his footing from his victory, however, before Brianne's blade came down on him. She jumped from foot to foot quickly, like a dancing flame, as she sidestepped his clumsy rush and brought him down.

They were down to three when they broke free from the main body of the fighting. Sergeant Bradford, Simone and Brianne almost stumbled at the sudden change, as the soldiers around them were focused on their own conflicts.

Before them, two women stood on a wagon bed. They wore matching white shirts and light blue, billowing skirts. One woman wore her grey hair pulled back in a tight bun, while the other had her long auburn hair braided, lying forward over her shoulder. The focused, determined expressions on the women's blue eyes mirrored each other as they stared down at Brianne.

A group of five Vodani soldiers rushed forward from the wagon to meet the new threat.

Brianne poured every ounce of her will towards the women. Straining, she tried to engulf them in raging flames. The women did not move, nor even seem to flinch but their eyes did not leave Brianne, as they grit their teeth in visible effort.

Screaming, Brianne pushed her will. It felt as though she was pushing against a stone wall and losing. The harder she tried, the larger the wall seemed to become, closing in on her.

"Do not lose focus, Kel!" she heard the older woman shout.

Brianne fell to one knee, the force exerted by the two women pressing down on her.

Between the duelling women, Sergeant Bradford took a sword to his leg, causing him to stumble. Swiftly he raised his sword to block a killing blow aimed at him but he was being overwhelmed quickly. Simone, beside him, was struggling to hold back two of the other soldiers. Though determined, she had been badly wounded and was becoming weak from the lost blood.

Brianne saw a new group of soldiers charge towards them from the camp beyond the wagon, where the soldiers who had been waiting to cross the river were now turning to face the threat at their backs.

Sergeant Bradford saw them as well. "Run, my Lady!" he shouted back at her. His words were cut short as the point of a sword emerged from his neck.

Simone took up his message. "Brianne! Go!" she screamed.

Brianne stared for a moment of indecision. Her power was useless with the women on the wagon focusing their own on her. The soldiers who had brought down Sergeant Bradford began towards her, grinning, with more approaching from behind them. The last thing Brianne saw before turning and fleeing into the horde of screaming, fighting men, was a Vodani soldier slash Simone's arm, causing her to drop her sword.

Tears began to flow as Brianne darted through the chaotic scene. She paid only enough mind to what was going on around her to avoid crashing into clashing soldiers or tripping over fallen ones.

She barely noticed when the crush of soldiers gave way to open plain. Her feet pounded under her, carrying her away.

CHAPTER 21

Blood trickled into Jahn's eye, threatening to distract him from the battle which raged around him. Early on he had been caught by debris, causing his helmet to cut into his brow. It was a minor injury but the trickle of blood was proving to be a major annoyance.

He found his thoughts wandering back to the Battle of Harten in the brief lulls between clashes. He had been so young, so innocent. He had killed one soldier by luck and spent the rest of the battle unconscious. Barely months had passed since that battle but it felt more like years. He had been a different person then; the training and raids in the time between had re-forged him, as the steel from a damaged blade could be salvaged and reshaped into a new weapon.

Feeling confident, he flowed from duel to duel. He was by no means a blade master but nor was he incompetent. Each opponent he faced fell to his sword after a brief match. His blade was dyed crimson with blood, which dripped over his fist and down the hilt, droplets falling to the ground from the pommel.

His squad moved with him. They worked well as a team, where most others seemed to have fractured in the chaos. By remaining close and coordinating their movements, they were able to defend each other and break up any concentrated efforts from the enemy rather than being overrun alone.

Only Amad was not directly with them, though he was close by. Using his speed and small size to his advantage, he continued the tactic he so loved of racing among the enemy, making quick strikes when possible but not allowing himself to be drawn into direct combat.

Omerin leapt forward, slicing at a Drevesine soldier who had been pushed back towards him by another Pohartan soldier. The Drevesine man was skewered between the two, as Omerin's sword slashed at his neck and the other man's pike thrust into his side.

As another soldier approached Jahn aggressively, Amad dashed out of the melee behind him. A quick slash at the back of the soldier's vulnerable knee and he was stumbling forward. Jahn brought his sword up into the space in the man's helmet with a grunt, knocking the helmet off as the blade emerged from the back of the man's head. Blood and brain matter spewed onto the muddied ground as Jahn withdrew his blade.

Behind Jahn, Megen let out a loud grunt as she was knocked to the ground by a large Drevesine soldier, dropping her sword. The enemy soldier raised his sword in two hands, preparing to plunge it into the downed woman. Before Jahn had the opportunity to react and help his friend, Megen had a knife in her hand and stabbed it into the man's thigh. She squirmed to the side, barely missing the man's incoming blade. Kicking him off of her, she wrenched the knife from his thigh, quickly digging it into his neck. With a flourish she sheathed the knife, collecting her own sword in one hand and the fallen enemy's in another.

A chorus of screams and horns rose over the already deafening roar of battle somewhere to Jahn's left, causing him to turn his attention. Their battalion had been placed on the far western edge of the Pohartan line, his own squad near the distance edge. The commotion could only mean the force from Stalius had entered the fight to support them, as Jahn had seen them charging in behind them across the fields.

Another attack brought his attention back to his surroundings, as he brought his arm up, catching the neck of a man who had been charging at Omerin's turned back. The soldier was pulled off his feet by the sudden obstruction, landing heavily on his back. Jahn kicked the fallen soldier severely in the helmet, raising his sword to strike. The man had gone still on the ground, so Jahn turned to face the next threat.

The swallowing horde of green-clad soldiers broke away in front of Jahn and his squad. Ahead, charging in their direction, a knot of leather-clad riders screamed, weapons raised.

Having only an instant to react, Jahn dropped to his knees, raising his sword as the lead horse leapt over him. The sword caught the horse in the chest, ripping the blade from Jahn's hand but causing the beast to fall and throw his rider.

The rider hit the ground gracefully, scythe-like blade drawn. He was a large, muscled, bare-chested man. His long black hair was tied back with a thin leather band around his head. Complex patterns of tattoos covered his chest and arms, most prominent among them the image of a strange, reptilian beast with large spread wings.

Tumas, who had narrowly avoided being skewered by one of the charging riders, rushed to the man with sword raised. The man moved smoothly, quickly. Tumas' first slash was deflected easily by the Zemiltaran's blade, then his second. With his free hand, the man caught Tumas' arm as he attempted to strike again. The scythe came down quickly, seemingly effortlessly severing Tumas' arm at the elbow. Tumas fell to his knees, a scream of pain ripping through the air. The man's blade whipped through the air with a sharp whistle as it smoothly sliced through Tumas' neck, silencing the scream as his head rolled to the ground.

Jahn picked up a discarded sword from the ground and screamed as he rushed the man wildly. His clumsy attack was easily pushed aside as he rushed past. Regaining his composure, Jahn faced the man, sword raised. Anger and vengeance pushed him, fighting with rationality. Tumas had been a far superior swordsman to Jahn, yet had been swiftly and easily downed by this opponent.

The man laughed as Jahn swung at him again. Jahn's blade was deftly knocked to the side as he was pushed away. Again Jahn turned to face the man, who beckoned him forward confidently, mockingly. So focused was he on Jahn, however, he paid no mind to those behind him.

Jahn rushed the man again. As he did, Amad raced in from behind him, slashing wildly at the man's weapon arm. The small soldier's blade dug hungrily into the flesh of the man's upper arm. At the same moment, Megen emerged from his side, her sword before her, digging into the man's abdomen. The man fell to one knee.

Frantically trying to fight through the pain, he grabbed his weapon with his other arm, reaching up to slash at his attackers. It was at that moment Jahn was upon him. With a scream of rage Jahn thrust his sword through the man's chest, severing the head of the beast tattooed there. Jahn withdrew his blade and stabbed again and a third time. Life had left the man before Jahn withdrew his blade from the third strike and the body fell limply to the ground.

More shouts rose near them and through the dust of battle, massive white shapes emerged, leaping through the air and falling on unsuspecting soldiers. The beasts growled and snarled as their jaws cut into their prey. Men of all nations fell to the beasts, the colour and style of their armour seemingly irrelevant.

A knot of men strode confidently through the chaos alongside the monsters. As they approached, their shouted commands cut through the din of battle and cries of fallen men.

"Drop your weapons and kneel! You will be spared!" a man in Pohartan armour with a black band around his arm shouted. Beside him a man in black-striped blue armour whistled, sending the beasts into another wave of violent attacks. The men were accompanied by a group of soldiers, some wearing the reds and oranges of Pohartan with the addition of a black armband, others in the blues and blacks of Stalius.

Beside Jahn, Megen immediately let her sword fall to the ground and dropped to her knee. The two men approached them, locking eyes with the remnants of their little party.

"I am Lukas Arhan. Your King has betrayed you and Pohartan. This is your opportunity to defend your home and end his tyranny."

A scream rose behind Jahn, as a Pohartan soldier rushed past, sword drawn. He barely made it a dozen paces towards Arhan and the Staliusian soldier before he was brought down by one of the massive tigers. The beast leapt at him from the side, the impact sending man and beast flying sideways. As the pair hit the ground, the beast's jaws were already closing on the soldier's head. The metal of the helmet caved in under the force as if it had been made of parchment, the man's scream cut short as the tiger's claws ripped at the vulnerable areas.

Amad fell to his knee beside Jahn, his sword thrown to the ground in front of him.

"Traitors!" Jahn heard Omerin shout. He turned to see the bald man raising his sword, intending to strike the kneeling Megen. Jahn spun, bringing up his sword to deflect the man's strike.

"Fucking scum!" Omerin spat as he rushed Jahn.

Jahn stepped to the side, barely moving his sword in time to block Omerin's attack. Before the man could prepare himself for another attempt, Jahn's blade was slicing the air. It struck Omerin's arm heavily, clanging against the armour and bouncing away. Omerin approached Jahn again and their swords locked together. For a long moment they strained, eyes locked, noses almost touching, pushing against each other in an effort to overpower their foe.

Suddenly, Jahn fell back, skipping to the side. With nothing to push against, Omerin fell forward. As he passed by, Jahn brought the pommel of his sword down into Omerin's back, pushing the man to the ground. Before he had the opportunity to rise, Jahn brought his knee down into the middle of the fallen man's back. Raising his sword over his head, he brought it down with a yell. The steel tip slipped in the gap between Omerin's helmet and armour, cutting through the flesh and bone of the man's neck before burying itself in the soft ground.

Jahn rose and stepped forward. For a long moment he stared at the Pohartan officer, Arhan. Jahn, of course, knew of him by reputation. The General of the Sixth Battalion offered him only a raised eyebrow in response. Jahn offered the Staliusian commander only a passing look as his gaze moved to the area around him. Tumas' body lay nearby, his head several paces away, fallen in such a way as to be looking towards Jahn.

Finally, Jahn looked down to what remained of the squad he had grown so close to. Amad looked up at him pleadingly, eyes anxious. Megen stared forward, looking at nothing and no one in particular. His sword already discarded—standing upright through the neck of the man who had turned on his squad—Jahn knelt.

*   *   *

Terrin screamed in fury, his sword slicing through the flesh and bone of the man before him. Richmond fought similarly beside him, axe head bloodied. The pair was again fighting back-to-back, carving a line of carnage through the enemy.

It was difficult to determine how the battle was going. Their knowledge was limited to the immediate area around them, which seemed an endless sea of green armour, at rare moments broken by a band of soldiers clad in white or tans. All fell the same before the blades of the King and Fire General.

Their progress forward had slowed, however. Where once they were surrounded by Pohartan allies pushing forward into the enemy, ever so slowly those friendly soldiers dwindled. They had pushed through the waiting lines of Drevesine soldiers, feeling victorious as they faced the backs of the soldiers attempting to flee over the river. However, those soldiers had turned to face the threat and seemed to number greater than expected.

Two Drevesine soldiers approached Terrin, one with sword drawn, the other hoisting a shield and mace the length of his forearm. Terrin glanced about for assistance. His nearby allies were already engaged in combat, including Richmond, who was facing off against a nimble foe who was keeping him out of arms' reach with a spear.

Terrin stooped to pick up a Drevesine sword from a fallen body and engaged the soldiers, attempting to deny them the opportunity to work together and control the clash. His arm shook as one blade caught the swinging mace. The weapon was heavy, swung by a strong arm; its head sporting large, crushing barbs. As he pushed back with that arm, he brought up his other blade to deflect an attack from the other soldier.

The soldiers took a half-step backwards to gather themselves and struck again. Again, Terrin deflected the strike of the swordsman, causing him to lose balance for a moment. However, as he brought his Pohartan sword up to meet the falling mace, the heavy weapon shattered the blade, jarring his arm. He dropped the hilt and blade stub, turning his focus to the other soldier.

In a few quick movements, he slashed at the man's elbow, causing him to howl in pain and drop his sword. Terrin continued his swing to strike his opponents leg, dropping him to his knees. Before he could finish the attack, pain exploded in his side. The mace had struck him in the side, denting his plate armour and, Terrin was certain, breaking a rib or two.

Terrin turned to face the grinning mace-wielder. He rushed the man with a flurry of strikes, gritting his teeth through the pain in his side. The man brought his shield up, deflecting the blows but being pushed back several paces by their intensity. In the moment it took Terrin to take a breath before launching another onslaught, the man swung his mace at the King's legs. With a quick hop, Terrin missed the brunt of the strike, which likely would have shattered his bones. The weapon did graze his leg, however, causing him to stumble and fall to one knee.

The attacking soldier stomped heavily on Terrin's sword, pinning the blade to the ground. As Terrin looked up he was reeling his arm back, preparing to bring the mace down on the King's head.

Terrin released the sword and rolled backwards. At the same moment, a massive war axe swung in, catching the falling mace in mid-air. Richmond stepped into the man, bringing his elbow hard into the soldier's head. The Drevesine soldier stumbled back, disoriented. With a growl, Richmond spun, using his entire body to add power to his swing. His axe whipped through the air, catching the man in the neck, severing his head from his shoulders.

Richmond reached down, offering his hand to Terrin, who grasped it and pulled himself to his feet.

"Thank you," Terrin said sincerely, nodding to his friend.

"Anytime," Richmond responded.

Terrin searched the ground. Spotting a fallen Pohartan soldier, he pushed the body aside with his foot. He reached down and pulled free the half-buried sword underneath. With a slight nod to Richmond, the two leapt back into the fray.

Terrin did not see the blow which took down Richmond. One moment his friend was fighting by his side; the next, he was gone. The King spun frantically, searching the area. There was a sea of bodies and fighting men around him. In the panic and chaos of battle, he had lost his direction. He did not know from which way he had come, in which direction he might find Richmond.

"Richmond!?" Terrin shouted into the calamity. He was rushed by a screaming soldier in green, who he swept aside easily, landing a fatal slash as he did. "Richmond!?" he shouted again. They had been through many battles and not always side-by-side; sense told him Richmond was well, fighting not far away. But sense was not always observed and a wave of dread washed over him.

Breaking through the melee came a band of Pohartan soldiers and Terrin felt a moment of relief as they surrounded him, offering him a brief respite. He did not know how long they had been fighting but he knew he was reaching his limits. His arms ached from swinging his sword, his chest heaved with heavy breaths, each one causing a shot of pain from his ribs. The adrenaline rush which accompanied battle was waning.

The rest was short-lived, however, as Terrin noted the black arm-bands worn by the soldiers. As they encircled him, they faced inward rather than out, ignoring the battle around them and being ignored by it in turn.

Two of the soldiers parted, allowing Lukas Arhan and a man Terrin recognized as Colonel Tronbul to enter the circle. They were accompanied by one of the great white tigers, which prowled calmly at Tronbul's side.

"Thank the Gods," Terrin breathed. "It is about time you men arrived. I think we just about have them." He extended his hand to General Arhan.

The General ignored the King's outstretched hand. "Terrin Dramen, I place you under arrest."

Terrin stood a moment, mouth agape. His mind raced, trying to piece together the events which had led to this moment. "Soldiers! Defend your King!" he shouted incredulously at the ring of soldiers around him. To his dismay, they stood motionless, simply staring at him.

"I am your King!" Panic began to grow in Terrin, creeping into his voice. "I command you, kill these traitors!" He thrust a shaking finger at Lukas and the Colonel. Again, none in the ring moved to heed his command. A smirk crossed Colonel Tronbul's face as he stood, stroking the tiger behind its ears.

A soldier from outside the ring did, however, answer the call. With a yell, he ran towards Lukas, sword drawn. Two of the men with armbands turned to meet him. The scuffle lasted only moments and the attacking soldier fell.

Over the shoulders of the men surrounding him, Terrin could see more soldiers turning their attention in their direction. While some Pohartan soldiers still clashed with those from Drevesine, Terrin noted that those wearing the black armbands stood side-by-side with the green-clad men who should be their enemy.

As seconds passed, quiet began to fall over the area. Even loyal Pohartans and their Drevesine opponents began to lower their weapons: none were eager to continue to fight and die. They could recognize something momentous was taking place before them and were happy to wait to see its outcome.

"These men have betrayed your King! They have betrayed Pohartan!" Terrin shouted, desperately. "Kill them!"

A brief roar rose as a few soldiers raised their swords against their countrymen, obeying the call of their King. Far too few, Terrin noticed. Those who rose up were quickly and brutally killed, either by Drevesine soldiers near them or by the soldiers accompanying Lukas. Too many simply stood motionless.

"I will do it my fucking self!" Terrin muttered, raising his sword and running at Lukas. He moved barely two paces before the massive tiger was upon him. Terrin attempted to get his sword into place to skewer the beast but the creature moved with unmatched speed. Hardly aware of how it had happened, Terrin was on his back on the ground.

He had lost his grip on his sword as he fell and the weapon had bounced out of his reach as the tiger stood over him. Its weight pushed down on him, pinning him, as it gnashed its teeth inches from the King's face, droplets of spittle falling.

"Good boy," Colonel Tronbul patted the snarling beast as he stepped up beside the fallen King. Terrin let out a groan of pain as the Colonel stomped his heavy boot down on his hand. Sickening cracks could be heard as he twisted his heel, breaking and grinding the bones of Terrin's sword hand.

Lukas stepped into Terrin's peripheral vision on the other side but was not looking at the King as he addressed the crowd.

"This privileged wretch has betrayed you all!" he shouted. "He nearly led you to ruin here on this field! You are here because of his childish temper! Your friends and comrades have died as he dragged you through Drevesine! And for what cause? Drevesine never threatened you!" Lukas stepped out of Terrin's view, pacing as he delivered his speech.

"Dramen lied to all of you! There was no alliance between Zemiltar and Drevesine until you crossed into these fields! The Zemiltarans who entered Harten were refugees! Innocents who disagreed with Matrel's rule and sought refuge!"

"Lies!" Terrin tried to shout. Colonel Tronbul kicked him in the face and Terrin winced as he felt his jaw crack. His vision began to blur.

Lukas stood over Terrin, looking down at him but still shouting to the crowd. "I, Lukas Arhan, General of the Sixth Battalion, hereby arrest you, Terrin Dramen, on the charge of treason against the Kingdom of Pohartan!"

A cheer rose from the soldiers immediately surrounding them, the men of the Sixth who served under Lukas. Slowly the cheer was picked up by others, spreading over the field of battle in a wave.

The General knelt beside Terrin's head, lowering his voice. "Now, where is my son?" he asked.

Terrin attempted to spit in the traitorous General's arrogant face. However, his mouth felt numb from Tronbul's kick and all he could manage was to spit blood over his own face.

"Take him," Lukas commanded two of the nearby soldiers. As they stepped forward and bent to grab his arms, a sharp word from Tronbul recalled the tiger, who stepped off Terrin and happily trotted back to its master. Terrin took the opportunity to twist, trying to free himself. His futile struggling was cut short, as one of the soldiers clutched his shattered hand, twisting his arm painfully behind his back.

The pain was too much for Terrin to bear and he felt a part of his will break somewhere deep in his mind. The soldiers stood him up but his legs were weak and he leaned on them heavily. His crowned helmet fell from his head, landing in the mud before him with a dull thud.

"He will be returned to Morim," Lukas was again shouting to the surrounding soldiers. "There he will stand trial for his crimes. It is time Pohartan was freed from the tyrannical reign of House Dramen and returned to its people! Let the Great Phoenix guide us all into a brighter future!" A chorus of cheers rippled through the field. Lukas bent and picked up the fallen helmet. For the briefest moment, he stared at the muddied symbol of power. Terrin thought the General might put it on his own head. Perhaps he was considering it but after a moment he merely tucked the helmet under his arm.

"The battle is over, this wasteful war is over." Lukas waited for another chorus of cheers to subside. "Return now to your commanding officers. Though some of you came to this field as enemies, you leave now as allies."

Lukas turned to Colonel Tronbul, speaking to him as the crowd continued to cheer. Pohartan and Drevesine soldiers who had minutes ago been fighting each other for their lives were now clasping arms in peace. Though disheartened by the apparently drastic and sudden change in their loyalty, Terrin had learned long ago that the majority of soldiers were welcoming of a reason to lay down their weapons and be able to claim some form of victory.

"Let us get him to Ordreg," Lukas said to the soldiers, ushering them out of the crowd. "He has been looking forward to this for a long time."

PART III
THE ASH

CHAPTER 22

"Hey, that one have anything good?" The voice was distant, muffled as if heard under water.

"They all have the same shit, you idiot," came the reply, sounding slightly closer, clearer.

"You never know! But it will be your loss if you miss something. More for me." There was a loud thud as if something heavy were being shifted nearby.

"They are soldiers. What do you expect them to have?"

Richmond's eyes opened sluggishly, as one of the voices neared him, shoving at his shoulder. A low groan escaped his lips.

"Hey, this one's still alive!" the voice shouted to its companion. Richmond felt the slight tremble in the ground as the other voice ran over.

"He's a big one. Let's get him up," the new arrival said. The two bent, hooking Richmond under his arms, lifting him out of the mud.

"Be careful, you idiot," one chastised the other. A jolt of pain shot through Richmond as he was jostled. His body ached, he could feel fractured and broken bones. The worst pain was radiating from his head.

"Gods be damned..." the first voice said. The pain in Richmond's head throbbed as his helmet was pulled off. The men had brought him to his feet and he swayed as the pain ran through him, leaning heavily on the other man. "I think this is their Fire General, Arhan."

Richmond struggled to blink the blur from his vision. Slowly the smear of colours in front of him began to gain crisp edges. He rolled his head to the side, eyeing the man who held his helmet and was staring at him. It was a young man dressed in Drevesine green, wearing the light armour of an archer.

"Arhan's the older one, isn't he? The one who came in with Stalius and took Dramen." The man on whom Richmond leaned looked him over, skeptical of the other's assertion.

Took Dramen? Richmond's thoughts were still foggy, slowly clearing. *What the hell does he mean by that?*

"No, you idiot. That was Lukas Arhan. I saw him when he came to camp to meet with General Navillus. This is his son, Richard, I think. Look at that badge." The man flicked the badge of rank on Richmond's chest.

"Rich…" Richmond struggled to speak. He spat a mouthful of blood, clearing his throat and trying again. "Richmond."

"The giant speaks!" the man supporting him cheered.

Richmond leaned away from the man, looking him over, struggling to maintain his balance on his own legs. He was dressed the same as his companion; as a Drevesine soldier in light armour. Scanning the area around him, Richmond found himself in the midst of the aftermath of a battlefield. All around him, bodies lay scattered. In pockets throughout the field, groups of living figures moved among the dead, collecting bodies and dragging them to waiting carts.

"What happened?" he managed. He was struggling to put the pieces together in his mind. Had the soldier mentioned his father meeting with the Drevesine General? The Drevesine soldiers clearing the field did not bode well but he saw people dressed in Pohartan colours working alongside them.

"You must have taken quite a hit." The soldier facing him crossed his arms for a moment, before dropping his hand to the hilt of a long knife on his belt. Richmond noticed the sudden change in tone. "Dramen was defeated," the hand tightened around the hilt of the knife. Richmond noticed the other soldier's change as he mimicked the pose of his companion. Tangible tension settled over them. "General Arhan marched in, turned his army on him and arrested the King."

Richmond wanted to react. His instinct was to draw his axe but he suppressed the urge: not least because he realized he did not feel its weight on his hip. He was far from fighting condition, struggling to stand on his own legs. The news shook him, as he struggled to make sense of it. He forced himself to focus. He was at a significant disadvantage and would need to choose his words and actions carefully.

"Good," he managed. The men seemed to relax, so Richmond assumed he had found the correct course and continued. "It was time for Dramen's reign to end." The words tasted so sour in his mouth, he felt his face must have visibly cringed. "I look forward to seeing my father again." Carefully worded truths were easier to stomach, he found.

"Well then, sir." The soldiers released their grip on their knives. "Why don't we get you something to eat. I am sure Major Kanneth would love the opportunity to speak with you." He gestured off behind Richmond.

Richmond nodded, his head still foggy and uncertain. He turned the direction the man had indicated and started walking. Stumbling, he nearly fell flat. The soldiers appeared quickly at his sides, steadying him. Richmond looked down, seeking out what had caused him to lose his footing.

The guilty object was the arm of a fallen soldier, separated from its apparent owner by a good four paces. Nearby, Richmond spotted his axe. He did not remember the later moments of the battle, uncertain whether his fallen weapon was responsible for the detached arm, nor whatever had happened to knock him down. As he bent and rose, retrieving his weapon, his vision went black for a moment. He shook his head in an effort to clear his thoughts, regretting it immediately as pain shot down his spine. The soldiers tightened their grip on his arms, guiding him towards their camp.

* * *

Richmond woke with a start. He sprang to his feet, mind racing, struggling to remember where he was. His body ached in revolt against the sudden movement.

Looking around, he found himself in a small tent, his head grazing the top of the canvas. Light outside suggested it was midday but he did not know how long he had been there. His armour—dented, scratched and muddied—lay propped against a tent pole with his axe. Beside it sat an emptied metal camp plate and pitcher.

He sat back on the cot he had been sleeping on, grasping his head in one hand. As he attempted to bring his left hand up, he found it restrained: strapped to his chest in a sling.

A dull ache radiated from his head. Gingerly, he reached his free hand back, testing his scalp. He found a large lump under his matted hair, sensitive to the touch. However, he was relieved to see his fingers come back free of blood.

Standing, more carefully this time, Richmond looked over his pile of belongings. Memories of waking after the battle came back to him: the conversations with the young men who came across him in the field. He supposed he must be in the Drevesine camp, brought to this tent to recover. The presence of his axe, however, suggested he was not a prisoner. He stooped to pick up the weapon, groaning. With great effort and complicated maneuvering, he single-handedly strapped the weapon around his waist.

For a moment he considered the rest of his armour. The breastplate and bracers were heavily damaged and would be near impossible to put on in his condition without assistance. The Pohartan flame on the tunic stared back at him but he left it where it lay: there was much going on he still struggled to understand but the beginnings of plans for his next steps were coming together and he was not certain such an obvious symbol would be beneficial.

So he stepped from the tent, bandaged arm over his chest and axe at his hip, dressed simply in non-descript shirt and trousers. He raised his good hand to his brow, blinking quickly in an effort to adjust his eyes to the bright sunlight.

"Send word to Major Kanneth that Fire General Arhan has risen!" a soldier shouted to his subordinate the moment Richmond emerged from the tent. A young man took off in the direction the tent was facing at a jog. Richmond could see the peaks of larger tents poking above the smaller, banners of Drevesine flapping above them.

Meeting with this Major Kanneth was not an appealing prospect to Richmond. The man could certainly provide him quick answers but Richmond doubted his own ability to maintain the ruse of loyalty to his father over Terrin. The reminder brought about by the thought shook him for a moment, as a part of his mind desperately tried to deny the evident reality that his father had turned traitor and captured Terrin.

Rather than wait for the Major to come to him, Richmond turned on his heel and started to walk in the opposite direction.

"Sir!" a soldier shouted, trying to stop him. "The Major will be here in a moment, if you will but wait here."

Richmond did not stop. "Are there any Pohartan soldiers nearby?" he asked a soldier as he passed. The soldier who had just spoken turned and ran after the original messenger, seeing that Richmond had no intention of waiting.

"Yes sir," the Drevesine soldier replied. "General Arhan left a small group to assist with the cleanup, like us. Your men are a short distance that way," he gestured off in the direction Richmond was already heading.

Mumbling thanks, Richmond continued on at a measured pace. As soon as he broke line of sight with the men who had been waiting outside his tent, he increased his gait. His injuries limited his speed, as his right leg dragged reluctantly at each step. He also did not want to raise any more suspicion than the unavoidable by running, so he hobbled along, focused on reaching the quasi-friendly Pohartan soldiers.

The Drevesine camp was not large—presumably, the majority of the force had been sent home—and he reached its edge quickly. He barely noticed the change as he moved from Drevesine to Pohartan tents, their lines separated by little more than a couple paces. The few Pohartan soldiers in the camp rose quickly as he passed, offering salutes. Richmond could see the surprise on their faces. Their weak ties to loyalty sickened him but he forced himself to put a neutral expression on his face.

Behind him, a commotion was beginning to rise in the Drevesine camp. Obviously, the Major was not pleased that he chose to leave.

He stopped at the first ranking officer he found, a Sergeant who stood quickly to greet him. Before Richmond could ask his question, he spotted the answer he sought: lines of horses off to the right.

Speaking quickly, he stood with his back straight, mustering all the air of command he could in his weakened state. His tone conveyed that he was not interested in questions of debate. "Sergeant, ready me a horse. I need to catch up to General Arhan."

The soldier saluted in response, turning and walking towards the horses.

"It is good to see you, sir," the young soldier said as they walked. Richmond wished he would move faster but dared not give the man reason to be suspicious. "We had heard you had not been seen since the battle. Rumours said you had attempted to defend the King and fallen to General Arhan."

"I was wounded, yes." Richmond was only half listening, his head swivelling. The activity was growing in the Drevesine camp as they searched for him. It would not be difficult for them to determine where he went and to reach him. "I missed the end of the battle and the fall of the King."

The soldier whistled and signalled to another as they approached the lines of horses. The young man disappeared between the beasts for a moment, then re-emerged leading a large, saddled, chestnut charger.

"You may take my horse, sir. Are you sure you would not like to speak with Captain Oiterna before you leave?" Richmond recognized the name—he was a Captain of his father's battalion. It was a safe assumption the man would be loyal to his father over the King.

Richmond shook his head. "I am in a great hurry, I am afraid. I have lost too much time already." Hoisting himself up with his good arm, he mounted the horse.

Without another word, he spurred the horse forward. The beast was well trained for cavalry riding and ripped over the plains like an arrow loosed from a bow. Galloping across the battlefield, surprising the soldiers and workers toiling at their gruesome work, he carved a path south. He did not yet have a fully fleshed out plan, only the barest skeleton of one beginning to form: the spine of which dictating he needed to help his friend, if he was even still alive.

* * *

Brianne rubbed her eyes with her palms. They were red and aching, made raw from the tears. The slight soreness of her eyes was but a tiny trickle alongside the roaring rapids of her shame. The scene played out in front of her, over and over. She had been so sure of herself, so arrogant. To show for it, the men of her Phoenix Guard had lost their lives for her. Simone had breathed her last breath defending her. And she had not even had the decency to stay and die with them.

She chastised herself for how little she knew about the world and how large her ego had grown in spite of that. She had thought herself invincible. The notion that there were others out there with powers anywhere near hers—powers that could render hers irrelevant—had never even crossed her mind.

At the moment she locked eyes with Simone on the battlefield, the moment after Sergeant Bradford had fallen and the moment before Simone did, she had felt her will break. Almost she had convinced herself that she was remarkable: that she was someone of note, worthy of standing alongside the likes of the King, the Fire General and Simone. The confident, in control, image she had created to fool others—and herself—had fallen away and all that remained was the scared young woman underneath.

Suddenly she was merely Brianne, a common village girl from a meagre village no one had heard of. And there she had been, standing in the middle of a battlefield, in the midst of a sea of carnage. A line of large, angry, armed and armoured men had been charging at her, so she did all she could think to do: she ran.

For the rest of that day she had run, as best she could, through the open plains. Instinct buried under her despair drove her south, hoping to find a road and piece together the route to Sastan, to home.

But is it home? she asked herself, silently. What awaited her there? Not family, not a livelihood. No, as far as she knew her mother and Ren were still in Morim and Jahn was somewhere behind her, hopefully alive.

She could not bear the idea of facing the army after abandoning those who had protected her. She dared not return to seek out Jahn, nor Terrin. So her best option, she decided, was to head for Morim. If her mother was there, she would find her somehow. If Ella had left the city it was likely she had returned to Sastan, giving Brianne a reason to do so as well.

As her legs began to fail her in her panicked race from the battlefield, she spotted tents, their peaks rising low over the gently rolling hills. She drew closer, slowing to a stumbling walk, to find an encampment similar to the one the forces of Stalius had engulfed. This one, however, had no signs of foreign soldiers.

From among the tents ahead, a group of riders emerged, charging towards her. Brianne struggled to embrace her power but found it was like trying to hold water in an open hand, the power slipping between her fingers and falling away. She did not know if the Vodani women had severed her connection to the Vein—if that was even a possibility—or if she was merely too weary. Regardless, she stood still and defenceless, the sword at her hip forgotten.

The riders broke their gallop suddenly, kicking up a cloud of dust that washed over her as they reined in. Their apparent leader pressed his horse an extra step forwards so he towered over Brianne. Pointing his spear in her direction, he began shouting at her in a language she did not understand.

The rhythm of his speech—short, chopped statements with rising intonation—suggested he was asking her questions but she could not recognize a word. Impotently she raised her hands, offering what she hoped was a universal sign of supplication.

He thrust his spear towards her, indicating the Pohartan Flame emblazoned on her chest, accompanied by more truncated statements. She offered him a look of weary sorrow which she could not control.

Stepping his horse back to his companions, the men spoke in hushed tones, alternating giving her sideways looks. Occasionally one would direct another statement to her, to which she could offer no reply.

As the men deliberated, three women approached from behind them. They dismounted their horses and pushed between the men, approaching Brianne. The woman in the centre was older: her tanned skin weathered, her grey hair cut short. The women flanking her shared similar looks but were younger, their long black hair framing more youthful versions of the same face. Brianne surmised they must be mother and daughters. Or, she looked closer, she may be looking at three generations but the women were undeniably related.

They stood in identical poses for a moment: feet spread, hands on their hips as they studied her. Brianne could feel their piercing gazes running up and down her body. Finally, their eyes settled on her own and their expressions softened.

One of the younger women approached Brianne, taking her face in her hands. Brianne flinched away initially but soon settled into the contact, lowering her hands and relaxing her muscles. She was tired and the touch was gentle. The woman was the youngest of the three, Brianne could now see. Her brown eyes gazed into

Brianne's green. The look lacked any malice and Brianne found herself comforted by it.

The oldest woman turned to the men, unleashing a tirade. Though Brianne could still not understand the words, she had seen her mother and the other women of the village chastise their husbands often enough to recognize the tones. The sheepish expressions which fell over the men's faces suggested they were not unfamiliar with such harangues from this woman.

Turning away from the woman, the men led their horses back in the direction of the tents. Their slightly bowed heads and slow pace gave them the appearance of puppies who had been scolded for misbehaving. Brianne lacked the spirit or energy to smile at the image, however.

The young woman was still supporting Brianne's face as she turned, calmly speaking a few quick words to the older woman. Replying, the woman approached Brianne, replacing the young woman's hands with her own. The older woman's skin was rougher; calloused from age and years of use. None-the-less, the touch carried the same comforting intent.

Continuing to speak to the young woman, the older brought Brianne's chin up, almost to the point Brianne had to rise to her toes but not quite. Distantly, on the periphery of her awareness, Brianne felt the sensation of someone nearby embracing power. As she tried to reconcile the sensation, a wave of power washed over her. She inhaled sharply as she felt the tingle run through her body. The woman had not stopped speaking, her younger companion nodding along, watching Brianne closely.

The tingle passed as quickly as it had begun. Brianne felt some of her weariness dissipate with it. Her legs no longer ached quite as much, her breathing came easier. The difference was slight but felt significant. Where before she had felt she would fall at any moment, now she stood firmly on her own legs, though she still felt she could sleep for days given the opportunity.

Whatever the woman had done, however, did nothing for her mental anguish. Still she fought back tears.

Looking at Brianne, the older woman offered her a grand-motherly smile and a comforting pat on the cheek. Without speaking, she pivoted to the side, stretching her arm towards the tents. Cautiously Brianne stepped forward, still uncertain of her footing but pleasantly surprised to find it firm. The woman wrapped her arm around Brianne's waist, supporting her should she stumble as they made their way to the tents. The remaining women fell into step behind them, their horses falling in with them without them needing to pull their reins.

As they entered the encampment, the men who had first approached Brianne were loitering about in front of a large tent. A sharp word and aggressive arm wave sent them scattering, doing their best to make it appear they were done their conversation anyway.

The women led her past a number of tents. People were scattered about, their daily routines briefly interrupted by the stranger being led through their midst. A group of children raced into the pathway chasing each other, only to stop short in front of the visitor. Most stared, blinking silently for a moment. One spoke to a nearby adult and received a sharp retort for their efforts. Growing bored, they resumed their game, pushing past Brianne and her escorts to disappear between two tents, their squeals of play carrying them away.

They stopped in front of a tent Brianne could not discern from those around it and the older woman ushered her inside while the youngest darted away. Within the tent were none of the furnishings she anticipated but instead a scattering of animal furs. To either side lay a simple mattress of woven field grass, with similarly manufactured cushions creating a small seating area in the middle.

Eager to fall onto the mattress, Brianne pulled at the straps of her armour, letting the bracers fall to the floor. The woman, seeing her struggle, offered her assistance, pulling at the straps around Brianne's hips. Brianne took a deep, relieved breath as the plated corset fell away: while she had enjoyed the appearance and confidence it gave her, she had to admit she hated wearing it. As quickly as the armour fell away, Brianne fell onto one of the mattresses. She was pleasantly surprised at the comfort she found and sleep came over her long before the younger woman reached the tent with an offering of water and food.

CHAPTER 23

She was not sure how much time had passed before the young woman rushed into the tent again, shaking her awake. Brianne blinked the sleep from her eyes as the woman waved urgently, speaking in that language unknown to Brianne.

Remembering her message was not getting through, the woman pointed to the flame on Brianne's chest, then pointed aggressively to the entrance of the tent. Brianne became worried but rose from the mattress and made her way out of the tent.

The other two women who had met her in the field were waiting outside for her and ushered her to the edge of the camp. It seemed the entire 'village' was gathered there, whispering to each other as they stared out into the fields. The women pushed their way through the group, dragging Brianne with them. Above, grey clouds had gathered, blocking the sun.

With a triumphant smile, the older woman stood proudly, pointing across the plains. Quickly cutting its way across the field was a long snake of marching soldiers. Brianne could see several wagons and carriages surrounded by mounted men at its head, above them fluttered and snapped banners of Pohartan and Stalius.

Brianne shrank back reflexively. The soldiers were moving fast, cutting across the horizon heading south. They showed no interest in the encampment but still, Brianne felt her heart begin to race with panic. The presence of such a force suggested Terrin must have won the battle, which was a relief, yet still Brianne could not imagine facing them again. She could not risk being spotted by the soldiers, her bright red hair standing out among the dark-haired crowd.

Instead of going towards the marching army, as the woman seemed to expect she would, Brianne took a couple quick steps backwards, bumping into the people behind her and trying to push in between them. The women were quick to catch her discomfort evident on her face, however, and parted the crowd for her with quick words and jabs.

Unable to look away from the passing soldiers, Brianne found herself sandwiched between two large men, deep in the crowd. From there she watched them pass for a long while. The column stretched as far as the eye could see and it seemed an endless flood of men stomping over the hills. As the head of the snake disappeared and it became obvious they had no interest in the camp, the gathered crowd slowly became bored of the spectacle. Members began to trickle away, returning to their routines.

Before the crowd could disperse enough to reveal her, Brianne too slipped back among the tents. She felt tears well behind her eyes once again as she weaved back and forth. Growing frustrated, she found herself soon lost in the forest of tanned hides and beige canvases. Letting the tears fall, she released her frustration in a growl, which was swallowed by a crack of thunder above. Grasping her head in her hands, she fell to her knees. She was not certain if the sky was mocking or commiserating with her as the rain started to fall, hiding the tears on her cheeks.

She was found there moments later by the three women, her new guardians and protectors. They ushered her up from the ground, wrapping comforting arms and a heavy blanket over her shoulders. Offering comforting coos, they led her back to the tent she had been sleeping in, guiding her inside to resume her rest and recovery.

* * *

The hooves of Richmond's horse plodded through the mud created by the previous day's rain, carrying him at a gentle walk through the field. Richmond was surprised he had not caught sight of any pursuers. The open, wind-blown nature of the plain was a mixed blessing. There were few places to hide or seek shelter, copses of trees few and far between. However, the wind blew the grasses about roughly, quickly covering the trail his horse cut through them. If he could remain low between the hills he had the best chance of passing unnoticed. He had cut a long path west—the least reasonable direction for him to go—in an effort to throw off any pursuers and was now returning southeast.

The path of the marching army was not so easily obscured. He had been surprised when he stumbled across it; a wide path of flattened grass and churned earth. The wind was less capable of erasing the passing of thousands of foot and hoof treads and the drag of wagon wheels. And so he followed it, letting his own tracks blend into the indistinguishable mass. His head swivelled endlessly as he scanned the horizon for soldiers ahead or pursuers behind.

A collection of tents came into view off to his right as he crested the next hill. Its stylings and banners marked it a nomadic Zemiltarian tribe. Hopeful, yet cautious, relief washed over him. He had been following the path of the army but with no clear goal in mind: he was not yet ready to actually catch up to the force. Without rations, however, he was losing strength. The small amount of rain he had been able to collect the previous day was insufficient sustenance. Perhaps this 'town' would be his salvation.

Riders emerged from the town as he split himself from the path carved by the army and approached it. He could not recognize the banners flapping above the tents and did not know which tribe this might be—though they had a tendency to change their names and symbols frequently as different men rose to power. However, he noted the absence of Foselak's new banner among them.

He reined in his horse calmly as the four riders reached him, encircling him with their horses. They rode around him several times, spears held high, eyes locked on him. Finally they brought their horses to a stop in unison, positioned at each point of the compass around him.

It was the man in front of him who spoke. "Who are you?" he asked in his native tongue. Richmond had spent enough time along the border with Zemiltar dealing with the tribes who frequented that region to pick up the basics of their language.

"My name is Richard," he replied, his use of their language slow and choppy but passable.

"What are you doing here?" the rider to his left asked. Richmond turned his head to look at the man as he considered his answer.

He did not know these men's allegiances, did not know what answer would provide him with the best chance of peace. Would they be more welcoming to a man who fought alongside or against Foselak and those with him? Was there any reasonable explanation for a foreign man to be in the area besides the war which had ripped into their territory? Would they be accepting or disdainful of a deserter from that war?

"I am a blacksmith," he said, tossing the dice. "I was serving the Pohartan army. I ran when the battle started to turn. Now I am trying to reach home."

The men spoke with each other, too quickly and complexly for Richmond to follow their conversation, only able to grasp a few stray words.

"That is a fine weapon for a blacksmith." The rider jabbed at the head of Richmond's axe, resting at his hip, with his spear.

"I was working on it for the Fire General," Richmond replied calmly. "A Pohartan noble. I took it with me for protection when I fled."

"We have heard of your battle. Our riders say your King has fallen and another man has taken control." Richmond craned his neck back to catch a glimpse of the man behind him, who had spoken.

"So be it," Richmond said simply. "I do not concern myself with what the nobles do. I would simply like to get home."

"How does a blacksmith know our language?" The sharp eyes of the man in front of Richmond stared into his as he turned.

It was a good question. Perhaps he would have done better to play ignorant. "I am from Erhindar. It is a city close to the border. I have traded with your people," Richmond answered quickly. As plausible an explanation as he could conceive at the moment.

The rider looked at him for a long moment but eventually lowered his spear to a more relaxed position, seemingly satisfied with Richmond's story.

"What do you want?" he asked.

"Refuge?" Richmond responded. "A night's rest, perhaps and a meal."

Looking to his companions, the man nodded. He indicated towards the tents with his head as he turned his horse, signalling for Richmond to follow. The other riders spurred their horses beside him.

"That is a fine horse, for a blacksmith," one of the riders noted, eyeing him sideways as they rode.

Richmond bowed his head in feigned guilt. "I stole it when I fled as well. It was being reshod."

"Well, he approves of you as a rider." Richmond was only able to reply to the comment with a confused expression.

"Might I ask your names? And what tribe this is?" he broke the silence which followed as they neared the tents.

"I am Lyrnod, of the Nagrain," the leader of the group responded. "These are Reharn, Wertar and Tynos." The three remaining men nodded in turn.

The party rode on to the encampment, dismounting just outside its border and continuing in on foot. Richmond looked about him as he walked, paying little attention to the rapid conversation happening amongst his escort. He had little experience interacting with the Zemiltaran people, aside from fighting against or negotiating with their warriors. He found himself surprised by what he saw.

In Pohartan, Zemiltar was often viewed and discussed as a wild, savage land and people. They were certainly fierce warriors and that ferocity evolved in the public mind into savagery and was extended to the entire population. Late nights of drinking in the border towns and cities often devolved into jokes implying an impure nature to the bond between the Zemiltaran riders and their horses.

Richmond saw no evidence of such savagery. He saw craftsmen and women working their wares. He saw younger children at play; older, seated with their parents, listening to their stories and learning their crafts. Through the gaps between tents, Richmond could see a circle of shirtless men, sparring with staves and spears. It was a difficult juxtaposition for Richmond to reconcile: the appearance and sounds of a military camp, with the warmth and community of a small town.

A group of women seated in a circle outside one of the tents caught his attention. Three of the women blended into the community easily enough, their black or grey hair and tanned skin matching those around them. Despite being dressed in the same fashion as the other women, the fourth woman, whose back was facing Richmond, stood out like a ruby among opals, her red hair and pale skin a stark contrast to those around her.

"Brianne?" he stopped and asked carefully, though he had little doubt who sat before him. Her back stiffened and her head turned slowly. Their eyes met for a moment before hers fell away, turning to look at the ground.

"Hello, Rich..."

"Richard," he cut her off quickly.

Her eyes returned to his, a glimmer of curiosity behind them for a moment. The light dimmed quickly, however. He was overjoyed to find her alive—he had had no indication of what happened to her on the battlefield. It must have been something terrible, he surmised, as he had not expected such a morose and distant greeting from her.

"You know her?" an elderly woman seated with Brianne asked. All eyes were on him now.

"Yes, she is a… seamstress' apprentice, with the army," Richmond answered confidently.

Lyrnod and the woman shared a long look which made Richmond nervous.

"May I speak with her a moment?" he asked. The group of women stood, Brianne following their example, not understanding the conversation happening around her. The older woman gestured to the tent in front of which they stood. Gently taking Brianne by the arm, Richmond led her inside.

Once inside, Richmond immediately recognized his mistake. Beside a grass mattress along one wall, Brianne's Pohartan armour sat in a heap: they were undeniably the garments of a fighter, not a craftswoman. Richmond chided himself for not thinking she would likely be still travelling in her armour.

"Shit," he muttered softly, as he heard hushed tones speaking quickly outside.

"You speak their language?" Brianne asked, looking up at him.

"A little. I told them my name was Richard and I was a blacksmith who abandoned the army." Richmond ran his fingers through his dishevelled hair then indicated her piled belongings. "And I am afraid I tried to tell them you were a seamstress's apprentice."

Brianne too looked down at her armour, reaching the same conclusion. "Shit," she repeated his curse.

With a rush, the flaps of the tent burst inwards and the men who had met Richmond in the field ran in. Two bore spears, one pointed at each of the occupants, while the others wielded the scythe-like blades Richmond had seen used in the battle. Lyrnod stood close to Richmond, holding his scythe in an aggressive stance, prepared to strike. But he did not attack.

Following the men came the three women. The eldest stepped forward between the armed men, while the two younger moved to the corners of the tent. The woman locked eyes with Richmond.

"I am Mirania, Haliness of the Nagraini. Who are you?" Her tone was firm; a tone used to being obeyed.

Richmond's mind raced. He saw few options: he had clearly been caught in a lie. Perhaps he could weave the lie deeper and find an explanation for Brianne's armour... Or, perhaps her being apparently welcomed into this community with her armour meant something.

Finally he sighed, deciding his course and prepared to accept wherever it led. "I am Richmond Arhan, Fire General of Pohartan."

The woman's gaze never left him as she nodded slowly. "And who is she?"

"Brianne. She is one of our soldiers." It was certainly a true statement but Richmond felt no need to reveal Brianne's abilities and the extent of her role.

To the untrained eye, the men around them did not seem to move. Richmond, however, had spent his life studying opponents and he recognized the signs of relaxation: the subtle shifting of weight, the slight shift in grip on a weapon. The men were still poised to strike but apparently were not further alarmed by his answers. Richmond released a breath he had been holding.

Brianne, however, did not understand the words, nor did she recognize the quiet shift in mood in the tent. Richmond offered her a comforting pat on the arm, moving slowly as to not alarm the group studying them so closely.

"Why are you here?" Mirania asked. Her tone had not softened.

"We were defeated. We are trying to return home, to our families." For Richmond it was a carefully worded truth, he did not know how true it was for Brianne.

"We saw your soldiers marching, they did not appear defeated." Mirania raised her eyebrow, apparently skeptical.

Richmond could not hide the anger from his voice, directed at the soldiers to whom she referred. "Those dogs are not our soldiers. They betrayed our King and turned to the enemy."

For reasons Richmond was not certain of the men now visibly relaxed, lowering their blades and raising their spears.

"Information travels quickly in Zemiltar," began Mirania, responding to Richmond's evidently confused expression. "Soldiers who fought for your King killed Matrel Foselak. He was no friend of ours and we are better for his absence."

Richmond was not certain how to respond. "Glad we could help," he said, a hint of bitterness behind his words. The death of Matrel was evidently the only good which had come from the battle.

"You may rest here. We will be leaving this area shortly. You will not accompany us when we do." Mirania nodded to the pair. She turned, ushering her companions from the tent. "I will have food and drink brought and water for washing," she said over her shoulder as she disappeared from the tent.

"What happened?" Brianne asked once they were alone.

"I told them who we were," Richmond shrugged. "Evidently they approve. It seems our soldiers killed their enemy."

"No, Richmond." Brianne grabbed the front of his shirt in both hands, staring up at him intensely. "What happened in the battle?"

"You do not know…" Richmond said softly, grabbing her hands in his and pulling them from his shirt. "Come, sit." He led her to one of the mattresses, guiding her down before taking a seat beside her. Her eyes were wide with worry and red from recent tears.

He watched her already distressed face fall deeper into despair as he relayed what little he knew: the last he saw Terrin on the battlefield and the information he had gained after waking of Terrin's capture and movement to Morim.

"I plan to follow them to Morim," he said. "I do not have much of a strategy beyond that, yet. Somehow find a way to free

Terrin. Maybe there will still be loyal soldiers who can help me but I will do it alone if I must."

The younger Zemiltar woman pushed her way into the tent bearing a tray piled with bread and dried meats, accompanied by a clay pitcher and two small goblets. Behind her came the other young woman, carrying a large clay basin, water sloshing over its edges. The two saw the pair of Pohartans sitting close on the mattress. They offered them quick, coy nods and smiles, placing their burdens on the floor and leaving the tent quickly.

"Do you know anything about these people, those women?" Richmond asked, moving to bring the tray closer to them.

"Very little," Brianne said weakly. "I am fairly certain those were the daughter and granddaughter of the older one, the one who was speaking to you." Richmond bit into a heel of bread as she spoke. He found the food surprisingly good: he had spent months now eating soldiers' rations, so the warm fresh bread was a welcome change. He ate greedily as Brianne continued.

"They have power, Richmond. All three of them."

"Like yours?" Richmond asked through a mouthful of bread.

"Yes. Well, from the same source, I think. Not fire, though. Or at least I have not seen them use it that way." She seemed to be becoming flustered. Richmond reached down and poured a drink from the pitcher. It was a colourful, slightly thick liquid. Richmond took a small sip before handing it to Brianne: a sweet juice, though he could not recognize the fruit.

"Take it easy Brianne, we are safe. For now." He rubbed her back for a moment, doing his best to comfort her.

"They used their power to help me. I was hardly able to stand when I first arrived. Grandmother—as I have taken to calling her in my mind—grabbed my face and I felt her power. It gave me a little bit of strength."

"I would not be surprised," Richmond mused. "The Zemiltarans are mysterious. They rarely deal with outsiders, except to fight them or very occasionally trade. Their bond with animals is well known, however, and generally considered to be mystical—likely brought about by this power."

There was a long silence as they both ate and drank. Richmond was bone-tired but relieved to have found an ally and friend. Since waking on the battlefield it had seemed the entire world had turned on its head and he was alone in recognizing it.

"What happened to you in the battle?" he asked Brianne, finally.

Brianne was silent and still for a long moment, her food just hanging in her hand, arm draped over her knee.

"Simone is dead," she said finally. He sighed, unsurprised. He would find himself more surprised to hear who had survived that chaos. "She fell alongside my Phoenix Guard, protecting me. We had tracked down two women in the fight, they were using power to block mine. I thought if I could find them, I could eliminate them." Brianne's voice was catching as she held back tears. "They were well defended and my power was useless... The soldiers killed Sergeant Bradford and Simone, then I... I just ran." She broke down into tears. Richmond wrapped his good arm around her shoulders, holding her close to him and letting her cry.

"It is all right, Brianne," he comforted. "There was nothing else you could do. Sometimes the best course of action is to retreat, to survive to face your enemy another day."

"They died for me and I just ran away," Brianne managed through gasping breaths.

"They gave their lives so you could survive and that is what you did. Do you think they wanted you to die needlessly beside them? What would their sacrifice have meant then?" Richmond hoped his words were being heard, for he knew they were true but he also knew it may take Brianne some time to accept them. He had seen many soldiers distraught at being alive while their comrades had died. "Besides, if you had died, you would not be able to help me rescue Terrin."

It took a few moments for Brianne to suppress her wave of tears enough for her to be able to speak. "I will not be much help. I have barely been able to touch my power since the battle. I think those women did something to me but I do not know."

Richmond pushed her away from him gently, grasping her shoulder and forcing her to look him in the eye. "You, Brianne Morette, are more than just your power. Maybe it will come back to you, maybe it will not. It does not matter. With or without it, you are the strongest, most determined young woman I have had the honour of fighting beside."

"No I am not," she refuted. "That was an act. I was trying to convince you—and myself—that was who I was. But I am not. I am just a stupid girl from a forgotten village."

"Hah!" Richmond expelled, his tone firm but supportive. "No one can pretend to be those things if they are not: no one is that good of an actor. You may not realize it but you have those qualities in you. You are that strong, confident, independent woman. In time you will realize that." He pulled her close again, hugging her as her tears subsided.

Finally, Richmond rose. The light from outside the tent indicated it was still afternoon but he was weary and drained from the recent days. He knelt in front of the large basin of water, splashing it over his face. He scrubbed his face and forearms, being gentle with his injured limb, rubbing away the grime of battle and days of riding. He longed for a proper bath, or at least a more thorough washing but his weariness won out.

He pulled his boots off and threw them aside, his shirt following after. Then he fell to the mattress on the opposite side of the tent. His rest in the military camp after being brought from the battlefield had not been enough to recover and the subsequent nights sleeping on the ground had only compounded his aches. The woven grass mattress seemed to embrace him like a long-lost friend.

"Richmond?" Brianne said from across the tent.

"Yes?" he replied groggily, sleep creeping upon him quickly.

"I will come with you, to help Terrin."

Richmond smiled, not bothering to open his eyes. "I know you will, Brianne." He shifted onto his side, the mattress adjusting to cradle him. In moments he was asleep.

As Richmond lay snoring, Brianne sat thinking. She hoped his words were true; both his justification of her leaving the battle and his claims about the value of her character. She did not feel they were but the seeds of recovery had been planted deep in her subconscious.

Finally, she rose and walked from the tent. Though she could not understand their language, the three women had been kind to her. They allowed her to sit with them as they spoke and Brianne could feel the tendrils of power moving between them as they did. From the flow of power and the rhythm of their conversations, Brianne believed Grandmother and Mother were teaching Daughter how to use her own power. It was comforting to be around women who were similar to her in such an unexpected way and perhaps, Brianne thought, they would be able to help her reconnect with her own power.

CHAPTER 24

Jahn's legs ached from the days of walking. They were being pushed at a fast pace, General Arhan apparently eager to return to Morim as soon as possible. They had been ordered to carry extra rations, as they would be moving too quickly for the supply wagons to keep pace.

Earlier that day they had crossed the border into Pohartan, or so he had been told. There was little indication of the change in ownership of the land. The plain they were marching across still looked the same, except they had found themselves suddenly walking on the packed dirt of a road, instead of stamped-down grasses.

Now they sat camped around the city of Erhindar, its tall spires and high walls dominating the horizon. The commanders of the army, including General Arhan and Ordreg, had found beds within the city, inviting themselves into the home of the local lord. The bulk of the army was left to fend for themselves in the fields outside the walls.

Those walls did not surround all the residents of the city, however, as Erhindar had grown out beyond its original design. Collections of buildings, towns in their own right, had sprouted surrounding the three main gates to the city, where those too poor to live within the walls but seeking the protection of proximity, had staked out homes and businesses.

Jahn's company were camped not far from one of those 'towns', known as Eastgate for the simple fact of its location. Now, Jahn found himself walking with Megen and Amad down the main road, the gates of the city closed in the distance before them. The sun was starting to set, yet the shops which littered the street to either side remained open, their proprietors shouting their wares, hoping to capitalize on the opportunity provided by an encamped army.

He was skeptical how lucrative that opportunity would prove for some of them: the officers who had coin, many coming from powerful or noble families, were inside the city walls. The common soldiers who remained outside had little coin and even less need for the silks or crafts many attempted to offer. Those who had food to offer, however, were certainly thriving. Lines of men bled into the streets from shops smelling of sweet bakings or roasted meats, soldiers eager to give up some of their sparse coins for a fresh meal.

"Let's go in there," Amad offered, pointing to an inn down the street. Its sign declared it the Horseman's Head, a caricature of a severed Zemiltaran head etched into the wood below the words.

"Are you sure they allow children inside?" Megen asked, not missing a beat.

"Hey, fuck you, Megen," Amad shot back but his tone and expression revealed the joviality he was feeling. Though the march was strenuous, for the first time since they had joined the military they were not marching towards war. Instead, they were marching home.

The three turned towards the inn, weaving between soldiers standing in small groups outside, tankards of ale in hand. The air was filled with a sense of joyful celebration, boisterous voices breaking into laughter at regular intervals.

Inside, the Horseman's Head seemed packed to the brim with soldiers, red tunics of Pohartan mixed in equal parts with the blue of Stalius. Serving girls wove through the masses expertly, flowing skillfully like dancers between the tables, trays full of drinks balanced high in the air.

The sound as they crossed the threshold seemed initially near-deafening. The deep buzz of a hundred conversations accented frequently by shouting emanating from games of dice and fists pounding on tables from games of drinking.

Megen scanned the room, then dove into the disorder, Jahn and Amad hurrying after. She had spotted three open stools at the end of a long table, sliding into one just a moment before it could be taken by another soldier. Jahn and Amad settled into the remaining stools, as the defeated soldier slunk away with a sour expression.

A haggard-looking serving girl moved in surprisingly quickly, one arm locked in place holding a tray of tankards. Even as she started speaking, she was placing three on the table before them.

"Ale, I am assuming," her tone was pleasant and she offered them a weak but sweet smile. However, her hair was in disarray, pieces escaping at odd angles from the bun she had tied at the top of her head. Behind the smile, Jahn could see she was exhausted. "It is a copper each. I apologize but we had to close the kitchen."

As Jahn reached into the purse at his belt, sifting through the few coins he had, he saw Amad reach his arm behind the server. She jumped slightly as he pinched her, stepping away from his hand but giving him an empty smile. Jahn realized her exhaustion was likely not just from serving but whom she was serving. A room full of soldiers who had just spent months on the road had to be an unpleasant clientele for an attractive young serving girl.

"And how much for your company, m..." Amad's question was cut short by a sharp kick to the shin from Jahn.

"Just pay for your ale and shut up," Megen elbowed the younger man. Amad glared at them both but silently dropped a copper piece onto the table. The young girl swept up the pieces and dropped them onto a pile on her tray. With another cordial nod, she turned away. Jahn watched as she weaved through the tables, looking for more patrons in need of fresh drinks. Every few steps she moved, he noticed, she had to dodge suddenly outstretched hands; with varying levels of success.

"So it is fine for you to stare at her ass as she walks away but I cannot pinch it?" Jahn grimaced as Amad returned his kick, bringing his attention away from the girl.

"I was not staring at her," Jahn attempted half-heartedly to defend himself: he did not feel any great need to convince Amad.

"I guess I am just stuck with you, my dear." Amad attempted to swing an arm around Megen's shoulders and received another sharp elbow in the ribs for his trouble.

"Not in a thousand lifetimes," Megen replied coolly before taking a long drink of ale.

"And why the fuck not?" protested Amad. "I know how to please a lady, you know. I would have you curling your toes in a minute." Megen feigned a violent wave of nausea in response.

"It is Jahn's pecker you are after, isn't it?" Amad questioned, raising an eyebrow. "I have seen it, you know. I promise mine's bigger."

"Just shut up, Amad," Jahn shot, harshly. He could feel his cheeks going red, despite his efforts to resist it. He had never been with a woman—though he doubted Amad had either, despite the man's boasts. The opportunity had not presented itself: in Sastan he had isolated himself from the young women his age—and everyone else in the village—and since leaving his home he had been constantly surrounded by men. He was only now realizing he had a future to consider, which would include such things.

Megen was eyeing him with a cocked eyebrow and sly smile and he felt the colour on his cheeks deepen, which seemed to amuse her further. "I am sure she is not interested in me either, Amad. She can do a lot better than her grubby squadmates."

"I will remind you, Corporal," Megen said, dragging out the title with a playful intonation, "you are more my superior officer than my squadmate. Besides, three soldiers do not really make a squad."

Jahn wanted to crawl under the table and disappear and felt as though his skeleton had already done so. His best escape was taking a long drink of ale, staring silently into the murky liquid as he brought the tankard back down onto the table.

He was jostled suddenly by a slap on the back from the soldier seated beside him. Jahn had not been listening to their conversation but it seemed it suddenly included them.

"You worry too much, Hank," the soldier was saying to his companion across the table. "These lads are our allies now!" The two were among a larger group, all dressed in the colours and sigils of Stalius.

"Well, they turned their allegiance pretty quickly. I am not sure how much their loyalty means," the soldier named Hank replied. Both men were slurring their speech heavily, obviously not on their first tankard of ale.

"Hank here says y'er a bunch'a cowards," the man said, now addressing Jahn. "But I don't think so. I think y'er smart, you see." He looked at Jahn, tapping his temple. "Y'er King was a madman, so you stabbed him in the back. Heroic, really. Now you can have our Hi'ral instead. He'll be settin' you right."

Jahn's stomach churned. He was still not confident in his decision to kneel before General Arhan, effectively breaking his vows to the King. Megen and Amad were both able to march with their heads held high, their consciences clear but the decision weighed on Jahn. More concerning was the man's implication that Ordreg would take control of Pohartan. Jahn could make peace with kneeling to one Pohartan to replace another but he would not bend knee to Stalius.

His planned response was cut short, as he thought he heard his name being called through the crowd. Ears now primed, he heard it again: "Corporal Morette?" a voice was calling over the din of the hall. Jahn rose and looked around the room, as it was difficult to discern the direction of the voice.

He met the gaze of a soldier standing in the doorway. The man stood in clean and polished Pohartan armour, the badge on his breast marking him a Captain, though Jahn did not recognize his face. "Corporal Morette?" the man shouted again, this time directed specifically at Jahn. Jahn nodded, leaving his friends with puzzled expressions as he made his way across the room. He was as confused as they were.

When he reached the man, Jahn snapped to attention with a sharp salute. "I am Corporal Morette, sir."

The Captain returned the salute quickly. "The General wishes to speak with you. Come with me. You better not be drunk," he commanded, turning on his heel and walking back through the door without waiting for a response.

Jahn cast a quick, uncertain look back across the room towards his friends. They were ducked in conversation with the Staliusian soldiers sharing their table. Megen glanced up for a moment, looking to Jahn and offering him a quizzical expression, as if asking for an explanation: she was unlikely to have heard the Captain's order. Jahn could only shrug in response before rushing out the door after the officer.

* * *

Jahn was awe-struck as he was escorted through the halls of the palace. He supposed it was a palace, anyway. He had little experience with such things but could not imagine anything so opulent being classified as anything less than a palace. Mirrored lamps dotted the walls, casting so much light Jahn forgot night had fallen outside.

It seemed every available space on the walls was covered with elaborate tapestries, depicting colourful scenes. Between the tapestries stood all manner of decor: sets of elaborately decorated armour positioned as if it were being worn by an invisible soldier, statues depicting the head and shoulders of proud-looking men and intricately designed vases and pots balanced on precariously thin stands. Several times Jahn had to speed to a trot to catch his escort as he had become distracted, transfixed by one artifact or another.

He had lost track of their path almost immediately, not paying too close attention. The Captain led him down winding corridors, taking turns so suddenly Jahn often took an extra step in the wrong direction before realizing.

Finally they reached a large wooden door, flanked by two Pohartan soldiers.

"Captain Poenath to see the General," his escort said as they approached the guards. He must have been expected, as one of the guards simply nodded and reached to open the door for him.

Before Jahn could take a step to follow, Captain Poenath raised his hand, stopping him. "A moment," he said, stepping into the room alone.

Jahn stood in the corridor at a loss. He looked at the guards but their blank expressions offered him no answers. It was only a moment before the Captain emerged again, holding the door open for Jahn. "General Arhan will see you," he said, ushering Jahn inside. To Jahn's surprise the Captain did not follow him into the room, instead merely closing the door behind him.

The room was large, a massive stone fireplace dominating one wall. Opposite the mantle, the wall was covered from floor to high ceiling with shelf upon shelf of books. The far wall was a bank of wide windows with the curtains tied back, showcasing a captivating view of the moon-lit city and night sky. All around the room banners hung; both the Flame banner of Pohartan and the bear banner of House Arhan.

In the centre of the room sat a gargantuan, ornate, polished wood desk. Behind the desk sat General Arhan, chin resting on his fist as he studied Jahn. His shoulder-length white-streaked hair was tied back in a short tail. His face was locked in a stern expression.

Gulping, Jahn stepped in front of the desk, offering his best salute. He was still uncertain why he had been summoned and his stomach churned with anxiety.

"So you are Jahn Morette, eh?" General Arhan asked, his voice surprisingly kind.

"Yes, sir," was all Jahn could manage.

"I will not waste much of our time, lad, there are a million more important things to be done." The General shifted in his chair, leaning back casually. "I remember you from the battlefield, re-member you killing that man as he raised his weapon against your companion."

"He had also been my companion, sir. Until that moment," Jahn stuttered at the moment of silence, not sure if the General had been expecting a response.

"I suppose he was," Lukas laughed ruefully. "But the moment he turned, you acted as you needed to. It was well done."

"Thank you, sir."

"There were many like him, you see. Not everyone was willing to believe the truth of Dramen's madness. We are in the process of dealing with them still." He waved a hand dismissively. "Naïve fools, we have no place for them. It seems your Sergeant—" Arhan leaned forward, shifting through some papers laid out on the desk, "—Morson, was one such fool. He professed his loyalty to Dramen and so was executed."

Jahn felt a pang of sadness strike him, hoping it did not show on his face. The Sergeant had been a good man, Jahn had liked him.

"We are working on replacing those cowards with good, strong, men loyal to the true Pohartan. Asking around, your name was brought forward and my interest was piqued."

There was no hiding the confusion from Jahn's face, he could feel it contort. He could fathom neither who would have recommended him, nor why. More confusing was why his name would have any meaning to the General.

"I see you are confused. I know your name because I knew your father. He was a Captain in my battalion and a good man. His loss was a tragedy to the army." Lukas gave Jahn a sympathetic smile. "You should be proud to have had him as a father."

"I am, sir." Jahn found himself standing slightly taller, back straighter. He had always known his father was a great man but it was empowering and vindicating to hear his praises sung by General Arhan.

"And now imagine my surprise as these pieces fall into place together." The General threw his arms up dramatically. "A name I have such respect for is brought before me and I find it is the same young soldier I was so impressed by on the field. The Great Phoenix is surely exerting Her will in these matters!"

General Arhan pulled a desk drawer open, fishing out a metal pendant and placing it on the edge of the desk before Jahn.

"Normally this would be a quick matter, done in the field. However, as I say, once your name was brought forward, I wanted to meet you myself. Congratulations, Sergeant Morette." General Arhan rose from his chair, extending his hand to Jahn.

Jahn stood dumbstruck for a moment. He had barely been promoted to Corporal—by Sergeant Morson, he reminded himself—and now he was taking the man's position. While doubt and confusion dominated his thoughts, he felt the faint glimmer of pride in the back of his mind as he shook the General's hand.

"Thank you, sir," he managed, picking up the badge. It appeared to be a finer quality metal than his Corporal insignia, shining brightly in the reflected torchlight of the room.

General Arhan returned to his seat. "You will do well in my army, Morette, I am certain of it. Keep at it and you will likely soon be a Captain, as your father was. Then, who knows?"

"Thank you, sir," Jahn stammered again.

"You may leave now. I still have much to prepare before I can rest: we will be executing the remaining officers loyal to Dramen in the morning. It will be quite the spectacle in the city square; an opportunity for the common people to see justice served. Ensure you are there." General Arhan was already returning to his work, looking down at the papers he was sorting through on the desk.

"Yes, sir." Jahn saluted, turning and walking towards the door.

"Sergeant," Lukas said behind him, looking up from his work. Jahn turned back. "Make your father proud."

"I will, sir," Jahn said, chin held high as he walked from the room.

* * *

Dawn rose quickly over Erhindar. Jahn had returned straight to camp after meeting with General Arhan the night before. He had found no sign of Megen or Amad and assumed they were still drinking in Eastgate—a suspicion confirmed in the morning, as they could be found in their bedrolls, groggy and near-impossible to wake. So Jahn had left them to their recovery and dressed in his armour, making his way to the city as the sun was still rising over the horizon.

Now he stood in Merchant's Square, the central hub of the City of Erhindar. It was a large cobbled clearing where the roads leading from the three gates converged. On a normal morning, the square would be dotted with market stalls and bustling with the activities of trade and commerce. This was no normal morning, however. The market stalls had been cleared and a large stage erected in the centre of the square. Soldiers and civilians stood shoulder-to-shoulder crowding the remaining space: word had been spread of the spectacle to take place.

A hush fell over the crowd in a wave as horns sounded. A column of men emerged from a fourth road which had been kept clear of spectators by lines of soldiers: Pohartan lining one side; Staliusian, the other. The road connected the Square to the palace Jahn had been taken to the previous night. The hush was replaced by a cheer as the men took to the stage, in view of everyone.

Four men led the group. General Arhan walked beside the Staliusian officer Jahn recognized from the battlefield. Behind them came an aged man in black robes Jahn believed to be Rodok Ordreg, accompanied by a younger man in grey robes.

Behind the leaders came the prisoners, each flanked by a pair of soldiers. None of the prisoners seemed to be resisting their fate, though some looked as though they would not have been able to stand without the assistance of their escorts.

First among the prisoners was the King. Jahn recognized him from their brief interaction before leaving Morim. He looked rough, his clothing in tatters and his hair in disarray, a scraggly, unkempt beard covering his chin. Dark bruises covered his exposed skin. Yet he walked with his head held high, ignoring an obvious limp and his arms bound behind his back. Jahn had arrived early enough to push his way to a spot close to the stage and could see the King's face clearly: through the bruised and swollen flesh Jahn could see fire blazing in his eyes.

So focused was he on the appearance of the King, it took Jahn some time to take notice of the men escorting him. He did not recognize one: a young soldier in Pohartan armour, the badge of Captain on his chest. The other, however, was General of his own battalion, Warsch. The General wore freshly cleaned and polished armour and an ornate sword strapped to his hip. Jahn could see the corners of the man's mouth turn up in a subtle, satisfied smirk as he and his companion dragged the King by the arms to one side of the stage.

Five prisoners followed, though Jahn only recognized the first two; the remaining likely being higher ranking officers of different battalions. The two he recognized were General Bartel, of the Third and General Furell, of the Fourth. Though not his direct commanding officers, the Generals of each battalion were easily recognized by all the soldiers of the army.

Where the King had been led to the side, the remaining prisoners were lined up across the centre of the stage and brought to a kneeling position. Some had taken a knee easily, willingly, while those resisted were brought down by a hard kick to their legs.

"Pohartans! Friends!" The crowd fell silent as General Arhan began shouting over their heads, pacing the length of the stage. He waited a moment for the silence to settle before continuing.

"We come together on an auspicious day! A glorious day! For too long Pohartan has lived under the cloud of war but today the skies are clearing!" He opened his arms to the blue morning sky, causing a ripple of cheers.

"For years Pohartan has suffered under the brutal rule of House Dramen." He thrust an accusatory finger at the King, who glared back. "He and his heathen lineage have scorched our land. Their rage and their greed, has kept us in a costly war against Stalius." The crowd was uncertain how to respond, though a weak cheer passed. For all of them, the war between Stalius and Pohartan had raged for their entire lives, they knew no different. Yet now their enemy stood before them, toted as a friend.

"What started that war? Minor bickerings over territory? Matters which could have been resolved with diplomacy, rather than the blade! How many of your fathers, brothers and sons died in that conflict?" An angry roar rose: there was no uncertainty about acknowledging the loss of loved ones.

"And then, just months ago, the King sent his dogs here, demanding more from you! More of your kin to die in his war! But this time, in his madness, he had started a war with our strongest ally, Drevesine!" The crowd turned to booing, any pieces of scrap which could be found suddenly being hurled at the King. Warsch had to dodge as a rotten piece of fruit narrowly missed him, striking Dramen.

"Peace!" Arhan called, calming the booing and throwing. "As I said, it is a new day, a new era of peace for Pohartan! The Mad King has been dethroned! He is to be taken to the capital, where he will be tried for his crimes and justice will be served."

"But here, today! The good people of Erhindar have the privilege of seeing the beginnings of that justice, the first steps towards a new Pohartan!" Arhan raised his arms for a long interval, revelling in the cheering of the crowd. Jahn still felt uncertain but heard his own voice rising with those around him, swept up in the fervour.

"The men before you are Dramen's loyal dogs, his mutts. They are leaders of his army. It is they who came to claim your sons and throw them to their deaths on the battlefield. When given the opportunity to acknowledge their crimes against the people of Pohartan and seek mercy, they refused! Their madness must match his, as they continue to beg for scraps at his feet."

One of the soldiers at each side of the kneeling men stepped away, moving the corners of the stage. The remaining soldiers each drew their swords, taking positions beside the prisoners.

"While this blade brings justice, with it comes forgiveness," General Arhan began to recite the traditional words. As he did, three of the men, including the two Generals, looked to Dramen. Arms bound behind them, they were unable to salute but each offered a firm nod which Dramen returned in kind. The remaining two men merely squeezed their eyes shut, their mouths moving in silent prayers. "Go now to the next life, free of the burdens of your failures in this. May you rise again in Her glory."

A thunderous cheer rose from the crowd as five swords sliced through flesh and bone. Only General Bartel's head came off cleanly, the remaining four being pushed back by the force of the blade before it could cut completely through.

CHAPTER 25

The wagon rolled to a slow stop, bouncing over stones in the road. The lone occupant was jostled out of his restless slumber. His body ached. He knew what was coming next: this had become the routine. In a moment, the gate at the back of the wagon would be dropped and he would be dragged out. He tried to roll as best he could, to stretch his muscles. His hands were bound behind his back and his feet lashed together. The covering of the wagon barely gave him enough space to roll, scraping his shoulders against the top and bottom; but he had learned it was best to be on his back when the wagon stopped.

As expected, the gate was lowered. Arms reached in, grabbing Terrin's ankles and pulling. He was dragged across the floor of the wagon to drop to the ground like a sack of grain. Repositioning himself as he had, he was able to break his fall with his arms and hold his head up to prevent it from smashing into the road.

The soldiers who had dragged him out roughly grabbed at his shoulders, pulling Terrin to his feet. He winced at the wave of pain sent through his body. He was not certain how many bones had been broken, how many cuts had been made into his skin but he did not feel there was any part of him which did not hurt.

As Terrin's eyes adjusted to the bright mid-day sun, he found Colonel Tronbul standing in front of him. Terrin flinched back involuntarily as he saw the tiger standing at the Colonel's side.

"Take him to his first appointment," ordered Tronbul, a sinister smirk coming to his lips.

Wordlessly the soldiers pushed him forward. Walking was a struggle for Terrin as his legs were reluctant to obey, instead screaming in pain at every movement. The soldiers were not interested in waiting for his slow gait and forced him forward, dragging him if he was too slow.

Terrin was not certain where they were. He had lost all sense of time, never certain whether it would be day or night when he was dragged from his wagon and losing any concept of how many days had passed.

It was difficult to see anything of the surrounding landscape, as he was escorted a short distance through the military camp. He noted that the grasses were lusher and the area more treed than the fields of Zemiltar. He craned his neck back to look around, cringing at the pain. In the distance, he could see a mountain range on the horizon, one peak shrouded in dark clouds poking above the rest: Mount Rhodal. They were getting closer to Morim, perhaps another two days of travel.

He did not know what would be waiting for him in the capital. Of course he knew what Lukas wanted him to find there: an executioner's blade. A voice in the back of his mind tried to reassure him, however. Surely he would still have allies in Morim. What about his wife Amiela and her family? Captain Oret, who commanded the troops left to defend the city? While Lukas led an imposing force, Terrin tried to convince himself he was not alone and abandoned. That voice of reassurance had grown increasingly quiet over the course of his captivity, however.

Terrin and the soldiers dragging him entered a large tent. Shoved roughly to the ground, Terrin struggled to rise. The soldiers pressed his shoulders down, limiting him to his knees.

"You may leave us," a familiar voice commanded. The soldiers turned from beside Terrin, leaving the tent.

"It is good to see you again, my Lord." The title hissed out of the man's mouth. "I wanted a chance to speak with you before you reached the city, for I do not believe I would have an opportunity after."

Rage filled Terrin as his eyes scanned the man in front of him. His vision was obscured and blurred from days of beatings but there was no mistaking the ornate red robes of the High Priest, or the beaked nose of Jermal.

"Jermal!" he spat. Terrin tried to rise, tried to rush the older man. His weakened body did not cooperate, however, and the King merely fell to the ground with a groan. "I should have known you were involved in this betrayal!"

Jermal laughed at his inept struggle. "My dear King. I work only to serve the Great Phoenix. It is Her will that your reign end." The High Priest folded his hands in front of himself, intertwining his gnarled fingers.

"You have sold Pohartan out to Stalius! For your petty revenge!" Terrin coughed, his lungs struggling with the deep breaths brought by his anger and raised voice.

"You fool." Jermal shook his head slowly. "You orchestrated this. You and those before you put the pieces in place. I merely tied the strings between them, as She directed me." He released his hands, counting out points on his fingers as he spoke. "You left your men isolated and disillusioned in the West. You then raided every village, town and city in this Kingdom for their young men. You turned on your greatest ally. You showed your hand and offered your throat to your greatest enemy. Perhaps She guided you to do these things, to provide the opportunity for one loyal to return the Kingdom to Her glory."

"Fuck you and your God," Terrin growled.

Jermal's face grew dark. Moving with the startling speed of a coiled viper, he crossed the floor and kicked Terrin in the side. Those ribs had already been broken and Terrin gritted his teeth, swallowing the pain.

"What now, Jermal. You take the throne? You become Ordreg's puppet?"

"I have no interest in such meaningless titles. I already serve Her in the highest capacity. And Ordreg will not be pulling any strings: he is dal'kar scum, a heathen who does not follow Her teachings. His involvement in these matters is merely a… convenience." The High Priest tucked his hands into opposite sleeves across his belly, slowly pacing the length of the tent.

"Who, then?" Terrin sneered, though he thought he already knew who would be reaching for the power which came with the crown and throne.

"One has been chosen but does it matter? It is one who the people will celebrate but one who recognizes Her influence and the rightful role of the Order." He spoke off-handedly as if it was an irrelevant, unimportant issue to him.

"So you are after the power," Terrin spat again, unsurprised when the glob which shot to the floor was crimson. The taste of blood was a familiarity to him, now. "Just not the title."

Jermal's brow lowered as his sharp eyes fell on Terrin. "I do not seek power for myself. I work for Her glory. I seek to restore Her presence in the hearts and minds of the people of Pohartan."

"Why did you bring me here, Jermal? So you could monologue about your victory? Gloat over me, weak and beaten?" Terrin returned to his knees with a struggle, his anger turning from the blazing rage to slow-burning coals.

Jermal stepped close to Terrin, stooping to bring their faces close together. The man's breath stung Terrin's nostrils, spittle hitting him in the face as the High Priest spoke. "Yes. You have been a thorn in my side for too long. Your arrogance, believing you are outside of Her plan, somehow above the Great Phoenix herself! I wanted to see you before you were dragged before the peasants of Morim. As you are dragged through the streets and meet your end, I wanted you to know you were there by my hand, guided by Her will. It is a small, selfish indulgence for which I will happily ask Her forgiveness."

"Now, King, tell me. Where is the Morette girl?"

Mustering his strength, Terrin lunged forward, snapping his teeth. He caught Jermal's nose, feeling a piece tear away as the man leaped back. Jermal released a howl of pain and rage, bringing the guards waiting outside rushing into the tent.

Terrin spit the piece of flesh to the floor. He could not help but laugh as the men started kicking him, one beating against his ribs with the pommel of a sword. The laughter subsided quickly, turning to choking coughs and moans. Finally, the beating stopped as he fell silent.

"Get him out of here!" Jermal screamed, a handkerchief pressed to his face, blood running down his chin and onto his robes.

The men grabbed Terrin by the arms, not bothering to try to lift him to his feet, instead simply pulling him backwards out of the tent, feet dragging behind him. He managed to smile back at a glaring Jermal before the tent flap fell closed behind him.

* * *

"You certainly angered that old Priest," Ordreg laughed, walking in a slow circle around Terrin, who had been bound standing upright to the central pole of Ordreg's tent. Ordreg dropped the iron poker he was holding back into the lit brazier in front of Terrin. "Took a good chunk out of his nose, too. I wonder if he will hold it so high still."

Terrin glared at the Hi'ral. His jaw ached from the beating he had taken after attacking Jermal and so he wanted to avoid speaking if he could.

"I cannot say I blame you for that move, nor do I hold it against you. That man is a rat: lurking in the shadows, only acting when none are watching. He lacks the balls to stand in the light," Ordreg sneered. "I do not know how you have tolerated him as you have. Once Pohartan is mine, with my man in charge, this Order of yours will be the first to face the gallows. If the old man is the standard, they would be no use in the camps."

Ordreg took up the poker again, its tip reheated and glowing a bright orange. He studied the point for a moment before dragging it across Terrin's exposed belly with a sinister smile.

Terrin flinched away from the burning pain but there was nowhere for him to go. A hatch pattern of fresh burns already criss-crossed his torso. His breathing became short, sharp breaths as he fought the urge to cry out, instead groaning through a clenched jaw. Ordreg gave Terrin a couple quick slashes to his sides before returning the poker to the flames.

"Hi'ral?" a soldier entered the tent outside Terrin's field of view. "The High Priest wishes to speak with you before he leaves for Morim."

"Send him in." Ordreg waved off the soldier, turning to Terrin. "Should I let him take his revenge?"

"Uh, Hi'ral..." Evidently the soldier had not left when dismissed. "He wishes for you to come to him."

Terrin could see the annoyance on Ordreg's face, his eyes rolling exaggeratedly as he let out a huff. "I promise you this, Dramen," he said quietly, head close to Terrin's. "As soon as this business is over, that meddlesome man will follow you into the afterlife."

Ordreg strode from the tent. "Have Mikale come clean up in there," Terrin heard him say as he walked away.

Some time later, Terrin heard the footsteps of the man enter the tent. The name had meant nothing to Terrin when he heard Ordreg say it but the man's face sparked a fuzzy memory. He had seen the man with Ordreg before the battle, then Brianne had come to his tent to pass along this man's message of support. Terrin had nearly forgotten the conversation, the remaining time he had spent with Brianne that day dominating the memory.

"King Dramen, I am Mikale Talode, First Sage of the Cereb'Ani." The man nodded his head politely as he moved to release Terrin's bonds.

"I know who you are," Terrin growled. "You were supposed to help us defeat Ordreg."

The man shook his head sadly. "You misunderstand. We were prepared to assist, once Ordreg was defeated. We had no means by which to bring it about. Nor did we foresee the treachery of your General Arhan."

Not satisfied with the answer, Terrin grumbled, "A lot of fucking good you are."

Mikale accepted the rebuke silently as he helped Terrin step away from the pole, putting the King's arm around his shoulders.

"Now Ordreg may be stronger than ever," Mikale lamented. "My people are at a loss: you were our best hope of removing him."

"Well, that will not be my problem," Terrin laughed, ruefully.

Mikale looked sideways at Terrin. "The Cereb'Ani may be uncertain how to proceed but I still believe you are our best hope for the salvation of Stalius. Or at least, I intend to keep you alive as an option."

They made their way slowly to the entrance of the tent, Terrin able to do little more than drag his feet across the rugs covering the ground. Outside, the sky was overcast with a familiar darkness. They were close to Morim now, the ever-present thin clouds radiating from Mount Rhodal blocking out a portion of the sun's light. Terrin found himself forming a slight smile. He had never felt comfortable under the bright sun away from the mountains; this is where he belonged.

The soldiers waiting outside eyed them uncertainly but were easily appeased by Mikale. "I am taking him to clean him up. The Hi'ral wants him presentable for our arrival in Morim tomorrow."

Slowly they shuffled their way through the camp. Terrin had no sense of which direction they needed to go but Mikale seemed to have a determined course. They were surrounded by Staliusian soldiers, who turned their attention to the duo as they passed. None rose to bar their path, however, and Terrin presumed Mikale's position gave him the authority to move freely.

Finally, Terrin saw a line of carriages ahead. As they neared the line Terrin could see the surrounding soldiers paying them more attention, their presence causing more of a stir. He pushed himself to move faster, steeling himself against the bolt of pain which passed through his body with every movement.

Mikale guided him to the closest carriage, opening the door and attempting to help Terrin step in. Lacking the strength to do so properly, Terrin fell to the floor of the carriage, wriggling his body further in.

As Mikale closed the door behind him, Terrin could hear the voices of approaching soldiers. "What are you doing?" a voice asked cautiously, attempting to balance their suspicion with their respect for Mikale's position.

The carriage shifted as Mikale jumped to the driver's seat at the front.

"The Hi'ral wanted me to take him to the next town," Terrin heard Mikale say, muffled through the walls of the carriage. He winced: it seemed the man was not well suited to espionage. Terrin knew it was a weak explanation, unconvincingly delivered.

With strain, Terrin dragged himself up to the seat, where he could look out at the soldiers. As he did so, he saw them lift their weapons.

"Step down from there!" one of the soldiers commanded Mikale, the ruse easily dispelled. A ring of soldiers began to tighten around them, as those nearby became alerted to the situation.

The carriage lurched forward suddenly as Mikale snapped the reins, throwing Terrin back against the seat. He watched through the window as they crashed through soldiers who had been standing in front of the horses. A thump and yell told him one of the soldiers had not jumped out of the way quickly enough, instead falling under the wheels.

A horn blared behind them, the alarm raised.

Terrin cringed as he was thrown about inside the carriage, Mikale whipping the horses into a frenzy. He could not see behind them but had little doubt they were being pursued.

They careened down a rutted road, trees moving by in blurs. It did not take long for the soldiers to catch up to them. Terrin heard the pounding of hooves come up beside them, the head of a galloping horse coming into the view of the window. The carriage horses were powerful animals but they were not bred for speed. With their burden in tow, they had no hope of outrunning the cavalry horses the pursuing soldiers rode.

Terrin realized those soldiers may be the least of their concern, as he heard a now-familiar growl. Leaning to look out, Terrin saw the blur of a large white shape running behind, closing the distance quickly.

He leaned back against the seat, accepting and awaiting the inevitable. It would be only moments before Mikale was pulled down. Terrin did not know if he would survive this encounter but was not certain if he cared. It would be better to die in the escape than be paraded about and butchered like a prize hog.

Terrin was thrown suddenly as Mikale attempted to turn too quickly. The carriage teetered on two wheels for a moment, debating which way to go. But the momentum was too much and it crashed down to its side. The torsion of the roll snapped the tack of the lead horses who, panicked, disappeared down the road at a gallop.

The carriage scraped against the packed dirt as it slid. A slight dip at the side of the road caused the carriage to roll onto its roof. Terrin felt certain any bones which had not been broken in his recent torment must now be shattered. His jaw had connected hard with the handle on the door and he knew immediately it was broken.

Weakly, he looked out the upturned window towards the road. He saw Mikale lying just off the pathway, having been thrown from the carriage. The man moved sluggishly, struggling to right himself as soldier and tiger moved in around him.

Mikale was looking in the direction of the carriage, locking eyes with Terrin. The King saw the man's mouth move but could not make out what he said.

One of the soldiers standing over Mikale raised his sword, bringing it down quickly. In the instant before blade met flesh,

Mikale seemed to wink out of existence. The blade continued through the now-empty space, clashing against the dirt.

Blinking rapidly, Terrin tried to make sense of what he had seen. At one moment, Mikale had been sprawled out on the road, looking at him. In the next moment, he simply was not there. Terrin would have doubted his sanity if the soldiers were not having a similar reaction.

"Fucking Cereb'Ani!" one of the men shouted. "The Hi'ral will not be pleased."

"Check the prisoner," he heard another soldier say, seeing him point towards the wrecked carriage.

The soldier walked towards Terrin, crouching to look inside.

"He looks alive," the man said, pulling open the carriage door. He grabbed Terrin roughly, dragging him out without any evident concern for his injuries.

"Wrap that gash so he does not bleed out and get him back to camp."

Terrin was thrown about by the men like a child's rag doll. He was barely aware of what was happening around and to him. The pain had moved into an ever-present numbness. His vision was beginning to go dark, those around him beginning to slip away into the distance.

One wrapped a swatch of cloth around Terrin's head, pulling it tight. A moment later he was being thrown over the back of a horse and tied in place.

* * *

He was not sure when along the ride back to the camp he lost consciousness but when he again opened his eyes, his view was filled with the face of Rodok Ordreg.

"Good, he is not dead," Ordreg said to someone else nearby, not looking away from Terrin. "You do not get to escape this life that easily, you piece of shit." He leaned in close to the barely-aware King, his voice coming out in a growl. "Your people will see you return to Morim in chains. They will see your life end. Those who have awaited this day since your family came to power will rejoice, celebrating their new shepherd. Those you have fooled into loyalty will see the way of things. They will see there is no resistance; a new day is dawning in Pohartan. Your pathetic Kingdom will be guided forward by the strong hand of Stalius."

Ordreg stepped out of Terrin's field of view and he lacked the strength to turn his head to follow him. He remained nearby, however, and Terrin could hear his conversation with the other occupants of the tent.

"What of Talode?"

"He must have gone back to Scrail," a gruff voice replied. Terrin heard the clink of metal and the pouring of liquid.

"Fucking scum. When we return to Scrail, I am burning that fucking temple of theirs to the ground." Ordreg must have kicked the cot on which Terrin lay, as he was jostled violently. He groaned weakly.

"Is everything in place in the city?" Ordreg continued.

"Yes, we will be ready in the morning," a third voice answered. Terrin distantly recognized its owner as Lukas.

"Has there been any more word of your son? Or that flaming bitch they were parading about?" asked Ordreg. There was no note of sympathy in his voice.

"None. We assume they died in the battle. Vodana reported seeing her during the battle but she was rendered powerless and ran." Lukas' tone was equally unemotional.

"Running and powerless is not the same as 'dead'," Ordreg shot back sternly. "But I suppose it is close enough. It is unlikely she made it off that field. If she did, she is probably whoring her way back to whatever shithole he dragged her out of. I knew immediately she was more appearance than use. Send word to the City Guard to keep watch for either of them, regardless."

"Drevesine claims she burned the Great Wood," the unknown voice offered.

"Ludicrous," responded Ordreg dismissively. "Those buf-foons are easily startled, complaining of phantoms in the night."

"A toast, men," Lukas's voice rose, changing the subject. "To the new Pohartan!" Terrin heard goblets knock together as the three men celebrated their victory.

As their conversation continued, placing the final pieces of the coming day's events into position, Terrin began to drift in and out of awareness, catching only disconnected snippets.

"What of his wife?"

"... men will remain outside the walls."

"... will build a camp on the slopes of Mount Rhodal..."

Finally, mercifully, a comforting darkness came over Terrin, surrounding him and isolating him from the world beyond his body.

CHAPTER 26

From nearly the moment the King had left with the army the atmosphere in Morim had been transforming. Men who had only whispered quietly in the back rooms of Inns were soon speaking openly in the common rooms, questioning the rule of House Dramen. Frustrations grew, as the demands of a marching army began to affect the city; their goods and grains being syphoned away to feed the soldiers. As the army moved from the forests of Drevesine to the fields of Zemiltar, dissenters moved from inn common rooms to street corners.

When news of the Battle of the Mad King — as bards had immediately taken to calling the events in Zemiltar — reached Morim, the transformation was complete. Houses once apparently loyal to House Dramen severed their ties, claiming to have always been working against the King in the shadows. Those truly loyal were suddenly outnumbered outcasts and criminals, driven to hiding or arrested in a bloodless purge, awaiting the judgement of the next ruler.

The council which had advised the King and governed in his absence disbanded quickly, its members bickering as each sought a means to maneuver themselves onto the now-vacant throne. As the structures of order dissolved, opportunistic criminals rose; looting and raping with relative impunity, the City Guard undermanned and under-motivated to adequately respond.

This was the environment Brianne and Richmond found when they made their way into the city. They had ridden hard to bypass the army they pursued, arriving in the city while they were still on the march. As much as Brianne knew Richmond wanted to simply storm the camp, confront his father and rescue Terrin, they both acknowledged it would be a suicidal road to take. Their best chance of helping their friend lay in Morim. Perhaps allies could be found and an opportunity for rescue created.

Entering the city was an easy matter in itself. The iron gates sat open, lines of people flowing through. Word had spread of an approaching army, the cargo they carried and the spectacle to unfold when they arrived at the city. People were flooding to the capital, eager to witness history. On the road to Morim Brianne had abandoned her recognizable armour, acquiring instead plain clothes in the fashion of northern Pohartan. Though Brianne still carried her sword and Richmond his axe, raised hoods on the long cloaks which concealed the weapons were enough to allow the pair of travellers to blend into the crowd and casually walk past the guards, who only passively surveyed those entering.

As they passed the gates, Brianne and Richmond quickly broke away from the throng and darted into the first alley they passed. They walked briskly, weaving between buildings to put space between themselves and the commotion of the new arrivals, finding a more quiet area of the city.

The noises of the crowd faded behind them and they slowed to a more comfortable walk, continuing deeper into the city.

"Where are we going?" Brianne asked after a few minutes. They were alone in an alley between the dark stone walls of a run-down inn and a farrier's shop.

Richmond stopped, leaning against the wall of the inn. "I do not know," he admitted quietly. "How do we know who to trust anymore?"

"What about the Captain of the City Guard? You said he may be able to help us." Brianne sat on an upturned barrel beside Richmond.

"Oret? Maybe. He is a good man." Richmond slid his back down the wall, sitting on the dirty ground of the alley. He looked up at Brianne. "But if he has turned against Terrin as well, then he is the most capable of arresting us and destroying any chance we have. I would hardly think I have the authority to stop him anymore."

"It is likely they will bring Terrin to the dungeons while they prepare to hold a sham trial and declare him a traitor. If we can get into the Fortress, our best chance may be to free him from there." Richmond hoped he was correct.

The pair sat in silence for a long while, each running through the available options in their mind. Brianne had little to contribute. Having only been in Morim for a short while and having spent the majority of that time under the eyes of Jermal, she had not had the opportunity to build many reliable connections. She certainly had no ideas of looking to the Priests for assistance.

As they pondered, a pair of figures crossed the opening of the alley. They moved quickly and had only flittered across Brianne's vision for a brief moment but something about the pair caught her attention. She rose from her seat and rushed to the mouth of the alley, looking down the street in the direction they had been going.

She caught sight of their backs for a moment before they turned down another street. One of the figures was nearly her height, with the hood of a rough cloak pulled up over their head. The other figure was much smaller: a child, kicking a stone along in front of them.

Brianne took off at a run after them. She could hear the thudding of Richmond following behind her.

Turning the corner after the pair, Brianne scanned the street frantically looking for them. The narrow street was dotted with people moving slowly about their daily errands, all dressed in the drab garb of the city's lower classes. Her heart lifted as she caught sight of the child, leaning against the wall of a bakery, looking down at something in his hands. She hurried to the boy at a quick pace, a smile spreading across her face.

As she neared, a commotion rose from the bakery and the second figure emerged in a rush. Close on their heels came a portly man in a flour-dusted apron, yelling and brandishing a cudgel. As the figure darted away, grabbing the hand of the boy and dragging him along behind, her hood fell back revealing a face Brianne knew well: her mother.

"Thief!" the baker shouted after them. He attempted to give chase but was not a man built for running, falling behind quickly.

Brianne broke into a run as well, with Richmond at her side. She caught sight of two other individuals dart out of the bakery with bundles clutched to their chests, running in the opposite direction of the blustering baker.

It was easy for Brianne and Richmond to overtake the baker, who half a block from his shop was bent over, hands on knees, wheezing. Brianne paid him no mind as she blew past, keeping her eyes locked on her mother and Ren as they pivoted and ducked into an alley.

Brianne skidded as she turned down the alley. The two were a short distance ahead, slowing as they knew the baker had abandoned his pursuit.

"Mother!" Brianne yelled forward as she continued to run, throwing the hood of her cloak back.

Ella broke into an instinctual run for a few steps before stopping. She turned slowly, uncertainty on her face falling away and being replaced by joy as she saw Brianne.

"Bri!" Ren shouted. He released his mother's hand and ran towards Brianne. She knelt and caught him in a hug as he crashed into her, nearly toppling her backwards. Brianne looked up to see tears in her mother's eyes as she approached.

"Mother!" Brianne repeated, standing and hugging Ella, squishing Ren between them. Brianne stepped back after a long moment, looking her mother up and down. Ella was dressed in tattered clothes, near rags. Her eyes appeared sunken, her face gaunt, a loaf of bread was cradled in her arm. Looking down, Brianne saw Ren had a similar appearance, though his eyes remained bright on his dirt-smeared face as he looked up at his sister.

"What happened?" Brianne asked urgently. Ella did not answer immediately, instead looking past Brianne suspiciously. Brianne turned, following her mother's line of sight to Richmond, who stood just inside the entrance of the alley. He was leaning casually against a wall, keeping an eye on those passing in the street while maintaining a respectful distance from the reunion taking place.

"That is Richmond, he is a friend. It is all right," Brianne reassured her mother. "What happened?" she repeated.

Ella's tired eyes returned to Brianne, "I could ask you the same. Where is Jahn?"

Brianne's heart sunk as she was reminded of the absent party in their reunion. "He was with the army last I saw him. I… I do not know where he is now, or how he is."

"If he is with the army I am certain he is well. He will be here tomorrow, from what we have heard." Ella's tone was hopeful. Brianne was not certain if her confidence was genuine, or a mother's practiced pretence for the benefit of her children and herself.

"Mother, tell me: what happened? Why are you not in the Fortress? Why are you in dirty clothes, stealing bread?" Brianne clasped her mother's hand, her eyes pleading.

Ella sighed slightly before she began her story. "Things started to change as soon as you left with the army. That very evening we were moved by the Priests from the guest to servant quarters. We were told we could remain, 'as guests of the King', if I were to work." She smiled down at Ren, who had wrapped his arms around Brianne, hugging her quietly.

"I thought there was little for us to go back to Sastan for, with you and Jahn gone; nor did I have the means to get us there. So I went to work in the kitchens. Surely life in the Fire Fortress, even as a servant, would be better for Ren than that hopeless mining village, right?"

Ella's tone darkened as she continued, "Then a few weeks ago, things changed again. One day guards came into the kitchen and pointed me out, along with a couple of the other ladies working in there and told us we were to leave. They barely gave me the opportunity to collect Ren. I still do not really understand why we were cast out, though speaking to people in the street we began to hear the news of the King's defeat, so maybe it had to do with that."

She looked down at the loaf of bread in her arm, a hint of shame flashing over her face before being replaced by the look of determination Brianne was accustomed to seeing on her mother. "I still did not have the means to get us back to Sastan. I have been trying to find work but the city has been becoming more and more chaotic, shopkeepers becoming more cautious. So I am doing as I must for Ren."

Brianne hugged her mother for a long, silent moment as she fought the tears which threatened to dampen her cheeks.

"It will be all right, mother," she said finally. "Richmond and I have come to rescue the King and he will set things right."

"Rescue that madman?" Ella shot back, incredulously.

"He is not what the people say about him, Mother. I have gotten to know him and he is a good man," defended Brianne.

It did not take Ella long to be swayed: the politics of the Kingdom were not of great concern to her. "Oh, what do I know, just the rumours in the streets. He was good to us. I trust you. But how do you plan to do that?"

"I can get Brianne and me into the Fortress," Richmond broke in, having moved from the alley entrance. "There are routes in and out that are not well known, nor patrolled. They are intended for the quick escape of the royal family. This way," he said, ushering them deeper into the alley, "a patrol of the City Guard is coming."

Moments before they turned a corner, a shout rose behind them. "You there, come out here!"

The group ignored the shout, moving further along the alleyway before they realized they had hit a dead end. Footsteps and grumbling could be heard approaching them from the street, the guards approaching.

"I suppose now is when we find out if we have allies in the City Guard," Richmond growled, pushing back his hood. He tucked the edge of his cloak behind his axe, resting his hand on its shaft.

Two soldiers of the City Guard rounded the corner. They were adorned in black tunics over silver armour, the Flame of Pohartan stitched on their breast. Each walked with a sword sheathed on their hip and a cudgel dangling in their hands.

"What do we have here then?" one of the Guards asked. "Are you causing trouble for these women?" He pointed his cudgel at Richmond.

"I am Fire General Richmond Arhan," Richmond introduced himself.

The two Guards shared a look and smiled. "Well, Sir, your father has sent word ahead of his arrival. We have orders from Captain Yinton to arrest you, should you arrive in the city."

Brianne heard Richmond sigh and saw his hand tighten on his axe handle. "What happened to Captain Oret?" he asked cautiously.

"He was arrested, for being one of the Mad King's dogs. Like you," the second Guard said, shifting his grip on his weapon. Both men took a wide stance, blocking the exit to the alley. "Now, will you be coming with us? Either way, we'll be due for a pay raise I think."

Richmond turned his head to them for a moment, speaking quietly, "Hide the boy's eyes."

Brianne wrapped her arms around Ren as she saw Richmond heft his axe. She buried her brother's face in her cloak, turning away from the fight as it began. Pulling her mother with her, she huddled her family into the corner, covering them both with her body as best she could.

She heard the sounds of a fight behind her: the clash of steel on steel, the grunts of the men and the thud of bodies crashing against walls in the confined space. Looking over her shoulder, she caught a glimpse of Richmond pulling his axe back, one of the Guards already lying motionless on the ground.

"We should get out of here," Richmond said to her moments later.

Brianne and her family rose. The second Guard was half-seated against a wall, his head lolling to the side, his eyes staring lifelessly at his fallen companion. Richmond was wiping the head of his axe on the man's tunic.

"Do you have a safe place for the night?" Richmond asked Ella, taking her hand to guide her around the fallen men. Brianne picked up Ren and followed.

"Safe enough. An inn near here has let us sleep in their stable the last couple nights."

"That will do," Richmond pulled his hood back up over his head, looping Ella's arm in his. The two gave the appearance of a casual couple out for a stroll. "Lead the way."

* * *

The main road through Morim was packed with waiting spectators. At the northern end, the massive iron city gates were thrown open. Shops along the corridor were locked and shuttered, their proprietors standing among the crowds out front, unconcerned with business. Citizens stood in anxious chatter, lining the thoroughfare from the city gates to the gates of the Fire Fortress, where the nobles and wealthy of the city gathered in the courtyard. While most shared the excitement which had spread among the populous, many huddled in hushed conversations. A significant change was underway and plans needed to be made as each House strove to benefit.

A large portion of the approaching army remained where they had camped the previous night: it had been determined the citizens of Morim would not appreciate Staliusian soldiers marching through the city like a victorious army. So the Pohartan portion of the army began the slow march into the city as the sun rose. Several Companies of the force had been sent ahead overnight, to secure the route and take firm control of the Fortress. They were welcomed with open arms.

Terrin jostled with the wagon as it lurched towards the city gates. The framework to which he was tethered had been constructed in the wagon bed the day before, forcing him to remain in a standing position, despite the protest of his legs. He had awoken in great pain but his keepers had forced a dark, foul liquid past his broken jaw and down his throat. The concoction did nothing for his pain but helped clear his mind: he was frustratingly aware of his surroundings.

Along both sides of the road nearing the gate crowds gathered and stared as he passed. The gate itself was surrounded by soldiers and those who had not arrived in time to enter the city were lining the way before, still relishing in their opportunity to see the fallen King.

Lukas and a small group of soldiers rode in front of him, waving and pandering to the cheering crowds. Banners of Pohartan and House Arhan fluttered above them. Smaller versions of the banners could be seen in the crowds, being frantically waved by adults and children. Those cheers faded to booing as his wagon passed each section, to return to cheers again at the lines of resplendent soldiers in full parade uniform behind him.

There was a brief moment of uncertain utterings between those cheers and boos, however, as directly behind the wagon bearing Terrin rumbled the black carriage of Rodok Ordreg. While acknowledging the presence of his soldiers would cast a shadow over the proceedings, the Hi'ral of Stalius himself refused to miss the end of his enemy. The carriage lacked markings to identify its occupant, his smiling face barely visible through a sliver of the pulled-back curtain. The crowd did not know what to make of the carriage but forgot it quickly as the shining soldiers passed.

Terrin tried to hold his head up, to meet the crowd's jeers with dignity. He stared forward coldly, refusing to look at the faces glaring up at him. When the first piece of rotting produce hit him, he flinched involuntarily but he steeled himself to the wave which followed.

It seemed an eternity before the parade made its slow way to the gate. The crowds gave way to ranks of soldiers. Terrin allowed himself to look down to the ranks of men and women in armour they passed, hoping to find a sign of support among them. Instead, in the faces which bothered to look up at him as he passed, he saw either glowers of anger or smiles of mockery.

He could not have prepared himself for the scene spread out before him as they crossed the threshold into the city. From his raised position he could clearly see the bare road cutting a straight path through the city to the looming Fire Fortress in the distance. Soldiers dotted each side of the road, people crushing against the invisible line created by their presence. Every window overlooking the road was crammed with more spectators, while others had climbed up to sit precariously on rooftops and watch.

There was no denying the air of celebration. People threw flowers at the feet of Lukas and his contingent, the roar of the cheering crowds as they emerged from the gateway was deafening.

Terrin felt the rage building in him. He fought it, wanting to remain calm, to appear dignified in apparent defeat. He could feel his rational mind losing that internal battle. This was his home; he had been born here, raised in these streets. The Fortress ahead was the only home he had ever known and he had grown up being taught to care for and protect the citizens of Pohartan. Now they stood in masses, cheering for those who had betrayed him.

Gaining strength from his anger, he pulled against his restraints. He wanted to shout and scream at Lukas, at the crowds. Had he not been a good King? His every decision had been in the interests of the Kingdom, in an effort to keep his people safe. His jaw, broken in Mikale's ill-fated rescue attempt, did not allow him to speak the words he wished, to make the demands of the people he wanted to make. Instead, he was able to utter only groans and growls.

While he caught sight of several children shrinking back, hiding their frightened faces behind the skirts of their mothers, the people laughed and cheered louder at his struggle.

Their cheers cut through Terrin's anger more efficiently than any release he had previously found. He saw himself through their eyes: the 'Mad King' they had been coached into perceiving. Here he stood, dishevelled, growling and thrashing like some caged wild beast.

The potential for support when they reached Morim had been his last source of hope. He had planned to ride in Lukas' position at the head of the victory parade, perhaps with Ordreg brought in chains as he was. The cheering crowds should have been for him and instead, the Kingdom and its people celebrated his fall.

Terrin felt the final remnants of fight and resistance leave him. No help was coming. There would be no popular uprising in defence of their beloved King. There would be no dramatic, last-minute rescue from surprise allies. What would be the purpose, if there were? Lukas had already won. He had the heart of the people.

He slumped against his restraints, letting them support his weight. His eyes scanned the faces of the joyous crowd but he no longer perceived them as the wagon rumbled along the cobbled street.

His mind drifted away as they neared the Fortress, leaving behind the sounds of the crowds and the aches of his body. Instead, it strove to find pleasant memories and images, reaching further back through his life.

First, his thoughts fell to Brianne. For a moment he remembered the passionate morning they had spent together most recently but that thought was quickly superseded by a more robust image of the young woman he had come to know and care for. Her bright eyes and warm smile as she looked at him. The strength and courage she showed from the moment he met her in the courtyard he was now approaching. Her soft laughter, heard so rarely in the trying times in which they had found themselves. He found himself lingering on the quiet memory of the two of them seated on a large rock, fingers entwined, staring silently into the starry night sky.

As that image faded, images of Richmond rose to the surface: his dearest friend, the man who had stood beside him through all manner of trial and challenge. Always he had been there, ready with a sharp joke or guiding poke, whichever was most needed. He could hear the combined echo of Richmond's deep laughter from a thousand occasions blend into a symphony.

Briefly, the picture in his mind flittered to his wife, the golden-haired Amiela. There was no room now for guilt, only fondness. He still cared for the woman, who had grown to be a close confidant and steadfast source of support. He could remember the warmth of her body against his as they slept and the subtle scent of flowers in her hair as it tickled at his nose.

His father followed. For perhaps the first time, Terrin recognized many of his own features in his father's face. He was stricken by the similarities as his mind's eye presented the image: it felt as though he were looking in the mirror at himself, aged the thirty years which separated them. His father's warm eyes peered back at him with a stern facial expression. Terrin could feel the weight of expectations and responsibility in that look, a look he had seen many times throughout his life. Buried beneath, evident in the eyes, was a deep-seeded love: the love of a father who was determined to do his best for his son after the painful loss of his wife but always felt he was falling short. The love of a father so entrapped in his own responsibilities he struggled to provide the proper care, affection and attention needed by his growing son. I *love you, Father*, Terrin whispered silently to the fading image: words he could not clearly remember speaking aloud.

As Terrin's physical form was carried by the wagon out of the city streets and into the courtyard of the Fire Fortress, a final image came before his distant mind: his mother. She stood before him in a simple blue dress, unencumbered by jewels or needless decorations. Her mouth was turned up slightly in a warm smile as she looked down on him. Her eyes shone in the source-less light. "Hello, my son," she said, her voice like a melody on the air. Terrin, feeling like the boy he had been when last he saw her, rushed forward into her embrace. The cheers and jeers of the crowds were locked away, not allowed to tarnish his new constructed reality.

CHAPTER 27

Richmond leaned back against the building, his breath caught in his throat. The towering outer wall of the Fire Fortress lay twenty yards from the building behind which he waited, the path between completely cleared of obstructions. A pair of guards made their way slowly through that clearing on their routine patrol. He dared not poke his head around the wall for a few moments, as he charted their progress in his mind.

Once he felt confident they had passed, he risked a look. As hoped, they had passed between him and the Fortress without concern and were continuing along the wall.

Silently, Richmond signalled for Brianne to follow and the two ran for the Fortress. Instinctively they moved in a hurried crouch, though it would not prevent them from being seen should the soldiers choose to turn around at that moment. They had only a few moments to move, however, as another pair of guards would be approaching soon—assuming they were still operating on the schedule Richmond was familiar with.

Directly ahead a line of shrubbery obscured a section of the wall. The branches were thickly packed, though bore only a few dried and brittle leaves. While the foliage rose well over Richmond's head, the wall continued above it for another twenty yards, its smooth near-black stone presenting an imposing barrier.

Through the twisted branches, Richmond could make out his goal: the outline of a door among the stone of the wall. The face of the door had been covered in the same stone as that of the wall, making it nearly impossible to notice behind the brambles, if you did not know to look for it.

The door's camouflage was not its only protection, however and Richmond felt his way along the wall, counting the bricks his fingers passed over. As he found the one he sought, he pulled his knife from his belt. Forcing the blade under the edge of the stone, he pried. At the point he thought his blade would snap and he doubted he had counted correctly, the brick gave way, sliding out.

Richmond caught it as it began to fall. He reached his hand into the created hole and pulled a lever he found there before replacing the brick.

The working of machinery could be heard dully through the wall and the door slid back into the wall several paces before angling inward.

"Someone's watching us," Brianne said quietly behind him.

Richmond looked at her, then followed her gaze. Sure enough, he spotted the man to which she was referring. He sat nearly directly opposite them, leaning his back against the building they had been using as cover before running for the wall. His face was dirty, obscured by a shaggy beard, his white hair poking in all directions under a layer of dirt. He appeared to be looking directly at them.

"Fuck," cursed Richmond, weighing his options. "There is no time," he declared, ushering Brianne to poke her way through the branches to the open door. "We will have to hope he keeps his mouth shut." He struggled to weave his way through the branches after Brianne, snagging his clothes but finally breaking through.

Together they pushed the heavy door back into position, hearing a heavy click as it locked back into place and plunged them into darkness. Richmond could not understand the mechanisms which operated the door but he silently offered a prayer of thanks to the engineers and smiths who had manufactured them centuries ago.

Their surroundings were shrouded in complete darkness but Richmond had spent time familiarizing himself with these passages within the Fortress, should he ever need to escort Terrin out. That day had finally come, he supposed.

He reached towards the wall on his right, offering Brianne a quick apology as he bumped her. Running his hand over the wall he found the small alcove he was looking for and retrieved the flint and steel he had left there years ago. To his left, he found an unlit torch, waiting in its bracket. It took several strikes of the flint and steel but finally the torch roared to life.

"I am sorry I could not help with that," Brianne mumbled dejectedly.

"Do not worry about it," Richmond said, hoping his voice was sincere and comforting.

Brianne had been unable to use her power since they were reunited. Each night as they camped she had spent long periods of time simply staring into the flames of their campfire. Though he did not see her move, Richmond could see the strain on her face as she watched the flames. Each night she would finally break the silence with a disappointed and frustrated sigh before lying down to sleep.

She had thought she had a breakthrough two days out from Morim. Richmond had been sitting across the fire, half watching her as he struggled in his mind to find a way to rescue Terrin. Suddenly she had stood up, excitement across her face. A moment later she sat back down and disappointment returned to her expression.

Richmond had barely understood her explanation, as she tried to describe to him how she had been able to hold her power for a brief moment but could not manipulate the flames before she lost her grasp on it. Now he could see that frustration in her face again, lit by the torch which she had not been able to light.

"This way. We better move quickly, they have entered the city." Richmond led Brianne through the darkness.

The outer defensive wall of the Fortress was thick to withstand any assault, which provided for a few strategically located narrow passages like the one they moved through now. The walls on each side brushed against Richmond's arms as they moved. His head did not touch the ceiling but he knew from experience it was barely a hand's width above him.

He nearly stumbled as they reached the stairway. "Careful," Richmond whispered back as he began to descend. At the bottom of the stairs, the pathway took a sharp right turn. They were now walking under the grounds between the outer wall and the main buildings of the Fire Fortress.

"Where is this going to come out?" Brianne asked as they continued along in the seemingly endless void of darkness.

"We have a few options," Richmond replied over his shoulder. "The kitchens will come first but they will be full of people. Nearly everywhere will. We could make our way right to the King's offices through these passageways, which might be best. There's nothing to guard in there right now, after all."

And so they continued for a long while: taking stairways up and down, passing some connecting passageways and turning down others. At each intersection Richmond stopped, holding the torch close to a wall and squinting, trying to make out the cryptic markings guiding their way.

"Here," Richmond said finally, as he pulled back from inspecting the markings beside a barely-visible door. Carefully, he slid aside a small window, allowing him to peer into the room beyond. The room was lit by the sun coming through the sole window and appeared empty, though his field of view was significantly limited.

He pressed the torch down into the dusty stone floor of the passageway, dousing the flame. Readying his axe, he pushed the door open as silently as he could manage. Brianne could be heard behind him drawing her own blade. Slowly they stepped into the room.

They emerged beside the massive, cold fireplace, the door blending seamlessly into the wall. The room was, in fact, empty and Richmond relaxed, though he kept his axe ready in his hand as he surveyed the chamber.

He had been in this room a thousand times, meeting with Terrin. It had been here they first received word of the army building in Drevesine on their border and had launched this ill-fated campaign. While he recognized the skeleton of the room, there was much that had changed.

The furniture was familiar: the massive desk and the sturdy chairs before it, the small tables and additional chairs scattered around the room. The differences came in the décor. While Terrin had kept the room simple and largely unadorned, it appeared its next expectant occupant had sent instructions to have his office prepared for his arrival. Everywhere hung banners, depicting the bear sigil of House Arhan over the Flame of Pohartan.

It was a jarring sight for Richmond to see. It had been Terrin who had raised Arhan to the ranks of the noble houses, deserving of their own sigil and Lukas had eagerly chosen the bear. Richmond had largely ignored the symbol for himself, leaving it for his father to wave so proudly. However, it was meant to be the silhouette of a bear on a field of indigo: placing the symbol over the Flame of Pohartan was reserved for the ruling family.

"What has he done?" Richmond muttered, mostly to himself.

"What is it?" Brianne asked.

"These banners," Richmond indicated around the room. "My father intends to make himself King, it seems."

He stood silently starring around the room for another moment. Though he barely identified with the bear, it still felt improper to him for it to be so prominently displayed. He did not share the ambitions of his father.

"We better hurry," he pulled himself away from his thoughts to the task at hand. They had learned from Brianne's mother that there were no plans to hold Terrin captive for a while. Soldiers had come spreading the word that the King would be executed the very day he arrived in Morim. They were running out of time.

Richmond strode to the main door, peering out through a small peephole into the hallway beyond. The view offered him little information, so he held his ear to the door, listening for any activity.

He heard the muffled clink of armour as a guard shifted his stance to the right of the door.

Returning to Brianne in the middle of the room, he whispered, "There is at least one guard outside the door. Potentially more." It was not a surprise: even unoccupied, this room was never left unguarded.

Brianne nodded, raising her weapon and waiting for his guidance. Richmond directed her to stand to one side of the massive door, out of the line of sight of anyone outside when he opened it. Moving to the other side, he grabbed the handle and took a deep breath.

He knew any action would put the guard on immediate alert. The question in his mind was whether the soldier would immediately raise the alarm and thus need to be rushed and silenced quickly, or if they would be foolish enough to investigate the mysteriously opening door before calling for assistance.

Choosing his course of action he released the handle, indicating to Brianne to take it. He raised his hand, silently lowering his fingers as he counted down. As his last finger fell, Brianne pulled the door inward. Richmond was ready and moved in a flash. His axe swung in a quick arc as soon as it was free of the doorway, striking bluntly against the helmet of the guard who was still in the process of reacting to the sudden movement.

Steel struck steel and the guard dropped to the ground in a loud heap. Richmond stood ready, his head snapping from side to side looking down the long hallway. There was no sudden pounding of footsteps or call of alarm and Richmond relaxed. Hurriedly, he pulled the limp body into the office.

"It is not too far to the courtyard now but there are no guarantees of who we will find in the hallways between here and there," he said quickly to Brianne as he replaced his axe at his hip and again raised his hood. She too raised her hood but kept her sword in her hand, hiding the blade under her cloak.

Their strategy now was to simply not draw attention to themselves as they passed through the Fortress. There were often strangers in the halls, visiting for a thousand different reasons. Only the highest ranking of the guards or staff would be bothered to stop anyone to ask questions.

Moving at a quickened pace just barely below a run, they moved through the corridors. As Richmond had expected, they passed scurrying servants who barely offered them a glance as they went about their business: certainly the arriving army and visiting nobles left plenty of work to be done.

A few times Richmond suddenly changed their course, pushing Brianne to make a quick turn as guards approached. While he expected most to have the same response to them as the servants—assuming they did not recognize him first—he would rather not take the chance if it could be avoided.

"You there!" Richmond's back tensed as he heard the call. It had come from a servant they passed, who he had not thought to examine too closely. He turned slowly to look now and recognized his folly. Before him was not a low-level page or cleaner but Mistress Ralos, the head of the Fortress staff. More than any soldier or spy, she knew all the happenings of the Fortress and ensured its daily operations ran seamlessly. If anyone would take notice of unexpected guests roaming the corridors, it was she.

Richmond put on his best smile as he looked at the ageing woman. They had gotten along well during his time in the Fortress, bonding over their similar positions as commoners working among nobles. Often when they passed in the corridors they would take a moment from their busy schedules to talk, at times joking behind their hands at the eccentricities of those around them who had been born into privilege. He did not know if the instructions given to the City Guard concerning him had extended to the Fortress staff, nor if his relationship with her would supersede such orders.

"Fire General Arhan!" she gasped. "What are you doing here? We have received instructions should you appear, you know." She wagged her finger at him, as she would a scullion who tried to steal a sweet-cake from the kitchens.

"We are here to try to save the King," he replied honestly. He was at his wit's end, desperate. With his plans for a dungeon rescue scrapped, he was reaching for straws to weave together into a new strategy, each step along the way more of a blind leap. He knew his reputation for cunning strategy but those who spread such stories rarely realized dumb luck could easily be confused with brilliance in hindsight. His failures had not been woven into enduring tales as his successes were.

Mistress Ralos considered him for a moment before answering. "Nice young man he is. Bit of a temper, though..." She stared at Richmond intently, as if judging his resolve. She had come to the Fortress before Terrin was born and cared for him as his mother's handmaiden since he was an infant. Finally she nodded, patting Richmond gently on the arm. "Good luck to you, my boy. Best be on your way."

Turning on her heel, she walked ahead of them with determination. Any servants she passed were pulled into her wake with an outstretched arm or sharp word, as she cleared a path for Richmond and Brianne to proceed.

After two more turns, their destination lay ahead. The heavy doors of the courtyard were thrown open and people were crowded through them. The common people had been kept from the Fortress so those gathered were all dressed in the fine silks of the nobility, yet they stood cheering in a mob, not unlike those outside. Over their heads, Richmond could see Terrin kneeling on a raised platform. To the side of the platform sat Rodok Ordreg and High Priest Jermal, while Lukas paced across the front. His words could barely be heard above the crowd, as they cheered with each flourish of his arms.

Lukas drew his sword and stepped beside Terrin as Richmond and Brianne crossed the threshold into the courtyard. The roar of the crowd rose in a deafening chant for blood.

*　*　*

Jahn stood on the balcony, hands clasped behind his back as he looked over the crowd gathered in the courtyard below. His Company had been selected to stand guard over the execution and so his soldiers were dotted throughout the crowd, as well as surrounding the room and forming a ring around the raised stage. The balcony provided him with the best view of the proceedings, though any incidents would need to be handled quickly by the nearest soldier.

General Arhan had recently taken the stage, presenting the bound King and welcoming the crowd. He was regaling the gathered nobles with the story of his heroic efforts in subduing the Mad King and they listened with rapt attention: cheering and booing at appropriate intervals as if participants in a practiced performance.

"He fell to his knees before me and he cried out! His words were nonsense, his mind had truly gone!" Lukas stood in front of the kneeling King, gesturing down at him as he spoke. "And so his foolhardy campaign was finished! The lives lost following his madness will forever be mourned and honoured but no more shall suffer their fate! The reign of the Mad King has ended!" The crowd erupted in cheers.

High Priest Jermal rose and approached Lukas. The two stood in the centre of the stage for a long while, waiting for the crowd to settle. The High Priest's nose was bandaged, his brows locked in a fierce scowl. Finally, Lukas brought up his hand and the voices quieted, allowing the presentation to proceed.

"General Lukas Arhan," Jermal began. His voice lacked the strength and projection of the General and the crowd was forced to quiet further to listen. "You have served your Kingdom with honour. You have acted under Her guidance and brought peace and light after a period of great darkness and war."

"While you began your life as one of the dal'kar, one of the common people, you have proven yourself to be of true blood, to be of the Fire-born." Jahn noticed the twinge in Jermal's voice, though he thought the man was attempting to suppress it. "We of the Order of the Great Phoenix have studied the ancient texts and we have traced back the line of House Arhan. We have been able to confirm the legitimacy of your House. Arhan stood proudly aside the great Houses of old." Again the crowd cheered, though their enthusiasm seemed to have lessened: most suspected the destination towards which this speech was headed and it did not bode well for their own ambitions.

"As such," the High Priest continued once they quieted again. "The Great Phoenix herself has spoken to me. It is Her will that Pohartan is led into this bright future by a man of strong character, a man of true heart and a man dedicated to Her teachings. General Lukas Arhan, please kneel."

Jahn could see an expression of surprise come over General Arhan's face as he knelt in front of the High Priest. From somewhere in his robes Jermal produced a golden circlet, which glinted in the sun which had cut through the overcast clouds to bathe the courtyard in light.

"Truly this is a sign of Her approval," decreed the High Priest, opening his arms to the sudden sunlight and inspiring a short burst of applause from the gathering.

"General Lukas Arhan," Jermal continued. "As guided by the Great Phoenix and in her name and glory…" he seemed to pause intentionally, adding gravitas to the words which followed. "I, as High Priest of the Order of the Great Phoenix, recognize you as King of Pohartan, Protector of the Flame, Guardian in Her Light and from this day forward: Champion of the People." As he finished speaking, a banner unfurled high on the wall behind the stage, revealing the bear of House Arhan over the Flame of Pohartan.

The cheer of the crowd which followed the proclamation began slowly, as the gathered nobles confirmed their own aims at the throne had been thwarted before they could be put into play. It rose quickly, however, as those same nobles quickly restructured their strategies, eager to gain favour with the new King to raise their own status and perhaps present future opportunities.

Jahn was struck for a moment by a confused thought: two factors which he could not make align. General Lukas had looked surprised when the High Priest began speaking and now presented himself to the crowd as bewildered and humbled by his sudden rise. But if it were such a sudden rise, how had the banner already been prepared?

"Hail King Arhan!" the crowd was chanting in unison. Lukas stood silently for a long period, basking in the energy as the High Priest returned to his seat. Finally, he raised his hand once again, producing a final roar from the assembled nobles before they settled.

"This honour is beyond any I would have foreseen for my humble family. If it is Her will, I accept this role with humility. I shall fulfill my duties as King with the interests of the people of Pohartan always at the forefront of my priorities."

He began to pace back and forth across the front of the stage as he went on. The voices of the crowd rose in support and would not be quieted, forcing Lukas to try to shout over the rumble. "Unlike my predecessor, I will forever work for the people, not my own selfish gain. Pohartan will no longer be led to ruin by the whims of a madman."

"As my first act, I hereby strip House Dramen of all its holdings and titles. They have done great harm to this Kingdom and have lost the favour of the Great Phoenix through their hubris and arrogance. For a brief period, their lands and estates will be held in trust by House Arhan until they can be redistributed to the people so harmed under their rule."

"Secondly, I declare the costly and foolhardy war with our neighbour Stalius to be over! From this day forward we will build to the future in harmony with the Steel Republic, working collaboratively for our mutual benefit. As you know, I have spent years of my life serving along that violent border, where I have been able to build the ties of alliance and save the lives of our Pohartan sons!"

"Finally, it is my honour and duty to end the tyranny of this man, Terrin Dramen." The crowd roared again as King Lukas stepped beside his beaten foe, drawing his sword. "Down with the Mad King!" the chant echoed through the courtyard.

Lukas planted his feet in a wide stance beside Terrin, who barely moved from the kneeling position in which he had been placed when brought in as if he was no longer aware of events around him.

"I declare you guilty of crimes against the people and Kingdom of Pohartan. Your sentence is death, to free this world from your poisonous, disastrous influence. You are not worthy of Her forgiveness."

As Lukas' sword rose, the crowd's chant broke down into an unintelligible roar of raw anger and righteousness. The blade slashed down through the air, striking an oblivious Terrin in the back of the neck. The blade continued through as if without resistance, severing bone and flesh. The tip of the bloodied blade sunk into the wood platform of the stage as the limp body fell to the side.

The head of Terrin Dramen dropped to the platform with a thud, rolling a short distance. It came to a stop with its empty eyes open to the shining sun above.

CHAPTER 28

Brianne screamed as the sword fell. The roar of the crowd swallowed the sound quickly but those immediately around them turned to find its source, including several of the soldiers standing in a ring around the courtyard.

She ignored everyone around her, focusing her attention on the struggle to embrace her power. Her thoughts were a frantic blur and she had difficulty achieving the focus she needed. They were too late. After all their efforts to get to Morim, all their hopes to save Terrin and they were too late.

Someone was pulling her back and it took Brianne a moment to realize it was Richmond. He was saying something to her, forcing her attention away from the horror on the stage.

"We have to get out of here!" he whispered harshly. Several of the guards were approaching them, suspicious of their unique reaction to the execution.

Brianne found it difficult to care if they got away or not but allowed Richmond to pull her behind him as he broke into a run. The guards, their suspicions confirmed by the pair attempting to flee, pursued them through the corridor.

Unencumbered by the heavy armour of the soldiers, Brianne and Richmond were able to gain a little bit of distance on them, though not enough to lose them entirely along the long corridors. Each time they were about to make a quick turn, their pursuers rounded the corner behind them, keeping them in their sights.

She knew she should be able to stop them. Only a short while ago striking them each with balls of flame would have been the simplest thing in the world for her, barely half a thought. Now she struggled again to collect her focus, trusting Richmond to lead her through the Fortress.

There, at the edge of her consciousness, she could see it, a small light on the horizon of her mind. While her feet led her physically forward beside Richmond, her mind broke into a run towards that little glimmer. It grew, painfully slowly. It seemed to be trying to move away from her but her approach outpaced it. Finally, it filled her vision and she reached out.

The familiar wave of warmth and strength washed over her. Her mind returned to the halls through which she ran, her legs feeling stronger, the fear and sorrow of what she had just witnessed being buried deep.

Turning to look behind her, Brianne saw the soldiers reach the intersection of hallways they had recently passed. There were four of them now and they paused for just a moment in the crossroads, their heads swivelling. In less than a heartbeat, they were running again, chasing their prey.

She let the power flow through her, walking the knife's edge between control and being swept away in the torrent. She envisioned a wall of flame stretching across the width of the corridor and hurtling towards the men pursuing them.

Nothing happened. "Fuck!" she cursed, trying again. Again, nothing happened. She had been able to open herself to the Vein — as Mikale had called it — yet still could do nothing with the power. Frustrated, she turned her attention back to running with Richmond. She did not release her hold on that power for the added strength it provided her and for fear of not being able to embrace it again if she did. For now, however, she was forced to rely on her legs and Richmond's guidance to see them to safety.

As they darted around the next corner Brianne saw a woman ahead turn suddenly, startled by the commotion rushing up behind her. She recognized her as the woman who had stopped them and spoken to Richmond before they reached the courtyard. Moving quickly, the woman pulled open a large door near her, ushering them through.

Richmond did not hesitate to follow the woman's suggestion and dove into the room. Brianne followed behind him, the door closing quickly as she did so, nearly catching her heel. The room they were in was windowless, with no lit torches or lamps providing light.

"That way! To the left! Hurry after them!" Brianne heard the woman shout a moment later, followed by the pounding of footsteps racing past the door and disappearing into the distance.

As Brianne and Richmond stood in the darkness struggling to regain their breath, the door opened a crack. The woman, silhouetted by the light of the corridor, slipped in and pushed the door closed behind her, returning them to darkness.

Brianne heard a soft shuffle and saw a couple quick flashes of sparks before an oil lamp blazed to life. The woman placed the lamp back in its mirrored holder beside the door, casting light over the room.

"Thank you, Mistress Ralos," Richmond said, his breath still short from their narrow escape.

"Of course, my dear. It is terrible what happened," she replied in a gentle voice.

"How do you know what happened?" asked Richmond. Brianne had the same question in mind: while they certainly had not run in a straight line from the courtyard, surely they were far enough away from it that this woman would not have been able to witness the execution and reach this room before them.

Her only response was a sly smile as she ignored the question and asked her own. "What will you do now?"

"I do not know," Richmond admitted.

"We have to leave," Brianne offered. Sadness welled up inside her but she suppressed it. There would be time to address those emotions later. "There is nothing else for us here. Your father has them wrapped around his finger. My family is still in Morim, we can at least get them out. Then… I do not know."

Richmond nodded slowly. "You are correct, Brianne. We cannot face down my father while he has the army behind him. Perhaps in time we can work with some of the nobles—surely many of them are not pleased he leaped over them to the throne. But for now… he has whipped the people into a frenzy of support for him."

"Very well," Mistress Ralos said. "There is no access to the secret ways from this room. Bar the door and I will come for you once night falls and things have calmed."

"How do you know about the secret passageways?" Richmond asked, his shock evident in his tone and expression.

Mistress Ralos responded with a pat to his cheek and a slight laugh. "Do not be naïve, dear Fire General." Without another word she opened the door, slipping out into the corridor after a quick glance and pulling it closed behind her.

Richmond moved to push the locking latch into place, then leaned his back against the door. He slid down against the wood with a heavy sigh until he was seated on the floor, legs splayed before him.

Brianne surveyed their temporary prison quickly. It was a small guest room, sparsely decorated and furnished: likely intended for the attendants of more important guests. A modest bed sat pressed against the far wall. To the right of the door sat a chest of drawers, while a small table with two chairs occupied the opposite wall.

Pulling out one of the chairs, Brianne dropped herself into it. With her elbows on her knees, she buried her face in her hands. The pair sat in silence as the hours ticked away, neither prepared to talk about their failure.

* * *

A quick, quiet knock at the door startled the room's occupants out of their daze. Without windows in the room, it was difficult to determine for certain how much time had passed but it felt like hours. Richmond was not positive whether he had drifted off to sleep during that interval or not.

He stood quickly, turning to peer through the small peephole in the door. On the other side stood Mistress Ralos, staring back at the hole as if she could see his eye through it. He unlatched the door, allowing her in.

"Put these on," Mistress Ralos instructed, thrusting forward the folded linens in her hand as she closed the door behind her.

Richmond took the offered pile, unfolding the top item to find the embroidered shirt of the Fortress staff. Under the shirt was a leather cap, the type worn by the stewards of the Fortress. He looked to Brianne, who was similarly investigating the livery dress she had been given.

"Go on then. The exit is not close and word has spread of the suspicious pair who fled the courtyard. Your best chance is to blend in with the staff. Most will not find you worthy of a second glance, though few of our stewards share your physique." Mistress Ralos stood staring at them, obviously accustomed to her instructions being followed without debate or delay.

Without concern for modesty, Richmond and Brianne changed into the provided garments, throwing their own travel-worn clothes onto the floor.

As Richmond bent to pick up his axe and reattach his weapon belt, a hand on his arm stopped him.

"That is no weapon for a steward. You will have to leave it here," admonished Mistress Ralos.

He stared down at the weapon in his hands. Its shaft was so familiar to his touch, worn to match his grip. The heavy double-edged head with its intricate designs felt like more of an extension of his own arm than a tool crafted by a skilled blacksmith. It had been his father who gifted the weapon to him, he remembered. Sneering at the memory, he threw the axe onto the bed.

"Your weapon too, Miss. Chambermaids in my Fortress do not carry swords."

Brianne looked to Richmond for confirmation, similarly reluctant to give up her weapon. He nodded and she too threw the blade to the bed, where it collided with the abandoned axe.

"Good, then. We will make our way to the Southern wing. The servants' quarters there provide access to your passageways and will provide the quickest…"

"Lead her there," Richmond interrupted Mistress Ralos, indicating to Brianne. "Take her all the way through to the exit, if you can, or at least tell her the way through the passages. I have something I must do first."

"Richmond, no!" protested Brianne.

"Brianne, do not worry. Once you get to the exit give me thirty minutes. If I do not come, leave without me. It will be easier for you; you will not be as easily recognized. Get your mother and brother out of Morim: that is your priority." He offered her a hug, too brief for her to even react and slipped from the room before either of the women could protest further.

He walked quickly down the corridor, tucking his hair under the cap Mistress Ralos had provided and pulling it low over his brow. Walking with purpose and with his eyes downcast, he did his best to present the image of a steward busy on an errand.

There was little chance he would see Brianne again. He was not certain if it mattered. Did anything matter at this point? It was true she would have an easier chance of making it out if she travelled without him. He was well known to the soldiers and nobles, while she had had little contact with most of them. Her reputation to those in the Fortress and city existed mostly in rumours, not first-hand encounters.

While they had sat waiting for Mistress Ralos to return, his mind had been running. He reached several conclusions during that time, foremost among them that his survival of this day was secondary to Brianne's. If he was going to survive, however, there was something he wanted to collect first. Taking the longer route through secondary hallways he made his way in the direction of his former offices.

The corridors were largely empty and most who saw him disregarded him immediately. For the few who turned their heads to get a second look at him as he passed, he moved away quickly, turning down the nearest corridor before they could ask any questions. None seemed curious or suspicious enough to follow.

Turning down the corridor where his offices lay, he breathed a sigh of relief. The doors were not guarded. Richmond did not know who would be occupying his former position but obviously, they had not yet been appointed or begun their work.

As he approached the door two soldiers appeared from the far end of the corridor, walking towards him. Rather than reach for the door as he had intended, he walked past it without a glance, continuing towards the soldiers.

Just before he passed them he turned, focusing his attention on a lamp hanging on the wall nearby, feigning checking the level of the oil. As the soldiers passed he caught a portion of their conversation; they were speculating on who would fill the position of Fire General, as well as the other high-ranking positions vacated by his father's recent purge.

Once the pair had passed a reasonable distance Richmond turned back in their direction, moving quickly to the door. With a quick check in both directions, he opened the door and slipped inside.

These rooms had become as much a home to him in his time as Fire General as any other he had ever known. His whole life he had moved from one location to another following the career and deployments of his father, never staying long enough to lay down roots. While he had only occupied these offices for a short while as well, it had been his first true experience of independence out from under the shadow of Lukas and thus had left a lasting impression.

The first room had served had his private office, as well as a strategic planning space. The middle of the room was dominated by a large oak table with eight chairs surrounding it: theoretically for the King, Fire General and six Battalion Generals to be able to meet. In a back corner sat a modestly sized desk, which he had used for his private planning and work. The other corner held a door, which led to his bedchamber.

Most of the décor had been in the room when he took it over from his predecessor, including tapestries of great battles and maps of various regions displayed on the walls. Above the cold fireplace which nearly filled one wall rested a display of two crossed swords, one of Pohartan, one of Drevesine: a gift from decades ago, signifying the alliance between the two regions.

Richmond's heart lifted as he saw a few of his own possessions in the dim light of a single lamp which had been left burning. On the mantle sat small carvings he had worked on while travelling. They were barely recognizable as what they were meant to depict but they represented to Richmond significant times in his life. Now, they represented the fact the room had not yet been purged of his belongings and what he sought would likely still be where it belonged.

He took the lamp from beside the door, carrying it with him as he hurried to the desk and pulled open the lowest drawer. There, glittering up at him in the lamp's light, lay the Crest of the Fire General. A plaque made of gold roughly the size of his hand, it was finely carved with intricate designs of flames and the crossed bars denoting the rank. Underneath it sat a letter, written and presented to him with the Crest by Terrin.

Together they were his most valued possessions, the latter made more so since Terrin's death. The Crest represented the culmination of years of work and dedication. The moment it had been presented to him was the proudest of his life. He distinctly remembered the brief ceremony and the nod of approval and the slight smile he had seen from his father. A small acknowledgement of pride but one he had not seen before and had always strived for. While that aspect of the memory was irreparably destroyed by

Lukas' actions, Richmond still found himself awed as he looked upon the Crest.

The symbol was about more than his relationship with his father. It was also representative of his relationship with Terrin and the trials they had been through together. He placed the Crest on top of the desk and took up the letter beneath it. Placing the lamp on the desk beside the Crest, he sat in his chair, opening and reading the letter for the thousandth time.

Richmond Arhan,

I, Terrin Dramen, King of Pohartan, Protector of the Flame and Guardian in Her Light, raise you to the rank of Fire General of the Armies of Pohartan. In accordance with this position of honour, under my authority, I recognize House Arhan to be of the Fire-born from this day onward.

King Terrin Dramen
Protector of the Flame
Guardian in Her Light

How about that? Even had to make you a real house, you bastard. The priests are going to be pretty upset but I will deal with them. Congratulations my friend

The formal section of the letter served as part of an official and compulsory record of his promotion. The message at the end, however, had been added by Terrin after the necessary authorities had seen and made their copies of the document. It was a private message, intended only for Richmond. Each time he had read it in the months since it brought a smile to his face. It was a perfect encapsulation of the bond he had shared with Terrin.

He loved the man. He had admitted it to himself years before but never to Terrin or any others.

"I thought you would probably come here." Richmond bolted upright at the sudden voice. Looking to the door leading back to the bedchamber he saw his father standing, arms crossed as he leaned against the doorframe.

"As soon as I heard reports of a blonde man and red-haired woman fleeing the courtyard, I had no doubt it was you." Lukas remained where he stood as Richmond rose quickly from his chair. "I will admit, I am glad you did not die on the battlefield."

Richmond vaulted over the desk and ran the few strides towards the fireplace, pulling both swords down from their display.

"I would rather it did not come to that, son. We have a great opportunity here, for our family." Lukas stood, one hand moving to his own sword at his hip but not drawing the weapon. "As little as two years ago we were nothing. We were mere soldiers. Now, Arhan is the most powerful name in the Kingdom!"

"Fuck your name," snarled Richmond. "You betrayed your rightful King. You are Ordreg's puppet."

Lukas let out a sharp laugh. "Hah! Ordreg is an old fool. He can barely run his own Republic. He puts on a powerful pretence but Stalius is on the brink of crumbling from within. No, Ordreg was just a useful tool, as was that High Priest."

"You, on the other hand," Lukas moved out of the doorway and along the side of the room, placing the centre table between himself and Richmond. "Son, we can run this Kingdom. No one knows for certain your loyalty to that foolish Dramen boy. You can stay here, remain Fire General and declare yourself loyal to me and we can launch a dynasty to last a thousand years!"

Richmond leapt onto the table, ignoring the empty words of his father. As Lukas drew his own sword, Richmond descended on him.

Moving quickly, Lukas sidestepped out of his path, turning and shoving Richmond into the wall behind him. For a moment Richmond struggled to detangle himself from the tapestry which fell over him.

"You have one last opportunity, son. Stand down and stand beside me." He stood with his sword upright in front of him, prepared for Richmond to strike. "If not, you will suffer the same fate as your friend."

Responding with a roar, Richmond charged at his father.

The younger man had the benefit of his speed and energy but was hindered by his anger, which overcame his training. His movements were not as smooth as they could be, his strikes coming in a flurry but lacking strategy. While Lukas did not have the energy or even strength of his son, his own training and experience had made him a master swordsman himself. The aggressiveness of Richmond's onslaught, however, forced him to remain on the defensive.

The two circled the room, locked in combat. The opportunity for conversation and negotiation was gone, each uttering only grunts of effort and aggression.

Again and again, Richmond slashed at his father. Images of the man's sword falling on Terrin crowded his vision. Beneath them lay indistinct memories built up from years of disappointment and frustration. The years he had spent striving for his father's approval felt wasted as he finally discovered the true merit of the man.

Lukas was beginning to slow, his breaths becoming more laboured. The skill behind his single blade was barely able to withstand the fury which drove Richmond's dual weapons. As they rounded the corner of the table, the older man's foot landed on the fallen tapestry. As he attempted to shift his weight, the tapestry slid beneath him and he fell to a knee.

Richmond did not waste the opportunity. He brought his boot against his father's chest, kicking him onto his back. As Lukas fell back, his sword clattered against the stone tiles of the floor. Richmond kicked it away and it sailed under the table.

Panting, Richmond stood over his father. He knelt, pinning Lukas to the ground with a knee.

"You killed him, you bastard!" Richmond growled, crossing his blades over his father's neck.

He looked down into the face of his father. His face was the stern, emotionless expression he had become accustomed to. However, Richmond stared deeply into his eyes. There he could see depth the man had never been willing to show. Most notably he saw fear there.

"Fucking do it then, take the throne for yourself," spat Lukas.

Conflict raged in Richmond's mind. This man below him, at his mercy, had killed his dearest friend. Yet he could not disconnect the fact he was kneeling over his defenceless father. Despite all Richmond had been through and the man he had become—despite all Lukas had done and the man he had proven himself to be—there was still a strong voice buried in Richmond's mind, craving the man's approval. He hated the voice but it would not be silent.

Richmond pulled back his blades, rising slowly. Freed, Lukas turned to his side, gasping for the air which had been denied to him by the weight of Richmond on top of him.

"You are weak," Lukas said, coughing.

"Next time I will not be," Richmond replied coldly.

Without looking back at his struggling father, Richmond ran to the desk. He grabbed the letter, tucking it behind his belt. For a moment he stared at the Crest but chose to leave it where it lay.

Lukas was beginning to rise as Richmond turned back. Though the man's movements were still slow and difficult, it would not be long before he regained his composure. Assessing his options, Richmond ran for the bedchamber. He slammed the door and pushed the latch into place. Through the cracks around the door, he heard his father laugh,

"Hah, still running to your room like a child," came the muffled criticism.

He ignored the goading and instead ran to the corner of the room. His father did not know of the passageways through the walls of the Fortress, nor did he know the Fire General's bedchamber had access to those ways.

It would not take long for Lukas to gain access to the room. When he entered to find Richmond gone, he would tear the chamber apart until he discovered how he had escaped. But Richmond needed only a few minutes to disappear into the labyrinth of tunnels and make his way to his rendezvous with Brianne.

CHAPTER 29

Brianne kept her eyes low as she followed Mistress Ralos through the corridors. Throughout their hurried trip Mistress Ralos was spouting instructions, as though Brianne was a new member of the staff receiving her introduction to the operations of the Fortress. At regular intervals Brianne would nod along, offering mutterings of "Yes, Mistress" to aid the illusion.

"We are nearly there," Mistress Ralos was saying, her voice lowered for only Brianne's ears. "The door to the servants' quarters is behind that banner ahead. We are in the Order's wing of the Fortress and they insisted evidence of our comings and goings be as discreet as possible."

Brianne had vague memories of being led through these corridors shortly after arriving in Morim months ago. It was not far from here that Jermal pushed her to first embrace and use her power.

As if summoned by her memory, a flash of ornately decorated red robe turning a corner caught her eye. Without thought, she broke away from Mistress Ralos in pursuit.

Her suspicions were confirmed when she rounded the corner and recognized the back of Jermal's head moving ahead of her. The corridor was empty save for them, with Mistress Ralos coming up behind Brianne.

Brianne had not released her power and it seemed to awaken from a slumber inside her at the sight of the High Priest. She longed to throttle the man and her power screamed to fulfill her wishes.

"Jermal!" she growled. Any sense of self-preservation had fled her as soon as she spotted the man. This man had been on the stage where Terrin died. He had stood with those who connived behind his back to bring him down. She did not know the extent of his involvement but had no doubts it was significant.

The old man turned as his name was called, his perpetual scowl growing deeper as met eyes with Brianne.

"So you survived," he said, approaching her. "Good, I suppose. You were promised to me. Now we will be able to find out what powers She has granted you and perhaps why you were chosen for such an honour." He looked at her without emotion, as one may study a small rodent. To him, she was an annoyance at best but one he would tolerate for the sake of research.

Brianne did not bother speaking to him. She closed the distance between them in two strides. Reaching up, she surprised him by wrapping her hand around his throat.

"Release me!" Jermal demanded, his eyes growing wide with rage. He clawed at her hand and arm but the power flowing through her gave her strength he could not overcome. She tightened her grip.

She watched his eyes as they turned from rage to panic, as his breaths became more of a struggle. Her memory moved back to the time she had been forced to spend with him, the abuse she had suffered at his hand and command. She thought of her conversations with Terrin, of the problems this man had caused him. Her mother and brother had been thrown into the street on the whim of this man and his Order. Finally, she imagined him pulling the strings of Ordreg and Richmond's father, laughing as the blade fell on Terrin.

Like steel striking flint, she felt a spark flare inside her. It disappeared instantly but then came again and again. Reaching inward with the power raging through her, she waited for the next spark. As it struck, she grabbed it. The flames exploded inside her, reawakened. She knew she lacked the strength she had achieved before that fateful battle but she was back in control.

Her eyes brightened as she looked at Jermal. Focusing her will, she channelled the flames through her arm and out the hand clasping Jermal's throat. His struggle rose to a fevered pitch for a moment before he fell limp, flames originating within his body burning through muscle and organs.

Soon white-hot flame emerged from his mouth as his body was engulfed. Brianne kept her arm out, holding the remnants upright as Jermal was consumed by the flames. She poured her will into the inferno, making it burn hotter and wilder, turning bone to ash.

She finally lowered her arm and recalled the flames as the final pieces of ash fell to a pile formed on the tiled floor. The sleeve of her dress had been burned away to the elbow, though her pale skin underneath remained unharmed.

"Gods help us," Mistress Ralos muttered behind Brianne, awed by the display of power she had just witnessed.

"He... was a bad man," Brianne offered weakly. She felt no remorse.

"Certainly he was..." mumbled the woman behind her, staring at the pile of ash which had moments before been the High Priest of the Order of the Great Phoenix. "Hopefully he does not just rise again."

Brianne found her mouth turning up in a slight smile at the woman's dry wit.

"Now we really must get you out of here," Mistress Ralos insisted. She reached out to grab Brianne's arm but seemed to second-guess the action and withdrew her hand.

"Lead the way," Brianne ushered, falling in behind Mistress Ralos as the woman returned them to their path.

As they reached the wall at the end of the corridor they had been in, Mistress Ralos pulled back the large hanging banner. It depicted the Great Phoenix, rising from ash and taking to the sky. Though the Priests had begun preaching the beliefs of the Order when they arrived in Sastan, converting the villagers had proven an uphill battle. The people of Sastan were skeptical of fantastical stories of creatures returning from the dead, or their flames somehow creating humanity. Sastan was a distant, simple, isolated village: its people believed in more tangible things, such as the earth beneath their feet and the crops which sustained them.

It was preached that true belief in the Great Phoenix was the key to eternal rebirth. When one died in this life, if they had accepted Her they would be reborn in the next. Surely Jermal was the most devout in these beliefs and she hoped for his sake the stories were merely the hopeful fantasy they seemed.

Behind the banner was a simple wooden door, which Mistress Ralos pushed open. Beyond was a narrower, less opulently decorated corridor intended for servants to move about unseen.

Mistress Ralos led her a short distance down the corridor before stopping at another door. They entered a long chamber, beds lining each side. Two of the beds were occupied by sleeping women.

"Oi, Merissa, Rebecca!" Mistress Ralos shouted at the women as they entered the room, startling them awake. "You layabouts! There is cleaning to be done and I find you asleep!"

Both women jumped to their feet in surprise. They were obviously confused by the sudden assault, as one attempted to point out they were intended to be off-duty until the morning. Mistress Ralos cut her off almost immediately.

"I will have none of your sass, Merissa! There is a new King in the Fortress and nobles from around the Kingdom have come to honour him! There is no time for your laziness. Get yourselves to the kitchen! Quickly!"

The two women did not dare protest or question further and scurried from the room, dropping quick curtsies to Mistress Ralos as they passed.

As the door closed behind them, Mistress Ralos moved to the wall between the third and fourth bed along the right side of the room. There she crouched, reaching along the bottom edge of the wall under one of the beds. Brianne could not see what her hands did but a moment later a section of the wall was released and swung inward into the darkness beyond.

"We are not far from the outer wall here," she began, grabbing a torch out of the darkness and lighting it on one of the lamps in the room before handing it to Brianne. "I have work to get to, so you will have to go on your own. There's a High Priest to clean up, after all."

"Take a left through here and follow the corridor as far as it goes. Be careful of the stairs. At the end take a right. You will then pass two intersecting corridors. Shortly after the second, there will be an alcove to the left: that is your exit. If the Fire General does not meet you there, the door is opened from the inside with a simple lever. Best hope there are not soldiers waiting outside."

Brianne used her power to douse the torch, smiling as she instead formed a ball of flame to float before her. She had just recaptured her abilities and was eager to exercise them.

"Thank you, Mistress Ralos," she said, hugging the woman. Mistress Ralos tensed for a moment at the touch but settled into it quickly, offering Brianne a supportive pat on the back.

"Good luck, my dear. Take care of Richmond for me," she said quietly into Brianne's ear before pulling away.

With a nod Brianne moved into the passageway, pushing the door closed behind her.

* * *

Brianne paced in the passageway, her little ball of flame floating peacefully in front of her escape route. She was not certain how much time had passed, or how much longer she should wait for Richmond. The indecision rattled her.

As she made the decision to leave, a glimmer of light appeared further down the corridor, where another passageway met the one in which she paced. She stopped to watch as the glimmer grew. Finally, a torch emerged into view, held by Richmond.

Brianne had to resist the urge to squeal and run to him but her relief was extreme.

He broke into a jog when he turned the corner and saw her waiting. A smile broke across his face as he approached but faded as his eyes scanned her, seeing the damage to her garb.

"What happened?" he asked with concern.

Brianne dismissed his concern with a wave of her hand. "I will save the story for once we are free of this dreadful place. Did you find what you were after?"

"I did," nodded Richmond. "That as well is a story for later."

Richmond turned into the alcove and was startled by the ball of flame he found waiting there. He looked at Brianne with a wry smile.

"So you have your power back?" he asked.

Brianne nodded with a smile, "Part of that story." She pulled energy from the ball, allowing it to wink out.

Richmond moved his torch around in the alcove, looking for the lever to release the door. Finding it, he reached out and pulled. The lever did not move.

"Hold this, please," he said, handing his torch to Brianne. He grasped the lever with both hands and pulled, pushing against the wall with his foot.

The lever resisted—decades of rust and disuse had locked it in place—but slowly it moved outwards. Finally it popped into its open position and the pair heard the machinery within the walls move. The sounds ended with a dull *click* as the door was unlocked.

Richmond took a deep breath and opened the door slightly to peer out. Brianne used her power to draw energy from the torch, dousing the flame.

"Fuck," uttered Richmond, pulling his face back from the door. "We are along the outside wall, as expected but this door is tucked into a corner. I cannot see if any soldiers are nearby."

"We will just have to take our chances, then," Brianne said confidently. "I should be able to deal with anyone who tries to stop us."

Richmond nodded to her, turning back to the door. Sharing a look with Brianne he counted down under his breath. As he finished he pulled the door inward, dashing into the night with Brianne directly behind. They did not concern themselves with closing the door behind them: it did not affect them who knew about those passageways now.

"Halt!" could be heard almost instantly as they broke away from the massive stone walls. Before she could register the recognition of the voice Brianne had a ball of flame in the air, hurtling towards its source.

The soldiers were close to the door and dropped to the ground as the flame hurtled towards them. The inferno winked out of existence an instant before it struck them as Brianne's mind caught up with her reflex and she realized whose voice it had been.

"Jahn!" she whispered harshly, torn between her desire to yell and her need to not draw attention. She turned on her heel and raced to her prone brother. Seeing her change course, Richmond followed cautiously.

Jahn's companion was first to rise from the ground, raising her spear threateningly towards Brianne.

"Megen, easy," Jahn said quickly as he rose. "This is my sister."

The female soldier did not relax, her eyes darting between Brianne and Richmond. "Jahn, that is the Fire General. We have orders to bring him in if we see him."

Jahn put his hand on his companion's arm, coaxing her to lower the weapon and step away. "I need you to trust me on this, Megen," he said, giving the young woman a long, meaningful look.

Brianne surprised her brother by wrapping him in a hug. "Thank the Gods you are alive," she whispered into his shoulder.

He seemed hesitant for a moment before returning her embrace. They stood silently in each other's arms for a moment as Richmond and Megen glared daggers at each other around them.

"Come with us," Brianne said as she pulled away. "Mother and Ren are in the city. I am going to get them. I... I do not know where we are going to go."

It felt like an eternity passed as Brianne waited for him to respond. "I cannot," he said finally and another eternity stretched as she processed what she had heard.

"What do you mean you cannot? Lukas Arhan killed the King! We have to get away from here!" Her voice was laced with panic and disbelief.

Jahn looked from her to his companion and back, the difficulty of the decision evident in his expression. "My place is here, Brianne. The army is my home. They are my family now."

"I am your family, Jahn!" Brianne argued. "And Mother and Ren!"

Her brother shook his head slowly, sadly. "We both know I never truly belonged in Sastan, Brianne. I have never really belonged anywhere until I joined the army. This is the best path for me."

Brianne continued to protest. "How can you say such things? Why would you..."

Richmond cut her off with a hand on her arm, gently trying to pull her away. "We have to go, Brianne. Before more soldiers come."

"I am sorry, Brianne," Jahn said sadly, though it was painfully obvious to Brianne that he was committed to this choice. As if to physically demonstrate his decision he took a step away from her and towards his companion, who still did not appear pleased with being prevented from attempting to apprehend them. "Take care of Mother and Ren. Keep them safe."

Richmond was still pulling her away gently and her feet began to allow him to. She felt tears come to her eyes as distance slowly grew between her and her brother. The soldier with him, who he had called Megen, glared at them. Brianne saw her stomp her foot in frustration and turn that glare on Jahn, who responded with a weak smile.

Finally, reluctantly, she broke eye contact with him and turned to follow Richmond. As it had been where they entered the Fortress, the land between the walls and the nearest buildings had been cleared for twenty yards. As they approached the closest line of buildings they heard a commotion rise behind them.

Turning, Brianne saw a second pair of soldiers approaching, pointing towards them in the moonlight. Before she and Richmond slipped out of view Brianne saw Jahn move to meet the new pair, confidently holding up his hand to forestall their pursuit. She and Richmond broke into a sprint, disappearing among the buildings before the soldiers could get a good look at them.

Richmond led them on a winding path through the city. Brianne had no notion of where they were, nor in which direction they needed to go and so trusted the man to lead them back to her mother.

It was a long journey through the city. While the streets were scarcely populated at the late hour, there seemed to be an excessive number of the City Guard and armed soldiers wandering the streets. Uncertain if they were searching for them, or if their presence was a coincidence—soldiers celebrating the day's events, or policing drunken revellers—Richmond and Brianne avoided encountering them at every opportunity. This meant spending long periods crouching in the shadows or alleys waiting for a chance to dart across to the next street.

Dawn was just starting to break as Brianne finally began to recognize their surroundings. She led them at a run the final blocks, practically crashing through the doors to the stable in which her mother and youngest brother were staying.

Ella awoke with a start, leaping to her feet and grabbing a nearby pitchfork before her eyes adjusted to the dark and she recognized her daughter. She dropped the improvised weapon and ran to Brianne, wrapping her arms around her neck and showering her with kisses in a rare moment of unbridled joy for the usually composed woman.

"I heard about the King and feared the worst for you," she said, stepping back to look Brianne up and down, presumably searching for injuries she could mend. She emitted a panicked sound as she spied the tatters of Brianne's sleeve but her expression turned to relief and confusion as she grabbed her daughter's arm and found no damage.

"I am not harmed, Mother. We were too late to save the King." Brianne heard her own voice catch in her throat. It had been a long day and night without rest and her exhaustion was beginning to catch up with her.

Reluctantly she released the power she had been holding and the exhaustion amplified. She swayed on her feet, her knees suddenly weak. Ren woke slightly as Ella guided Brianne down onto the pile of hay they had been using as a bed. The young boy's eyes opened for a moment. He smiled slightly as he caught sight of his sister before closing his eyes again and drifting back to sleep.

Brianne welcomed the relative comfort of the hay. The power she had been holding had not only suppressed her exhaustion but also her emotions. With that protection gone, the events of the day washed over her. Finally, in this moment of safety, she could allow her mind to drift to the thoughts she had sought to avoid.

"Did you see Jahn?" Her mother's sudden question startled her for a moment, shifting her mind from one sad thought to another. Brianne attempted to keep the tears back from her eyes, to present a strong face to the mother who had always seemed to be able to do so for her.

"I did. He is well," she started. She had to clear her throat to maintain the strength of her voice. "He is with the army and wishes to stay there."

Ella nodded slowly as she took in the information. "Perhaps that is best for him," she said finally as if the act of saying the words was helping her believe them. "Your father was a proud soldier; I am not surprised Jahn would follow in his footsteps."

"He seemed... happy when I saw him. He has grown so much. He truly seems a man now." Brianne managed a smile as she looked up at her mother.

Her mother smiled back, her nodding growing more confident. "I do wish I could see him. What will we be doing now?" She looked from Brianne to Richmond.

As Richmond hesitated a moment, it was Brianne who replied. "We have to leave, Mother. There is nothing for us here and the new King will be searching for Richmond and me."

"We have to leave soon, today," Richmond added. He looked out the door towards the sky, still mostly dark with a hint of orange beginning to peak over the rooftops. "In a few hours the streets will be crowded. Shopkeepers in Morim will be eager to open and catch the visitors they missed yesterday before they leave the city. Our best chance will be to blend into those crowds."

"Very well, let me pack my things," Ella said, raising her chin in the air. Despite the sorrows of the day, Brianne could not help but laugh at her mother's joke as she looked around the dirty, empty stable.

"You can rest, Brianne. It will be a while yet before the city wakes." Richmond was leaning against a pillar, arms crossed in front of him.

"Yes, please rest," her mother agreed.

Brianne felt conflicted but could not resist the call of the hay on which she sat. She lay back, shifting her body around to create a comfortable divot, ignoring the errant pieces poking through her borrowed dress. As soon as she settled Ren shifted beside her, pressing himself close against her side. She found herself smiling as she held him close.

"Do you have any different clothes for us?" Richmond was asking her mother. Ella thought a moment before nodding and disappearing from Brianne's line of sight. She returned a moment later carrying two tattered cloaks.

"These belong to the grooms here," she said, handing the articles to Richmond.

He looked them over quickly before nodding his approval. "Good enough. We will find something more permanent outside of the city."

Brianne felt sleep settle over her sluggishly, though she continued to resist it. As her eyes began to grow heavy and finally close, she was left with the image of Ella and Richmond standing side-by-side in the doorway to the stable, looking out at the slowly brightening sky.

CHAPTER 30

Jahn lay awake in the darkness, staring up at the ceiling. As a Sergeant within the Division stationed at the Fortress, he had been given a small private room just off main barracks where the Company under his command slept.

He did not know what the hour was. The perpetual darkness of the nearly windowless Fire Fortress was a bizarre and disorienting divergence from the months he had spent sleeping under the stars. As often as possible he assigned himself duties allowing him to leave the suffocating walls of the Fortress and walk under the open sky.

The pure coincidence that had led him to be there the moment his sister and Arhan had emerged from their secret door was one of the thoughts dominating his mind and preventing him from sleeping. He did not consider himself a spiritual man but the sheer unlikelihood of the event raised serious questions.

Primarily, the thoughts which robbed him of sleep were of his sister and his family. While he had made his decision to remain with the army, parts of his mind were still struggling to accept it. Would Brianne get his mother and brother out of the city? Where would they go? What challenges and dangers would they face? King Lukas had reissued orders regarding his son, adding a bounty for any who brought Richmond to him: dead or alive. If his family was travelling with the former Fire General, surely they were at greater risk now.

Despite these greater risks, Jahn remained confident in his decision. The words he had spoken to his sister were the truth: the army felt like a family to him now, more than anyone had before; despite the bonds of blood and genuine love he shared with Brianne, Ella and Ren.

Megen shifted on the bed beside him, as if to remind him of her presence during his moments of doubt. Their relationship had become a poorly kept secret among the soldiers. He was worried it would cause animosity towards her but she insisted she was not concerned. Being a woman among the primarily male soldiers created enough of a divide, another factor to add to it was of little concern to her.

He reached to the table beside the small bed, striking flint to steel to light the small portable lamp placed there. Admitting defeat, he abandoned thoughts of getting more sleep this night.

Again Megen stirred beside him, her own sleep disrupted by the sudden light. Jahn looked down at her in the soft glow and smiled. The small bed he had been provided was not intended to fit two, so she was pressed close against his body, her soft skin warm against his. Her dark hair was obscuring the facial features he found so beautiful. The blanket they shared had been pushed down by his move to light the lamp, exposing her bare breasts. Jahn smiled as he admired them.

He appreciated Megen's company and companionship. Their relationship had begun after the army left Erhindar, on the road returning to Morim. She had initiated it, slipping into his tent one night. While nervous and inexperienced, he had not turned her away that night, nor those that followed.

What had begun as a physical relationship quickly blossomed into something more for Jahn. Each morning as he woke he found himself more glad to find Megen beside him and more disappointed the mornings she snuck out before he woke. While he had always found her beautiful, he began to notice smaller details which he found irresistible: the way her eyes creased when she smiled, or the slight bend to her nose which she professed an utter hatred for.

She had saved his life, in a sense. Without her influence, he would likely have been among those who fought in the name of King Terrin: he would have been on the losing side, dead in the mud. She had warned him of the potential uprising and the sight of her kneeling before then-General Arhan had been the final push he needed.

Uncertain if she shared his deeper feelings, he dared not discuss them. The previous two days had, however, given him hope she did. Megen had been irate at him for letting Fire General Arhan escape. Yet, she had said nothing of the matter to others. Even in the moment, as other soldiers approached, she had supported his story of the figures they saw disappear into the city being mere beggars looking for handouts.

In the hours which followed, during private moments between them she would occasionally grumble about it to him. Each time he would make the case that he could not have turned in the younger Arhan without turning in his sister and Megen would again settle. It had been a while now since she mentioned it and he hoped she had finally accepted his decision. Or perhaps it was simply that it no longer mattered. At this stage, Arhan was long gone and revealing they played a passive role in his escape would only end with them meeting the headsman's blade.

They also shared the secret of the passages. After sending the other soldiers to continue their patrol, he and Megen had grown curious and investigated from where Brianne and the Fire General had emerged. They had not gone far down the passages but were delighted by the discovery, vowing to keep it between them. Unfortunately, they foolishly pulled the door closed behind them as they stepped out again and had not been able to discern how to reopen it.

"Excuse me, Sergeant. That is hardly appropriate," Megen sleepily admonished him, catching his leering gaze, still directed at her chest. She pulled the blanket up to her chin but offered him a smile as she snuggled closer. "What time is it?"

"I do not know. It is impossible to know here," Jahn yawned.

"I should probably dress and get back to the barracks," Megen said into his shoulder, though she did not move to do so.

"You know, if it's morning, I think it might be my birthday," Jahn said wistfully as the thought came to him. Most of his birthdays had come and gone with so little notice for him—despite the best efforts of his mother—that he barely remembered the day. It had been difficult to keep track of the date on the march, each day seeming a seamless continuation of the last. But during the ceremonies which surrounded the crowning of a new King, he had heard the date mentioned.

Megen's eyes gleamed, a mischievous smile coming to her face. "Well, we should probably celebrate," she whispered into his ear as she slid her hand up his thigh and shifted her body down, her head disappearing under the blanket.

* * *

Brianne woke to the chirping of birds. It was an oddly pleasant sound, a jarring contrast to how she felt; as though the little creatures were unconcerned and unaware of the worlds' events.

They were somewhere northeast of Morim, making their way towards Zemiltar, intending to continue on to Vodana. It had been Richmond's idea, as it was the furthest they could get without attempting to travel the barren lands across the mountains to the southwest. He hoped his father's influence did not reach into the Water Kingdom to the north and perhaps they could find a semblance of peace there.

Her mother and Ren were still sleeping quietly beside her, so she slipped from the small improvised tent carefully. Outside, Richmond was checking the packs of their meagre belongings on the two horses they had managed to acquire, tucking his bedroll alongside. He insisted on sleeping outside and Brianne was not certain how much sleep he ever got.

"Good morning," she said, rubbing her arms and looking out to the sun, just beginning to show itself over the horizon.

"Good morning Brianne," Richmond replied, not turning from his work until his bedroll was secured. His face was sombre, as it usually was now.

It had been two days since they fled Morim. Brianne was not certain how Richmond made it past the guards at the city gates: he had insisted they separate briefly to make it through more easily. Brianne was able to walk through with relative ease, she and her family keeping their heads down and blending in with the rest of the travellers. Without offering much in regards to explanation Richmond had rejoined them shortly after, as he promised he would. Perhaps it had been as simple for him as well.

For the first day, the road was littered with other travellers, whom they had been able to barter with for goods they needed such as new clothes and rations of food. Richmond had acquired the two horses from a man after a quick discussion—and a gold piece passed discreetly into his pocket.

Now, however, they were travelling along a less populated route, as most others had branched off towards their own homes. They too had turned off the main road, preferring the less travelled rabbit trails through the lightly forested region, where they were less likely to meet soldiers.

"Breakfast," Richmond said, handing her a small packet as she noticed the remains of a recently doused fire. "The snares I set last night caught us a couple of rabbits. We better eat on the road as soon as your family wakes. I want to get out of Pohartan as quickly as we can." Brianne opened the packet to find the still-warm meat and tore off a portion.

"You need sleep, Richmond," she said with concern as she looked up into his weary eyes.

Richmond turned away, dismissing her concerns with a wave. "Maybe I will be able to sleep more soundly once we cross a border, or two. I try, Brianne, I really do. But sleep often refuses to come. I cannot get the images of Terrin out of my mind, or the voice of my father."

The previous night she and Richmond had stayed awake a short while after Ella and Ren retired to bed and he had told her the story of his altercation with his father—in barest detail, she was sure. Her heart ached for him. While she had lost her father over the course of years as he became a different person, she could not imagine the struggle of having one such as Lukas Arhan.

Then she had shared the story of her encounter with Jermal and while they shared a moment of levity and victory, it was short lived. Soon their conversation faded away and both merely stared at the flames before Brianne joined her family in the tent.

Brianne heard her mother emerge from the tent and turned to see her bringing a yawning Ren with her. Richmond went to them immediately, offering a quick greeting before he went to work tearing down their shelter to be packed away for another day of travel. Ren pulled on his mother's arm, drawing her attention down. After a few whispered words, Ella pointed into the trees and the boy ran off to relieve himself.

"Looks like Richmond's ready to go already," Ella said, hugging Brianne quickly.

Brianne offered her mother the meat Richmond had given her. "He wants to get as far as we can as quickly as we can. I cannot say I disagree."

Ella nodded, "Me neither, I suppose."

Ren came running to them, wrapping Brianne's legs in an embrace. Ella offered the food to her son, who eyed it suspiciously for a moment before eating hungrily.

"Ready to go, ladies," informed Richmond, patting the neck of one of the horses. Brianne was surprised to see how quickly and efficiently he had dismantled their camp, leaving little trace they had ever been there.

"Can I ride the big one today, Uncle R?" asked Ren with excitement as he ran towards the horse beside which Richmond was standing.

"Well, are you sure you are big enough?" Richmond replied playfully.

Ren ran up beside Richmond, measuring his height against the man's side, thinking he was being discreet as he lifted his heels and rose onto his toes. Richmond put his hand out, moving it horizontally just brushing the top of Ren's head.

"Looks like you are big enough, though just by a hair," said Richmond. Ren's expression filled with pride. He squealed with laughter and delight as Richmond hefted him into the air and onto the back of the horse.

"I will be coming with you, then," Ella said up to her son, causing his expression to sour.

"But Mum, Uncle R says I'm big enough!" he protested.

"Well, Uncle R is not your mother. It is not up to him."

Richmond cupped his hands, giving Ella a platform from which to boost herself onto the back of the horse behind Ren.

"Well I'm going to steer," declared Ren, unfazed as he picked up the reins.

Cupping his hands as he had for her mother, Richmond offered to assist Brianne onto the remaining horse. "No, thank you," she waved him away, grasping the horse's bridle. "I would like to walk for a while this morning."

Simply nodding, Richmond grabbed the bridle of the other horse and led them out of the trees and back to the path they had been travelling. As eager as they all were to be away from Morim, he insisted they not over exert the horses by all four of them riding. He wanted them to maintain their strength, should they need to escape quickly.

They walked for a long while in silence, listening to the sounds of the forest around them. Brianne was certain Richmond was listening keenly for any sign of pursuit but none came.

Finally, Ren began to sing, as he often did. His song was made of nonsense, the lyrics inspired by the things they passed: be it an interesting crooked tree, or a deer dashing into the underbrush as they approached. The melody similarly lacked any sense of cohesion, yet it made Brianne smile regardless. While easily dismissed as the naivety of youth, the song was one of innocence and joy. Brianne looked over to Richmond and for the briefest moment thought she saw him smile as well.

* * *

King Lukas Arhan opened his chamber window, allowing in the warm breeze. He breathed deeply, enjoying the relative freshness the open window added to the ordinarily stale and stifling room. He smiled as he looked out over Morim: his city.

"Tell me about events in Stalius," he said over his shoulder. It had been months since he had been crowned King and his neighbour to the West had fallen silent in the intervening time. He was anxious for news of Ordreg.

"The Cereb'Ani are leading a revolution, it seems," the soldier reported. He sat comfortably in one of the chairs provided, enjoying the chilled water Lukas had offered him as the King turned away from the window and returned to the table.

"I would not expect the peaceful Cereb'Ani to be leading a revolution," Lukas mused. Their Order was well known throughout the continent for their vows of pacifism. Though based in Stalius, they had often been brought in as neutral arbitrators in disputes; a service which likely would have been beneficial to the fallen Dramen.

"Forgive me, my Lord. I suppose 'leading' was not the correct term. They are certainly a part of it, however. Another man, not of their beliefs, is the figurehead." The messenger placed his goblet back on the table.

"Who is this man in charge, then?" Lukas asked, taking his own seat and leaning back, crossing his heels on top of the table.

"His name is Reaban. We do not yet know much more about him."

Lukas nodded. "Reaban, eh? Well, keep an eye on matters. We need to know who comes out on top of this mess. Anything else?"

"No, my Lord," replied the messenger, standing and bowing deeply.

"You may take your leave. Send in the next messenger." Lukas offered the man a pleasant smile as he waved him away. This news of revolution in Stalius was certainly intriguing. There had been murmurings of such things for years now but until recently he had been certain Ordreg's iron grip on the Republic was so firm revolution would be impossible. He wondered where his friend Henrik had decided to lay his loyalty.

A second messenger entered the room in place of the first, bowing deeply as he approached.

"Please, take a seat," offered Lukas, indicating the recently vacated chair. "I hear you have news from Drevesine?"

"Yes, my Lord," the messenger said nervously, choosing not to take the offered seat.

"Well, on with it then."

"Nightcloak's rebellion appears to have been destroyed. A rider arrived just moments ago with the report." The messenger dropped a sealed letter onto the table.

Lukas looked at the letter. "I do not suppose you know the contents? Save me the reading?" he asked.

The messenger shook his head. "No, my Lord. It is meant for you, I dared not open it."

"That is a good instinct, of course," Lukas nodded. "Thank you for your report, you may go."

Bowing as he walked backwards, the messenger left the room, closing the door behind him.

Lukas stretched his arms out, clasping his hand behind his head as he lounged, a smile splitting his face. He would read the details contained in the letter soon enough but for the moment he chose to merely bask in the good news.

He had learned weeks ago from Fire General Warsch that Nightcloak had aligned with King Dramen, helping the Mad King harass Drevesine's army in exchange for a promise of future support in this rebellion. Lukas could not help but laugh at the unfortunate outcome for the man. Instead of having the forces of Pohartan on his side under the Mad King, Nightcloak had been overwhelmed by the combined force of the legitimate rulers of Drevesine and their Pohartan allies.

Rising from his seat, he poured himself a small glass of whisky from the decanter at the back of the room. It was Kalmak, a label he was familiar with and fond of, left behind by the previous King. Moving to the window, he sipped it as he looked out over the city once again.

To the northwest, Stalius was in chaos. He did not yet know how that would resolve itself but he was not concerned. If Ordreg managed to destroy his opponents and maintain his grasp on control, Lukas had built a positive relationship with him. If this upstart Reaban instead stole power, Lukas was certain he could forge a new, fresh alliance. The new ruler would be happy to guarantee peace with those around him as he solidified his control within the Steel Republic.

Off to the east, he had just received confirmation of their victory in Drevesine. HardOak and her council remained secure. Pohartan and Drevesine had a long history of alliance, only briefly interrupted by Dramen's insanity. With HardOak indebted to him for not only bringing down Dramen but now Nightcloak, he had been able to mend that bridge.

Lukas was counting the other nations and Kingdoms off on his fingers now, his pleasure growing as he eliminated each as a concern. To the north, Zemiltar lay largely unchanged. Matrel's son has risen in his father's place and was still struggling to unite the region. As far as Lukas was concerned, the squabbling of those savage tribes had not changed in centuries. He maintained the forces along the northern border to monitor the situation and turn back any errant raiding parties who dared cross south. As long as they remained in their region, the dogs could fight among themselves for another century.

Beyond Zemiltar lay the Water Kingdom of Vodana. While they had arrived at the Battle of the Mad King as an ally to Drevesine, he had had little contact with them. Rarely did Pohartan and Vodana interact, separated as they were by the barren expanse of Zemiltar. To his knowledge, Queen Gracia remained on the throne uncontested. Perhaps he would have to extend an olive branch, he mused. He was looking to remarry, to create a worthy heir to follow him and Vodana noblewomen were said to be unequalled beauties.

Thoughts of heirs soured his mood. Richmond had escaped and was now out in the world somewhere with that flaming bitch of his. Lukas would need to be mindful of that until his son was located and brought to him or killed. His rise to the throne created an automatic line of succession, with Richmond at the top. Regardless of his own efforts to delegitimize his son by recognizing him as a traitor, that claim could serve as a rallying cry for any fools still quietly loyal to Dramen. Lukas would not feel truly secure until his eldest son was dead and he had a new son to follow him to the throne.

Beyond the vague and distant threat of his son, Lukas felt confident in his hold on the throne, which returned the smile to his face. The nobility who dared question his rise had been quietly paid for their support or removed if they did not seem to approve of the price offered. The Order of the Great Phoenix had also been neutered, their High Priest disappearing into the night. Still they remained insular and secluded, as they squabbled among themselves to determine who would take the vacant position.

Lukas swallowed the last dregs of the whisky, placing the empty glass on the sill. He stared out over his domain. The city below was bustling with activity, the final remnants of the celebrations which followed his coronation only now being cleared away and life returning to normal. With relative peace on all borders—

something not even the oldest among them had experienced—and the excitement of seeing a man who was once a commoner able to rise to the throne, the people were overjoyed with the reign of their new King: a reign which promised to be one of unequalled growth and prosperity for the Fire Kingdom of Pohartan.

THE END

Thanks for reading!

Available books in the **Legends of Myr** series:

Pohartan
A Peace of Steel

Three currently untitled works forthcoming
Visit www.legendsofmyr.com for more information

Note: Books are listed in publication order; there is no prescribed
reading order. The books in the series may be read in any order.

NOTE FROM THE AUTHOR

Hi! Thanks for reading my book!

I had started writing an "about the author" here, but it was painfully boring and formal. Calling it a "Note from the author" at least gets rid of the formality. There's nothing I can do about the other part. If you really want to know the basics: I live in Saskatoon, Saskatchewan, Canada. I have two university degrees, and a technical school diploma. Woo hoo.

My love for fantasy started in my pre-teen years. The first fantasy novel I read was actually book four of Robert Jordan's *Wheel of Time* series. Though confused at first (I did not realize I had missed three books), it sparked a life-long love of fantasy. The worlds of Tolkien and Jordan and Goodkind and Brooks and so many more provided a welcome escape from the troubles of those turbulent teen years.

I started developing the ideas for this series and writing this novel in 2011, while working as a "supply" (substitute) teacher in London, England. It took six years and a convenient bout of unemployment to actually get it done.

I hope you enjoyed it, and are looking forward to more.

Matt Kalesnikoff